Tempting the Heiress

"Pierce does an excellent job blending danger and intrigue into the plot of her latest love story. Readers who like their Regency historicals a bit darker and spiked with realistic grit will love this wickedly sexy romance."

—*Booklist*

"Masterful storyteller Barbara Pierce pens captivating romances that are not to be missed!"

—Lorraine Heath, *USA Today* bestselling author of *Love with a Scandalous Lord*

"I love *everything* about this book. The characters are like friends you cheer for, and the story draws you in so closely you will dream about it."

—*Romance Reader at Heart*

"*Tempting the Heiress* is the latest entry in the Bedegrayne family series and it is an excellent one. Known for the complexity of her characters, Barbara Pierce doesn't disappoint in this aspect of *Tempting the Heiress* . . . I should warn new readers to the Bedegrayne series that they will find themselves eagerly glomming the previous three novels in the series. Highly recommended!"

—*The Romance Reader's Connection*

"This story is so touching . . . An excellent read."

—*The Best Reviews*

MORE . . .

A Gentleman at Heart

"This story includes a strong touch of action and . . . sensual encounters . . . A novel of the era that fans can definitely enjoy."
—*Romantic Times*

"The second in a series featuring the Bedegrayne family highlights a hero and heroine willing to risk scandal and brave danger for love, and the tangled passions and sensual desires that ensnare them."
—*Booklist*

"*A Gentleman at Heart* is a beautifully written, absorbing and complex Regency historical that will compel the reader to keep turning the pages."
—*The Romance Reader Connection*

"Ms. Pierce's portrayal of high society lifestyles and the 'taboo' of mixing with a commoner are refreshing and delightfully off the beaten track."
—*Romance Reviews Today*

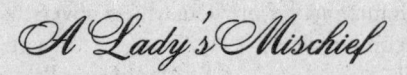

A Lady's Mischief

"Delightful, vivid, exciting! Barbara Pierce's star continues to rise!"
—Gaelen Foley, author of *Lady of Desire*

"Looking for a dark, enigmatic hero? He's here in the handsome Viscount Tipton and ready to ignite your imagination. Different and original, this dark and sometimes brooding tale will intrigue and fascinate and definitely keep you turning the pages."

—*Romantic Times*

"*A Lady's Mischief* is an absolutely absorbing diverting historical romance. Once I began reading, I could NOT put it down!"

—*The Romance Reader's Connection*

"This is a wonderful book of love and the fears that accompany it, making this an author to watch for!"

—*Romance Reviews Today*

A Desperate Game

"An exceptional debut! Destined to become a favorite among readers."

—Lorraine Heath, author of *Love with a Scandalous Lord*

"This is an excellent presentation of the Regency era . . . Very innovative."

—*Romantic Times*

"Barbara Pierce's first historical romance is a romp, an adventure, and a suspenseful drama, peopled with compelling characters and a believable plot. A worthy debut."

—*Affaire de Coeur*

St. Martin's Paperbacks Titles
by Barbara Pierce

Tempting the Heiress

Courting the Countess

Courting
the Countess

Barbara Pierce

St. Martin's Paperbacks

COURTING THE COUNTESS

Copyright © 2004 by Barbara Pierce.

ISBN: 0-312-98622-X
EAN: 80312-98622-3

Printed in the United States of America

St. Martin's Paperbacks edition / November 2004

St. Martin's Paperbacks are published by St. Martin's Press, 175 Fifth Avenue, New York, NY 10010.

10 9 8 7 6 5 4 3 2 1

"True love has ten thousand griefs, impatiences, resentments, that render a man unamiable in the eyes of the person whose affection he solicits."

—Joseph Addison, *The Spectator*, No. 261 (1711)

Courting the Countess

Courting the Countess

London, June 1809

When Brook awakened she knew her husband, Lyon, had finally succeeded in what he had once threatened. He had murdered her. Confused by the unfamiliar surroundings, Brook rubbed her temple while she fought to remain conscious.

Pain, sharp and blinding, made her heart stutter while an iron vise mercilessly squeezed her abdomen. Arching her back in agony, she gritted her teeth trying to keep from crying out. Lyon despised weakness and would be furious if someone heard her. She flinched in fear at the competent hands that came out from the encroaching darkness. They soothed her while implacably preventing her from rising.

"Milord, her mind is as broken as her body," a woman said mournfully. "Shall I call yer mon and have him get something to bind her to the bed?"

"I doubt leather cuffs will be necessary," was the dry masculine retort. "The lady is too ill to be troublesome."

The threat of being tied propelled Brook into action. Turning away from the disembodied hand that stroked her brow with a moist cloth, she rolled to her side. She was so weak the attempt to sit was halfhearted. The quick movement made her retch. Someone caught hold of her before she pitched headfirst off the bed. When that person discerned Brook's need, a chamber pot appeared under her nose. Feeling like she was being torn from the inside out, her stomach rejected its scanty contents.

When she was finished, she pressed her face into the muscular chest of the man who held her, too miserable to feel something as simple as humiliation.

"There is no shame letting one's body set itself to rights," the man murmured sympathetically in response to the soft mewling sound she did not realize she was making. "Milly, dispose of this mess while I see to our patient."

"Aye, milord," the woman replied, clearly not impressed with her companion's decision. Gathering up the chamber pot and soiled linens, she quit the room.

Unperturbed by the woman's sulky exit, the man eased Brook back into the small mountain of feather pillows. "I am pleased you are back with us again, Lady A'Court. Miss Bedegrayne has been inconsolable since your initial collapse. She blames herself, you see."

Obviously, she did not. She shook her head as if to clear her confusion. "Bedegrayne. Miss Wynne Bedegrayne?" She had a sudden flash of sitting in her friend's drawing room. Brook rubbed her temple, attempting to recall how she had managed to get herself to the Bedegrayne town house.

"Ah, I see you are beginning to remember. The fever and your . . ." he hesitated, judiciously picking his next words, "condition upon your arrival left you insensible. You will recall more as you improve."

She stared up at the man who had no connection to her and yet had taken care of her during her illness. "Are you a physician?" His size was imposing, and he appeared to be fully capable of wielding his physique if it suited his needs. She tried not to stare, but the shock of white hair sprouting from his right temple drew her gaze up to his face. The eyes that returned her scrutiny were composed of the lightest blue, although at times his eyes took on a pewter cast. She shivered, feeling the coldness of the odd hue.

"I am a surgeon by trade. Wynne summoned me because I am also family. Her younger sister, Devona, is my wife."

Le Cadavre Raffine. That was the childish sobriquet the *ton* mockingly called him behind his back. The Refined Corpse. She had not recognized him, but she had heard the rumors about him.

Brook audibly swallowed. "I am acquainted with your wife," she said faintly, not certain if she had been formally introduced to this gentleman. Regardless of the gossip, her friend would not summon an incompetent quack to care for her. "I am indebted to you, Lord—my lord," she amended, flustered that all she could recall was that ridiculous name.

"Tipton," he corrected. He heightened her embarrassment by pulling down the sheet covering her. She was wearing only a borrowed chemise. "Forgive my impudence, Lady A'Court. My interests are purely of a medical nature." He gently pressed down on her abdomen. "Tender, hmm?"

Brook sucked in her breath and held it a few seconds before she exhaled. "It hurts." Every part of her hurt. She frowned, staring at the top of his lower head. He was too focused on his examination to notice her regard. There was something in his manner that seemed reminiscent of another time he—what? "Is this the first time I have been conscious since my collapse? Did I say anything?" She could very well imagine what truths she might have uttered. A moment of weakness might have placed them both in danger.

"Hmm." Tipton's head came up and his light blue gaze cleared as his thoughts aligned to her question. "Oh, our conversation was brief. You were feverish and suffering. It might be kinder if you cannot recall it." He pulled the sheet up and tucked it around her shoulders.

His brisk movements and the grimness she sensed in his statement alerted her that he was keeping something from her. "My lord, tell me, am I dying?"

The question startled him. "No." He emphasized the denial

with a quick shake of his head. "You collapsed almost a day and a half ago. Although I confess that the seriousness of your condition concerned me, I am heartened by the fact that we are having a coherent conversation. It indicates you are improving."

Brook glanced down at her clasped hands resting on her chest. A missing day was excusable, but it would take more than a fever to blot out the last few months. Closing her eyes to escape, she realized whatever lies she had spun for Wynne Bedegrayne would be a wasted effort on Lord Tipton. He had examined her body, and much to her shame, the viscount knew the truth.

Regret swelled within her chest. She should have never sought out Wynne Bedegrayne. Her selfishness had placed them all in an awkward position. Slipping a hand lower, she gingerly stroked her cramping stomach. "This . . . this fever could not be good for my baby," she said, tears filling her eyes. The warm gush of blood between her legs already revealed the truth her fragile mind had shunned.

"The fever," Tipton said, tasting the word. If possible, his expression grew even grimmer. "No, Lady A'Court, the *fever* was not."

Chapter One

The transition from sleep to wakefulness was so sudden it was almost painful. A surge of nameless fear pumped through him. Muttering an oath, Mallory Claeg attempted to rise, but something anchored him to the bed.

Or someone.

Bracing himself on his elbows, he glanced down at his forgotten companion. Even asleep, his current mistress, Mrs. Carissa Le Maye, kept him securely manacled to her side. The telling action would have angered her. Twice widowed, she had garnered a rather unladylike reputation for seducing and carelessly discarding her lovers.

Mallory had made her acquaintance when her last lover had commissioned him to paint a portrait to immortalize her beauty. At their first meeting, the naughty gleam in her eyes foretold they would be lovers before he finished her picture. Always serious about his work, he had intended to behave himself until he concluded the task. A sensual and playful hussy, she had ignored his gentle rebuffs. While her much older protector awaited her return in the comfort of Mallory's drawing room, Mrs. Le Maye had boldly unbuttoned his breeches, cupped his testicles, and slid his engorged manhood into her eager mouth. He had climaxed almost immediately, surprised by her aggressiveness and creativity. Their first encounter had established a routine that lasted for weeks.

Instead of discarding Lord Quercus, she had insisted that the gentleman escort her to every sitting. It had given her a perverse pleasure to rut with Mallory like an insatiable animal on the sofa while her other lover was just beyond the door. The risk of getting caught elevated their passion, and Mallory had been fascinated enough with her beauty and body to permit the lady her games.

Those games ended when he finished her portrait. In her typical manner, she had told the fifty-year-old earl that she was bored tutoring him in the bed. She offered her portrait as a remembrance of what he had lost and suggested that someone younger might be more forgiving. The gentleman paid Mallory his commission and quietly departed with his possession.

Carissa Le Maye was a dreadfully heartless woman, Mallory thought, grinning affectionately down at her. Sleep seemed to enhance her beauty. Her face devoid of artificial adornment made her appear younger than her twenty-nine years. The fact her eyes were closed helped in the illusion. Whenever she focused her direct brandy-hued gaze on him, he noticed the cynical edge and polish of experience. Most of her lovers, himself included, were dazzled enough by her beauty and earthy lust to overlook such a tiny flaw. However, Mallory was not foolish enough to fall in love with the likes of Carissa Le Maye. He shuddered at the ridiculous notion. A tigress in and out of bed, she would devour the tasty morsel of a man's heart without hesitation and leave him bleeding. The artist in Mallory began sketching the image in his head.

"Mon cher," Carissa murmured sleepily, nuzzling against him. "Again, you rogue?"

They were a fair match in bed, Mallory silently admitted. He was enjoying their affair immensely, and her exotic dark looks stirred the artist in him. He tensed as she placed her hand on his stomach. Already his body started to react to her musky scent; his mind could imagine her expression when he entered her. Mallory shook the image from his head. "I did not intend to wake you. I thought I might take advantage of the morning light and sketch the cliffs." He needed to put distance between them before she claimed more than he could spare of himself.

She rolled toward him and allowed her hand to stroke his growing erection. "Mmm . . . this does not feel like a desire to sketch." Her eyes were half-closed, giving her the appearance of a pleasure lady.

"Not now, Carissa," he snapped, feeling that his stance was already weakening as her hand slipped lower.

"You and your temper do not frighten me, *mon cher*."

She pushed him on his back and he found himself responding to the sultry expression she affected. Allowing the sheet to slide down to her waist, she straddled him. Gloriously naked, he unwillingly cupped her breasts with both hands. She rolled her eyes back in pleasure as he slipped inside her and used her inner muscles to squeeze his rigid manhood.

"You may sketch your boring cliffs," she said imperiously, her black hair tickling his face, "but not now." She moved up and down the length of him, proving her power over him.

The organ she wanted to engage was not the heart. Relieved, all his thoughts about escaping faded. Tightening his hands on her hips, Mallory spent the next pleasurable hour showing Carissa that her perception of control was simply an illusion.

Brook Meylan, Countess of A'Court, was too occupied in planning a tactful retreat from the morning room to bother with the pretense of eating. A mindless exercise, the crisp linen on her lap had been transformed into an unrecognizable contortion, while she maintained a polite mask of interest for her guests. Guests who had arrived uninvited five days earlier, trespassing upon her solitude. The fact that she was related to the lot was inconsequential.

"I miss London," her half sister, Ivy, moaned, although it had not affected her appetite. She had just turned fifteen and was anticipating her come-out ball. "It is too quiet here. I have not heard the sound of a single carriage since our arrival. Your closest neighbor must be a day's journey from here and, just my rotten luck, older than Mrs. Byres." She winced at her mother's glowering disapproval. Swallowing the poached egg she had been chewing, Ivy sent the elderly woman an apologetic smile. "No offense intended, madam."

"None assumed, dearie," Brook's deceased husband's grandmother assured her sister. "I am very old."

Mrs. Byres's dry comment elevated the warmth of the room. Brook's mother smiled at her husband, Mr. Ludlow, who was attempting to conceal his chuckle behind his hand. Their children demonstrated no such restraint. Ivy's gaze locked with that of her older brother, Tye, and they burst with laughter. The baby of the family, thirteen-year-old Honey, mimicked her older siblings, joining in with an infectious giggle that forced a reluctant smile even from Brook.

A quick glance at Lyon's mother quelled Brook's brief spark of mirth. The elder Lady A'Court found little amusing in life and considered most spontaneous displays a vulgarity. The slight compression of her thin lips made Brook feel as if she had swallowed her knotted table linen.

"If you had not lost my son's heir, we would have reason for celebration. My grandson would have been born this month."

Brook abruptly stood at her mother-in-law's calm announcement while the butler served the older woman her morning hot chocolate.

"Oh, Lady A'Court," her mother said, uncertain who was more deserving of her comfort.

"Madam, I . . ." Brook's mind blanked of any polite defense she could have made. Mortified, she glanced helplessly at her table companions. Mrs. Byres, too familiar with her daughter's rants, continued to eat her meal undisturbed. Brook's family returned her stare with varying degrees of discomfort. Honey had the audacity to giggle.

Sipping her chocolate primly, her mother-in-law dismissed Brook's silence with a flick of her wrist. "Keep your own counsel. Countless apologies will never heal a grieving mother's heart." Burdened with the pain of loss, she bowed her head and shuddered.

Relieved the two women had solved her awkward dilemma, Mrs. Ludlow left her seat and embraced the older woman. "There, there, madam," she crooned. "We both shoulder the sadness of our tragic loss." She discreetly gestured for Brook to leave.

Her eyes filled and blinded her. "Let it not be said that I tarried where I am clearly not wanted!" Brook slapped her knotted linen onto her chair.

Her stepfather, Mr. Ludlow, stood, attempting to soothe her hurt feelings. "Brook, my dear, there is no need to add to the dramatics."

"Sir, I respectfully disagree."

Passing the footman in the doorway, she ordered him to stand aside so she could slam the door.

" 'Keep my own counsel,' " Brook mimicked; her black cloak flapped about in her agitation. Too hurt and angry to be reasonable, she had remained in the house long enough to collect her cloak and departed without a word to anyone. The beautiful scenery she rushed past was perceived as a colorful blur, but she had traversed this course a thousand times. She did not require her sight to find her way.

Open meadow was swallowed up by a grove, which thinned as soil was replaced by rock. The higher she climbed, the more barren the landscape became. Only pockets of wild grasses and flowering weeds brought color to the edge of her world.

Panting slightly, she widened her stance instinctively as

she peered over the edge down at the churning sea below. She could not explain to anyone the lure of the cliffs when there were prettier aspects to the land she claimed as her own. To the left beyond her view there was a narrow path that descended to a small cove. On warmer days, she might have walked along the water's edge or enjoyed a sea bath in one of the tidal pools that were hewn from the rock by one of her father's ancestors. Today she was content to remain aloft and brood.

"A mother's grieving heart," she scoffed, stomping her foot with enough force to send a spray of sand and pebbles over the edge. She clenched her right hand into a fist and pounded her chest. "What of my grief? My heart?" she raged at the thundering sea below. "I have been left with nothing." Brook took a deep breath, feeling the cold wind pull at her skirts, coaxing her closer to the edge. She resisted the seductive tug and closed her eyes. "What more must I sacrifice before they are all appeased?"

The next gust of wind struck her, stealing her breath. She took a hasty step forward in an attempt to keep her balance. A reply to her question did not float down from the heavens on the fickle wind. Brook stood alone, already feeling the oppressive weight of the truth. Her sins were too great. There would be no peace for her in this life.

Mallory had been drawn to the intriguing vision of the lone woman in black challenging the sea he had glimpsed while searching for a location to sit and sketch. He had been too far away to hear her words, but her gestures were violent and poignant. He would have left her undisturbed if the silly creature had not been determined to kill herself. As he dropped his sketching book and small box of supplies, his quick stride erupted into a full run when he realized she was fighting the wind for her balance.

He caught her arm and spun her toward the safety of firmer

land. The momentum sent both of them falling. It was too late to be noble. The woman landed on her back with him on top of her. He grunted, taking the brunt of the fall on his forearms. Gazing down at her ashen face, he adjusted his initial impression that she was an older woman. The lady underneath him was quite lovely and familiar. He blamed the unflattering black she was bundled in for his error. She was short in stature. Grief had whittled her slender frame, enhancing her fragility. Even tragedy could not steal her beauty.

She pushed him away and he willingly rolled off her. "Are you mad, sir, or simply drunk?" she demanded in a trembling voice. Still shaken by the encounter, she remained seated on the ground.

"Neither. I was sparing your family the grief of searching for your broken body this afternoon amidst the rocks below," he said, irritated that his heroism was perceived as lunacy.

Her anger changed to stunned outrage. "I was not—I could not." She gazed weakly at the edge before struggling to her feet.

Mallory measured the doubt he noticed in her eyes in silence. He only allowed her a moment to deduce her legs were still too wobbly for the grace he had always attributed to her. "Here. Take my hand, my lady."

He pulled her roughly onto her feet. To make certain she was paying attention, he tightened his grip on her arm until she winced. "No trouble is worth casting yourself into the sea." He released her and put a respectable distance between them.

"I was not throwing myself off the cliff. The notion sounds painful, not to mention messy. I will have you know that I walk here daily and am quite familiar with the dangers—" She broke off, realizing she was explaining herself to someone she considered an underling. She shivered as the wind buffeted them. The spring air had put a healthy bloom on her cheeks. "Besides, what would you know about me or my troubles?"

He gave her a slow, roguish grin. "Well, Countess, the answer to that particular question might take some time. Why don't you let me escort you home and I will make my confession over a pot of tea?"

Mallory was quite used to women who acquiesced to his dictates without question. It was a rather novel experience to observe that his limitless charm had altered her expression from mistrust to blatant hostility.

"Who are you, sir?"

He mockingly patted the imaginary wound over his heart. "Why, Lady A'Court, your forgetfulness smites a lethal clout on my self-love. During your absence from London, have you forgotten your old friends?"

She glanced away at the mention of London. "I have few friends in town these days, sir, and *you* are not one of them."

"Perhaps not," he acquiesced. "We, however, are connected by friendship. A lady in your position should be basking in the affection of her companions." He let his gaze roam the bleak landscape. "Not praying for an early death in the remoteness of Cornwall."

"Who sent you?" she demanded with unexpected bluntness.

Surprised by her intensity and the impact of her blue gaze focused on him, Mallory shifted his stance and concealed his visceral reaction to her proximity with a grin. "Such ferocity! Dear madam, you make me want to confess everything, but alas, only my selfish pleasures have brought me to you."

She blinked at the double entendre, uncertain if it was deliberate. "You claim you know me."

"Indeed. I believe you once honored me with a dance at your come-out ball. There were so many admirers that evening, I could hardly fault you for not recalling." He offered his arm, wanting to get her away from the cliff and out of the cold before her teeth began to chatter. "You mentioned tea."

"*You* mentioned tea," she countered. "As well as plunging

from cliffs, forgotten acquaintances, selfish pleasures, and a ball I barely remember. I warrant you have spoken more words than I have in the past week. Do you ever hush?"

Mallory sat down on a nearby flat stone and laughed, enjoying the way her brow wrinkled in exasperation. Whatever her intentions before he had gained her attention, he was satisfied that the dark moment has passed. "Occasionally, my lady. I treasure the awakening colors of dawn, the sound of the wind rattling the windows, spring and the new life it yields. When I awaken each morning, I lie abed listening to the soft breathing of my lover and savor the warmth of our embrace. I expect I appreciate my moments of silence like any other man."

She made a choking sound that she quickly muffled with her gloved hand. It was terribly mischievous to speak so boldly, yet the widow sparked something in him. Her reactions were too charming to resist.

Clearing her throat, she said, "My mother always said that rudeness begets rudeness, and she is correct. Regardless of your playful objections, you are a stranger to me, sir, and my speech was most forward. Please accept my apologies."

"No," he said, shaking his head. "No, I do not believe I will." He crossed his arms, awaiting her response.

"Y-You must!" she stuttered, flustered by his refusal. She started pacing in her agitation. "No gentleman ever leaves a lady obligated."

Briefly an image of Carissa flickered in his mind. "I have never been one for polite rules, Countess."

Noticing his enjoyment, she stopped and sighed. "You are teasing me."

"Beautiful ladies are always so much fun to tease." He stood and clasped her elbows lightly when her expression blanked. "You are supposed to smile when a gentleman gives you a compliment."

"I have tarried too long. My family is expecting me," she

said in a breathy rush, finally noticing their close proximity.

"And what of your expectations?"

"I have none. Good day, sir." She stepped out of his embrace and turned to leave.

"My name!" he shouted to her departing figure.

She hesitated at his words.

"Claeg. Mr. Mallory Claeg. I believe you claim my younger sister, Amara, as one of the few friends you have left in London."

He had truly managed to shake her with his announcement. Something akin to shame moistened her gaze. "You do your sister no favor by connecting our names. In remembrance of old friendships, I beg of you to forget that we ever met."

Watching her hasty retreat, Mallory crouched down to retrieve his abandoned sketching book and supplies he had dropped earlier. Well, well, who would believe he and the pretty widow would be sharing secrets? Forget? He rose, brushing off some grit that clung to his left knee. "Not bloody likely!"

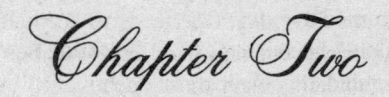

Chapter Two

Cornwall, April 1811

"Brook!"

The woman who bore the name winced at the shrill quality her younger sister managed to inject into the single word. Having observed the activity below from her bedchamber window, Brook already knew the reason for her sister's excitement. The door swung open with a resounding bang.

"There you are," Ivy said, clearly exasperated by her search. "You are not dressed. And your hair!" She gestured, clearly at a loss for words. Brook's sixteen-year-old sibling was a tidy creature, with her freshly scrubbed face and her straight blond hair plaited into a single braid down her back. There was not a smudge of dust or a careless wrinkle pressed into her dress.

Brook unconsciously tucked the wisps of hair that had strayed from their confines. The unremarkable dress she had donned was several years old. The countless washings had leached the black dye, fading it into an unflattering indescribable color. The life she lived beyond the critical eye of polite society was isolated. She had long lost interest in obtaining the current fashions. Regardless, her face warmed at Ivy's unspoken censure. "I spent most of the morning in the company of Miss Bee and she did not complain of my attire."

Ivy crossed her eyes. "Miss Bee is a cow. You have enough hired help around here that you should not be forced to consort with the farm animals." She leaned closer and suspiciously sniffed. "At least you washed."

"Naturally, I washed," she countered, offended by the comment. "This is a farm, Ivy. One tends to keep animals on it. Besides, I will have you know that I find Miss Bee's conversation more stimulating than most duchesses'." She swatted away her sister's hands when she attempted to pluck the pins from Brook's hair. "Leave it be."

Ivy stepped back and laughed. "Mama is correct. You are hopeless."

The innocent observation stung more than it should have, considering that she had heard her mother say those three words hundreds of times in the past eight months. Brook grabbed her sister by the shoulders and guided her toward the door. "I can see to myself. Why do you not entertain our unwelcome guest until I can join you?"

Her younger sister huffed. "How can you be so unkind when he is the only one from London who bothers to visit? Mama says Mr. Claeg has risen in her estimation since his father was promoted to a viscount and that you should not so easily discard the gentleman's friendship."

"Mama speaks too freely in front of children." She pushed her sister through the doorway. "Out!" she said, shutting the door on her annoyed sibling.

"Does it matter to anyone in this house that I do not *want* Mr. Claeg's friendship?" Disgruntled, Brook rang for her maid and began savagely snatching the pins from her hair. She peered into the mirror on her dressing table and groaned. Her guest would just have to wait.

The chaos his impromptu visit had created amused Mallory greatly. The indulgent half smile remained even after Miss Ivy Ludlow's whirlwind appearance and departure. Painfully young and too impressed with him, the beautiful child had managed to stammer out the message that her sister would be joining him shortly and then dashed off to supervise their refreshments.

Turning his back on the closed door, Mallory used the time alone to appreciate the treasures in the front parlor. It had been his understanding that Loughwydde had been part of Lady A'Court's dowry, bequeathed by Lord Lanston, the dear lady's father. Mallory doubted the A'Court family with their vast holdings had viewed the small farm in Cornwall as possessing much value, which might explain why the countess had chosen it as her dowager residence.

Mallory idly tapped his finger along the mantel in ticking cadence with the clock on a nearby table. Centered above the hearth hung a Chinese mirror picture portraying an elegant mid-eighteenth-century pastoral scene. Being a man who savored all tactile explorations, he could not resist sliding his fingertips over the gilded flowers and leaves that framed the scene. The carved gilt wood frame had been added later and was obviously English in origin. Five smaller pictures were positioned below. Mallory studied the tiny watercolors depicting various landscapes. He dismissed them as tasteful, if not rather boring.

Somewhere in the house, someone began to play a pianoforte. The composition was cheerful and reminded him of spring. It certainly enhanced the ambience of the room. He wondered which of the Ludlow sisters was honing her musical skills. There were at least two, and a brother, though Mallory had yet to meet the seventeen-year-old. Humming along with the music, he picked up a pretty little vase and checked the bottom to view the potter's mark.

The air around him stirred as the door opened. The lady of the house entered, her cheeks flushed from what Mallory assumed was a harried dash to join him. He found the color in her cheeks very appealing. There was something about her sweet, wary face that had him returning to Cornwall, even a year after he and the mistress who had brought him to the locale for their dalliance had parted ways.

The dress she wore was atrocious. Still, the garment could not diminish her natural beauty. In fact, she appeared rather matronly in a gray dress made of jaconet muslin. The drab color was relieved with the addition of a white lace collar high on the throat and a frilly white lappet cap over her blond hair. Mallory was not so arrogant to assume by the countess's flustered entrance that she was eager for his companionship. The wary speculation in her expressive blue eyes was there again and had never dimmed in his presence. He credited good manners and a certain amount of bullying from her family for her appearance. However, he was not one to dwell over the particulars when he benefited from the results.

The soft blond curls around her face bounced when Lady A'Court curtsied. She gestured for him to be seated. He found her regal manner simply enchanting. "Mr. Claeg, please forgive my tardiness. I was not expecting visitors this afternoon."

The subtle reprimand added a touch of stiffness to her walk, but it did not shame Mallory into an apology. His high-handedness was necessary. He did not doubt the lady was not above disappearing if she had been given forewarning of his visit.

"I require no apologies, my lady. Your graciousness in receiving a weary traveler is in itself a soothing balm." He heard her teeth click together as she fought to contain her frustration. Mallory's lips twitched in amusement. It had taken only minutes to needle a reaction from her. Indeed, he considered that progress.

Silence descended between them. The music floating down the hallway from the pianoforte smoothed over the awkward lapse in conversation. The quiet did not bother him. It was understandable. They were in many ways essentially strangers. Besides, one could learn much about a person without the distraction of polite speech. Some of his favorite hours with a lady evolved without a single word spoken.

"How inconsiderate," Lady A'Court blurted, rising on her feet. "You must be parched from your journey. My sister—"

"Is already seeing to the refreshments. Sit," he commanded, cutting off her words and feeble attempt at escape. His eyes narrowed when she hesitated. Realizing there was no polite option but to comply, his companion sat. He rose from the chair he had been reclining in. Crossing the distance between them, he deliberately sat on the sofa beside her. In the past, he had been careful to keep a respectful distance. Regrettably, he did not possess a vast amount of patience. His visits to Loughwydde had convinced him that the lady was quite content in keeping him forever in the chair across the room. Mallory had known by the end of their second encounter that he desired a much more intimate position with the widow. A true scoundrel, he was not above using seduction to attain her.

Lady A'Court gave him a long, considering stare before sliding away from him. Perhaps she intuitively sensed his carnal intent or found his proximity unsettling. Either way, he silently applauded her pluck to remain on the sofa when he wagered her instincts were telling her to run from the room as she had run when he had encountered her on the cliffs a year earlier.

"I must confess I am astonished by the timing of your visit, Mr. Claeg. I would have assumed the season would have lured you back to London," she said, struggling to conceal her discomfort.

"Oh, my plans will eventually lead me back to town." He positioned his body toward her and braced his right arm along the back of the sofa. She subtly flinched when he deliberately brushed his leg against her skirt. "For now, the cottage I leased suits my needs. Is it not fortuitous that until my departure we will be more or less neighbors?" He was already anticipating the *more* aspects of their new friendship.

"How splendid," she faintly said. If she moved another inch away from him, she would be perched like a heron on the armrest. "Is it your art that brings you here?"

"My art," he said, tasting the words on his tongue. "I suppose you could say that that I find my current surroundings inspiring." She glanced swiftly down at her clasped hands. The pale rose blooming in her cheeks at his equivoque created a lovely picture before him. A rough sketch of the scene formed in his mind. Lady A'Court slanted her cat eyes demurely in his direction, curious about his stillness. He wondered if he would ever be immune to the impact of her stare. It impaled him and roused a possessiveness within him that he never had known existed. Puzzling over his reaction, he murmured, "You wear the mantle of innocence too effectively for a married woman." He reached out to see if his touch would shatter the illusion.

She abruptly rose and moved out of his reach. "I find your observation offensive, Mr. Claeg. Neither do I wear or shed my emotions like a shawl or toque. I have never been one for games; however, I believe you are well acquainted with deep play." Magnificent in her anger, she straightened her shoulders and pointed to the door. "Since we will be neighbors, I must respectfully ask you to keep to your property. If the solitude is less than *inspiring*, might I suggest that you summon your current mistress from London? Considering your past, I doubt anyone would be shocked by your impropriety."

So she had learned of his dalliance with Carissa Le Maye last spring. He concealed his wince by rubbing his neck. A year ago he had been too focused on enjoying the pleasures of his lover to quibble about discretion. How could he have predicted that meeting her that day at the cliffs had planted her in his thoughts? After his affair with Carissa had ended, had he not returned to Cornwall just to see the countess again? While he had lain in his bed alone, the seed of a notion had rooted itself in his brain. What if? The possibility of enticing the prim widow into sharing her bed had kept him awake well into the darkest hours of the night.

As he rose to comply, the haughty tilt of her head made him act on impulse. Before she realized what he intended, Mallory hooked his arm around her waist and hauled her up against the length of his body.

She had to tip her head back to meet his gaze. "Mr. Claeg, if you please—" She sucked in a quick breath when he lowered his head so that his mouth hovered just above hers.

"Have you not guessed, Countess? I always do what pleases me." She wet her lower lip with a flick of her tongue. The tiny nervous action drew his attention. "Such ripe lips. Are they as sweet as confections? Let us find out."

She squeezed her eyes tightly shut and visibly braced herself. The lady obviously expected him to behave as the worst kind of scoundrel. Instead of ravaging her mouth, Mallory laved her lower lip with his tongue. He tasted the plump curve with a tenderness that made them both shiver. Although she was not screaming for her servants, she was not exactly relaxing in his arms. Undeterred, he licked the heart-shaped bow of her upper lip. "Hmm . . . sweeter than marshmallow and richer than bonbons. I have always had a weakness for sweets." He released her.

Lady A'Court stumbled back a step to regain her balance. There was no doubt her liberation from his embrace had surprised her. "You," she said, sounding breathless. She removed a lacy handkerchief she had tucked within her sleeve and dabbed the wetness from her lips. "You will not kiss me again."

"My dear lady, that was not a kiss . . . just merely a taste."

The distinct whine of wheels from a cart and the excited murmur of feminine voices drew closer. Startled, she glanced nervously at the closed door. He had heard their approach long before she had. Her family's imminent arrival had been the only deterrent keeping him from deepening their kiss. It definitely had not been his mastery over restraint!

"It appears we are about to lose our privacy for a proper demonstration. Be patient; I promise I will give you another chance to muddle my good sense with your enthralling wiles."

Her eyes flared at the outrageous suggestion. "You arrogant coquet! I am not attempting to enthrall you. If you have any decency, sir, you will make an excuse to leave and then keep away from me."

The door opened and Miss Ivy Ludlow cheerfully bounded into the room. A footman pushing the rattling tea cart followed behind. The countess's mother, Mrs. Ludlow, and a girl of fourteen who from her looks Mallory deduced was another sibling joined them.

"Mama, I thought you were resting in your room," the countess said, uncomfortable at being caught alone with Mallory in the front parlor.

"Bosh, how can one sleep with such activity in this house?" In Mallory's opinion, Mrs. Ludlow did not appear to need a nap. Placing her age somewhere in the late forties, he noted that she was alert and sensed that she was shrewder than her eldest daughter credited. The older woman focused her cheerfulness on him. "Mr. Claeg, it is so kind of you to visit us again. Has my daughter been treating you properly?"

The countess had turned away and was busy preparing the tea. He could not see her face clearly, but he noticed her ears were pink. "Madam, your daughter knows how to make a gentleman feel welcome." The lady he could not resist teasing shot him a look of pure loathing. "I confess, my small cottage will seem inhospitable after basking in her warmth."

"Oh, please spend the afternoon with us, Mr. Claeg," Miss Ivy Ludlow entreated. "My sister Honey can play the pianoforte for you and later we could take a walk in the woods."

Mrs. Ludlow handed him his tea. "Do stay, sir. The remoteness of this farm denies us visitors of quality." If she heard the countess's sigh, her mother ignored it. "You can tell us the latest news about your family. How is your sister? I have been out of circulation, but the fuss regarding her marriage to Mr. Brock Bedegrayne last summer reached even my old ears. You must tell me everything."

Mallory brought the cup to his lips and looked over the rim at Lady A'Court. She met his stare directly and a silent promise of retribution was delivered. The countess was not a gracious loser. Her family did not seem to notice her upset. While they nibbled on cakes, sipped their tea, and laughed at the stories he shared about his travels she covertly studied him. She viewed him as an adversary. Mallory was not disheartened by the revelation. He had her attention. Soon he would have her in his bed.

Chapter Three

Standing at the edge of the cliffs, Brook stared down at the beach below with her fists clenched. She had felt nothing for so long that it took her a few minutes to recognize the churning in her stomach as resentment. The man perched on one of the large, flat rocks near the shore was to blame. Blissfully ignorant of her presence, he had drawn one knee up and was using the limb as an easel for his sketching book. For the moment, his art commanded all of his attention. Brook had felt the force of his blue-eyed intensity and knew she was safe from being discovered. Even so, prudence had her stepping away from the edge and returning to the woodland path. She did not have the strength to endure a confrontation, nor did she want to be alone with him. Mallory Claeg was a careless bounder who disregarded propriety. If an opportunity presented itself, there was no telling how outrageous he would become.

Like kissing.

Brook ducked to avoid a small tree branch. The man wanted to kiss her. She had sensed his interest almost from the beginning, although she had no clue why someone like her would interest him. He was a sleek, sensual beast who reveled in decadence. The women he chose as companions and bedded were equally outlandish and sophisticated. Brook understood her true worth. She was as exotic as a sparrow. Lyon had voiced his disappointment often enough during their short, turbulent marriage. Gentlemen like Mallory Claeg rarely spoke to women of her sort, let alone desired to steal a kiss from them. No, she would not play his cruel games. If he was bored, Mr. Claeg could return to London.

"My lady—Brook."

Brook blinked, surprised as much by the newcomer as she was that sometime during her dark musings she had stopped. She glanced down at her fist and saw she had snapped off one of the branches she had passed.

"They told me that I would find you out here," the gentleman said, his voice filled with indulgence. Without permission, he took her hand and kissed it, handling her like she was composed of delicate glass. "You should not wander alone. Even here, it is not safe, Cousin."

She looked away, letting her companion think she was properly chastised. Brook treasured her quiet walks. Her outings were small acts of defiance in a world that was at times too confining. She doubted anyone could dissuade her from taking them. "My lord, your appearance is unexpected. Mother A'Court's letter did not mention that you would be joining the party."

A fortnight past, Brook's mother-in-law's letter had arrived, announcing their intentions for a brief visit. Brook dreaded these encounters and assumed Lyon's mother found them equally unpleasant. However, the dowager considered it her duty to occasionally check up on her son's widow. There had definitely been no mention that the elder Lady A'Court had invited the cousin who had inherited the A'Court title after Lyon had died.

"I—we wanted it to be a surprise. My sister, May, has also joined our little gathering." He clapped his hands together and rubbed them together, pleased by his lighthearted mischief. "Come let us return to the house. May has been eager to see you again." He hooked his arm through hers and they continued down the path. Brook was content to let him dominate the conversation, adding the appropriate sound of approval when he gazed expectantly at her.

Seaton Hamblin, affectionately nicknamed Ham by family and friends, might have shared a superficial resemblance to his deceased cousin, but that was where the similarities ended. Ham was average in height, and build. His clothes were fashionable, an indulgence of his new rank, and his straight brown hair had been recently cut. He had not been reared to be the next Earl of A'Court, but his hands had the softness of privilege. He had spent the years strengthening his mind with books and lectures rather than his body. Lyon and Ham had not been close. However, before her marriage Brook had encountered Mr. Hamblin and had formed a conversational acquaintance with him. The new earl possessed a sincerity that warmed even the gray hue of his eyes. Lyon's eyes had also been gray. Odd, how the same color could represent kindness in one man and the frigid depths of hell in another.

She had chosen to return to Loughwydde after Lyon's death because her wounded spirit had craved the wild isolation. The farm had been part of her father's estate. At his death, her mother, unable to cope with the financial disarray, had turned to their solicitor, Mr. Horatio Ludlow. He had assisted the family in selling off most of their landholdings and had invested the proceeds in mining prospects so they had not been left destitute. Loughwydde had been retained as the family's residence.

Another man might have taken advantage of her mother's confusion and grief. Mr. Ludlow, seven years Lady Lanston's senior, had instead fallen in love with the beautiful widow. Her mother had initially refused the solicitor. Two years later, practicality had outweighed her grief. She was a woman alone in the world with a five-year-old daughter. Marrying Mr. Ludlow provided the stability she had needed.

Their joyful union had given Brook three half siblings: Tye, Ivy, and Honey. There had been a place for Brook in the Ludlow family. Mr. Ludlow gave her the affection and discipline he bestowed on his own children and yet she was not allowed to forget her legacy. She was, after all, Baron Lanston's daughter.

"Good! You have returned. Ham, you were so gallant to find my wayward daughter," Mrs. Ludlow said, leaning out one of the second-story windows. "Brook, darling, take your fine gentleman into the parlor. Once the ladies have settled into their rooms we will join you." The excitement of having guests had boosted her vivacity.

Passing the two carriages in her front yard, Brook sighed. Unlike her mother, who had convinced Mr. Ludlow to move the family closer to London once they had married, Brook preferred leading a solitary life. Perhaps old memories were ruling her decision; not that she cared. Only she understood that she had paid a dear price for her freedom.

"We have our orders, my lord," she said, giving him a little smile. In the foyer, she removed her toque and wool cloak and handed them to her housekeeper. Ham surrendered his hat and walking stick. "Thank you, Min. I assume preparations for a celebratory supper are under way."

"Yes, madam. Cook has a gooseberry tart baking in the oven even now," the housekeeper briskly said, hustling them into a parlor so she could continue with her chores.

"Gooseberry tart, eh?" Ham said, choosing the chair closest to the fireplace. "You know how to make a man feel like he is returning home after an arduous journey."

The innocent compliment gave Brook a frisson of alarm, but she brushed off her reaction. The earl was just being kind. "My mother keeps the staff on alert with her frequent visits.

Often she has one or all of my siblings in tow, so we have learned to adjust to the unexpected."

Ham cleared his throat. "Speaking of the unexpected—"

"Miss Hamblin." Brook crossed the room and embraced her. They touched cheeks and separated. "How good to see you again. I trust your journey was bearable."

"Just," the young woman admitted wearily. May Hamblin was two years younger than Brook. Her hair was darker than her older sibling's and she wore it short, letting her natural curls frame her oval face. At the moment, she was scowling at the chair her brother offered her. "After spending days in that awful carriage, I vow I cannot face sitting for at least a day, maybe an entire week."

"I doubt it is your *face* that pains you, pet," Ham quipped.

"Beast," she replied affectionately. She kissed him on the cheek and turned back to Brook. "Your mother told us that you spend your days exploring the wilds here, Lady A'Court. You must take me with you on one of your adventures. I adore anything right now that does not involve sitting."

"Please call me Brook, Miss Hamblin. There will be enough confusion with so many family members assembled under one roof."

"And you must call me May," she countered, seeming relieved to shed the rigidity of manners. "Besides, we are family. Ham has been filling my ears with endless praising of your virtues. I am pleased we will have the time to become better acquainted."

Brook's half sisters, Ivy and Honey, burst into the room. Their lively chatter masked Brook's soft reply: "We will?" Lyon's grandmother, Mrs. Byres, shuffled into the room using Brook's stepfather's arm to steady herself.

"Papa, when did you arrive?" Brook lifted her brows in surprise. She had not expected him to journey so far from London at this time of year, when his business demanded his attention. His arrival explained her mother's joy.

"When Lord A'Court expressed a desire to join his family at Loughwydde, I decided to travel with him. How are you, my girl?"

"Pleased to see you, Papa," Brook said. She waited until Mrs. Byres was seated before she gave him a quick hug and peck on the cheek. "Welcome back to Loughwydde, Grandmother Byres."

The elderly woman beckoned Brook closer with a gnarled hand crippled by arthritis. She had been a renowned beauty during her youth. Age had caused her proud carriage to stoop with the burden of the years and had weathered her skin into wrinkled parchment. Patting Brook's cheek fondly, she said, "You've added a bit a flesh to your bones since last we met."

"Ah yes," Brook said, flustered that the observation had invited everyone to scrutinize her body. The loss of Lyon and her baby and then the ensuing scandal had ravaged her slender form. It had taken more than a year to recover her appetite.

"Good. It is a sign you are healing," Mrs. Byres rasped, focusing her faded blue eyes on Brook. "You have color in your cheeks again. Do we have a certain gentleman to thank?"

The image of Mallory Claeg flashed in her mind. She could recall how it felt, his crushing embrace and the tender caress of his tongue on her lips. It was madness to contemplate a union, even a brief one, with such a man. Ruthlessly she doused the memory. "I do not believe—no, not a gentleman," Brook corrected herself, not interested in explaining to the family that each day without Lyon had been rewarding.

"Madam, have a care," Ham entreated, visibly uncomfortable with the old woman's question. "You are embarrassing the lady." He removed a handkerchief from the inner pocket of his coat and dabbed at his upper lip and brow.

"Dare I hope you have resisted springing the surprise in our absence?" Mrs. Ludlow demanded, clearly frustrated at being excluded.

Lyon's mother, Lady A'Court, was an imposing presence behind Brook. The warmth she had experienced from the rest of the A'Court family was noticeably absent in the dowager. Duty had Brook straightening and showing her respect by curtseying. Her mother-in-law returned the courtesy with a slow nod. Nothing in her expression or posture invited intimacy.

"What surprise are you referring to, Mama?"

Mr. Ludlow touched Brook's shoulder to gain her attention. She glanced up and was comforted by the gentle squeeze. "Sweet wife, unlike the rest of the family, you are fairly bursting from the suspense. Why not share your news with our daughter?"

Honey poked her head through her father's arm and clung to his waist. She was still a child and had a child's impatience. "Can I tell her, Papa? Can I?"

"Absolutely not," Mrs. Ludlow objected. "And I cannot see how it is any of your concern, since you are too young to join us." Defiant, Honey stuck her tongue out at her sister Ivy. Mrs. Ludlow frowned, her face losing its eternal zeal. "Any further impudence will result in your taking your meals in your room. If you remain here, you must conduct yourself with decorum."

Honey pulled away from her father, her countenance sullen. "Yes, Mama." The notion of Ivy having fun without her was unacceptable.

Satisfied that she had won their latest battle, Brook's mother looked to Lady A'Court for her approval. The dowager had chosen the sofa to accommodate her generous proportions. She met Mrs. Ludlow's gaze with indifference. Anything that did not involve the elder countess held little interest for her.

"What were you saying, dear?" Grandmother Byres asked. Since she was speaking to the empty space to the right of her, whom she was talking to remained in doubt. The elderly woman had claimed on several occasions that spirits visited her. Her particular favorite was her husband, who had died over twenty years ago.

"Yes, m'dear," Mr. Ludlow encouragingly prompted, deciding Mrs. Byres was speaking to his wife. "Share our news with Brook."

"Yes, Mama, tell me the news."

Dispelling the dark mood Mother A'Court's silence had summoned, her mother seized both of Brook's hands, obviously brimming with excitement. "Brook, having lost your father at such a tender age, I above all others understand your grief."

No, you cannot. She quickly glanced at Ham and May and found their expressions sympathetic. "Mama, this is not the appropriate occasion to discuss the matter." She silently pleaded with her mother to end this conversation.

Mrs. Ludlow shook her head. "No, it must be addressed. You are not the only one here who misses Lyon. It is laudable that you wish to honor his memory—"

Covering her mouth with her hand, Brook made a small choking sound. She had spent the past two years trying to forget what he had done to her—to all of them. The man had chosen to marry her because she bore a physical resemblance to the woman he lusted for and could never have. Brook had paid for his disappointment in ways no one would ever know.

Her mother ruthlessly forged ahead unaware of her daughter's turmoil. "Rusticating out on this farm is no life for a young woman. It is time to bury your grief, and we all intend to help you."

The comment sounded like an ominous threat. "Your help has not been asked for, nor is it needed," Brook said, deliberately keeping her voice level, but the hint of steel was apparent.

"Lyon lamented over your mulish temperament," the elder Lady A'Court interjected, gaining and holding Brook's attention. "You were so much less than he expected."

Brook gasped at the unexpected cruelty. She had no defense against what she perceived as the truth.

Mrs. Byres tugged on her skirt. "Lyon was a beautiful boy. The pair of you would have made handsome children."

Ham stirred from his chair. "Ladies, there is no use speculating on a past that cannot be altered. Not only is it spiteful, it is in my humble opinion a complete waste of time." He touched Brook lightly under the chin. "Cousin, your pallor concerns me. Perhaps a turn in the garden will restore your health."

She allowed Ham to lead her out of the room away from their good intentions and pitying expressions. They did not linger for their cloaks, but walked out the front door. Ham was correct. Being outdoors helped.

She lifted her face to the breeze and enjoyed the coolness. "My lord, you may release me. I shall not faint on you," she said, a feeling of calm slipping beneath her skin.

The earl hesitated. Critically judging her appearance, he must have decided she had not lied, and released her. He locked his arms behind his back, and they walked the yard. She sensed a struggle within him. Finally, he said, "I apologize for the pain my family has caused you. Elthia, Lady A'Court, well, her life was built around Lyon. She will never see that he had a hand in his destruction. It is simpler for her to believe that the rumors circulating after his death were malicious lies."

She tasted the bitter bile of injustice. "You do not need to justify her reasoning for me."

"I am not excusing her behavior." He matched her short stride and kept a respectable space between them. "I suppose I am not explaining myself well." He boldly took up her hand and compelled her to halt. "I would find it regrettable if you thought my opinion and the dowager's were in alignment."

Understanding softened her features. "I knew it was not

so, my lord. Your friendship has meant something to me."

Boyish delight lit his handsome visage. "Truly? I am glad to hear it is so, Cousin. And when we return to London, I will be steadfastly by your side. No one will dare speak out of turn."

She wrinkled her face in confusion. "London?"

"That was what your mother was attempting to explain before my aunt made a hash of things. Your family is opening the town house. They are expecting you to join them for the season."

Brook pulled her arm from his grasp. "I have no intention of traveling to London this season or the next. I thought you understood!"

"I do. You are afraid."

"I am not!" she snapped. She was not afraid; she was terrified. "You were not even in London when Lyon died. What do you know of the matter?"

"I have heard all of the rumors, even though Mr. Milroy and his then betrothed, Miss Wynne Bedegrayne, have always been close-mouthed about the final minutes of my cousin's life before he fell to his death at Mr. Milroy's town house. People will speculate. You cannot control human nature."

She pushed him away, unable to contain her anger. "You have no notion of what you speak of, my lord."

Undeterred, Ham pressed on, "You were too weak from the loss of your babe to endure all the curious speculation and cruelty. You are stronger now. Return to London with your family and I vow it will be different."

"A touching promise," Mallory Claeg drawled, casually making his way toward them. "Though it lacks the poetry of romance. Perhaps you would be more convincing, sir, if the delivery was made on bended knee?"

Ham glared at the intruder who so easily mocked his sincerity. "Who the devil are you, sir?"

Chapter Four

This man would never be his friend.

Executing a quick bow, Mallory said, "My name is Mallory Claeg, sir, though I doubt I have answered your question."

"Ham is my guest, Mr. Claeg."

Behave. Mallory heard her unspoken warning but was not inclined to indulge her. "What you really want to know is, who am I to Brook?" He deliberately used her Christian name, insinuating an intimacy he desired and had yet to achieve. Of course, Ham was not aware of it.

"Mr. Claeg, please."

He retrieved the bouquet of wildflowers from behind his back and handed them to her. "I thought of you when I picked these."

Brook buried her nose into the colorful mix of spring blooms and inhaled their fragrance. "These are lovely. Thank you." Her catlike eyes narrowed. "Why are you bringing me flowers?"

Mallory expelled an exaggerated sigh. "You are too young to be so cynical," he mournfully replied. "Consider them a bribe—or an apology. I will accept whichever will get me some tea. My exploration of your lands has left me parched."

Not liking the familiarity of their conversation, Ham interjected, "As a matter of fact, Mr. Claeg, I would very much like to know about your relationship with my cousin."

"Cousin?" Perhaps he had misunderstood the other man's possessive posturing. Jealousy made men foolish indeed.

Lady A'Court, being the proper little hostess, provided the introduction. "Mr. Claeg, may I present Seaton Hamblin, the ninth Earl of A'Court. Ham, Mr. Claeg, a renowned artist, is also Viscount Keyworth's heir."

"Your name is, I confess, unfamiliar to me. However, I did have the honor of listening to your father speak once in Parliament. He is a remarkable gentleman."

"I will pass on the compliment." Mallory assumed the lady's motive for mentioning the connection to the Keyworth name was to elevate his status. He could not thank her for it. He had spent most of his life distancing himself from his father. It was not a subject he dwelled on, so he focused on more important matters. "So, Countess, do my flowers gain me admittance to the castle?" *The flowers had been a thoughtful touch,* he mused, watching her inspect the various blooms.

"Your imagination is as delusional as your self-love. Join us if you must."

"Yes, please do join us, Mr. Claeg," Lord A'Court echoed the invitation with false sincerity. "Mayhap you could use your influence to help us convince my dear cousin to return to London with us."

"No one has that kind of influence," she darkly muttered.

Watching Mallory Claeg interact with her motley family was a tiring affair. Her mother and sisters had been thrilled by the artist's arrival and his simple token of spring flowers. Elthia, Lady A'Court was not so easily won over. As she glanced from Brook's face to Mr. Claeg's, the wheels of speculation were grinding out their own conclusions. From her thin-lipped expression Brook guessed the lady's opinion was unflattering. Mr. Ludlow was affable yet reserved, while Grandmother Byres insisted that Mr. Claeg sit beside her at supper. Ham was acting petulant. He hovered in a fawning manner around Brook that changed from flattering to downright annoying.

Then there was his sister May's behavior. Mr. Claeg's presence had revived her flagging spirits. As she sat beside him on the sofa with Ivy on the other side, the pair took turns flirting outrageously. A stern look from Mr. Ludlow curtailed Brook's half sister's poor manners. Regrettably, no one thought to restrain May Hamblin.

Mallory Claeg seemed immune to the tension. After supper, Mrs. Ludlow had suggested that they adjourn to the small music room. Ivy and Honey, both competent on the pianoforte, took turns impressing the group with their skill. Mr. Claeg praised both girls and swore when pressed that he was unable to dub one girl superior over the other. His evasion did not prevent them from squabbling. Brook also was able to play the instrument but did not volunteer, nor was she asked. A slender book of verse in hand, she feigned interest in it while her parents, Mother A'Court, and Mrs. Byres played whist. With his arms crossed, Ham watched Mr. Claeg as if he were a stray mongrel he mistrusted. May Hamblin's intentions were so clear that Brook felt a pang of pity for the young lady.

So lost was Brook in her musings, it startled her to find Mr. Claeg staring directly at her. Another man would have glanced away once he had been caught. Mr. Claeg was proving to be something other than predictable. Peeking over her unread tome, Brook lifted her brow, letting him know in her own way that she was not intimidated. Unabashed, the scoundrel simply tucked his fist under his chin and continued to study her. Ham had noticed their silent exchange and scowled at them both.

May Hamblin lightly stroked Mr. Claeg on the coat sleeve, interrupting his deliberation. "Being a connoisseur of art, you must live a fascinating life, Mr. Claeg."

Ham shifted his stance. Perhaps he had finally noticed his sister's keen interest in the artist. "Mr. Claeg is in trade, May. He makes pictures. It is connoisseurs who make it art."

."It is an old argument, my lord, and both sides are passionate," Mr. Claeg said, smiling at May. The gaze he directed at the earl held no amusement. Mallory knew he was being baited and yet could not leave the subject undefended. "Naturally, I am in favor of the artist. It is his vision, his blood, that is ground into the pigment and mixed with linseed oil. The artist puts a part of himself on that canvas." He shook his head as if deriving conclusions from a private argument with himself. Brook suspected he had said more than he intended to his unappreciative audience. "I lose respect for the gentleman who claims to know art because he had traveled to Italy and viewed several dozen pictures. All that proves to me is that he can traverse the seas without disgracing himself."

May giggled and applauded her companion. It was a dreadful simpering sound, Brook thought. The woman was also making a fool of herself.

"The artisans should allow the educated gentlemen to create a standard of excellence. They need guidance, a moral and decent aspiration. Mr. Claeg, even you must concede that you do not have to be a potter to appreciate a porcelain vase, or a silversmith to recognize good plate," Ham stubbornly argued.

"I do not criticize aspiration, Lord A'Court, just the man who judges its value," Mr. Claeg astutely countered.

Ivy's hands froze over the keys of the pianoforte while she listened raptly to the gentlemen's debate. The players of the card game had also suspended their play. Despite his casual airs, Mr. Claeg took his art very seriously, and it was an imprudent man who provoked him.

"Ha! Only those who embrace mediocrity fear the power of the connoisseurs. Talent survives the ages."

May was not the only Hamblin who was acting outrageously. Brook had credited Ham for having more sense than he was illustrating.

"Not when the varnish blackens and the paint begins rotting off the canvas," Mr. Claeg drawled. She noticed his white teeth when he smiled. They were straight and very sharp, the sign of a true predator.

"If this argument has been debated by learned men for generations, I doubt we will find a resolution this evening," Brook said, and everyone laughed with the exception of the earl and Mr. Claeg. She was putting an end to their conversation before they took their disagreement outdoors. "Ivy, play something soothing."

"Play one of Handel's works," her mother called out before returning her attention to the cards in her hand.

The gentlemen continued to scowl at each other while Ivy began playing. Ignoring the hostility between her brother and Mr. Claeg, May said, "I saw your submission to the Royal Academy last year, and *mediocrity* was not the word to describe it."

Losing interest in the earl and his plebian tastes, Mr. Claeg focused his eerie light blue gaze on May. "What did you think of my *Pandora*?"

Flattered, she checked her reflection in the large mirror on the wall across from her and preened. "Extraordinary, sir. One could empathize with her anguish."

Exasperated by his sister's attempt to intellectualize on a subject out of her depth, Ham rolled his eyes, mumbled, "God save us."

"Were you shocked by her costume?" Mallory asked innocently.

May pursed her lips. "No. Was that your intention?" As they sat side by side together on the sofa, her curly dark hair and classic beauty complemented Mr. Claeg's masculine grace rather nicely, Brook sourly mused.

The artist idly scratched his chin. "Well, for the sake of symbolism she was stripped of her civility."

The young woman looked perplexed.

"His *Pandora* was naked, May," Ham dryly replied at his sister's gasp. "She was probably some prostitute he dragged off the street."

The earl's snide tone had Brook rising to Mr. Claeg's defense whether he needed her to or not. "It is a high honor to be chosen by the academy. Are you an associate?" Brook asked, attempting to cast him in a responsible light.

His head snapped in her direction. All the friendliness she always associated him with was quickly doused by her question. "No," he said, stating with that one word that pursuing the subject would be futile.

If having an artist in the house had not captured her younger half sister's imagination, the notion that he painted naked prostitutes was positively titillating. "Ladies truly pose naked for you?" Honey asked, her eyes wide with awe.

"Honey Ludlow!" her father shouted.

"Sweet Honey, I assure you—" Mallory winked at Brook. "I kept my eyes firmly shut."

The clock chimed the tenth hour. The house was still active with the sounds of its temporary inhabitants. If they had been in London, they would have been preparing for a late supper or a ball. Here it was easier to conform to nature's schedule. Everyone was going through their various nighttime rituals before they went to bed. Brook smiled at the feminine shriek that was followed by infectious laughter. She had paired her half sisters in a bedchamber. Brook envied their closeness. Too many years spanned between them for her to share in their merriment.

She pushed open the door they had not bothered to close. Honey was chasing Ivy around the room, both were dressed in their nightclothes. The few pieces of furniture posed no obstacles for them. What they could not run around they climbed over. Brook opened her mouth to chastise them and then thought better of it. The room would survive the abuse.

"Pleasant dreams, girls," Brook said.

Ivy narrowly escaped her sister by rolling off the bed. She used the post to right herself and swing herself in another direction. "G'night," she said, not breaking her stride.

Honey skidded to a halt and exhaled a sigh of relief that it was not mother or father who had come to check on them. "G'night, Sis." She lunged for Ivy and the chase resumed again.

Brook closed the door. She continued down the hall and listened to the indistinct murmur of voices. Recognizing one of the voices, she deduced that her personal maid, Morna, was still tending to Elthia, Lady A'Court's needs. The older woman traveled with her own personal staff; however, she was a woman who was used to an army of servants seeing to every whim. If Brook wanted assistance with her dress, she might have to seek out her housekeeper, Mrs. Gordy.

The door abruptly opened while Brook stood there wavering about whether or not she should open the door. The solemn face of her housekeeper popped into view. So the dowager had absconded with her Mrs. Gordy, too. Chagrined, Brook wondered if she would be forced to seek assistance from one of the bailiff. She could just imagine Lady A'Court's reaction to that plan!

Brook looked at the large pot of steaming water in her housekeeper's hands. "Is there a problem?"

"Aye, madam," she huffed, tossing a perturbed look back at the women in the room. "Too many people in this house. Demanding this . . . complaining about that—I am too old for this nonsense!"

Since Mrs. Gordy was younger than the woman she was complaining about, Brook fought back a smile. "What is wrong with the water?" she calmly asked.

The older woman sniffed. "Too cold, Her Ladyship says, as if she can't see the steam rising from it. Why, I could scald a babe in this water!"

"Housekeeper, who is keeping you from properly heating my water? Put aside your idle chatter for your own time. My feet cannot wait."

"Go," Brook whispered. "I will handle her." The thought startled her. There was a time when she did not believe she could handle anyone with the A'Court name.

"You'll be able to cook an egg in it," Mrs. Gordy promised, a malicious gleam lighting her gaze. "A good night to you, my lady."

"Do not dawdle, Housekeeper. I cannot—" Seeing Brook, the dowager halted her rant. "Oh, it is you, Lady A'Court."

She sat in front of her dressing table. Brook's maid, Morna, was at the older woman's feet removing her stockings. The dowager's personal servant was in the act of peeling off her wig. Brook had never seen the lady without her wig and found the vision disconcerting.

Not meeting her sharp gaze in the mirror, Brook said, "I have spoken with Mrs. Gordy. She will return shortly with your water. I hope it will be more to your liking." Conversing with her mother-in-law had never been easy, especially since Brook was treated like a servant who had transgressed.

"Your household is a mess, Lady A'Court." The dowager let her head fall back while her servant massaged her scalp. For practical reasons her graying hair was cut short as a gentleman's. "Your servants cannot carry out even the simplest orders, and one or two of them border on insolent. That housekeeper of yours must go. I suppose it is difficult to find competent help in these remote areas."

Brook and her maid exchanged looks. On Elthia, Lady A'Court's last visit she had suggested that Morna should be sacked. Brook had naturally ignored the dictate, because her maid was clean, pleasant, and had served her well. If she had listened to the dowager's commands she would have replaced the entire household staff three times over.

"It is good of you to worry about the management of my household, madam. However, do not trouble yourself on my account. I will handle the matter." She gracefully inclined her head. "I will bid you good night. Rest well."

"I know one or two families locally who might be able to assist you in this area. Let me think on it and we will discuss it tomorrow."

Sometimes Brook wondered if the older woman could hear her. She looked into the mirror half-expecting to see nothing. "Till tomorrow then." She quit the room feeling no better than when she had entered.

Brook passed her parents' room, barely pausing at their threshold. Since she heard no sounds from within, she assumed that they had already retired. Heading for her own bedchamber, she considered her duties concluded for the night. She had already spoken her "good nights" to the earl and his sister. Brook needed her rest for the arguments she would face tomorrow. Her family had not given up on the notion of her returning with them to London.

They had respected her decision to remain in Cornwall for two years. Elthia, Lady A'Court, should have been thrilled with the idea of her beloved son's widow spending the rest of her life mourning him. She had been less than satisfied with the match; however, Lyon had had his way. Brook closed her eyes, letting the pain flood her. Why had she not seen past his handsome face? He had seduced her with poetry and compliments and she had foolishly believed him. The sting of tears burned her eyes, but the tears never fell. She had not cried since the day Lord Tipton had told her that her husband had murdered the child in her womb.

Walking into her bedchamber, she placed the lamp on the table along the wall. Her maid was not likely to return anytime soon. Resigned, Brook began the task of removing the pins from her hair. Sensing that she was not alone, she turned toward her bed and blinked in surprise. May Hamblin was sitting on her bed.

"Forgive me, Cousin. You seemed so lost in thought that I did not want to startle you," she said, hopping off the bed.

Like Brook, she had not dressed for bed. "Do you need me to summon a maid? Mother A'Court should be finished with Morna by now." Brook reached for the lamp.

"No, the maid can tend me later. That is not why I am here," May said, fidgeting with the ribbons at her waist. The nervous gesture seemed contrary to her nature. "I wanted to discuss Mr. Claeg."

He was the last person Brook wanted to think about before she climbed into bed. Nor did she want to listen to May romanticize the scoundrel. As she removed one of the last of the pins from her hair, the heavy blond length cascaded over her shoulders and down her back. Brook did not consider herself a vain creature, but she thought her hair was her crowning beauty. Lyon had often complimented its thickness and color. Blindly in love with him, she did not suspect early on that he was thinking of another woman when he reached for Brook's hair. Later he had shown her that the one thing she prized could be wrapped around his fist and used to subdue and punish her.

"My goodness! You are plucking more hair than stray pins out," May said, coming up behind her. She guided Brook into the chair in front of her dressing table. "Here, let me play maid for you." Biting her lower lip and with more care than Brook had been managing, May removed the remaining pins that had been concealed in her hair.

"Mr. Claeg just recently leased his cottage. I am not certain I can tell you much about the man," she said, feeling obligated since May had been kind and helpful.

Reaching around her and picking up the brush, the young woman began the task of smoothing out the snarls left behind from Brook's rash pin search. "Oh, he explained all about coming here to paint the cliffs. Mrs. Ludlow was telling me that Mr. Claeg has been visiting you on and off this past year."

Brook and her mother were going to have a talk about her lack of discretion. She managed a small shrug. "He is not the first artist who has come to sketch and paint the landscape."

From May's frustrated expression, it was not the explanation she had sought. "When he comes here, he always calls on you."

"True. Being a gentleman, he feels obligated," she said, not even believing her own words.

The other woman laughed. "Have you not heard what they say about him? From all accounts, the man shirks duty. Gracious me, the man actually married his mistress!"

Being friends with his sister, Amara, Brook had learned bits and pieces about Mallory Claeg's life in the extraneous manner one does about a stranger. She could recall that she had sympathized with the family, since they had been scandalized by his actions. "I heard it was a love match. Besides it being none of our concern, the lady in question died many years ago. Tragedy can change a person," she said, thinking of her own losses. Odd, she had never considered that she and Mr. Claeg shared that in common. "Why are we discussing this?"

May had ceased brushing Brook's hair. Clutching the hairbrush to her breast, she said, "My brother has spoken to me at length regarding Mr. Claeg's presence at Loughwydde. He worries that the gentleman's attentions toward you might be less than honorable. You have been so fragile since your husband's death."

Considering she had watched May flirt with Mr. Claeg all afternoon and evening, Brook thought this lecture on her behavior reeked of hypocrisy. However, May was only the messenger, she reminded herself. It was the new Lord A'Court who was overbearing.

"You may tell your brother that Mr. Claeg has never be-
haved in a questionable manner." There was no need to point
out that he had almost kissed her in the front parlor. "He also
happens to be the older brother of one of my dearest friends,
someone whom I have neglected since I departed London.
His sister would never have forgiven him if he had not paid
me a call or two."

The explanation was reasonable if Amara had known
where Brook was. Only Mr. Claeg had discovered her small
sanctuary, and he had kept her whereabouts a secret. He had
not asked her why or even mentioned his sister since his return to Cornwall. Perhaps because of the promise she gained
from him, he had deduced that speaking of Amara would be
too upsetting. Did he, like Ham, believe Brook was too fragile? The thought was mildly irritating.

"Please forgive my prying," May begged. "Our connection is not of blood; nevertheless, when Ham inherited the
A'Court title your well-being also became a matter of interest
to him. He is a good man. You have been through so much
and deserve a little happiness in your life."

Brook rose and twisted in the chair until she was facing
May. She offered her hand and the other woman clasped it
within her own, accepting the silent apology. "I treasure
your friendship. Please convey to your brother that his fears
about Mr. Claeg are groundless. Like you, he will be returning to town for the season."

"I am not so certain."

She managed a small smile. "Of course he will. He came
to paint. Once he has finished his task, he will move on."

"You misunderstood me. I was referring to Mr. Claeg's
interest in you. My brother was not just being overprotective. On more than one occasion, his gaze strayed in your
direction."

Brook parted her lips in surprise. How could the man

make her feel flattered and annoyed in the same moment? "You are lending credence to coincidence."

May put the brush down on the dressing table. "Possibly. Just be careful, Cousin. Mr. Claeg has the notorious habit of choosing widows for his mistresses."

Chapter Five

The countess was altering her daily routine. He would be flattering himself to think she was deliberately avoiding him. Mallory did not mind her edginess. Nonetheless, he was guessing her family was distracting her. The new Lord A'Court did not trust him, and with good reason. The pompous earl sensed from the very beginning what Mallory wanted from the lovely widow because he wanted her, too. How ironic the recipient of their mutual lust was blissfully ignorant of the chaos she was causing.

Then again, maybe she was not so blind. There had been awareness in her eyes when Mallory had hauled her slender body against his. She may prefer that he seek his affections elsewhere. Miss Hamblin was a sweet, fine-looking woman who hinted by her actions the other day that she would have welcomed a brief dalliance. It was a pity her classic beauty did not stir him. One day he might immortalize her on canvas, but she would not grace his bed.

He had risen early. Mallory used the morning light to appease his muse. He had finished several watercolors of what he considered the countess's cliffs and one stark seascape. It was not his favorite medium. He preferred working in oils. However, watercolors were advantageous for outdoor work because he required fewer supplies and there was a quicker drying time. Satisfied with his morning work, he returned to his thatch-roofed cottage and dropped off his supplies. He had hired a local woman who tidied up after him and prepared his meals. Mrs. Whitby arrived late in the morning. She remained there as long as it took to clean up, restock his pantry, and leave him with enough food so he would not starve to death. He tried to explain that he required very little when he was painting, but she was determined to earn the generous wages he paid her. Mallory grabbed the small basket of food she had assembled for him and waved farewell to her. More out of habit than plan, he retrieved his sketching book and a few black lead pencils and tucked them into the basket.

The walk to Loughwydde was not arduous. The cottage's proximity suggested that it might have once been part of the property. Perhaps some of the surrounding land had been sold off at the baron's death. Whistling a tune, Mallory strode across the open area past the stone barn. From the corner of his eye he saw a blur of muted hues coming at him. The impact was not particularly painful. Dropping the basket, he wrapped his arm around his prize to steady himself. Mallory was pleased with his good fortune.

"Countess, there is no need for these outrageous stratagems," he said into her shocked face. "If you want me to touch you, all you have to do is ask."

Sputtering incoherent denials, Lady A'Court placed her hands on his chest and shoved. Hard. "I was not trying to touch you, oaf! What are you doing skulking about on my lands?"

Her straw bonnet had been dislodged and dangled by its ribbons down her back. The careless knot she had twisted her hair into was coming undone around her face. She wore a lilac spencer trimmed with swan's down at her wrists and across her bosom over a practical brown dress. Mallory gave her feet a passing appraisal and was pleased the ankle-length skirt revealed half boots.

"Good, you have something sensible on your feet. Let us go," he said, taking her by the hand and leaning sideways to grab the basket in the other.

"I am not going anywhere with you, Mr. Claeg."

"Of course you will." He nodded at the house. "You have the choice of walking in the woods with me on a fine spring day or returning to the house and allowing your family to badger you into something you do not want to do."

She resisted his subtle tug by keeping her feet firmly locked in place. "And why do you presume you would be the better choice?"

He took a step toward her and leaned close so that she could feel his breath on her face. She shivered in reaction, confirming what he had sensed. Beneath all that ice, the lady hungered. "Because any sensible lady would rather spend the afternoon with a handsome scoundrel than being lectured by disapproving relatives."

Mallory Claeg was correct. She had been delaying her return to the house for that very reason. Not that she would admit it to *him*. He already looked so pleased with himself, smiling down at her with those sorcerer eyes, daring her to defy convention for a few hours. Oh, she was tempted! Brook was biting a hole in her tongue to keep from giving her consent.

Her inner turmoil must have been apparent on her face. His jaw tightening in determination barely registered as a warning before he bowed low and threw her over his shoulder.

She clawed at his back seeking purchase in her upside-down circumstances. "Put me down!"

He shifted her with a series of bounces, trying to find a comfortable balance. She groaned, losing her bonnet. Her stomach roiled from the abuse. "Settle down, Countess. I predict things could become awkward if you alert anyone."

Awkward was the least of her worries. He spun them once around, testing his balance. She covered her mouth with her hand to silence any sound. It might have been laughter, but her corset was digging into various parts of her and it was making her a little queasy. Mr. Claeg had a firm hand on her backside. The pressure kept her in place, although she could have sworn he had caressed the round curve of her bottom. His gait should have been unsteady with her on his shoulder and the basket in his other hand. Somehow he managed both. He did not appear to be overburdened with muscles and yet he felt hard beneath his clothes. No one noticed as he carried her away from the house and toward the woods.

One of them had to be sensible. "You have had your jest. Enough, Mr. Claeg. Put me down."

He twisted his face toward her and pressed a kiss into her corseted side. "I like where you are. Besides, Countess, I thought you would enjoy having me be your beast of burden."

The journey had shaken out many of the pins securing her hair. The loose knot bounced against the side of her head. "What do you hope to accomplish with this nonsense?"

He did not answer her straightaway. When he spoke, he said, "I was looking for someone to share the sun with and I thought of you."

Brook did not have an acerbic rejoinder for what on the surface seemed like a reasonable, if not sweet, explanation. She winced, instinctively ducking when a low branch snagged some of her hair. Her hands clutched fistfuls of his coat. "Another minute like this and I shall lose my breakfast, Mr. Claeg. I demand—"

Her world twirled again as he set her on her feet. The remaining pins could not support the weight of her hair. It tumbled free down her back. He had to hold her upright until the dizziness subsided. Brook glanced around, noticing that the woods concealed them.

"Feeling steady?" he asked, rubbing his hands up and down her arms. "I have you until some of the blood leaves your face and pumps back into your limbs."

She shook off his hands and staggered back a step. "You most certainly do not have me." Brook gave her spencer a furious jerk. There was nothing she could do about her hair. It was hopeless to try to fix it without her pins.

"Well, not in the manner that first comes to mind," he conceded, grinning at her useless attempts to rectify her disheveled appearance. "Then again, my hand was on your rump. You cannot imagine my delight, Countess, to discover that you were hiding a bit of flesh under all that fabric and whalebone. At first glance, you have the build of a boy."

A boy! Oh, the nerve of the man. She had always been slender and, in truth, had lost too much weight after she had lost the baby. However, she had slowly recovered and likely weighed slightly more than she had before her husband's death. Pure feminine ire radiated throughout her body. "I refuse to remain another minute and discuss my inadequacies with you, Mr. Claeg." Expecting resistance, she charged him.

"Hold, you little fury," he commanded, picking her up off her feet. The indulgence in his expression faded when she kicked him. Dropping Brook onto her feet, he backed her up against the nearest tree. He blatantly used his body to keep her from escaping. "I used to believe you were a sweet little thing. All fancy lace and meringue. . . ." He let his words trail off. "Did anyone ever tell you that you have the devil's own temper?"

She could see his pulse beating in his throat. During their struggle, his hair had come free from its queue. The luxuriant mass with rich hues of browns threaded with honey curled slightly as it rested on his shoulders. She was amazed by how much she wanted to reach up and touch his uncivilized mane.

"I have been complimented countless times for my agreeable nature." Mr. Claeg snorted in disbelief. "I speak the truth. If you find me disagreeable, you can blame your uncanny ability for provocation. You could goad a saint into committing violence."

He was looking at her with that brooding intensity that seemed to penetrate her skin. Inside her half boots her toes curled. "Ah, that explains it," he said, pulling away from her.

It was immediately apparent that their proximity had inflamed him. The impressive length of his manhood swelled notably despite his snug breeches. Brook remained against the tree as if he still held her in place. She could barely breathe, wondering what he was planning to do to her. They were alone in the woods. Encumbered by her skirts, she could not hope to elude him. Would he throw her down onto the leafy loam and slake his lust?

Lyon had explained to her that a male could not control his reaction to a willing female. On the eve of their wedding, dressed in a white nightgown, she had expected a night of gentle touches, whispered assurances, and passionate declarations of love. Instead her new husband had come to her drunk on whatever spirits he and his friends had been toasting their nuptials with. Without ceremony, Lyon had unfastened his breeches, pushed up the fabric of her nightgown, and forged himself into her virginal body. She had sobbed during his rough invasion. Afterward, he had told her that she was to blame for his fierce ardor. She had looked so beautiful waiting there so patiently for him to pluck her virginity that he had succumbed to his baser instincts. He had accused her of trying to manipulate him with her tears. Angry, Lyon had stormed out of their bedchamber. She had spent the rest of her wedding night alone.

"I pray I am not the reason for that sorrowful look."

Startled, Brook wondered how many minutes had passed while she stared through him into the past. "I beg your pardon." Had she been gazing at his crotch all this time? If she could expire from embarrassment, she would have happily surrendered.

She flinched at the hand he offered her. Muttering something under his breath, Mr. Claeg said, "We have tarried here long enough, Countess. Besides, I have a better spot in mind."

Numbly she put her hand in his larger one. He led her farther into the woods, obviously comfortable with his surroundings. Why was he waiting? Mr. Claeg strolled with her hand in hand as if he were blissfully ignorant of his arousal. He was not demanding that she ease his pain, nor was he railing at her for placing him in this awkward predicament. The man had a notorious past and a string of mistresses. He was not the sort of man who denied himself anything. Her back was so stiff she hardly needed a corset. She felt like she was bracing for an expected blow that was never delivered. The anticipation was making her crazy.

"We'll stop here," he said, abruptly snapping her out of her private musings.

"Here," she echoed, looking at where he had brought her. It was a small clearing, not unlike countless others, with the exception that spring had added color to the landscape. In this section of the woods, bluebells had created a fragrant carpet for them. "I had not realized the bluebells were blooming. It is a lovely spot, Mr. Claeg."

Brook tried not to panic when he set down the basket and began to remove his coat. He shook it out and laid it on the bed of flowers. Mr. Claeg looked up sharply. She was terrible at subterfuge. Everything she was feeling was there for him to read.

"For you," he gently explained, motioning for her to be seated. "I do not mind a little dirt." At her hesitation, a wistful quality dimmed his natural exuberance. "Nor do I invite a lady I admire out into the woods so I can cruelly ravish her."

Lady A'Court sank onto his coat. Her rapid descent hinted that her compliance was dictated by a slight fainting spell more than her willingness to please him. Mallory wished he had not spoken his dark musings aloud. He had just grown weary of her staring at him ever since she had noticed his inopportune arousal like he was a vile debaucher of virtuous widows. Was it his fault that bumping up against her sped up his heart and pulsed his blood into his nether regions? The countess was a prickly lady, but he had no desire to terrify her.

Mallory crouched down beside her. He stretched his long legs out in front of him and braced himself upright with his arms. From his side view he could see that her color was improving and she was not dragging in air like a winded horse. He was content to listen to the birds and the soothing creaking and rustling of the trees.

"I have been behaving horribly. Will you accept my apology?" she quietly asked.

"I am afraid not, Countess." She gasped at his rudeness, extracting a rueful smile from him. "I meant that you do not owe me one. I am an impassioned, sometimes selfish man who shares my joys and sorrows with whoever happens to be around. I understand bad temper," he said, keeping his demeanor friendly. "We can discuss what upset you earlier if you like."

Lady A'Court clutched and released the fabric of her skirt. "I do not like. Thank you, I appreciate your kindness."

"As you please," he said, unwilling to upset her further. He rummaged though the basket he had brought. "Ah, saffron cake. I have a weakness for sweets and Mrs. Whitby has yet to disappoint me. Here." He handed her a thick slice. Mallory took out another for himself. He broke off a small piece and popped it into his mouth. Chewing thoughtfully, he said after he had swallowed, "If I could convince the old girl to marry me I would have freshly baked cakes every day."

The countess choked on the mouthful of cake she had been chewing. She covered her mouth with the back of her hand and coughed again. As she waved away his assistance it was then that he grasped she was laughing. The sound reminded him of her; soft, throaty, and hinting of shyness. She cleared her throat and said, "Mr. Whitby might have something to say about you absconding with his wife."

In Mallory's wild youth, something as mundane as an irate husband would not have stopped him from claiming a willing woman. There was no point in inspiring Lady A'Court's imagination about his misdeeds. She already viewed him as a scoundrel. "Well, then I shall have to find another lady who will satisfy my sweet cravings," he said innocently.

Naturally, she was not taken in by his guise of innocence. Tilting her head upward, she managed to look down her nose at him despite her small stature. "You like to play games."

Finishing off the last of his cake, he nodded. "There is no rule that having fun is for the young. I looked it up in a book once."

She delighted him by laughing again. "Are you ever serious?"

"Why? My father makes up for my lack," he said dismissively. He and Viscount Keyworth had been at odds long before Mallory had run off to marry Lord De Lanoy's mistress. Unlike his younger sister and brother, he had not sought his sire's approval. His cavalier attitude rankled his father more than his acts of disobedience. "Thirsty?" He uncorked the small jug and sniffed. "Nothing stronger than apple cider," he said with some regret. Mrs. Whitby, bless her, had the foresight to include a small cup. He filled it with cider and handed it to Lady A'Court. For himself, he drank straight from the jug.

"It is good. Mrs. Whitby is a treasure," she said, relaxing under the warmth of the sun. With her blond hair down, she seemed younger than five and twenty. "Did you know that when Mrs. Whitby is not looking after temperamental artists she comes to Loughwydde and helps her daughter with the laundry? Our laundress is carrying her third child."

Mallory picked up his sketching book and dug around in

the basket for his lead pencil. Without asking permission, because people rarely gave it when asked, he began a rough outline of her face.

"What are you doing?"

"I am sketching the bear behind you," he quipped. The only bears roaming England had human masters. "No, sit still!"

She huffed but complied with his order. "Are you always so overbearing when you work, Mr. Claeg?"

"Yes." He thickened the line defining her jaw. While he sketched her face, he could imagine another one in oils. This one would be full-figure with the countess lying on her stomach counting the bluebells. Naturally, she would not have a stitch of clothing on. He would position her so that her long hair and the flowers concealed more than they revealed. Mallory grinned at himself. Lady A'Court would slap him if he suggested such a picture. Later, perhaps. Recalling her question, he added, "Or so my sister complains. Did I mention that I convinced her to sit for me the summer last? She became Eris, the goddess of discord, for me." Saying not a word, Lady A'Court plucked some bluebells and brought the blooms to her nose. "I was rather pleased with the results. Amara had intended to give it to our mother. Regrettably, her marriage to Mr. Bedegrayne has created a rift in the family. To my knowledge, neither my mother nor father has spoken to her."

Mallory blew a frustrated breath out. He was losing patience with the countess's refusal to speak of anyone or anything that was connected to London. Something akin to slyness slid into his grim expression. "She will make me an uncle by summer's end. Brock's father, Sir Thomas, is thrilled there will be a new generation of Bedegraynes. I suppose I should be grateful that I did not murder Bedegrayne the second I suspected he had put his hands on my sweet sister."

No reaction.

"Confound it, woman!" he roared, slamming down his

book and lead pencil. He lunged for her before she could roll away. Seizing her by the shoulders, he shook the indifference from her face. The fear that replaced it was an improvement from the doll-like mask she had donned.

"How long?" he harshly demanded.

"W-What? I do not understand!"

The tremor in her voice made him feel despicable. Still, it did not stop him from pressing onward. "How long will you pretend that you did not have friends and a life in London?" They were both on their knees face-to-face. She was trying to pull away, but he was meaner and stronger. "When you ran away, Countess, did you even think of your friends? Amara was hurt by your silence."

Genuine pain mixed with her unshed tears. "I did not— oh—please, Mr. Claeg, I cannot talk about this."

"With me or anyone?" Disgusted with himself that he was bullying her, he released her.

She rubbed her arms but sat down on her folded legs instead of attempting to flee. "I thought I was dying," she said, her voice so soft he had to lean closer to hear her words. "My first clear recollection when I woke up was that my husband had murdered me." She laughed wearily. Bitterness had replaced joy. "I was partly right. Lyon murdered my baby."

Now that she was talking, he wanted to stop the flow of words. She sat on the forest floor hugging and rocking in a gesture of comfort. Mallory pulled her into his arms, coaxing her to lay her face against the warmth of his chest.

Lady A'Court pulled back and saw the apology in his gaze. "Why do gentlemen marry, Mr. Claeg? For wealth, position, an heir to pass on their prosperity to? Love?" She curled her lip in derision. "Lyon married me for none of those reasons. Do you want to know why I was so appealing to the handsome Earl of A'Court?"

"Hush. You have said enough. I am more sorry than I can say."

She ignored his plea. "Lyon married me because I bore a passable resemblance to the woman who had become his obsession. Miss Wynne Bedegrayne, a woman whom I considered one of my best and dearest friends. I was so young, so *stupid*. I loved him." Fighting back her tears, she pushed away from him and climbed to her feet. She paced and fought back the natural release of her grief. Lady A'Court did not speak again until she had vanquished what she considered a weakness. "I was already married when I learned the truth. Every time he whispered that he loved me, he was speaking to her. The clothes and jewels he lavished on me were to show Wynne what she had spurned. During the nights when he came to my bedchamber, it was Wynne's spirit he tried to break, her thighs he pried open, and it was her name he cried out as he spilled his seed into me. Even then, he found me lacking because I was not *her*!" She pounded her breast for emphasis.

"Damn it, Countess, enough!" Like everyone else, he had heard rumors that Lord A'Court had mistreated his young bride. Hearing a few of the less savory details sickened him. Mallory wished the earl was still living so he could have the pleasure of snuffing out his vile existence.

She rubbed her temple in frustration. "I was ill those last days. Most of my recollection is a confusing mix of what others said and a little supposition on my part. I know Lyon kidnapped Wynne and he had prepared a trap for her betrothed, Mr. Keanan Milroy. Whatever happened in the Milroy town house ended with Lyon's death."

The wind picked up, sending waves across the carpet of bluebells. Tendrils of her blond hair danced on the wind. "Perhaps I did run away, Mr. Claeg. If I had remained, the gossip would have flourished, hurting not only me but Wynne Bedegrayne as well." She stared at her bare fingers. "My friends would not have benefited from my association. Besides, they have gone on with their lives. Wynne married

Mr. Milroy. My mother told me that they have twin daughters. As for Amara, well, I am happy she has found love with Mr. Bedegrayne." Lady A'Court appeared to be struggling with her tears again. "A baby, you say?" Her trembling hand came up to her mouth.

"The babe will come in August." He came up behind her and enclosed her in his embrace. Resting his chin on the top of her head, he said, "I was wrong to pry, Countess. I hope Loughwydde has brought you a measure of peace."

She shuddered. Perhaps she was also thinking of the day he had found her near the edge of the cliffs daring the rock to crumble beneath her feet. "I have been comfortable."

It was Mallory's opinion that comfort was a poor substitute for happiness. She may not view it as such, but he thought it was fortunate fate had thrown him in her path.

"Are you finished with your sketch? I should return to the house before they start searching for me." Not waiting for his reply, she slipped out of his embrace. She walked over and retrieved his book. The countess studied his sketch of her in silence.

"It is an adequate representation," he said, defending his work. "I would like for you to sit for me again. A beauty such as yours deserves to be immortalized beyond a simple sketch." She looked up at him blankly. Or mayhap she did not believe he was sincere in his compliment. Indeed, he had seduced countless women into his bed with false flattery and they had tumbled eagerly. It wounded a bit that she thought he was low enough to take advantage of her vulnerability. "You, of course, may refuse if you find my work mundane."

Lady A'Court handed over his sketching book. "Do you honestly believe that drivel or are you playing on my sympathies? No, do not answer. Right now I do not know what to believe about you. One minute you are a flirtatious bounder and I see you for what you are. The next, I am telling you things I have never confessed to a soul while you let me cry on your shoulder. Which man is the real Mallory Claeg?"

He agreed with her assessment except that she had not cried on his shoulder. She had not permitted those tears to fall. Hell, he understood her confusion. Years ago he could have answered her with confidence, but over the past year and a half there had been some changes in his life. His first step had been to reestablish a bond with his sister, Amara. It had been too late to make amends with his younger brother. Four years ago, Doran had gotten involved in a coining scheme and had landed in Newgate Prison. He had died there. Losing him had reminded Mallory that he had allowed pride and his selfishness to destroy his ties to his family. Amara had been generous with her love. His father had no use for love. He wanted respect but had none for Mallory's art. Lord Keyworth's rigidity reminded Mallory why he had broken with his family all those years ago. Molding oneself into someone else's ideal destroyed one's soul. Doran had died trying to appease their father's expectations. Amara had almost given up the man she loved. Who was Mallory Claeg? Wicked seducer or jovial confidant? For Brook Meylan, Countess of A'Court, alone, maybe he could be both men.

"Countess, who do you want me to be?"

She sighed, disappointed in his flippancy. "More games, Mr. Claeg? The difference between a child playing games and an adult playing them is that a child never tires of them. I can see my way home on my own. Thank you for the cake and the flowers." She began threading her way through the trees toward Loughwydde.

He slapped the palm of his hand against his forehead. She had asked a simple question in an attempt to understand him and he had mocked her with a flirtatious reply. What arrogance! He had poked at her old scars to discover the wounded, passionate woman beneath, but he had denied her the same courtesy she had offered him.

"Countess, when can I sketch you and the bluebells again? It must be soon, for the blooms will not last."

"Beauty never does, Mr. Claeg!" she shouted back over her shoulder. "Tomorrow, possibly, if I can get away." She kept walking. There was no coy look or explicit promise that she would join him in the woods.

Mallory scooped up his coat and brushed off the dirt. If she had been any other woman, he would have suspected that the countess was playing her own game.

Tomorrow, possibly, if I can get away.

Oh, he would be waiting for her. If she showed, maybe he would tell her that she was naked in the picture he was planning.

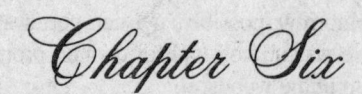

Chapter Six

Rushing down the stairs, Brook checked the clock. Goodness, she was late again!

"My lady, your bonnet!" Morna said, chasing after her.

Reversing directions, she met her maid in the middle of the staircase. Brook squelched her impatience, waiting for the young woman to place the bonnet on her head. Her patience lasted mere seconds. "I will tie it. Thank you, Morna!" She waved farewell and proceeded to tie the bow as she hurried down the stairs.

Ham ambushed her when she reached the landing. "Where are you running off to, Cousin?"

The inquiry was polite. Still, she bristled at his assumption that she owed him an accounting of her whereabouts. "Where I always go, Ham. My cliffs and perhaps the beach today." She gave her bow a firm tug. Brook was not concerned how the bonnet looked, since she planned on removing it once she reached the woods.

Ham surprised her by placing his hand on her shoulder. He had never acted presumptuously. "I speak not only for myself but for the family. You spend too much time alone." He lowered his voice as if he thought anything loud would frighten her. "Elthia, Lady A'Court and your mother worry that my presence has somehow upset you."

"I am not upset," she assured him, ducking under his arm.

"I am a creature of habit, my lord. I prefer keeping to a schedule."

If Ham delayed her too long, Mr. Claeg might assume she was not coming. Eight days had passed since their first meeting in the woods. Each day she had vowed not to go and yet each afternoon she put on her bonnet and dashed off to meet him.

"Why do I not join you?" the earl suggested, pleased with his brilliance.

Brook stifled a groan and turned around to face him.

"We could discuss your return to London without the interference of the family. And as we walk, you can show me the finer aspects of your land."

She had been deftly avoiding the subject of returning to town for days. If her luck held, she could evade it another day, and another, until she was bidding her guests a safe trip. "These solitary walks comfort me, Ham." Brook made a vague gesture with her hand. "Having all of these people in my house is slightly overwhelming. It is usually so peaceful here."

"Of course."

She gritted her teeth at his condescension. "The quiet and the air clear my head and ease my nerves. We will take a walk together another day."

"Very well, Cousin." He took her hand and bowed. "I will await your return."

Brook had almost reached the edge of the woods when she realized she had been practically running. If Ham had watched her from one of the windows, his suspicions would have been aroused. A woman did not rush out of the house for a solitary walk. She rushed to meet—a lover! Horrified by the unbidden thought, she deliberately slowed her pace. There was no reason to give Mr. Claeg any encouragement. Spending a few hours with him each day was already giving him ideas.

"Caught you!"

Mr. Claeg encircled her waist and spun her around until she laughed. "I thought you had forgotten me," he whispered in her ear, making her shudder. He kissed the side of her neck and released her.

"Not likely," she said, untying the bow under her chin. "Tell me that you were not on your way to the house." Removing her bonnet, she let it dangle at her back while she retied the ribbons.

"Is there a reason why I cannot pay my neighbor a visit?" he gruffly demanded.

Did he want a list? There was May, who wanted him. Ham despised him. Her sisters and mother adored him. Mr. Ludlow did not trust him, and the dowager considered him unworthy of her exalted presence. As for herself, she was uncomfortably aware that each day she was looking forward to his companionship. Trouble? "None at all," she lied.

He gave her an odd look. She started breathing again when he took her hand, saying, "Come along, Countess. I set everything up while I waited for you."

Hand in hand they ran through the woods like children on an adventure. Mr. Claeg had replaced the quiet of her walks with discovery, humor, and color. His enthusiasm for reveling in his surroundings was contagious. She had haunted these woods for almost two years, but it was with him that she had learned to appreciate their beauty.

Brook was panting by the time they had reached the clearing. Waving her hand in front of her face, she said, "I need to rest before we start."

"All you do is laze under the sun while I slave away on your picture," he complained good-naturedly. Retrieving a flask from the basket, he poured some water into a cup and handed it to her. "If the heat is troubling you, I would not take offense if you chose to remove that burdensome dress."

This was one of his games. After her initial shock, she had gradually gotten into the spirit of the game, if not applauding his single-minded tenacity. Each afternoon he artlessly suggested that she allow him to paint her in the nude. She always politely refused and he never took offense. However, she had conceded his point that her spencer was unnecessary.

"You are tarrying. Here, let me assist you before the clouds consume the sun." All business, Mr. Claeg began to unbutton her spencer, ignoring her murmur of protest.

"This is hardly appropriate."

He lifted his brows. "It is if I am trying to get your dress off."

She tossed her cup of water in his face. "Degenerate! Your charm may be boundless, but you will never convince me to model nude for you." Brook backed up, not trusting the gleaming challenge in his eyes.

"Care to wager on it?" he taunted, swinging an arm out to grab her.

She jumped backward, picked up her skirts, and dashed to the left. He chased her, the pair of them zigzagging through the trees. Brook squeaked, barely avoiding capture by ducking low and doubling back. She laughed at his oath when he scraped his arm against one of the trees.

"Shall I summon Mrs. Whitby to bandage your wound?" she called out, glancing back to see how close he was.

Mr. Claeg had disappeared.

Stunned, she skidded to a halt and whirled around. Where was he? "My lord, where—oof!"

Brook fell neatly into his hands when he sprang his trap. Concealed behind one of the larger trees, he had circled around it and rushed her from the other side. They fell to the ground, but Mr. Claeg had been prepared for the possibility. Pulling her against his chest, he took the brunt of the fall on his side.

"Damn, I landed on my injured arm," he groaned, rolling on his back. Both lay there, staring up at the treetops, panting from the chase.

"You deserve the pain." She turned her head and glowered at him. "You nearly scared five years off me when you charged me. Will you look at my dress? When I return to Loughwydde, they will think I threw myself down a hill."

He rolled onto his side and propped his head up on his fist. The hair around his face was wet from the water she had tossed at him. His tender gaze had her thickly swallowing. "We never did get this garment off," he murmured huskily. With one hand, he unfastened the remaining buttons. He splayed his hand possessively across her waist.

"Mr. Claeg, w-what are you doing?"

As he leaned over her, the tips of his wet hair swirled crazy brushstrokes on her cheeks. "Brace yourself, Countess. I am about to claim a kiss."

Brook squeezed her eyes shut, anticipating him ravishing her mouth. The butterfly caress he gave her was more devastating to her senses. His lips swept lightly over hers. He repeated the motion again and again. Her nipples tightened painfully and a wave of sensation rippled down to her knees. Parting her lips, she inhaled sharply, seemingly pulling him closer with her breath alone. She felt his tongue slide into her mouth, silently coaxing her into another one of his games.

Brook tentatively brushed her tongue against his. Mr. Claeg growled his approval, slanting his mouth so their connection deepened. Warmth and need coiled in her loins. She curled her tongue around his and her fingers speared his hair, pulling him closer. He complied. Sliding one leg between hers, he positioned himself so his arousal was pressed against her hip. What had begun as a gentle kiss was gradually escalating into a frenzied eagerness. She sucked his tongue deep into her mouth, but it did not satisfy the need rising in her. Frustrated, she bit his lower lip.

He drew back and stared down at her face. The light blue color was merely a slim ring of color and his mouth was red and moist from her dedicated effort to devour him. "Again," he said, pressing a hard kiss to her mouth. Still bracing most of his weight with his left arm, he trailed kisses along the line of her jaw. Brook arched her neck, giving him access. He licked the pounding pulse at her throat while his free hand traced the contour of her body. Mr. Claeg nibbled at the tender flesh of her throat and chills moved just under her skin. Using his right hand to anchor her to him, he set his teeth into the soft swell of her right breast.

She choked in surprise. Brook had never considered breasts particularly sensitive, but under Mr. Claeg's expert mouth the flesh swelled and tingled. He reached up and tugged at the edge of her bodice. She tensed for a moment, fearing he intended to rip her dress. Both her breasts popped free of the confining corset.

Murmuring what she assumed was praise, he laved first the right nipple and then the left. She moved against him restlessly, uncertain what her body wanted. Mr. Claeg understood her needs. Teasing one of her nipples with his tongue, he tilted his head, his eyes meeting her unfocused gaze.

"Has no one ever sampled these lovelies before, Countess?"

Brook shook her head. Lyon had taken pleasure from her body, but he had never bothered to show her that there was pleasure also in giving.

Mr. Claeg gave her a slow, enigmatic smile. Keeping his gaze on her face, he lowered his mouth to her breast and suckled her. It was an incredibly wicked sensation. A part of her was appalled that she was lying on the ground like a depraved hussy allowing him to touch her in any manner he pleased. The other half of her was afraid he would stop.

He cupped the underside of her breast and feasted as if he were withdrawing rich milk from it. The suction bordered on exquisite pain. Releasing that breast, he chuckled and nipped her other one. He did not bother to share what amused him. Before she could ask, he covered the areola of her left breast. Pleasure was a lightning bolt. It struck her between her legs. She would have crossed them in response if his body were not pinning down her right leg. Brook curled toward him, digging her fingers into the back of his neck. Mr. Claeg stiffened as if the electrical charge had jumped from her and into him. As he dragged her closer, she was not aware of his hand beneath her skirt until his fingers tested the wetness between her legs.

She squeezed her legs together, but those talented fingers had already breached her feeble defenses. "No," she whispered, but her traitorous body rose up eager for his touch.

He was merciless. Using the wetness, he boldly rubbed his thumb over the sensitive nubbin hidden within her feminine cleft. It blossomed beneath his skilled touch. Panting, she twisted under him, her body uncomfortably warm.

When he lifted his head, she noticed he was breathing heavily. There was an intensity she had never seen before in his light blue eyes that was akin to madness. "Do not fight it!" he ordered, plunging his fingers deep into her. She gasped at his invasion, but there was no pain. She sensed a growing tension in her body as well as his. The kisses and suckling of her breasts became less practiced and more frantic while his hand between her legs stroked and penetrated her rhythmically, driving her to the edge of sanity. Earlier she had feared the rigid flesh concealed within his breeches. Now she longed for him to end her torment. She blamed his sorcerer's eyes and magical touch. They had woven a spell over her. It was the only thing that made sense.

"I want you inside me," she said through clenched teeth.

His head jerked up at her rough command and his nostrils flared, taking in her scent. "I am, Countess. Feel me." He flexed his fingers within her feminine channel, pressing his damp thumb against her nubbin simultaneously. Increasing the pressure, he quickened his strokes. "Come for me," he ordered, biting her earlobe hard.

Brook embraced what he was offering. She cried out his name, and her hips bucked as his fingers ruthlessly plunged, wringing out a spiraling ecstasy she had never known existed. He had shattered her. She pressed her face into his neck and felt him shudder. Neither of them moved from their shameless position. As the blood pounding in her ears receded, the normal sounds of the woods returned.

She felt his fingers spasm before he slowly withdrew them from her moist channel. "Are you all right?" he politely asked, covering her exposed legs. "Was I too rough?" He rolled off her.

Lyon had never asked her humiliating questions. He had simply used her and then left her alone. She almost wished Mr. Claeg were as inconsiderate. "I am unhurt, my lord." Brook sat up and fought the weakness in her limbs that was making her tremble. Her breasts were still swollen and tender. Stuffing them back into her bodice, she knew her flesh would bear the marks of his teeth for days. She blushed at the thought.

He picked several twigs out of her hair. "You never found pleasure in the marriage bed?"

She winced at the question. A minute earlier she was cavorting with him on the ground, not caring that she was half-naked. How could a simple question make her feel more exposed? "Is this necessary? I would rather not discuss the particulars of my marriage with you, Mr. Claeg." Standing, she gazed up at the sky. "It appears you have lost your sun, after all."

He stepped in front of her. "To hell with good manners. You shouted my name while in the throes of your pleasuring. I want to hear it again."

Brook shook her head, shyly refusing. Now that she was

thinking more clearly, her own brazen behavior embarrassed her. Dear God, she had actually begged the man to compromise her. Thank goodness he had refused, else she would have become one more woman in his long history of scandalous seductions.

His temper flared at her reluctance. "What troubles you, Countess? That you let me touch you?"

She walked around him, buttoning her spencer with unsteady hands. Mallory Claeg refused to be ignored. He manacled her upper arm and forced her to halt.

"Or is it that a few minutes ago I proved that you were no better than every other lascivious female who has parted her legs and begged me for a superior fu—"

Brook slapped him hard across the face. It was a stalemate on who was more surprised by her violence. She had never committed violence against another person. Horrified, she heard his teeth audibly clamp together as his hand curled into a fist. His restraint was commendable, but she might have felt better if he had retaliated and hit her.

A muscle in his jaw twitched. The imprint of her hand appeared like a sunburn on his cheek. "We were both painfully accurate, it seems."

She blinked, taken aback by his cruelty. Brook looked down, unable to face the burning blue ire in his eyes. She did not comprehend the duality of men. What had she done to provoke him? It was almost as if she had somehow hurt his feelings. "I see no reason for us to meet again. You have more or less accomplished what you set out to do. Forgive me if I do not remain and watch you gloat over your victory."

"And the picture?"

Ah, the bait he had used to lure her out into the woods each day. No matter how long she had begged, he had refused to show her his work until it was finished. She had no idea how far he had progressed, since he seemed to spend most of their time flirting with her. Her ignorance did not prevent her from replying, "Paint another face over mine. I care not what you do. As you have so crudely pointed out, you see no distinction from one woman to the next."

Mallory Claeg did not reply to her insult. He just stared at her with an unfathomable expression.

She pulled the loop of ribbon over her head and shook the debris from her bonnet. "Oh, and one more thing, Mr. Claeg. Keep off my land."

Ham crouched down using his walking stick for balance and leaned his back against the trunk of a tree. His hands still trembled, but he had escaped unnoticed. The man and woman he had seen in the clearing were too caught up in their passion to hear him. At first, he had believed he had come across one of the housemaids with her lover.

As he had crept closer to the couple, he had recognized the man to be no servant but none other than the notorious Mr. Claeg. Curious about the lady who had been ensnared by the gentleman's charm, Ham had stealthily moved from tree to tree in an effort to improve his view. Although he had only glimpsed her face, he had immediately recognized her hair and the dress. Lady A'Court had lied to him. She was not taking solitary walks as she had told her family. Instead, she was rushing off to meet Claeg. Immobilized by his shock, he watched the artist pull on the front of her dress and feast like a starved man on the lady's exposed breasts. She had moaned and the sound of pleasure pierced Ham's gut like a lead ball. His cock had thickened and it was not his fault that he had had to unfasten the falls on his breeches and adjust his swelling length. Ham had expected Claeg to do the same. Those throaty mewling sounds his cousin made would have stiffened the rod of a sodomite. Yet the artist had kept his breeches closed, an act that most likely had spared the gentleman's life.

If he had touched her . . .

And yet Claeg had claimed her. Ham had watched the man's hand slip under her skirt. Lady A'Court had whimpered and risen to meet those thrusting fingers. Sweat had beaded Ham's brow. He had stroked his rigid cock imagining that he was the one who was pounding into her tight passage. That she was grasping his shoulders and begging him to spill himself into her. He had collapsed against the tree that concealed him, and muffled his hoarse cry as he brought himself to climax.

Ham had used his handkerchief to clean himself. Sneaking a peek at the couple, he had recognized the frenzied motions of completion. Buttoning his breeches, he had slipped away unnoticed with Lady A'Court's cries echoing in his ears.

Thirty minutes had elapsed since he had crouched down and begun waiting for his cousin's return. Hatred burned his throat for the artist. Envy was a weight on his heart. Ham dropped his head on top of his clasped hands, which rested on his walking stick, and despaired.

Mallory had let her go. It was for the best. Both of them were feeling angry and prideful. There was nothing to be gained in exchanging further insults. He threaded his hand through his tousled hair. The countess had removed the leather strip he used to tie back his long hair. Searching the ground, he picked up the narrow strip and tried to put order to his appearance.

The lady had surprised him. They had spent days dancing around the witchery between them. How had a harmless kiss ignited into a conflagration of need? Once he had put his hands on her and she had responded, he had waged an internal battle not to finish what both of them had wanted.

Yet the little widow had found satisfaction in his arms, he smugly mused. She had resisted, not understanding it was her body and desires she was fighting, not his. Her release had been an irresistible siren's song to the long-denied needs he had leashed on her behalf. Like a green lad reacting to his first taste of a naked breast, he had ground his arousal against her hip and ignobly pumped his release into his breeches. Damn, his hands were still shaking, he noted with disgust.

Fisting them, he stared off in the direction in which the countess had departed. Enough time had passed for him to follow at a discreet distance. She might have a low opinion of his bloody nobility, but he was not going to let her traipse around the countryside unescorted.

For a tiny woman, she slapped like a tough costermonger, he wryly thought, picking up her trail. That flash of temper had been unexpected. He would have wagered everything he owned that she had never struck a man before. Mallory rubbed his injured cheek. She had been horrified by her action, but the slap was well deserved. He had been deliberately provoking; however, he was willing to lay some of the blame at Lady A'Court's feet.

She could not bring herself to say his name.

Her reluctance had hurt. It was an unwelcome vulnerability. Since his wife's death, he had been selective when choosing his lovers. They were all beautiful, covetous, ambitious wenches who had been willing to share their bodies with him for a price. He had always been willing to pay it whether it was jewelry, new clothes, a small house in an affluent section of town, or even an introduction to a richer protector. He had adored each one in her turn. Still, none of his lovers had left a permanent impression on his heart. When the affairs ended, there was never regret.

Mallory had already figured out the countess was not so shallow as to sell herself for trinkets or his protection. He had offered her more of himself than he had anticipated, but at what cost? At the moment, he was not certain this lonely, unhappy woman was worth the trouble. He could return to

London and find another lady to amuse him, someone who was prettier and more confident. A naughty minx who muddled his senses but not his damn heart.

Why was he stalking the one woman guaranteed to ruin him?

Mallory had been observing her progress at a distance as they walked through the woods. Another woman would have cried after fighting with her lover or at least made a noisy exit. Lady A'Court had too much dignity. However, the lady had made a mistake in allowing him to get so close. What most gentlemen thought was ice was hot and quivering when stroked. He had discovered she had a weakness, too.

Him.

Keeping out of sight in case she glanced back, he stopped as she exited the woods. Mallory became alert when a male suddenly appeared from behind her and motioned for her attention. The countess halted, allowing the man to catch up to her. At this distance, it was difficult to see the man's face, but it was someone she knew, maybe the new earl.

The man had been waiting for her. The notion did not sit well. Mallory watched them talk for a few minutes and then continue walking toward the house together. Poor Lady A'Court. For a woman who shunned company, she had an abundance of male suitors. He brought his hand up and inhaled. Her musky scent still clung to his fingers. All thought of packing up and traveling to London faded. With the gift of clarity, Mallory grasped that he was willing to pay whatever price to have her.

Chapter Seven

"Cousin, walk with me in the apple orchard?"

Brook lifted her gaze from her needlepoint. Ham had positioned himself behind her and she had to squint to see his face. "Certainly, my lord." She rose and nodded to her companions.

The ladies had decided to use the sunlight to their benefit and had set up a table outdoors to work on their various endeavors. Her half sisters had complained of the ennui, and exasperated with their complaints, their mother had given her blessing. The last she had seen of them, they had been running off to see the lambs.

"Do not keep her out in the sun too long, my lord," the elder Lady A'Court said, finishing off a stitch. "Lady A'Court is beginning to freckle. Remind me later, dear, and I shall write down a reliable recipe even your housekeeper cannot spoil."

"You are too generous, madam." The freckles were the dowager's way of reminding Brook that she had been neglecting her duties. It hardly mattered that she had not gone farther than the stone barn for the past three days. It was cowardice that had kept her so close to home. By the second day, she figured out that it was not fear of seeing Mallory but, rather, fear of *not* seeing him that kept her away from the woods.

Ham did not offer his arm while they walked. She had not been the only person at Loughwydde who was petulant these days. His hands crossed behind his back, the earl seemed preoccupied with his thoughts. The day she had quarreled with Mr. Claeg, she had encountered Ham near the woods. Despite her refusal, he had been searching for her in hopes of joining her. The thought of him accidentally discovering her activities with Mr. Claeg had been alarming. Without protest, she had accepted his escort back to the house.

"My lord, I can tell something is troubling you," Brook said, breaking the silence. "You may not view me as a confidante; however, you have been kind to me. I can do nothing less than offer you the same."

They had reached the orchard. The air was fragrant and the branches were pregnant with white blossoms. When the breeze shifted, the low branches showered them with tiny white petals.

"Lady A'Court, I will be leaving for London tomorrow morning."

Odd, Mother A'Court had not mentioned leaving. "Of course. I would not wish to interfere with the duties of the title or any business prospects." She cocked a glance in his direction. "Did you think I would be angry?"

"No. Yes." He shook his head in confusion. Ham took up both her hands. "What I had hoped was that you would be disappointed in my departure."

"You will be missed."

"By you." His light gray eyes reminded her of silver in sunlight. "You will miss me?" he asked, the distinction seemingly important.

"Certainly. You are a good man."

He was not going to let her dismiss him with a few polite words. "Good enough to be your husband?" he countered, carefully judging her reaction.

She stopped under one of the oldest apple trees in the

grove. "Ham, I do not know what to say." Brook was stunned. She had not considered that the earl had thought of her in any romantic manner.

"S-Say you will," he stuttered, wearing the tortured expression that every man wore when forced to declare his matrimonial intentions. He cleared his throat. "I can see my revelation has shocked you."

The orchard needed a few stone benches, Brook decided. If one had been available to her she would have collapsed on it. "I consider you a friend."

"Friendship is as good as anything to base a marriage on," he reasoned. "We could keep things as they are. You are fond of Loughwydde, and I would not keep you from it. Naturally, we will have to spend part of the year in London. It will be expected, but you will adapt."

The old panic about London tightened her chest. "I told you, Ham. I do not want to reside in town. If I return, there will be gossip about Lyon." And her. She could not bear the stares and whispers. There was also Wynne. How could she face her old friend again after Lyon had done his best to hurt her?

The earl was unaware of the fears he had resurrected by mentioning London. "The *ton* will accept you. You will not be Lyon's countess; you will return as mine."

"Ham, I cannot talk to you about Lyon—or my life with him." She genuinely did not want to hurt this man. "After my husband died, I vowed never to marry."

"And you think you are the first grieving widow who has made such an oath and later regretted the impulsive words? Dearest, no one will mock you for embracing life again."

He was forcing her to speak the words that would crush him. Brook took a deep breath. "Ham—"

He had yet to release her hands. Maybe he feared she would run off. "Wait! Do not say it. In my eagerness, I have not allowed you time to adjust. You see me as Lyon's cousin and a friend. You have never looked at me and seen the man."

"If I had known—" She would have sought a gentler way to dissuade him from this notion.

"Hush; forget about your answer. Put it aside. I have to leave tomorrow. Being around you without expressing my feelings has been . . . difficult. When May and the rest of the family follow, I want you to come to London. Come to me and allow me the privilege of courting you properly. I swear you will never find a man who adores you more than I."

Ham bent down and pressed a hasty kiss on her open mouth. Holding her firmly against him, he tried desperately to prove without words the high sentiments she stirred in him. Brook stood stiffly in his embrace. She could have pushed him away, but curiosity had overruled her usual caution. When Mallory Claeg had kissed her, she had felt the humming response all the way to her toes. She hoped Ham's kiss would inflame her, too. It would ease her mind, viewing her moments with the artist as a natural reaction to any male rather than offering the scoundrel a true part of her heart. Brook concentrated on Ham's mouth. His lips were clammy and a little too soft.

"Very touching," Mr. Claeg mocked with false cheerfulness. "Children, is there good news to share?"

Where the devil had Mr. Claeg come from and how long had he been observing them? Groaning, Brook closed her eyes. She placed the blame entirely on him. It was fortunate that Ham was still holding her, because she was reeling from her discovery. Nothing. She had felt nothing at all when Ham kissed her! Could it be that she actually had *feelings* for that miserable trespassing scoundrel?

The countess looked thunderstruck. Mallory might have drummed up a pang of sympathy if he had not caught her kissing another man. He scowled at her. The duplicitous witch had the audacity to return the murderous glare. What had he done? She was the one caught in a compromising embrace.

"Mr. Claeg," the earl greeted him, releasing the lady's arm and respectfully edging away from her. "Your timing is regrettable, sir. My cousin and I were hoping to say our farewells in private."

His meaning was a tad too obvious for Mallory's liking. Neither was the countess pleased. Though he benefited nicely when she switched her glower from him to Lord A'Court.

"So you are leaving us," Mallory said, cheered by the news. He did not perceive the man as a threat, but having him skulking after the countess at inopportune moments certainly dampened one's ardor.

Lord A'Court frowned at both of them. "Tomorrow. Was there something you wanted, sir?"

Oh, he could not get rid of a Claeg that easily. He sent the lady a sly look, which had her bristling. He smiled. She understood what he wanted even if the earl was obtuse. "My muse," he said, spreading his hands out in a gesture of helplessness. "She has summoned me to Loughwydde."

"You actually hear voices?" she asked, her tone ringing with skepticism, pretending that he was not referring to her.

He gave her a patronizing look. "The summons is not a voice and yet it is a call." He was always willing to talk about art. When he could get her alone, they would discuss the reason he had come to Loughwydde.

"Truly," the earl said, fascinated in spite of his and Mallory's mutual dislike. "Does the call come to you in dreams?"

"Sometimes. Most days, it is—I suppose one might describe it as a restlessness. In the beginning, it feels like a tickle in your stomach."

"Eating a slice of Mrs. Whitby's saffron cake should take care of your problem," the countess suggested, convinced he was playing one of his games.

She was partly correct.

Mallory reached out and lightly pinched her shoulder in

warning. "You have a petal," he apologetically explained, removing it. "Hunger is a part of it, but not for food."

He raised his brows in a telling manner. The countess blushed, recalling as he had hoped that she had briefly experienced one of his other aspects of hunger.

"The tickle if ignored becomes thrum. It expands outward and is all consuming. One must obey its call."

The earl idly twisted his walking stick into the soft ground, contemplating Mallory's words. "And if one does not?"

"A kind of temporary madness."

The countess choked on what he suspected was laughter. "Now that does explain a few things," she said, managing to keep her amusement from her expression.

He had yet to forgive her for kissing the earl, so he ignored her. "You lose the taste for food. There is no comfort to be found in the oblivion of sleep. You wander about with a cauldron of unfathomable turmoil bubbling in your belly, which provokes you into seeking a means to ease the discomfort."

Riveted, Lord A'Court asked, "What guides you to the solution?"

Mallory shrugged, struggling to put into words something that was unique to each individual. "For me? Maybe it is an artist's acumen. It is difficult to explain. Sometimes it is a glimpse of an image, a flash of color, or even music."

"How do you know when you have appeased this muse?" the other man inquired.

"When that thrumming recedes into nothingness and I can think of something other than my art."

"It sounds like a selfish way to live," the countess said flatly.

The blue eyes gleamed like sunlight on winter ice. "Oh, it is, Lady A'Court." Leave it to the widow to unerringly find and poke one of his old wounds. Her observation was too reminiscent of his father's and several bitter mistresses who had never accepted that they had been secondary in his life.

"It can be a solitary one as well." Mallory shook off the dark thoughts with a cocky grin. "However, it also has its rewards."

The earl cleared his throat. "I imagine it does," he said with a trace of envy. "So what has brought you to Lough-wydde?"

"A picture," Mallory said mysteriously.

As she recalled their last encounter and her warning that he should stay away, the countess's temper flared. "I have no interest in sitting for you, Mr. Claeg."

"Then we are both fortunate, since you are not the lady who kindles my inspiration," he smoothly countered, smug that she had fallen so neatly into his trap.

The countess had been so arrogantly convinced she was the reason for his appearance that his admission left her speech-less. He had ruined the clever dismissal she had planned for him. Though the flash of pain she swiftly concealed tugged at his conscience.

"Who do you wish to paint?" she asked, her earlier spirit subdued by his snub.

Mallory gritted his teeth. Hurting her had not been part of the plan. Perhaps he did want to unsettle her a little, but he was not cruel. "Miss Hamblin. With your permission, natu-rally," he said to the earl.

"Well, Cousin, I see no reason to deny Mr. Claeg his muse. My sister will be departing with the dowager, so you will have a few days to indulge in your craft. What is your opinion, Lady A'Court?"

"I believe your sister will be extremely flattered, since she admires Mr. Claeg's . . . uh, talent," she said, being diplo-matic. "Even her departure for London in a few days will not be a hindrance, since Mr. Claeg had plans to return once his work here was concluded. There is nothing keeping you here, is there, sir?"

He could not interpret her expression, but he wagered he would have hated her private thoughts. Instead of showing

envy or anger, the damn woman was just letting him go without a fight. Her emotions were muted, just like her dress and
the boring life she had set up for herself. He wanted to shake
her for that apathy.

Mallory willed her to look him in the eyes. "You have it
right, Countess. I will return to town once I have finished my
work."

"That is what I thought." She offered the earl her arm.
"Let us go share the good news with the others."

Lord A'Court stilled. The hope brimming in his boyish
face had Mallory tensing. "Does this mean—are you by
chance giving your consent?"

The earl's anticipation shattered the mask of calm she
had donned. She bowed her head. "I was referring to your
sister's good fortune, my lord. As for the other, you spoke of
giving me time. If you cannot, I—"

"No, no," the man hastily cut off her refusal. "I was being
thoughtless. Forgive me, dearest."

"Oh, Ham, so am I," she said, her face poignant with regret. "If you both will excuse me." The countess separated
from the earl. Picking up her skirts, she ran toward the house.

Watching her run away, Mallory figured both he and
A'Court were at fault. He knew why he was feeling lousy,
but he was very curious about Lord A'Court's question. "I
assume there was more news."

They continued in her wake, not making any effort to
catch up to her. Mallory sensed the earl was deciding how
much he should reveal. "The family wants her to return to
London. She is . . . stubborn."

Yes, indeed. One could see it in her stance and the way she
lifted her chin. She had not always been strong, so what she
had become after her grief waned was all the more remarkable. Though one thing was certain: the countess was not
about to let another man rule over her. Mallory was not about
to presume that he understood the logic of the feminine

mind, but he had figured out that the past was tied to London. She had snipped those threads, and the decision had held for two years. With everyone clamoring for her to change her mind, the next few weeks were going to be interesting.

"The countess has a rather fierce opinion about not returning to town. Why are you convinced you can succeed where her mother has failed?"

"Her fears are groundless and I can prove it if she would just allow me the chance. As my bride—"

"Bride," Mallory silkily echoed. "She has accepted your proposal?" His intuition told him it was not true, but it seemed fair to hear A'Court's denial before he murdered the man. How dare the man propose marriage to his soon-to-be mistress!

"No." He scrunched his face in disgust. "She was not ready to hear my declaration. In my haste, I had forgotten how fragile she is. I hate to speak ill of family, but my cousin Lyon was not a patient man. Anyone could see that his marriage to Lord Lanston's daughter was destined to be an unhappy one. Her youth and effervescence were contrary to the exacting, somber nature of my older cousin. It was clear that she adored her husband, but his need to control her bruised that gentle spirit. On reflection, I can see my error. I was too forceful." Lord A'Court turned to Mallory in horror. "Mayhap I reminded her too much of Lyon?"

Only if fate was generous, thought Mallory. Well, now he knew it was A'Court's proposal rather than his appearance that had astonished her. "An intolerable quandary. I do not envy you, sir. If I may offer a suggestion?"

"I would welcome your counsel, Mr. Claeg."

"Grant her the patience denied her in marriage to your cousin," Mallory suggested. "Go slowly. Let her set the pace." If he interpreted the countess's quick escape correctly, her pace would be a snail's shimmering glide into never.

"You have offered sound advice. I thank you, sir." Lord

A'Court inclined his head. "The day Lady A'Court accepts my proposal, it will be you, Mr. Claeg, whom I will praise for the success of our tender courtship."

He smiled and accepted the earl's appreciative pat on the back. Guile was akin to betrayal and Mallory had mastered both at an early age. He did not feel a twinge of guilt for his interference. A'Court would not be the first man who had lost the lady he coveted to Mallory's charming subterfuge. Although he had thought he had outgrown it, the skin of a rogue fit him perfectly.

Chapter Eight

Mallory Claeg was up to mischief. Brook could not shake the nagging suspicion, even though his behavior was irreproachable at Loughwydde. Ham had been unconcerned about the artist's daily presence when she had mentioned it to him. The morning he had departed for London, he had commented that it eased his mind that a gentleman was nearby to check on them. She had managed quite well on her own these past two years and she had not needed or wanted Mr. Claeg's lauded presence.

"Countess, have you fallen asleep again at the window?" Mr. Claeg winked at May, who giggled. Brook winced, wondering for the hundredth time how a pretty young woman could have developed such an obnoxious laugh. "I can hear your soft snores from here. Are you having difficulty sleeping at night?"

She did not bother to acknowledge his teasing with an irritated glare. The man was immune to them. "I sleep quite adequately, thank you. Grandmother Byres must have fallen asleep again." Brook checked on the elderly woman and she had indeed nodded off in her chair. "Sleeping like that cannot be good for her."

"Let her be," he ordered. "Her back is troubling her again."

"How do you know?" she asked, annoyed that he had been included in the intimate dealings of their family.

"She told me," he said, peering over his sketching book at her. "That particular chair is comfortable. She is bothering no one by sleeping in it. Now why do you not tell us what is so troubling that you have spent the past hour sulking about it in silence?"

May, who had been sitting in the same position, risked Mr. Claeg's wrath by stretching her stiff arms. "Perhaps, she is pining for my brother." She closed her eyes and concealed a yawn with her hand. The young woman was unaware that her explanation had put frowns on both of her companions' faces.

"I am not sulking, nor am I pining for your brother, May," Brook argued, her crossed arms and frown noticeably belying her statement.

"Ennui, then," May suggested. Poised on a chair, she had chosen a white muslin dress with an orange band around the waist for the afternoon. A matching orange ribbon was threaded through her curly black locks and tied into a jaunty bow on the left side of her head. She represented youth, beauty, confidence, and ingenuousness. She had everything Brook felt she lacked. The chasm of their ages seemed to span decades instead of a mere two years.

"Maybe," Brook said, not really interested in pursuing the source of her agitation. She had figured out the answer days ago. Nothing short of torture would gain a confession.

"Miss Hamblin, you have strayed from the position we had agreed upon," Mr. Claeg chastised his model.

"Sitting is tedious," the young woman complained.

He was unsympathetic. "Endure."

She repositioned her hands until he grunted his approval. "This is no longer fun," she rebelliously muttered.

"I never promised fun. I promised art," he replied, distracted by the woman on the paper.

Brook recalled him mentioning that his sister, Amara, had sat for him. She could not imagine her friend had displayed any more patience than May while the artist within the man demanded perfection.

Too absorbed in his work to notice, she allowed her gaze to move away from the scenery outside to his bowed head as she had done numerous times during the past hour. He possessed a male beauty deserving of an artist's study. She would have been amazed if he had not received an offer to model.

He was not vain. She had encountered gentlemen who were enamored with their own beauty and how others responded to it. Mr. Claeg was not oblivious to the female admiration his good looks gathered. He simply used them like another man might use his hands. His face was a beautiful tool that he could manipulate for his benefit.

She had ordered him to leave her alone. In his typical manner, he had complied, but on his terms. They spent their afternoons together, but the rapport he had teased her into had cooled. He had told her that sketching May was his reason for visiting Loughwydde. Several hours later he had convinced her and the rest of the family. Since Mr. Claeg refused to display an unfinished sketch, most of the family had lost interest in their guest. It had fallen on her shoulders as mistress of the house to act as chaperone for Ham's sister. Being relegated to something not worth protecting from blackguards and fortune hunters had been depressing. No one seemed to worry that Mr. Claeg might take advantage of her, and why not? He showed more affection to Grandmother Byres than he did to her these days.

Maybe that was the explanation for her distrust. The drastic change in his affection was *too* convincing. *Unless he had feigned his passion,* she mused, rubbing her temples. No, she did not believe it was possible for a man to fake his physical response. Alas! It was all too confusing.

"All that frowning would give anyone a headache," Mr. Claeg said from behind his sketching book.

"Are you speaking to me?" She flinched, realizing her fingers were digging into her temples. Brook let her hands drop into her lap.

He made a concurring noise in his throat as if he were giving her a portion of his attention. "Your eyes have always reminded me of a cat. A brilliant blue fire that sears a man's soul. They are hell on my concentration, Countess."

She had yet to glimpse his face and yet he had been aware of her actions. Brook felt the tingling heat of mortification.

May moved out of position again and glanced back at Brook. Her eyes narrowed, trying to see if her assessment agreed with the artist's. She was not happy with her conclusions.

Brook came up from her seat in a flurry of motion. Mr. Claeg's head jerked up and his gaze locked onto hers. There was no doubt she had gained his entire concentration; perhaps she had it all along. A thousand excuses fluttered in her mind, but her tongue felt thick.

"Grab your mantle, Miss Hamblin," Mr. Claeg directed, not taking his gaze off her. "The air is stale in this room. Soon I will be napping alongside Mrs. Byres if I do not act. A walk will cure your headache, Countess. Dress warm and wear sturdy shoes," he warned both of them as he rosé and stretched. "The beach will serve our purposes."

Mallory was pleased the ladies had heeded the unspoken impatience in his voice and had rushed to complete their tasks. Miss Hamblin was exuberant to be free of the pose he had confined her to and was willing to partake in the adventure he had presented. The idea had come to him as he discreetly observed the countess at the window. What had she seen through the glass panes? Was it a reflection in the past, where the specter of regret haunted her, or was it the future, where she imagined how splendid her life would be once she rid herself of family and undesired neighbors?

The Ludlow sisters had joined them. Honey—or was it Ivy?; he had difficulty recalling which one was which—was distracting Miss Hamblin with her animated chatter. He was secretly grateful. The earl's sister was a shameless minx. If Mallory had been younger, he would have enjoyed her favors immensely. Her directness was refreshing, but he predicted the worldliness she faked would lead her to heartache. Despite her bravado, the young woman owned a tender heart. What kind of brittle creature would she become if a callous gentleman shattered it?

"You are not filled with your usual vigor, Lady A'Court," Mallory said, slowing so she could catch up. He suspected she was deliberately putting distance between them. After all his plotting to gain an invitation to Loughwydde, the telling action was intolerable. "Take my arm," he commanded. "Miss Hamblin, continue on toward the beach."

"You are joining us, Mr. Claeg, are you not?" The sisters giggled at the demand May had threaded into her question.

"Naturally. I am just too old to be skipping across the meadow picking spring flowers." The trio collapsed into one another laughing. He encouraged them away with a gesture. "Begone, children. Your elders will eventually hobble their way down to the beach."

"Who are you calling elderly?" The countess sneered, shaking off his assistance. "Miss Hamblin is two years younger than I am. She scarcely qualifies as a child."

"And I am six years older than you. Positively ancient from your sisters' point of view," he reasoned, preferring her surliness to the polite indifference she had bestowed on him each day since their amorous play in the woods. "You can relax, Countess. With three impressionable young ladies underfoot I am not likely to seduce you."

She smirked. "It was not even a concern, Mr. Claeg."

The air and the lady's prickliness had restored his good humor. Stepping in front of her, he leaned in close, allowing his mouth to hover invitingly above hers. "Shall I give us both something to worry over?"

"Keep away," she whispered, not realizing she had instinctively tilted her mouth up to his.

He let loose a low growl of frustration and pulled away. "I have and see where it has gotten me."

"Showing up daily to sketch and flirt with Miss Hamblin is not my definition of restraint."

"The devil it is not," he grumbled. "Have I not kept my hands off you, woman? I think about touching you with each passing minute and still I have managed to resist."

"Why is it an ordeal? I figured women were interchangeable, like a pair of shoes or a frock coat."

Mallory stared her down in mute fury. Temper had pushed him to say something similar and he was honest enough with himself to concede there was some truth hidden within the mocking exaggeration. "Not all women." *Not you*. The admission remained lodged in his throat. "My wife, Mirabella," he said hoarsely, looking ahead and checking on the young ladies under his protection, "she was unlike any lady I had met. Untamed and possessing a daring that rivaled my own, she seemed my natural mate. It mattered little that she had belonged to another gentleman. When I claimed her as my bride, I willingly forfeited my honor."

It had been the first of many losses he had suffered as the result of their passionate alliance. The countess was not the only one who had loved unwisely. "So, you see, even I occasionally looked deeper than the delights of the flesh."

"You must have loved your wife very much," she wistfully said, after a thoughtful period of silence.

Mirabella's death had almost destroyed him. "I have had over six years to learn how to live my life without her," he said, feeling an echo of the old grief.

"You had broken with your family back then; however, I do recall there were a myriad of rumors about the party you and your wife had attended and her death. It was an accident, was it not?" she asked, sneaking a quick glance at him, judging his willingness to speak of the matter.

She was not the first woman to ask him questions about his dead wife. Their scandalous marriage and Mirabella's tragic accident were the stuff out of which foolish young maidens spun their romantic fantasies. Even one of his poet friends had innocently offered once to immortalize their love in verse. Mallory's companions had to drag him off the frightened gentleman. No one had understood that there was nothing romantic about being covered in your wife's blood and gore while she bled to death in your arms.

"If my goal had been merely to steal Marquis De Lanoy's mistress from him, I would have been heralded as a hero in the gentlemen's clubs scattered about London. For loving a woman who had been selling herself to the highest bidder since she was fourteen, most considered me moonstruck. As for the marriage"—he opened his arms in a defenseless motion—"it closed many fashionable doors, including my family's. While it also opened others, still fashionable and yet reserved for the less savory characters of the *ton*."

"I am not certain I understand."

"I would have been astonished, Countess, if you had." She had been sheltered, first by her family and then, as Lord A'Court had explained, by her unyielding husband. How could she possibly understand the decadence and debauchery that idleness and too much money instilled in some gentlemen? "Our notoriety as a couple had granted us entrée into a society ruled by the perverse."

"You were outcasts."

He smiled slightly. "On the contrary, we had found people who were like us. It was a garish world I readily immersed myself in because it scorned everything my pretentious family valued."

They had come to the cliffs. The other ladies had reached

the beach, and their distant shrieks of laughter while they played rose up with the muted roar of the rushing sea. "Here, take my hand." Giving her no choice, Mallory guided her down the stone stairs one of her ancestors had hewn from the natural slope of one of the lower outcroppings of rock. The countess moved cautiously, but her ease revealed she had maneuvered the stairs countless times on her own.

Miss Hamblin, who was near the water's edge, spotted them and waved. Mallory returned her greeting. Neither he nor Lady A'Court made any effort to join the girls. She climbed up onto one of the large rocks and sat. He was content to stand. They both stared out at the water.

"This new life you had created with Mirabella," she said, continuing their conversation. "Were you happy?"

Leave it to the lady to condense what he had viewed as a complicated debacle into a simplistic balance of joy and sorrow. "I was never one who scrutinized my actions too closely," he lied, and then caught himself. He had begun telling her about one of the darkest years of his life as a test, both for her and for him. "That is not quite true. I told you that I thought Mirabella was my natural mate. A female copy of myself, if you will. We were both selfish, indulgent beings who brought out the worst in each other."

She frowned, trying to understand what he was telling her. "That does not seem like love, Mr. Claeg."

"Mallory," he corrected. "I never share my secrets with strangers."

She accepted his justification with a nod. "Fair enough."

He shook his head in disappointment. "That is what I have been trying to explain, Countess. Rarely have I indulged in fair play. My time with Mirabella was spent painting by day and the nights in profligacy."

Mallory refrained from confessing the nasty particulars of those evenings. They had lived like nomads, moving from house to house, party to party, always the same circle of people challenging one another, escalating their devilment. Some of his singular recollections were tainted with a smoky haze. In hindsight, it seemed he and Mirabella had taken turns nudging each other toward the precipice of their own destruction.

"Are you unwell?" Lady A'Court inquired, staring down at him from her higher perch.

He was sweating despite the cool breeze. Mallory removed his hat and used his sleeve to mop his forehead. "Just thinking about how different my life might have been if I had chosen another path. Regret," he said, the word rising like bile in his throat. "It is the cruelest emotion." He faced her and wryly smiled. "Perhaps you have the right of it, turning away from your old life. Incising the past like a surgeon does the flesh when he removes a tumor."

She leaned over and placed a comforting hand on his shoulder. "You accused me of hiding or running away. You are too strong to take a coward's path."

"I am unworthy of your praise, Countess." His eyes squinted against the blinding sunlight that surrounded her head like a radiant halo. "I had done my share of running. Do you know who really murdered my wife?"

"You do not have to tell me."

Lady A'Court pitied him. He hated pity almost as much as he did regret. These were not the feelings Mallory wanted to awaken in this woman. He could have accepted her offer and ended his tale. However, the countess was right: he was too strong to take the coward's path.

"Yes, I do. I murdered Mirabella."

Mallory Claeg had a distinct flair for melodrama. His chilling confession had effectively doused her rising sympathy. Brook did not believe he had murdered his wife, but he had unquestionably slain their tête-à-tête.

"No words of comfort, Countess," he softly taunted.

She slid off the stone she had been sitting on. He automatically caught her by the waist and set her on the ground.

"How am I supposed to reply to such an outlandish boast?" she demanded. " 'Oh, good for you, Mallory! She likely deserved it! Share all the grisly details, if you please'?"

As he heard the false sweetness and light of her delivery, Mallory's brow quirked in disbelief. "Well, I was not expecting the sarcasm. Who knew you could be a bloodthirsty little fiend?" He held on to the bottom edge of her spencer, keeping her close.

She had managed to surprise him by not reacting in the manner he had anticipated. The flash of humor had diminished the grim bleakness that had been brewing in his demeanor.

"You did not shoot your wife, Mr. Claeg."

"Mallory," he absently reminded her. A few seconds later, his body visibly jerked and his pale blue eyes glowed with a burning attentiveness as the meaning of her statement became clear. "You seem awfully certain for someone who was not present that night."

"You loved Mirabella. It was not feigned like my—" Honey had caught her attention when her pursuit of a sure-footed seabird ended with the bird taking to the air and her sister almost falling on her face. The antics had Brook smiling mistily. Glancing at Mallory, she shrugged apologetically. "Anyway, I sense you blame yourself for not preventing her death. That part of the gossip about her participating in a duel was correct, was it not?"

As if his legs could not bear his weight, he slid down onto the sand and dragged her down with him. She braced herself with his shoulders to keep from toppling over and then settled beside him. The sand was cool and dry to the touch. Her housekeeper, Mrs. Gordy, was not going to be pleased when they returned bringing half the beach with them into *her* house.

Mallory was not worrying about the sand or watching Brook's sisters play in the surf. Pensive, he stared unseeing into the past she had dredged up with her questions. "Our nomadic existence had led us north to Mr. Justus Henning's country house."

"Who is he?"

"Someone whose name you should forget. He and his wife fit nicely into our odd circle of friends. It was our mutual passion for art that garnered an invitation to one of their exclusive summer gatherings. The circle had an inner circle and Mirabella and I were naively flattered that we were included in the upper echelon." He took up her hand and idly traced a pattern on her palm.

He was unaware of what his touch was doing to her. Considering the trouble she had gotten into the last time, she was grateful he was distracted by his story. "Was the invitation less than you expected?"

"Quite the opposite. It was much more than promised. There was a reason why Henning kept his gatherings remote and exclusive. It was a feast of appetites, Countess. There were no limits; a man could let his creativity soar into ecstasy or mire in the filth of brutal self-indulgence."

Brook felt he was choosing his words carefully, as if he was worried of divulging too much detail about the life he had shared with Mirabella. It also seemed he needed her to understand this piece of his past. "I thought we had established that you are the kind of man who thrives without limits."

"Yes, an unfettered existence held a great amount of appeal," he said, his expression subdued. "At first, my days were spent exploring and appreciating his extensive collection of art. Those hours fired my imagination. I took notes, sketched, and planned."

"And your nights?"

He hesitated. "Lavish suppers. Music. Beautiful women and men fulfilling our every whim. There was enough food and drink available to feed half of London's poor. Amusements both public and private tailored to his guests' peculiarities."

She crinkled her nose. "Peculiarities?"

Mallory dismissed the word with a gesture. "Indulgences . . . obsessions, if you prefer. Our host, for example, not only had an enviable art collection; he also could sit discussing color and technique for hours. He also developed a habit of taking young boys into his bed."

"Good heavens!" she exclaimed.

"Heaven had nothing to do with the Hennings. Mrs. Henning preferred men to boys. Any gentleman would do. Another *friend* thought it was entertaining to have a young maid flogged in front of us. There was another fellow who relished the lash on his own flesh."

She was aghast. "You considered these people your friends?"

"These were their dark secrets, Countess. They went about their daily business like you or me. You could have sat beside one of them at a late supper or consented to be their dance partner at a ball."

"I *know* some of these people?"

Mallory did not reply to her question. "You are missing the point," he said, grimly amused by her horror. "Those intimate gatherings were an outlet for the darker pleasures. It was merely fantasy for some of the meeker players, exquisite pain for a few, and overindulgence in many guises."

The notion of such a gathering sickened her. She touched her stomach, trying not to think how Mallory had entertained himself those nights. Brook frowned. "You cannot convince me that you and your wife . . . that you were like the others."

He studied her; his enigmatic expression gave her no hint of what he was thinking. "No, Countess, we were not like them. Nevertheless, we had a child's curiosity for things beyond our experience. No one was bullying us to do anything other than observe their wicked play. Henning had hoped access to his art collection would smooth over my discomfort and, regrettably, it had. Mirabella and I remained."

Mallory dug into his inner coat pocket and removed a small flask. Removing the top, he drank. She wondered if it was dryness or fortification. He offered her the flask, but she refused.

"I blame no one but myself. The Hennings had provided the arena; we seduced ourselves into playing their games. Of course, the soporifics helped us along." He took another healthy sip.

"Your host drugged you?"

"I cannot prove it," he said quickly. "Maybe something was slipped into the wine. It is still a little hazy, but I seem to recall a pungent incense fouling the air. Perhaps a hypnotic was common practice to relax everyone. All I know is that I lost interest in Henning's art collection and the long night never ended."

"What happened to you?"

"Who knows? Even I cannot be certain what parts I dreamed and what was real."

He was lying. Brook did not have the heart to press him. He was right. Everyone had secrets. "And Mirabella?"

Thrusting his hand through his hair, he did a thorough job snarling it. "We were . . . separated. I cannot tell you for how long, since time had no meaning. When I did remember to look for her, the duel had commenced. The pistols discharged before I could fight off the hands that held me back. There was nothing anyone could do. The ball had hit her in the chest." He stared down at his empty hands. "She died in my arms."

The tears Brook could never cry for herself streamed down her face for a woman she had never known. "Please tell me that someone was punished for her death?" No one deserved to die for a game!

"For an unfortunate accident?" He made a tsking noise. "No one was sober and everyone had gone without sleep for days. Witnesses said it was Mirabella's idea to stage the duel. She chose her opponent. I was assured the pistols had been loaded with only gunpowder. There would have been an impressive discharge of fire and smoke, and very little risk. Who is the villain, Countess?"

She felt a smidgen of his frustration. "But . . . what about Henning and his penchant for exclusive parties? The hypnotics?"

"No proof. And even if I could prove that I was drugged, Henning could always claim that I had ingested it freely," he explained, obviously having considered all the angles of his situation. "Oh, there is something else I should tell you."

"What?"

"That night." He cleared his throat. "The reason . . . why I was not there with my wife when she proposed the duel . . ."

"You can tell me."

"I was in bed, Countess." He threw back his head and laughed. The wild, hysterical sound tickled down her spine. "While my wife was setting the stage for her own death, I was diligently slamming my hard member into Henning's wife as he and his young lover watched."

Chapter Nine

What was she to do? The man was making her crazed, she mused hours later. The horrible tale he had told her was remarkable. It would have been simpler to brush it aside as a manipulative ploy to gain her sympathy. She certainly would have slept better at night. However, his anguish had been genuine. Whatever her opinion of the man, he had recounted the tragic events that had led to Mirabella's death as he recalled them.

He had seduced Mr. Henning's wife.

Brook had tried to be open-minded. Why had she acted like he had betrayed her? Her reaction had bordered on ludicrous. Her only excuse was that she had been ill prepared for that aspect of his story. The immediate revulsion she had felt was plainly evident on her face.

Mallory had solemnly waited for her to pass judgment. He had anticipated her response, which explained his previous hesitation to reveal the entire sordid tale. She had been speechless. Accurately interpreting her silence as condemnation, he had politely thanked her for listening to his ramblings and had abruptly departed for his cottage. May and Brook's sisters had called out for him to wait, but he had ignored their jovial pleas to return. He left it up to Brook how she explained away his rudeness.

It shamed her that he thought she had judged him so

harshly. When had she turned into a smug paradigm of perfection? Lyon was constantly telling her—no, she was not
going to think about what he thought. He was dead. She had
control of her life again.

Or did she?

Nothing made sense to her anymore. Ham wanted her as
his countess. Mallory longed for a less permanent arrangement with her. Her mother-in-law expected her to dedicate
her remaining life to mourning Lyon. All her mother wanted
was for her eldest daughter to return to London. Somewhere
along the way she had stopped listening to her own needs
and filled the emptiness with everyone's desires.

Although it had not been his intention, Mallory had opened
her eyes about the stagnancy that had become her existence.
The man had known loss, and yet it had not prevented him
from continuing on. Brook might disapprove of how he had
gone about it, but she admired him for trying. She should have
told him that, instead of condemning him like everyone else
had when he had run off with an inappropriate woman.

The need to correct her mistake agitated her empty stomach. She lifted the drapes and grimaced at the fading light. If
she hurried, she might reach the dwelling before the last of
the sunset slid into the sea.

Mallory dragged a chair in front of the picture he had finished,
sat down, and studied the work he had completed an hour earlier. As he worked by candlelight, the absence of his model
had not deterred him. The image of her lying in the bluebells
had been scored into his brain. He reached for the bottle of
port and refilled his glass.

Holding up the glass to the picture, he said, "To you, Lady
A'Court. The most exasperating, humorless, puritanical hypocrite I have ever had the pleasure of meeting." He emptied
the glass, wondering why he had told her about the Hennings

and Mirabella. Others had asked and he had given them just enough details to satisfy their ghoulish curiosity. When the widow had kindly asked, he had held nothing back. He still could not believe he had told her about his ignoble activities with Mrs. Henning. God, what a fool! Mallory reached for the bottle again and poured. He closed his eyes as if the act could erase Lady A'Court's revulsion from his mind. What demon had prodded him into revealing that old ugliness? If he had wanted to drive the countess away, he had succeeded remarkably. Even if she allowed him into her house again, his sordid history would stand between them.

I murdered Mirabella.

Lady A'Court had not believed him capable of killing his wife. Even now the knowledge warmed the inner depths of him that had grown cold years ago. How had he repaid her generosity? He had ruthlessly smashed the illusion that he was worthy of her precious gift. Mallory stared into the shy blue cat eyes that gleamed at him from the portrait. After what he had told her, she must despise him.

Used to having servants around him, Mallory did not immediately react to the faint knock at the door. Mrs. Whitby was gone and likely in her own bed. He could have hired someone to attend him in the evenings, but it seemed too much trouble for a man who neither expected nor craved company. When he finally managed to stumble to his feet, the knocking had ceased. Curiosity prompted him to open the door.

The wind had picked up. He fought to maintain his grip as the blustery currents buffeted his face and the wooden door. The sketching book he had left on a chair fluttered its pages. Peering into the darkness, he did not trust the apparition he saw.

"Good, you are awake," Lady A'Court said, clearly relieved to see him. "When no one came to the door, I feared you had retired for the evening." She cocked her head and looked behind him into the cottage. "You can smell the rain in the air. Do you mind if I step inside before it blows onto land?"

Leaning on the door for support, he widened the gap, allowing her enough space to slip through. She threw back the hood on her cloak and moved to the center of the room. Under the cloak she clutched a small leather satchel. She looked at him expectantly.

"Forgive me, Lady A'Court. My manners are rusty. Usually the women who see me alone in the evenings are not particularly fussy about pleasantries."

"Please, do not belittle yourself," she entreated, making him feel ashamed. "I am the one deserving of your derision. I would have waited for the morning, but I worried that you might leave before I had the opportunity to apologize." She held up her satchel. "I brought a peace offering."

Mallory closed the door. He did not want her apology any more than he wanted her pity. Brooding, he crossed his arms and leaned against the door. "Leave? I assumed the drifting clouds of dust from my carriage wheels leading away from Loughwydde would give you cause to rejoice."

Her soft lips quivered. "Not when it was my heartlessness that drove you away."

Her eyes were sad and luminous in the candlelight. Lady A'Court was melting his resentment by just looking at him. She had left her braided hair down, but the wind and hood had done their damage. Wisps of blond hair swayed free. His fingers itched for his black lead pencil. "Impossible. If anything, Countess, you have too much heart." The wind surged, rattling the door at his back. "It is rather late for you to be wandering about the countryside alone. Did you walk?" The area seemed safe enough during the day, but there were unseen dangers, especially at night.

"No, I rode one of the horses." She held out an appeasing hand at his curse. "I am a capable rider, I assure you. I thought about hitching the horse to the cart. It just seemed too much trouble."

He fought back the urge to scold her. Throttling her had merit, too, for the risk she took in visiting him. In this gusty wind, a fallen branch could have spooked the horse and caused it to throw her. Sitting in a tiny cart would not have spared her if it had overturned.

"I could have walked," she admitted, growing steadily wary of his strained silence. "But the sky was darkening and the wind showed signs of worsening."

Yelling at her served no purpose except to vent his spleen. "Sit," he ordered. "I will see to your horse. Let us hope that if it has run off it has more sense than its mistress and returned home."

"Hey, I resent that, Mr.—Mallory," she meekly amended when he took a threatening step toward her.

Ah, now she chose to be prudent. "Stay out of trouble. I will return as soon as I am able." He did not give her a chance to argue.

Stomping off, he opened the door and braced his body against the wind. The first icy droplets of rain hit his face. The storm she had worried about had arrived. It appeared his fondest wish had been granted. He and the countess would be sharing a bed.

Brook pushed aside Mallory's discarded coat and sat down on the overstuffed sofa. Remembering the satchel, she unfastened her cloak and pulled the leather strap over her head and placed the bag on the table. She jumped up and then sat back down. Should she remove her cloak or was that presumptuous? He was seeing to her horse. Maybe he wanted to check the saddle before he plopped her backside on it and sent her on her way. No, he was angry with her. He was not being cruel. Sometimes she forgot that not all men welded those two emotions together.

The door burst open and rebounded against the wall. She jumped up and rushed to it. A startled scream came out as a squeak when Mallory filled the dark entrance.

"Are you crazy? Get back inside, woman!" he roared over the storm.

There was no point in replying. Together they pushed the door closed again. He put his hand on the frame to brace himself. He was drenched from the rain, and his lungs were puffing like bellows from his outdoor exertions.

"I was not leaving. The door popped open and I got up to close it."

He fingered the edge of her cloak near her throat. "You are still wearing your cloak."

Her grin was sheepish. "You said that you would see to my horse. There was no mention about what you had planned for me."

He let his head drop onto his damp sleeve and groaned at her logic. "Only you, Countess."

She softened at the gentle teasing. Brook realized he was dripping on the floor. Suddenly all business, she crisply said, "Where is my head? You need dry clothes and something warm to drink before a chill settles in your lungs." She moved to get him a towel to dry off his face and then realized this was not her house. "You can see to yourself. I will put the kettle on and tend the fire."

Mallory returned minutes later. She glanced back at him before adding more coal to the hearth. "You must have raced up and down those stairs to be dressed in the short amount of time you have been gone."

He bent down and removed her cloak from her shoulders. She had forgotten that she still had it on. "I did not want to give you too much time alone. I was afraid you might talk yourself out of staying." He tossed the outer garment on a chair.

He hunkered down in front of the hearth and nudged her

away. Mallory had untied his dark brown hair from its queue. The wet, dark length had twisted down like hundreds of tiny snakes and dangled in front of his face. If it bothered him, he showed no sign of discomfort. Brook moved out of his way while he made adjustments to her efforts. In front of the fire, he seemed wholly a primitive male, with his broad shoulders defined without the covering of a coat and his feet bare.

"I would be as crazy as you accused me of being to go out in that foul weather. I am safer here," she said, her tone huskier than usual.

"Are you?" was his soft reply.

"The kettle!" She grimaced, chastising herself for being so thickheaded. "I forgot—"

"Leave it." He stood and dusted off his hands. "I prefer my tea cold." He stalked across the room, his sharp gaze searching for something.

Understanding lit her gaze as she observed him retrieving his abandoned glass of port.

"I have another glass, if you would care to join me."

"No, thank you," she said, cringing at how prim her refusal had sounded. "It makes me sleepy."

Mallory lifted his brow at her confession. "Well now, we wouldn't want that." He winked at her and moved closer to the hearth.

They were friends again, she thought, not grasping why she wanted to weep. Recalling what had impelled her to seek him out, she leaned earnestly forward. "Mallory, I never thanked you for trusting me with your accounting of your ordeal with the Hennings and your wife's death. I swear that I regard what you told me as private. You do not have to concern yourself with gossip."

He shrugged negligently. "If I was worried about gossip I would have never told you."

Mallory loomed over her, his expression forbidding. Perhaps mentioning their discussion had not been sensible. She

tried smoothing over the awkwardness with another explanation. "You told me this extraordinary, horrifying tale. Did
you think that I would not have any reaction to it?"

He scowled at her. "No, Countess, your response was entirely predictable."

She was positive he was being deliberately offensive. "I
still do not agree with your ridiculous statement that you
murdered your own wife."

He contemplatively sipped his wine. "No. But even you
wonder why I was fornicating with my host's wife when I
should have been protecting my own."

She was having trouble getting past that part of his tale.
"Why did you tell me? You could have omitted it. I would
have never known."

"My sin was so grievous. Maybe I needed a confessor,"
he helpfully suggested.

"I doubt it." She rubbed one of her fingernails with the
pad of her thumb as she reviewed the facts in her mind. "I
got it wrong. You let me think you seduced Mrs. Henning. It
was just the opposite. With the assistance of her husband,
she seduced you."

Mallory turned away, leaving her guess unconfirmed.

Curling her legs under her, she was confident she had hit
upon the truth. "You were drugged. It was not your fault."

"That will always be debatable, since I cannot trust my
own recollections." He kept his back to her, broodingly staring into the fire. "Is that why you risked your neck coming
here? To offer absolution?"

Brook was risking her neck in more ways than one. She
had provoked the beast and waited for him to pounce. "No.
That was not what you were seeking from me."

He finally turned and faced her. The intensity rolling off
him was overt. "What was I looking for, Countess?"

Emboldened by his lack of anger, she said, "Confirmation.

You wanted someone to speak aloud the inner whispers in your head."

"Pray continue. What do these whispers say?" he lightly mocked.

Ignoring his attempts to intimidate her, she forced herself to hold his gaze. "They tell you, Mallory, that you always had a choice. No one coerced you into Mrs. Henning's bed. You could not resist because you have always been a selfish, wanton beast. The pattern was set long before your arrival at the Hennings' estate." She counted off each offense with her fingers. "You chose your art above family duty. You wanted Mirabella and you took her. Bedding Mrs. Henning was just another indulgence, one in which your wife forfeited her life."

Grim amusement seemed to ignite Mallory's light blue eyes from within. "I see you have given my indiscretions some thought."

"I thought of little else." Her family had thought she was moping about London. She had been content to let them think she was considering their command. "At first I admired you."

"Admired?" The corner of his mouth crooked up. "An odd sentiment."

"No, truly, I found how you had continued with your life after your wife's death admirable. Comparing it to my own, I found myself shamed that I had chosen a coward's path."

He peered over his glass of port at her. "It is rude of me, I suppose, but I happen to agree."

"Then I realized I was wrong—"

"Imagine it."

She refused to let him provoke her. Intent to have her say, she attacked, "There is nothing admirable about your life."

"Thank you, m'dear," he murmured, unfazed.

Brook shook a chiding finger at him. "You have been running away, too. You escaped the restraints of your overbearing father. You mocked polite society and all its rules. You could not even be faithful to Mirabella when tested, and the life you have led since her death has been far from pious."

"You must find me loathsome."

She exhaled noisily. "No, Mallory. You are the one who believes that."

"Absurd," he scoffed. "I am content with the life I have built."

Brook studied his back silently while he wielded the poker with a little more enthusiasm than the fire warranted. "Are you? Then why are you here alone in this cottage, instead of London with two mistresses fighting over you?"

He chuckled. "Your imagination conjures a fascinating predicament. I almost wish I could confess it were true." Setting the poker aside, he crawled over to her. "As for being alone, how can that be when I have you?"

The wind howled, reminding them both that she was his guest until the weather relented. She shifted to the side and reached for the satchel on the table. "I brought you something."

"You said it was a peace offering."

"After you left the beach, I believe nothing short of bribery would convince you to let me into your cottage."

She untied the leather string and flipped open the top. Pulling out a drawstring bag constructed out of cheesecloth, she presented her gift. Tentatively he accepted her lumpy bundle. "My housekeeper does not possess Mrs. Whitby's culinary magic. Still, she has managed to fatten me up with her sweets. These are a favorite."

With undisguised delight, he tugged on the drawstring and worked his fingers into the bag. Looking inside, he said, "Sugar puffs?"

"Lemon," she confirmed, thrilled he was genuinely pleased with her gift.

"My housekeeper in town serves them up with fruit fool," he said, looking hopeful.

"So does Mrs. Gordy. Unluckily for you, I do not. I had enough to manage between the increasingly foul weather and the horse. Be grateful I was feeling guilty enough to filch sweets on your behalf. My housekeeper is a formidable foe. Who knows what diabolical punishment she will concoct for my crime?"

"So do not tell her," he advised, shaking his head in disappointment that Brook had not come up with it on her own.

"There is no help for it. The woman has the sight."

He popped the small sweet into his mouth. "Ridiculous."

"So true," she said, closing her fingers around the lemon puff he had placed in her palm. "When I am scrubbing dishes in the wooden sink alongside the scullery maid I will be certain to recall your sage advice."

"Poor little countess," he teased, getting up but not relinquishing his bag of sweets. "What you need is for someone to teach you how to shed some of that burdensome virtue." He held out his hand.

"Are you offering me lessons in wickedness?"

He reached down. Seizing the hand she hesitated in offering, he hauled her to her feet. "You could do no worse, I wager."

May listened to the storm outside battering the house. The wind yowled, feral and hungry. The tree branches near her window tapped persistently at the glass panes, making her think of skeletal fingers. She shrank down in the bedding trying to fight her rising fear.

She hated being alone in a strange place. Loughwydde lost most of its charm at nightfall. She pitied Brook for having endured this wretched place for two years. Once they returned to London and renewed acquaintances, her friend would never want to return to this isolated place.

Sitting up, May pulled one of the blankets off the bed. Wrapping it around her, she imagined that Brook was lying awake in her bed, too. May doubted anyone in the house was sleeping through this nasty storm. She hopped off the bed, warming to the idea. While Ham was away, he would appreciate her looking after the woman he intended to marry. Oh, he was too private to share his plans, but May had observed them together. If Ham had not asked the widow, he was preparing to do so in London.

With a lit candle in hand, May slipped out the door. She liked Brook. Her shy manner and intelligence complemented May's brother rather nicely. Moving down the hall, she could imagine how much fun they would have in town. May could talk Ham into taking them to the theater. She muffled a gleeful giggle imagining how lovely it would be if Mr. Claeg joined them. Naturally, she would be spending a large amount of time with him while he painted her portrait. All of the *ton* soon would realize how taken he was with her beauty. May had noticed how he had stared at her. Those marvelous eyes had made her insides all buttery.

It was a shame Ham had asked Mr. Claeg to watch over Brook. A man who obviously had a keen sense of duty, he had remained by the countess's side instead of playing with the girls on the beach. Well, once they returned to London, his obligation to Ham would be finished.

She knocked on the door softly. "Brook, it is May." Pressing an ear to the door, she listened. The storm made it impossible to hear anything. Undeterred, she pushed down on the latch.

"Are you awake? I could not sleep and hoped we could talk." Puzzled, she held the candle over the bed. It was empty and the bedding bore no sign of its owner. "Where is she?"

Chapter Ten

"I have something to show you."

Lady A'Court locked her feet together and stalled. "Where are we going?"

"Little craven," he affectionately ribbed. "This cottage is too small for a large painting room or a dungeon, so we will have to be content with walking across the room."

"Oh, I see," she said, finally noticing he had set up a small work area near the window. "The smell of your alchemy permeates the air. I had wondered where you worked when the weather fouled or the light waned."

"This is less than I prefer," he explained, missing his London town house. "However, I have learned to make allowances when traveling."

She gestured at the picture perched on the easel. "Are you working on Miss Hamblin's portrait?" she asked, approaching the picture from behind.

Mallory was nervous. He put the bag of sugar puffs down and wiped his damp, sticky hand carelessly on the front of his shirt. "This one is finished."

Sending him a quick smile at his ambiguity, she walked around to view his work. Pleasure lit her face. "Why, this is me!"

"In spite of what was said, I could not burn it as you had suggested. Nor could I replace your likeness with another woman's face. Each time I sat in front of it, all I saw was bluebells and you."

He moved closer so he was standing behind her. She was quiet in her perusal, her somber eyes analyzing each detail. Straining his patience until he thought he might explode, she finally said, "Your efforts are remarkable, sir. You have succeeded in capturing the afternoon."

"And you, Countess?"

"A credible representation, although you have improved upon your subject."

Mallory felt the tension in his jaw first. "Explain yourself."

He had flustered her with his demand. Her hand made a sweeping gesture at her image. "I meant no insult. All artists fall prey to flattering their patron."

He took an intimidating step nearer. "Firstly, you are *not* my patron, Countess," he said, shifting her chin so he had her complete attention. "I painted this picture because it called to me. Secondly, my work may provoke the viewer, but it does not flatter. Do I make myself clear?" He looked hard at her.

"Yes."

Women who did not recognize their own beauty baffled him. The vain Carissa Le Maye and the nonchalantly confident Miss Hamblin were the sort of women he usually preferred.

His own sister, Amara, had reacted in a similar fashion when viewing the portrait he had painted of her. He placed the blame on their father for treating her like an article of trade to be presented to the highest bidder rather than a daughter. Marrying for gain was not uncommon; however, it was not until recently Mallory had learned that at sixteen his sister had been trapped alone by one of their father's approved suitors and raped.

Amara, too frightened of the consequences, had told no one in the family of her violation. Only Brock Bedegrayne had known and guarded her secret. Mallory was still resentful that Bedegrayne had kept silent. Then again, he could hardly blame him. The man was in love with Amara. Her father had been in favor of Lord Cornley, so her defilement would have ensured marriage to her abuser. Mallory had abandoned his sister when he had run off with his mistress. Presented with those conditions, he could understand Bedegrayne's reluctance in trusting Amara's family.

The countess also had trouble with trust. She had suffered at the hands of her husband. Mallory had treated her little better, even though hurting her had never been his aim. She had been surrounded by people who had flattered her for the sole purpose of taking something from her. The bitter experiences had left their mark.

He pushed aside his irritation. "Forgive me, Countess. Talking about Mirabella fouls my disposition. I confess it comes in second to people criticizing my work."

"I was not criticizing your work, my lord."

"Well, you were disparaging my model, and I take offense to anyone who is blind to the beauty that I see."

She stared at the picture. "When you look at me, this is what you see?"

Mallory gently rested his hands on her hips. Pressing a kiss on her right earlobe, he murmured, "What did I get wrong? Your hair? The color is not a common brown. It is a rich blend of hues, reminding me of honey and caramels. And you know how much I like my sweets." He swayed them side-to-side while he nuzzled her ear.

"Uh . . . ahhh, my eyes?" she asked, letting her eyes flutter shut.

"Mmm, your eyes. Azure." He kissed her neck and moved so that he was blocking her view of the picture. Discovering her eyes were still closed, he lightly kissed each lid. "Inquisitive and yet wary. When you smile, I feel like I am soaring the cloudless heights of a summer sky."

She opened her eyes when he pulled away. "And my mouth?"

He heard the invitation in her voice. Elation and need roared through him, similar to the whipping fury beyond the walls of the cottage. "Mouth? Right, your mouth," he whispered inches from her face. "Tender. Plump, rosy petals that beg a man to nibble and suck." He dipped his head closer. *Just a little taste,* he thought. *What harm would it do?* His blood heated and raced through his body and his cock twitched between his legs in response.

"Damn!" Mallory groaned, chagrined at his unruly body. Squinting his eyes shut, he lowered his forehead to hers. "Does anyone know where you are?"

Unprepared for his question, Lady A'Court opened her eyes and blinked in confusion. "All that running about on the beach had tired the girls. Everyone retired to their rooms early. I saw no reason to disturb them, since I would have returned before my absence was noticed."

The little fool! What was the purpose of having servants if she kept them from looking after her? She had been wandering about these lands alone for so long she had forgotten that the dangers had not diminished with familiarity. He would have never forgiven himself if she had had an accident on his behalf. Mallory drew back and gave her a shake. "You wild, mad girl. You have been running wild for too long. Someone has to rein you in before you get hurt."

"On my own lands?" She snorted in disbelief. "You are being ridiculous and sounding like Ham. I like being by myself and refuse to change my routine to please two arrogant twits."

A man was in a sad state when a lady's huffiness aroused him. "It isn't arrogance but common sense." Desperate to make her understand the risks she had taken to soothe him, Mallory hauled her up on her toes. She emitted a tiny squeak when he backed her against the nearest wall. "Not all of the risks are outdoors, Countess. You are alone and trapped with a true scoundrel. If the tale I told you earlier did not prove what a scoundrel I can be, then you are the *twit*!"

She laughed down in his face. His mouth went slack in surprise. "Oh, what a big, nasty scoundrel you are, Mallory Claeg," she mocked in feigned terror. "I doubt warning off your victim is in the scoundrel's handbook."

"Mouthy little witch. You chew a man to bits for acting noble."

"Did you actually *read* the handbook, sir?" she demanded, unperturbed that he still had her dangling off her feet. "Nobility is not part of a scoundrel's code of ethics. In fact, neither are ethics!"

She was not afraid of him. If anything, she was goading him into action. Although easing her fears had been one of his goals all along, he found this side of her bedeviling. "You are correct. To Hades with my bloody nobility!"

He fastened his mouth to hers before she could take her next breath. Her lips tasted of the lemon sugar puff she had been nibbling on while she studied her picture. "Open your mouth."

The second she relaxed her mouth he slipped his tongue inside and tickled hers. She recoiled, but he was not interested in coyness. Having seen how bold she could be when facing his temper, Mallory wanted to cultivate that courage in the sensual arts.

"Taste me, too," he coaxed.

Lady A'Court licked her lips. "Like this?"

His groan was laced with humor when she stuck her tongue out at him and then leaned into his face for the kiss. The lady was a novice at love play, but he was a patient man if the reward was worth the effort. The Countess was deserving of his best effort. He captured her tongue and sucked on it, showing her how pleasurable her daring could be for both of them. Inexperience had made her content to let him guide her every move. He preferred being dominant.

However, he also wanted a partner in his bed, a woman who was as hungry for him as he was for her. Someone who was too impatient to lie passively for her gratification.

He jerked his mouth away from hers. Aroused to the point of pain, he said, "There will be no going back for you tonight." He meant the storm and much more.

"I know. I smelled the change in the air. I could have turned back," she replied, assuming the burden of responsibility for her being trapped with him.

"Yet you did not."

She smiled down at him. "No." Lady A'Court wiggled in his arms. "This does not sound worldly, my lord, but could you set me down? Your grip is making my corset dig into my flesh and it is terribly uncomfortable."

He did not return her smile. Mallory was so unused to the fresh sincerity that was an essential part of her character that he considered it something to treasure, not mock. "I can do one better," he promised as he set her down and scooped her into his arms. The wind attacked the cottage again, making the glass shudder in its wooden casings. "You are safe with me."

Mallory Claeg promised safety and then carried her away from the warmth and the light. Perhaps she was lacking common sense, because if he had been any other man she would have started screaming. The fact that she had not gave her pause. When had she begun to trust this gentleman and, graver still, want him? The quick pecks Lyon had pressed on her lips during their brief courtship had been abandoned for the other amusements he had gained by taking her body. Once she had naively viewed those tight-lipped kisses as feverish longing. The recollection made her feel silly now. Mallory might not crave a lady's heart, but he had proven that he wanted her body, her mouth on his.

Cradling her, he carried her up the spiraling stairs and into the closest bedchamber. She clutched him tightly, the darkness and the unfamiliarity of where he was taking her making her anxious.

Lifting her head from his shoulder, she noticed that the steady glow of the fireplace provided some light. "I am about to drop you on my bed," he warned before the gentle landing onto softness. "I will light a candle."

She thought about the ugly marks Lyon's possession had left on her pale body. *If Mallory saw them—* her mind snuffed the appalling thought. "No. Please, the light from the grate is enough."

Even in the dimness, she could sense he was attempting to discern her reasons for refusing his offer to light a candle. A quick nod and he returned to the bed. She supposed he had assumed it was shyness that prompted her odd request, and she was content to let him think thus.

He climbed onto the bed. "I recall you were here." He pushed her onto her back. Before she could sit back up, he crawled on top of her. "And I was about here." He adjusted his position several times, aligning them so that his mouth was just above hers. "Yes, exactly right."

With him so close, she saw the determined gleam in his light blue eyes and then she saw nothing at all. This man's kisses made a mockery out of her husband's miserable efforts. Mallory moved his mouth over hers with the easy glide of silk over silk. Brook sighed and let him explore her mouth. Well, mayhap *let* was not correct. He claimed what he wanted and she did nothing to hinder him.

"Are you tied into this dress?" he asked, kissing her ear. What was it about her ears that he could not seem to resist? He nibbled the tender flesh of her earlobes and tickled the inner recesses with the tip of his tongue. She shivered in his arms.

"My maid assists me," she weakly explained.

"Roll over," he commanded, turning her over himself. As

he straddled her buttocks, she felt his hands move over her back. After a muffled oath, he murmured, "A candle would hasten my work."

"I thought all scoundrels could undress a lady blind-folded."

He lapsed into silence. The partial weight he held her down with shifted. She heard a drawer from a small table near the bed open. Brook heard him search for something within the contents of the drawer and utter a soft exhalation of satisfaction. "Countess, I will show you what real scoundrels do with cheeky wenches." His weight returned. She felt a tug at her back and then another. It took her a moment to guess what he was doing.

"How dare you cut my laces!"

"Oh, I always dare when provoked," he growled in her ear. "Now hold still. I do not want to slice a finger off." A forceful tug and the dress parted for him.

"Not my corset, too," she complained, already feeling the dull side of the blade slide against her chemise. How did the man expect her to return home with her clothing in pieces?

"You are too slight to need such a confining device."

Suddenly she was free from her bindings and the relief she felt was immense. She twisted her head back and glared at him. "You have ruined my dress. How will I get home? Wrap myself in a blanket?"

"I will think of something," he replied, unconcerned by the predicament in which he had placed her.

She pushed up on her arms and her dress slid down to her wrists. Brook removed her fabric cuffs and tossed them to the end of the bed. Most of her body was covered by the loose-fitting chemise, and that gave her comfort. "I cannot fathom why you felt it was necessary to cut off my clothes," she muttered.

"A fancy I had always wanted to indulge," he said, im-mune to her annoyance.

"Truly? Perhaps I should brandish a knife near what you hold dear and see how cheery you feel afterward, Mr. Claeg." She froze when he cupped her face in his large hands.

He did not bother correcting her slip. "You do not have to fear this. I will not hurt you, Countess."

To see him distinctly, she had to get nose-to-nose. He kissed one cheek and then the other. Mallory seemed to believe what he was telling her. "Are you speaking of the act? I am no longer a virgin; that sort of pain has passed." She could not begin to explain to him that there were other kinds of pain that lasted far longer than those of what was done to her body.

He unfastened the tiny buttons on her chemise. She was grateful he had lost interest in the knife. "The act," he mused. "What a pitiful phrasing for something so wondrous. I think for that alone I could strangle your dead husband."

It was strange how a declaration of murder could fortify her. "I was not—"

"The former Miss Bedegrayne," he said, finishing her sentence. "Your friend is a lovely lady. Nevertheless, so are you, Countess." He kissed her softly on the mouth. "Definitely worthy of an obsession," he murmured, nipping her lower lip. "Your husband was an utter ass for not appreciating you."

"Are you—" she said, and then tried again. "Will you appreciate me, Mr. Claeg?"

"Mallory," he implored. "Oh, most thoroughly and most definitely." He lifted the hem of her chemise.

She stopped his movements. The notion of being stripped of her clothing and laid out on the bed like a virginal sacrifice for a pagan god disconcerted her. "What about your clothes?"

He rubbed his nose against hers. Kissing the tip of hers playfully, he said, "I was not certain if seeing a man's body would frighten you."

The notion that he had considered her fears loosened the knot in her chest. She shook her head in denial. Brook was with him on the bed. She preferred not discussing Lyon's odd predilections with a man who genuinely wanted her. That concept alone was something she was still struggling to grasp. When Mallory gazed at her, he made her feel desired for herself, not what she could pretend to be.

"Allow me to assist," she offered, reaching up to unfasten his buttons before she completely lost her daring. He had never bothered putting on a coat, so her task was over too quickly. Together they lifted and removed his linen shirt. His physique was as spectacular as his face. Unable to resist, she stroked his muscled chest. "No wonder the ladies whisper about you behind their hands. You are a beautiful man."

Instead of preening, he looked ill at ease at her praise. He captured her stroking fingers and kissed each one in turn. "I am not interested in other women, Countess."

She understood his meaning. He was hers for now. That was more than she had expected from him. Grateful, she gave in to one of her yearnings and leaned forward to lick his flat pap. He moved his hands to her head and encouraged her exploration by guiding her. She felt the flesh under her tongue react to her caress. It was a heady feeling, discovering she had the power to make his lean body respond.

"Enough," he groaned, pulling her face up to his and kissing her. "You will have me rashly spilling my seed in my breeches again."

"Again?"

"Yes, you potent witch," he said, pushing her down on her back. "I had my hands all over you, my fingers inside you. Your response pushed me beyond my limits. Rubbing myself against you, I peaked like some inexperienced lad. What did you think, Countess? That I was impervious to you?"

His control had seemed formidable. She had wondered several times since their encounter if he had not been trying to manipulate her. The ends of his long, dark hair tickled her nose. Brook twitched it, resisting the urge to scratch.

"Silly woman," he chided. Reaching between their bodies, he unbuttoned the falls on his breeches. Taking her hand, he slid it down his torso until her fingers closed around the rigid length of his manhood. It felt hot beneath her fingers. Covering her hand, he encouraged her to squeeze the velvet flesh. "This is proof of my desire. Interest cannot be faked." He flexed, displaying his strength in a different manner.

Brook wanted to argue, but Mallory extinguished her protests by sliding his hand under her chemise. She tensed when his hand glided up her thighs seeking the soft nest between her legs. His thumb pressed into her womanly cleft.

"We have barely begun and already your body is preparing itself for me," he said, appearing as surprised as she was. His gaze locked with hers. "Take off your chemise. I want to see all of you."

Brook sat up partially and with his assistance removed the remaining barrier concealing her from his hungry gaze. The air was cool on her overly warm skin. She glanced down at her legs. "My stockings."

Mallory saw humor in her quandary. "With your permission." He untied each garter above the knee and slipped off her stockings. Once she was completely vulnerable to him, he stood and appreciated the tableau she presented. "You are exquisite, Countess," he said, his voice husky with awe. "I could spend the rest of my days painting you like this and never be bored."

"A lovely sentiment," she replied dryly, imagining her family's horror on viewing in public dozens of pictures of her sans clothing. "The artist will have to be content with the man's good fortune. I will never pose naked for you."

Undefeated, he inclined his head. "A pity, truly. Your breasts are inspiring."

"You must find your inspiration elsewhere," she said,

regretting her thoughtless words. She did not want to think of the other women who displayed their bodies for him without fear or coyness.

Misunderstanding her suggestion, he stood and shucked his breeches. Aggressive as his nature, his manhood jutted from its dark nest of hair. "Oh, I shall, my lady."

He covered her with his heat. Parting her legs, he made a place for himself there. Mallory curled his hand around one of her breasts while he nuzzled the other. A moan escaped her lips when he sucked vigorously on her nipple. He was rapidly mastering her body, gauging the degree of her pleasure by occasionally testing the moisture between her legs.

"You must stop?" she begged.

He mischievously bit her stomach and gazed up at her. "Why?" To prove his point, he slipped his fingers into her soft, womanly channel.

"I cannot take it. These feelings." She could not understand the tension he was building in her body. Her flesh felt taut and close to bursting. He had succeeded in making her want him, that part of him she had thought she would never crave from a man. She moved restlessly against him.

"Easy. I can help you," he crooned, sliding lower down her body.

He parted her feminine cleft with his fingers and put his mouth on her. His mouth was even more devastating than his fingers had been. She dug her fingers into the bedding, trying to fight back the sensation he was cleverly building.

"This is wrong. You must stop."

Mallory sucked on the swollen nubbin of flesh. If he had heard her frantic plea, he ignored it. Slipping his hands under her buttocks, he pulled her closer. She unthinkingly opened herself to him, granting him deeper access, and he readily claimed it. Brook arched back against the mattress while his tongue lapped the intimate core of her.

"Mallory," she said, his name a plea upon her lips.

Gliding his tongue in a tantalizing pattern, he responded to her plea by plunging his fingers into her wet feminine channel, ruthlessly driving her toward the pinnacle she was unknowingly beseeching him for.

The wild wind of the storm was suddenly within her. It spiraled, battering her insides. Rising, she shook from its questing intensity for release. Helpless, Brook opened her mouth and surrendered, freeing the storm with her scream.

She fell back into the bedding. She was so shaken by her experience, her eyes filled with tears. Mallory rose up between her legs. He appeared grimly satisfied with what he had accomplished until he saw her tears.

"There, there." He crawled up and covered her back with his body. She sank against his overheated flesh, needing his warmth. Concern furrowed his brow as he pulled the blankets over them.

"Why the tears, Countess? Did you not enjoy my pleasuring?" he murmured in her ear. He stroked her hair, trying to soothe her.

"It was beyond anything I have ever experienced," she whispered, choking on a sob. "I thought I might die of it."

He kissed her hair and snuggled her closer. Neither spoke. Brook listened to the wind and realized Mallory had kept his promise. She was safe with him. Weary, she closed her eyes and let sleep claim her.

Chapter Eleven

Mallory awoke with an undefined sense of urgency.

Opening his eyes, he realized his arms were wrapped around the source. Brook was still tucked close. He pressed his nose into her hair and inhaled her scent. The subtle shift in position made him painfully aware of something else. During their slumber, his rebellious body had ruined his noble intentions of giving her pleasure while taking none for himself. His defenses weakened in sleep, he had instinctively buried himself deep in the countess's welcoming heat. How long they had been joined like this Mallory could only guess. Her rhythmic breathing subtly massaged the engorged head of his cock and he groaned at the exquisite torture. He flexed inside her and the easy glide revealed that the sleeping widow was as aroused as he was. Unbeknownst to her, her body had accepted his penetration and on some level wanted the completion he craved.

Mallory had resisted because he understood Brook had never been given the proper loving she deserved in her marriage bed. Lyon, her bastard swine of a husband, had shown her only the selfishness of a man's lust. Overcoming his need to lose himself in her, Mallory had wanted to gently lure her into passion. The notion of *her* demanding that he pleasure her had aroused him immensely.

There was torment in stillness, he decided as sweat

gleamed on his brow. He was already half-mad from his restraint. Awakening to the discovery that he was inside, actually inside, her was enough to make him shed his veneer of civility and take her like a mindless rutting beast.

His nostrils flared taking in their combined scent. It was a heady aphrodisiac. Quivering with need, he flexed again. A tiny murmur passed through her lips. She shifted and took him deeper.

The dam of restraint broke at her unspoken invitation. Moving his hands lower, Mallory clasped her hips and guided his cock deeper into her silken passage. Quickening his short thrusts, he used her hips to keep him anchored. He felt Brook's subtle transition from sleep to awareness. Her breath caught in her throat and her body tensed. He took hope when she did not fight to get away.

"I need you, Countess," he said, his rough voice almost guttural. If she asked him to pull out when he was so close, he was afraid he was about to prove to her that he was just as selfish as her husband.

Getting over her initial shock, she reached back and touched his face. "Need me, Mallory," she offered.

He needed no further prompting. Pulling out of her long enough to roll her onto her back, Mallory fitted himself against her opening and let her take him. The depth of the penetration after countless shallow, inadequate strokes shattered his control. Hammering himself into her, he gritted his teeth and threw back his head against the fury of his orgasm. He surrendered to the onslaught zealously, holding himself deep as his cock rhythmically pumped his seed into her womb.

Mallory blinked, stunned by his recklessness. He had always taken care not to leave his seed within a woman. Although he enjoyed numerous women, he had no desire to populate England with his bastards. He had even denied Mirabella his essence, since they had not desired children so soon after their marriage. Somehow Brook had destroyed all his good intentions and years of rigid restraint in one cataclysmic moment. As he stared down at her sweet face, it was not the stirrings of regret that thickened his voice.

"I have never awakened so perfectly. I am of the mind of never letting you return to Loughwydde."

The countess was also struggling with her composure. Mallory was not certain, because he had been too focused on his own release, but she had the look of a woman who had found completion in her lover's arms.

"The storm has passed on and dawn is almost upon us. You know I cannot stay," she said, softly reminding him of their impropriety.

His body was feeling too good to dwell on the troubles an affair with her would create. Mallory had wanted her almost from the beginning. Claiming her had only intensified his hunger. "We have a little time left before I have to take you back."

The walls of her feminine passage had thickened around him as if trying to keep him lodged within her. He retreated slightly, reveling in the snugness of their fit, and then surged upward. Her eyes widened in pleasure and she lifted her hips to meet his thrust.

"Yes, there is time."

Brook felt like a thief in her own house. *A very daring criminal,* she mused as she walked through the front door. The advice had come from Mallory when he had escorted her home and taken care of her horse. They had encountered no one in the barn. Before he had departed, he had told her that most of the servants would be eating or going about their duties at the back of the house. No one would be watching the front door. It was a very clever plan.

She moved quietly from the entrance hall to the stairs. The first step had the tendency to squeak, so she stepped over it and pulled herself up with the railing. Her dress and corset had caused her some concern when she recalled how he had cut the garments off her. Mallory had kissed her soundly when she complained. They had just staggered out of his bed and he was far too pleased with himself to allow her to dampen his outlook with tedious details. He had teased her out of her sulks by tickling her mercilessly and then searched the cottage for some kind of cording to temporarily hold her dress together. Although the cloak she wore concealed his handiwork, she felt completely indecent. He had not bothered securing her corset. Mallory had even suggested initially that she forget the unnecessary contrivance. She had flatly refused. In the end, she had put on the corset and used the lacing of her dress to hold everything in place. He had deliberately kept the lacing loose and the ties within reach so she could undo them herself. If she made it to her room undiscovered, no one would ever know she had left the house.

It was not until she had closed the door to her bedchamber that she dared to breathe again. Relieved, she unhooked the clasp of her cloak and discarded it on the chair. Reaching for the ties at her back, she untied the strings and slipped out of her dress and corset.

Brook glanced down at her bare legs. Dear heavens, she had forgotten her stockings. Or had she? Mallory had helped her dress. Perhaps his odd humor this morning had encouraged him to hide them. He probably laughed on his return walk to the cottage thinking about how she would react. Oh, he would pay later for his mischief.

Leaving her chemise on, she pulled back the covers and climbed into bed. Weariness weighed her eyelids down as she laid her head onto the pillow. She did not regret her night with Mallory Claeg. He had treated her with tenderness and his skillful touch had caused her to transcend to such enchanting heights. Keeping her eyes closed, she smiled. He thought she was beautiful. When he said the words, he made her believe them.

The pleasure he had given her was so dizzying and wondrous, she would have granted him anything. Letting him rut upon her body had seemed inconsequential. He had held her while she had cried in response to the joy he had given her. Afterward, she had expected him to slake his own needs. Mallory, instead, had curled himself around her and had promptly fallen asleep. She had lain there, confused and hurt by his disinterest. Eventually, she had fallen into a dreamless sleep.

When she awakened, he had managed to once again confuse her. Not only had he remained in the bed through the night, but he had seduced her while she had slept. It had been disorientating to awaken with his breath hissing in her ear and his arousal warming her from within.

I need you, Countess.

His husky plea had touched her. She was not about to turn him away when he had awakened the hunger within her, too. Brook touched the sensitive flesh between her legs. Her insides constricted with desire as she recalled how he had clutched her desperately to him and she felt the warm flood of his release. She squeezed her legs tightly together, feeling an echo of her earlier response. The gentle pulse of his completion had triggered an answering need. The velvet muscles within her had milked his manhood, taking his seed deep into her body as he willingly emptied himself into her.

Both of them should have been satisfied.

She should have gotten up and quietly dressed as Lyon had always done after he was finished. Mallory should have wanted her to go. Neither had climbed out of the bed. Instead of softening, his manhood had remained firmly lodged within her. He began stroking her slowly, rekindling the waning passion, and her body had responded. The darkness in the sky had been creeping toward dawn when they had clung to each other and surrendered to a second release.

Slipping into sleep, she was too practical to believe her

dubious charms would keep him near Loughwydde forever. She was already missing him when she finally let go and drifted off.

Mallory was in excellent spirits and he owed the beautiful widow his thanks. Walking along the shore, he picked up a section of driftwood blown in by the storm and swung it back and forth merrily.

He had remained at Loughwydde until he was satisfied Brook had slipped into the house unnoticed by the other residents. Since he did not hear any screaming accusations coloring the air, he had returned to the cottage. His muse had called to him this morning. A night holding the mortal incarnate of Aglaia, the goddess of splendor, in his arms had stimulated his creativity. Mrs. Whitby had arrived around nine, expecting him to still be in bed. He had flirted with her outrageously while she fixed his breakfast. His joviality had been contagious. Laughing, the flustered old woman had shooed him out of the cottage so she could do her chores.

Mallory took up his chalks and sketching book and chose to spend part of his day at the beach. Later he would return to Loughwydde on the pretense of working on Miss Hamblin's picture. Who he truly wanted to see and if he could arrange it put his hands on was the countess. He had never guessed the generosity and passionate fire she had hidden from herself and the world. Mallory had tapped that wellspring and tasted the pure, sweet water of her ardor. God, he wanted her again. One sip and he was thirsting eternally for his next swallow. If that was his price for bedding his earthbound goddess, he was willing to pay.

"Mr. Claeg," a disembodied voice called down to him. "Mr. Mallory Claeg."

He shielded his eyes and searched the cliffs. He spotted the corpulent gentleman slowly making his way down the stone steps. Mallory acknowledged the stranger with a wave.

There was no point in having a conversation from a distance, so he reversed his direction to shorten the man's walk.

"Good day to you, sir. Your servant told me that I might find you here. My name is Stand. I have come from Truro. Mr. Claeg, you are a difficult man to locate," the man confessed earnestly, his plump face suffused with pink from his exertion.

"I was not trying to be found, Mr. Stand. How may I help you?"

"Two riders arrived in Truro eight days ago. Each carried a missive with orders to find you. One continued east. The gentleman who intended to ride here fell from his horse three days earlier. I am a cousin of the surgeon who was summoned to his bed. He was so certain that you were residing and painting somewhere on this section of coast that I offered to assist him in his quest." The harried explanation left him winded.

Mallory could not think of anyone, except Amara, who cared where he wandered. How the devil had she found him? "The letter?"

"Oh yes, quite right." He dug into the inner pocket of his coat. "Here it is," he said, handing it to Mallory.

Mallory stared down at the wax impression of the Keyworths' seal. "You must be parched, Mr. Stand. If you return to the cottage, Mrs. Whitby will give you something to drink. Do not offend her if she insists on filling your belly. She is an excellent cook."

The man tugged on his hat. "Your generosity is most welcome, Mr. Claeg. I pray you are the recipient of good news."

He stared out at the sea, observing a ship in the distance. The letter remained clutched in his hand unread. What news was so important that his father had sent two riders to find him? He glanced down in resignation. If the pompous Lord Keyworth had exerted himself to locate his errant heir, Mallory was certain the news in the letter was likely to douse his good cheer. The man had often done so, with ruthless efficiency.

"G'morning, my lady," Morna said, rousing Brook from her deep slumber. The maid opened the curtains and the window, letting in the morning air to clear out the staleness of the room.

Brook did not open her eyes. "The time. What is the time?" she asked groggily.

"Eight or thereabouts," the young woman replied, gathering up the discarded clothing. "Lo, what a beastly storm we had last evening. Though it certainly cleaned the air." She paused, shifting the bundle in her arms to get a closer look at the dress. "Here now, what happened to your dress? And corset?"

The stunned amazement was as effective as cold water on Brook's face. She sat up and rubbed the corner of her right eye. "The storm kept me up. I had retired so late, I did not want to disturb you. Since I could not manage the lacing myself, I simply cut them." The blatant lie came easier than it should have.

"My lady, you should have summoned me. I wouldn't have minded helping you get comfortable."

"Nonsense," she dismissed the maid's protest. "The laces can be replaced. I regret that the dowager keeps you on your feet most of the day with a thousand biddings." Brook scooted to the edge of the mattress. She stifled a groan. There was not one part of her that did not ache.

"Do not fret about that ol'—" Gasping, Morna stared at her in horror.

"What?"

The maid chuckled. "Oh, my lady, you gave me a fright." She clucked her tongue at her own foolishness. "'Twas all the blood, you see. It's your curse."

Brook looked down at the front of her chemise. The large

bright red bloodstain was indeed startling. She gave her maid a rueful glance. "I have always considered it so."

Breakfast did little to restore her spirits. She ached and had the beginnings of a megrim. She blamed her mother and Mother A'Court for the headache. Their blissful assumption that Brook was returning with them to London made her clench her teeth. The servants had already started packing for the journey. Honey and Ivy were fighting again. Brook was not even paying attention to Ivy's current ire. May was also in an odd mood. The woman kept sending pensive looks at her that were quite frankly annoying. One more problem or irritant was likely to upset the delicate balance of her restraint.

"Before your daughter can contemplate rejoining society," Elthia, Lady A'Court expressed with authority, "we must see to her wardrobe. Those dresses might be adequate for rural life, but for polite society they are several years out of fashion."

"Madam, I have been out of society for several years. I saw no reason to waste money on evening dresses and ball gowns," Brook said, stuffing a spoonful of poached egg in her mouth before she lost her temper.

Sensing her eldest daughter's disagreeable disposition, Mrs. Ludlow tried to appease both women. "Lady A'Court, naturally Brook will purchase a wardrobe befitting her station. Ham spoke of his desire to reacquaint her with the amusements town has to offer. Together we will see to it that she has everything to make the proper impression." Her mother patted Brook's hand. "You always loved new dresses, my dear. You will look radiant in the fashionable colors of the season." She lowered her voice confidentially. "Mourning colors have always given your skin a sickly cast. Your looks will improve greatly without them."

"Mrs. Ludlow, no one expects a widow grieving for her

husband to look anything other than sickly," the dowager said, embracing her favorite subject. "I cannot heartily agree with you and Lord A'Court's notion of thrusting Brook back into society."

Brook choked on her egg at the word *thrusting* and slumped lower into her chair. She never thought she would hear that particular word uttered by her mother-in-law. "I agree with Mother A'Court."

"Bosh," Brook's mother said, rejecting her opinion. "You are just shy."

"However," the dowager said, calling attention to herself, "if you must insist on this business, then I will not have her shaming her husband's memory. People are bound to speak of the tragedy of his death. I feel we must resist sharing our sorrow with the *ton*. All of us will be under scrutiny. I pray our decorum will uplift the A'Court name."

"Why does Ham have to marry Brook?" Honey asked aloud. "She is the A'Court widow. It sounds like bad luck marrying the widow of your namesake. One would think that if he wanted to marry another member of the family, one of us would be up for consideration."

Mrs. Ludlow pounced on her daughter before Brook had a chance. "Honey Ludlow, what would your father say if he heard your impertinence? For the benefit of clarity, you are not invited to partake in this conversation. Furthermore, you and your sister are too young to marry Lord A'Court."

If their mother's lecture had not silenced Honey, the dowager's jaundiced stare had her swallowing her tongue. Grandmother Byres cackled with glee for no particular reason.

"Speaking of sickly," May interjected casually, "I have been meaning to comment on your complexion, Cousin. Your pallor is more pronounced this morning. Did the storm disturb your sleep?"

Brook tightened her grip on her spoon. The friendliness

she usually attributed to the young woman was absent, making her wary. "Some."

"The wind was dreadful," Brook's mother wailed. "I awoke in the middle of the night and had to fortify myself with a small glass of brandy."

Honey straightened in her seat. "It was a banshee, coming to warn us of death." She mimicked the mournful call of a spirit in torment. Ivy added her voice, creating an eerie atmosphere.

Grandmother Byres, the oldest member of the family, was spooked. She made a fretful noise.

"Girls, we have endured a sufficient amount of your mischief," Brook said, glaring at both of them. She pointedly glanced at Mrs. Byres, hoping they were clever enough to reason out her meaning.

Mrs. Ludlow clapped her hands rapidly. "Honey and Ivy Ludlow, you may both retire to your bedchamber until you are summoned."

"Mum," Ivy implored, frustrated that she had been caught up in her sister's web of disobedience.

"Not another word from either of you," their mother commanded. "Go!"

"Although I disapprove of her method, I have to agree with her sentiment. The wind, indeed, sounded like something from the mournful and supernatural." May deliberately settled her gaze on Brook. "I scarcely slept at all."

Elthia, Lady A'Court, sniffed. "Storms rarely trouble me."

"Oh, you poor dear," Mrs. Ludlow fretted. "Did you suffer through the night with your covers over your head?"

Brook dropped her spoon. She waved away the footman and leaned over to retrieve the utensil herself. Her clumsiness had been deliberate. The wariness she felt around May was bubbling into complete alarm. She was disturbed by the young woman's uncharacteristically sly expression. Snatching up the dropped spoon, Brook sat up hoping her mask of composure was in place.

"Actually, I—"

Mrs. Gordy bustled into the room. "Sorry for disturbing you, my lady. You have a visitor. Mr. Claeg is asking to see you."

Brook did not miss the flash of hostility in May Hamblin's eyes. It seemed her disappearance last night had not gone unnoticed and assumptions, albeit correct ones, had been made.

"It is awfully early to receive gentleman callers," Elthia, Lady A'Court, said with disdain. She had long ago judged Mr. Claeg and found him lacking.

The man was inviting trouble coming to Brook in this bold manner. If she had wanted to draw attention, she would have slammed the door when she had entered the house. Putting her concerns about May aside, she addressed the most important one. "Did Mr. Claeg mention his reasons for his visit?"

The housekeeper shook her head. "No, madam. He was most insistent on seeing you alone right away."

"Very well," Brook said, gaining the dowager's disapproval for not turning him away. "Put him in the formal parlor. I will join him immediately."

"I already tried," Mrs. Gordy protested. "There is no time for formality, he says to me. He and his horse are on the front lawn, awaiting you. Do you want me to tell him that you are indisposed?"

Everyone seemed curious about Mr. Claeg's rudeness. May was interested in Brook's response to his odd request. Avoiding everyone's gaze, she stood, saying to her housekeeper, "Never you mind. I will address him directly." Head high, she reminded herself that she had done nothing shameful and exited the dining room.

Brook kept her slow, regal pace until she was out of view.

She then picked up her skirts and ran. Mallory climbed
down off his horse the second he noticed her. Holding on to
the reins, he walked her around to the other side of the horse,
using the animal's body to conceal them from prying eyes.

"What are you doing here?" she demanded, slightly hurt
that he had not thought to kiss her. "Everyone knows you
have asked for me. What happened to being discreet?"

"I have little time to explain. After I leave here I am racing
off to London," he said, his light blue gaze encompassing her
entire body as if he was committing her to memory.

"Why? What have I done?"

"Nothing," he harshly snapped, reacting to her melancholy. "If I had a choice I would remain by your side, Countess. It is my father." His throat worked while his speech
failed him. "He has had a stroke. It took the messenger more
than a week to deliver this message. My mother wrote that
she fears that he will not survive his injuries. I *have* to *go!*"

Mallory was the viscount's only surviving son and heir. It
was his duty to leave her. She could not prevent the start of
tears from adding brilliancy to her gaze.

"Look, I could not leave Cornwall without seeing you. I
needed to explain. I did not want you to think for one moment that I was abandoning you."

"Of course. Did you want me to wish you a safe journey?" Her attempt at being worldly was failing miserably.

He stepped forward and captured her chin with his fingers.
"I cannot guess when I will be able to return to the cottage. To
you." He bent down and rubbed his forehead against hers.
"There is another way. One I hesitate to ask but am too selfish
to deny myself. Come to London, Countess. I cannot offer
promises until I have learned of my father's condition and
what will be required of me. If we are both residing in town, I
can satisfy the demands of my family and you. I most especially look forward to satisfying you." He lifted her mouth up
to his waiting lips.

"Mallory—"

"Damn you, say that you will come!" he ordered impatiently. "I have no more time for this. I must get under way. This I vow: Whatever your fears, we can face them together. Give me a chance to prove myself." He coaxed her with another kiss.

"Prove what?" He was pushing her. Brook detested being rushed or manipulated by anyone. "I have made my feelings clear about returning," she said weakly. She could not prevent the old fears from choking her, not even for him.

Her response infuriated him. Scowling at her, he walked around to the other side and mounted his horse. "The woman I shared my bed with last night was not cowed by what other people thought about her." His closed countenance was merciless. "The choice is yours." He leaned down and seized her by the back of her dress. Hauling her off her feet, Mallory savagely devoured her mouth. He released her when he had finished, letting her fall and find her own balance.

"Choice, you black-hearted villain . . . what choice?" She wiped her mouth; it stung from his abuse.

His eyes narrowed derisively. "The choice of whether you are my woman or some pitiful lonely widow I fucked for sport."

She backed away, feeling the blood leaving her face.

"Come to me in London, Countess!"

He pulled harshly on the reins, steering the horse away from the house. The animal stomped and moved sideways, disturbed by the cutting bit. Mallory spurred his steed into a gallop and the animal leaped into the air to avoid another kick. Man and horse rode away, leaving Brook standing alone in the swirling dust. He had warned her; his challenge lay at her feet like a verbal gauntlet.

She truly despised him.

Chapter Twelve

If he had traveled by post chaise, the journey from Cornwall to London would have taken him at least seven days. By horse, he reached his parents' town house in less than two days. He was dirty, tired, and he had worn out three magnificent horses to answer his mother's fearful summons.

The Keyworths' butler, Buckle, wearing formal livery, answered his knock. The servant's solemn face creased into a grateful smile. "Mr. Claeg. How good to see you, sir. The viscountess was concerned that neither of her messengers had located you."

His mother had probably feared that he might ignore her curt request to return home. The family had viewed his nature as defiant more than dutiful. "Does my father live, Buckle?"

"Aye, sir. He is resting upstairs with your mother at his side. She will want to know of your return."

Mallory started to follow him up the stairs. The servant held out his hand. "Madam might need a moment to compose herself. The viscount's collapse has devastated her. Why do you not go into your father's study and wait for my return? Pardon me for saying so, my lord, but a bath appears to be in order. I am certain we can find something of His Lordship's that will cover you properly."

Descending the stairs, Mallory headed in the direction of

the study. With shaking hands, he realized he was not prepared to face his father quite yet. Some of the viscount's brandy might steady him, and the butler's suggestion of a bath was welcomed, too. Mallory's family had always prided themselves on appearances, and his resembled that of a brigand rather than a viscount's heir.

He walked through the arched doorway of his father's study and was stunned to see he was not alone. A woman had her back to him as she peered out the window.

Brook.

The lady, sensing his presence, whirled around and cried out in startled joy. "Mallory!" She rushed into his arms. "Oh, Mallory, where have you been hiding?" his sister, Amara, demanded. "No one knew where you had wandered off this time and I have been so frightened." She sniffed and dug into her reticule for a handkerchief.

"You have made my wife cry, sir," a masculine voice interrupted their tearful reunion. "I have throttled men for less."

Brock Bedegrayne seemed capable of inflicting any damage he promised. Tall, his lean build reminded Mallory of a hungry wolf. The faint jagged scar on Brock's left temple was a warning that the gentleman had not spent his youth studying life through books. His blond hair and pale green eyes were a legacy of his mother, Anna Bedegrayne. His younger sister, Wynne Milroy, also shared his good looks. Two years younger than Mallory, Brock had been close to him when they were boys, but they had grown apart. Even as a young man, Mallory had sensed Brock's interest in Amara had been less than sisterly. Fortunately, the gentleman had waited until she had grown into a woman before he acted on those impulses. Even so, Mallory had wanted to murder Brock for kidnapping his sister and seducing her.

"Bedegrayne, how have you been treating my sister?" Mallory was too weary to add credibility to his frown.

The younger man snorted. "Better than you have been

treating yourself. Sit before you collapse. Amara, get your brother something to drink."

Amara smiled sweetly at her husband as she passed him and complied with his order. "As you can see, my husband still has the tendency to act like a scolding older brother." She handed Mallory the brandy she had poured.

Unable to resist, he reached out and spread his hand across the swell of her burgeoning belly which even her skirts could not conceal. The child growing in her kicked him. He snatched back his hand and laughed. "The act that planted your daughter in your belly was scarcely brotherly, Amara," he said dryly.

She smoothed the fabric covering her abdomen, revealing how large his little sister had grown in his absence. "Why do you think this is a girl and not a boy?"

He stared down into her heart-shaped face, knowing those stormy blue eyes as well as his own. Pregnancy had softened her face and plumped up her bosom, though as her brother he was pretending not to notice such things. The glow she seemed to radiate had been there longer, at least since Bedegrayne had returned to her and declared his love. Amara's shoulder-length mahogany tresses were pulled up into a dignified knot. He had been mildly surprised to encounter her and Bedegrayne at the Keyworth town house. Their father had threatened to disinherit Amara if she accepted Brock's proposal of marriage. As far as Mallory knew, his parents still had not forgiven their daughter.

"Her quick temper and retaliation remind me of you, puss."

Brock pushed him into the nearest chair. "Care to wager on it, old man?"

Mallory cocked his left brow. "Later. Sisters get a mite testy when brothers start placing bets on their progeny."

Amara sank down onto the sofa. "Brock, do not encourage him."

"How can I resist, dove? He is so weary, he will be babbling in a few minutes," Brock argued.

Mallory was tired. In spite of their angry parting, he had regretted leaving Brook. He had been deliberately provoking, hoping her ire at him would allow her to focus on him and not her fears. Somehow, he doubted the countess had appreciated his thoughtfulness.

"Where were you, Mallory?"

Since he did not have to open his eyes to have a conversation with his sister, he did not. "Cornwall. West coast."

Amara made an exasperated noise. "Why there?"

He brought the brandy to his lips and drank. "Pursuing my muse, I suppose," he said, appreciating his humor even if his companions did not.

"I cannot fathom why you would choose the remoteness of Cornwall to paint," she said, not understanding why he disappeared for weeks sometimes. "Why, I cannot name one person who claimed a love for such a—"

He opened his eyes when she did not finish her thought aloud. She was looking beyond him; the contemplation on her comely visage would have made a less courageous man wary. "What? Spit it out, puss. I am too tired for puzzles."

"Nothing, I suppose. I was just thinking of someone I knew who liked your Cornwall as much as you. A random thought."

"She gets a lot of them, I fear," Brock admitted, coming up behind his wife and circling his arms around her neck. She pinched him in retaliation for his teasing.

"Have you seen Father?" Mallory instantly regretted asking when both of them sobered. Amara pressed the handkerchief she clasped to her eyes.

Brock answered for her. "Your mother merely tolerates our presence, Claeg. We showed up as soon as we learned of your father's collapse and she was too distraught to recall that she should turn us away. Since then, we have been allowed entry into the house simply because of appearances. We wait here in the study. When Lady Keyworth feels we have overstayed our welcome, she sends Buckle to send us away."

"Mama told me on the first night that she was afraid that if Papa saw me at his side, it might kill him. Why does he despise me so much?" Amara sobbed into her hand.

Mallory forgot about his own fatigue and stumbled out of his chair and onto the sofa beside her. "No crying. You will upset your daughter and she is likely to kick you and ruin your supper."

Amara laughed as he had intended. She buried her face into his shoulder. "How I have missed you. Will you be staying?"

Mallory would remain as long as his father needed him. He wanted, no, needed, the countess by his side. If she ignored his command and he was satisfied his father's recovery was in sight, he planned to return to Cornwall. Lady A'Court would not discard him so easily.

"I will be around to spoil my niece, if that is what you are asking," he said, willing Amara's tears to cease. His sister was an emotional creature. Tears were part of her nature, whereas the countess viewed them as a weakness, an adversary she had to vanquish.

"Sir Thomas is insisting that the child be male. He will be disappointed if we have not given him a boy to carry on the Bedegrayne name." Brock produced a handkerchief out of his pocket and cleared all traces of her tears. "You realize, dove, that if my father does not get his grandson he will be badgering me into begetting another child."

They smiled at each other, imagining Sir Thomas's antics. "For you, my love, I will endeavor to cooperate."

Mallory smiled, feeling the bitter sweetness of envy. Had his wife survived, they most likely would have had children by now. His thought jumped from Mirabella to Brook. She had experienced briefly the feeling of life within her womb, until her husband snuffed out its tiny life. She understood loss. A tremor moved through him as he recalled with stunning clarity how it felt to spill himself inside the countess. Not just once, he reminded himself, but twice. Had their passion fortuitously created a child? The notion spun dizzying possibilities.

"Mallory."

The crisp matronly voice snapped him from his fanciful musings. He saw his mother in the doorway. She had changed very little since he had last visited. Her hair was tidy and the dress might have been worn to receive afternoon visitors. Amara sat frozen beside him, waiting for their mother to acknowledge her only daughter.

"I had hoped you would have received my summons quicker. Nevertheless, in light of not knowing your whereabouts I should be content the letter reached you at all."

Mallory rose from the sofa. He crossed the room to reach out to his mother, since she seemed disinclined to enter the study. She did not relax in his embrace. "I was preparing for my departure minutes after reading your letter. Father." He glanced back at his sister, including her when their mother did not. "How is he?"

"Not well, Son." Lady Keyworth's lips trembled, betraying the emotion she refused to share with anyone else. She stared blindly at the wall above Amara's head. "Thank you for coming today. You will understand why I cannot remain and visit. Buckle will show you out." She touched his wrist. "Come, Mallory."

Bedegrayne accepted her dismissal with mute fury on his wife's behalf. Amara was clearly devastated by her mother's daily rejection. Mallory was tempted to shake his mother and force her to reconcile with the couple.

Amara must have gleaned his thoughts from his brooding countenance. "No," his sister said, rising regally. "If you will allow it, we will come tomorrow, Mama. Please give Papa my love."

Mallory and his mother passed Buckle as he entered the study to escort Amara and Bedegrayne out the door as if they were unwanted guests instead of family. He climbed the stairs in his mother's stiff wake, fighting the urge to confront her on her callous treatment of her pregnant daughter. It took him several minutes to calm down. Amara would not appreciate his meddling. His mother, although misguided, was protecting the man she loved. Upsetting him would not endear Mallory to anyone.

"You said in your letter that he collapsed. Did something trigger it?" Mallory asked, focusing on the present. He planned on sharing what he had learned with Amara.

Lady Keyworth stopped in front of her husband's private chambers. "My lord did nothing out of the ordinary. He went to one of the commons with his falcon, Ellette. Later he had supper at one of his clubs. He had been preparing for bed when he collapsed. I heard his valet shouting for Buckle. When I ran into the room, I thought he was dead. Mallory, his face was a horrifying blue." This time she bowed into his embrace and sobbed. He held her, letting her rid herself of the grief she had held in too long.

"You said, Mother, that he is improving," Mallory prompted once the worst of her grief had passed.

She dabbed her eyes. "Yes. You will see for yourself." Lady Keyworth opened the door and gestured for him to enter.

There was no sound expect the soft, raspy breathing coming from the man in the bed. The drapes were closed as if the brightness of the afternoon would disturb the ill man. The man whom Mallory recognized as his father's valet sat in the chair positioned close to the bed. The servant closed the book he had been reading.

"I will leave you now," he whispered out of respect for his sleeping employer. "I will await your summons downstairs, my lady." He quietly shut the door behind him.

"Go on and take the chair," Mallory's mother encouraged. "I pray seeing your face when he awakens will improve his spirits."

Mallory sat down, his knees colliding into the mattress. At first glance, his father appeared no different. Lady Keyworth nodded approvingly and sat in one of the chairs pushed against the wall. He had no idea how long he would have to wait until his father awakened. Shifting in the already-uncomfortable chair, Mallory bumped the mattress again.

Lord Keyworth's eyes were mere slits, as if testing the dim light to see if it pained him. Aware he was being observed, he let his head drop to the right. His eyes widened, but Mallory noticed his father's right eyelid drooped lower than his left.

"Mawry," the viscount said, mangling his name. Lord Keyworth spoke as if his tongue had been paralyzed by his apoplexy. Sadness and pity rose up within Mallory for his sire.

"I am here. Mother's messenger found me in Cornwall. It took me a few days to get here. Buckle has promised me a hot bath, but I wanted to see you." He found it awkward to talk to this enfeebled likeness of his father. This man looked like a harsh word might crush him.

"G'in' t'die," the viscount mumbled.

He leaned closer, attempting to understand his father. Scrutinizing him, Mallory noticed the muscles on the right side of his body were lifeless. Not only did his right lid droop, but his mouth was slack also. His breath was a slurping hiss between his lips.

Mallory gave his mother an appealing glance. "I—I do not understand, sir."

"Dot . . . rahda die t'en liblike t'is." He repeated the garbled sentence a second time. He struck his chest with his left fist.

Mallory's concern escalated. He wondered if Lord Keyworth had been robbed of not only his speech but his intelligence as well.

"Gllma," he said, growing more agitated by his son's puzzled expression. Tears streamed from the corners of his father's eyes. "Gllma, gllma, gllma!" He let his head flop to the left as if the sight of Mallory pained him.

"My lord," Lady Keyworth said, finally interrupting their reunion. "We have tired you, and your son needs a bath and rest from his journey. I will return to you shortly." Her grip reminded Mallory of an iron clamp as she guided him out of the room.

"Buckle is efficient. Your bath most likely awaits you in your bedchamber."

"Mother, is he—is he insane?"

Her expression grew incredulous. "For heaven's sake, no. Whatever made you think such cruelty?"

"I have no desire to hurt you with the truth, Mother," Mallory said, positive anything he had to say would accomplish the deed. "The man on that bed is just a shell of my father. He was agitated and spoke gibberish. There is reason for me to conclude that even he does not know what he is saying."

Lady Keyworth covered her mouth, shocked by her son's rash conclusions. When she pulled her hand away, her lips were compressed into the thin line he had seen often enough in his life. It indicated that he had managed to disappoint her.

"Mallory, you need to be patient with your father. His right side was injured when he collapsed. The physician said that his speech would improve over time."

And what of his confused, agitated, damaged brain? Mallory silently asked. "Then I suppose you understood what he was saying to me?"

"Not every word, but his meaning was clear," she said, daring him to contradict her.

"What was he saying over and over, madam?"

She looked away, not meeting his probing gaze. His mother was silent for a few minutes. Reluctantly she admitted, "He asked you to kill him."

Chapter Thirteen

The chaos and smells of London nauseated Brook. Arriving eleven days after Mallory's abrupt departure, she was not positive who had bullied her into leaving Loughwydde. Maybe there was no one to blame but herself. One day she was telling the inflexible and boorish Mr. Claeg that she was remaining in Cornwall. Several days later she was riding in the carriage beside her sisters.

Initially, the journey had roused her curiosity. It had been long since she had explored beyond her lands. Passing through the various villages and meeting fellow travelers at the inns they had rested and supped at had fulfilled a longing she had quelled. She had forgotten that once she had craved adventure. Mr. Ludlow's business had required that he travel often, and he had brought his family along.

Lyon had ruined it for her, she acknowledged. Their honeymoon to Italy had been a private nightmare. Only realizing that she had returned to England carrying his child had eased her pain. At least for a while.

She buried her recollections as she had ruthlessly buried her love for the man some considered a monster. The pleasures and curiosities of her journey faded for Brook as the distance she had put between her and her past shrank. Everyone was so excited about seeing London and making plans, no one had noticed her subtle withdrawal.

Once the wheels of the carriage were rumbling through the congested streets of town, she had worked herself into a state of despair. She had a hundred grievances, but she kept them to herself. The air was too thick and reeked of excrement. The sky was too gray. There were so many people that she thought she might suffocate.

What spared her from entirely breaking down was that she was not returning to the town house she had shared with her husband. The house belonged to Ham as the new Lord A'Court. He and May were welcome to it. Brook could not bear to walk down its opulent halls. Her mother was confused by her decision until Brook had pointed out that without a house filled with chaperones, residing with the new earl would cause undue speculation. Mrs. Ludlow readily agreed. She had convinced her husband to lease a house for them.

The square was older and not as fashionable as Brook's mother had desired for herself and her girls, but Mr. Ludlow's calm practicality overruled his wife. Honey and Ivy were too young, in their father's stern estimation, for the tawdriness of the *ton*. His girls could enjoy the town's amusements without descending into the muck Brook's mother was so eager for her elder daughter to embrace.

"Are you missing Loughwydde?" her stepfather asked from behind as she observed a hawker peddling her fruit. Several hours had passed since their arrival, and everyone was still occupied with settling into their rooms.

"Some," Brook conceded when in truth her thoughts were closer to London. She looked up and could hear the muffled argument her half sisters had engaged in about a pair of embroidered stockings. "With everyone out of the house, I would have relished the peaceful silence." She frowned, listening to one door slam and then another. Next she heard her mother's determined stride overhead. "Papa, do they ever quit fighting?"

Rare humor glinted behind his spectacles. "Only when they fall asleep." They both laughed at his joke. He opened his arms and she willingly embraced him. "I am pleased you listened to your mother. Spending a season in town is just what you need." He kissed the top of her head and released her.

Drawing away, she asked, "And what do you think I need?"

His gesture was vague. "A new adventure, pretty dresses that have you dreaming of dances and a handsome gentleman for a partner . . . old friends, new friends . . . someone to help you discover your smile again."

"I smile, Papa," she protested, stunned by his whimsical list. She pasted a smile on her face to force him to retract his complaint.

Mr. Ludlow pushed his spectacles back into place on his nose. He did not return her smile. "Not often. Not as effortlessly as you used to, Daughter."

She slumped against the window frame. "Of late, there has not been much going on in my life to have me grinning like a loon."

"Be considerate when you speak of your sisters, Brook," he chided, coaxing her to laugh. "There, that is what I mean. Perhaps you had some romantic notion of you mourning your Lyon forever, though it is wholly idealistic."

"Oh," she said, deflated that her stepfather had reduced her escape to Loughwydde as a step away from sulking. "Is that what I have been doing? Mourning Lyon?"

Realizing he was a man straying away from his expertise, Mr. Ludlow pulled uncomfortably on his cravat. "You are your mother's daughter. I would not presume to understand the complicated workings of the feminine brain."

"Papa, I am no longer mourning my husband." She had stopped shortly after his death. Brook pulled her stepfather's fussing fingers away from his cravat before the poor man strangled himself. "I was not ready to resume my old life after his death. Two years away from all of this and now I do not believe I will ever want to be that person again. Am I making sense?"

"Of course. You are the most logical of all my girls, including my wife." Realizing his error, he said, "Though I would be obligated to deny it if ever questioned by my lady wife."

"A laudable view," she conceded, secretly amused her stepfather was awed by her sprightly mother's temper. Brook kissed his cheek. "I would never place you in such an awkward position."

"Daughter, you have a good heart. It would be a pity if you could not find someone to share it again." She stared down at her feet.

"Just mull over my words. You are a great deal like me in that regard," he said with some pride.

He wandered away unnoticed, leaving Brook to wonder when her fears had distorted prudence into stagnancy.

Ham looked up from the book he was reading as his sister walked into the room. The young woman was truly vexed about something. "Do the dowager and Mrs. Byres approve of their rooms?"

"Approving leaves Elthia, Lady A'Court, no room to improve upon her situation," May said, feeling the strain of Brook's absence. The old crone, deprived of her usual fodder, had focused her discontent on May.

The earl chuckled sympathetically. "She is our late cousin's mother, pet. Abandoning her would be cruel. Besides, I need her on my side. Her approval of Brook as my betrothed will still the gossips' tongues." He understood his lady's fears and was trying to anticipate the obstacles of their future together.

May approached his desk. She turned his book around and read enough to discern the subject. Wrinkling her nose, she said, "Ham, are you positive you want Brook for your countess? As you are now Lord A'Court, the title would lure other ladies of wealth."

Her jealousy of his affections being divided was a natural response. "I had asked her to come to town, May. She heeded my request, so I assume she has embraced the idea of being my Lady A'Court."

"There is something you do not know. After you departed Loughwydde, a terrible storm struck the land."

He knew of his sister's fear of storms. "Poor lamb, did you quake beneath your sheets until dawn?"

"No," she replied, insulted that he had thought so little of her. "I went to Brook so I could extol your impressive merits."

"Why, thank you. I am undeserving to have you for my sister."

"There is more. When I went to her bedchamber, her room was empty. Her bed had not a wrinkle."

"So she was somewhere else in the house."

"I do not think so, Brother. There is something going on between her and Mr. Claeg. I dare not add supposition to what I know as fact."

Ham conjured the disturbing image of them entwined in the woods. "What proof do you offer?"

"None." May bit her lip in dismay. "Except that before our departure Mr. Claeg arrived at Loughwydde and demanded to speak with Brook. He refused an invitation to await her in the parlor. He insisted that she meet him outdoors *and alone*."

The way May described their encounter, it sounded suspicious even to Ham. "What happened?" Had he dragged her into the woods again? Did she go willingly?

"Nothing."

Relieved, Ham was not above some brotherly retribution. "May, you are not making much sense."

Defensive, she said, "Well, they were not together very long. She returned to the dining room and explained that a summons from his family had called Mr. Claeg home."

"And?" Ham pressed, losing patience.

"And then Brook agreed to join the family in London." May shrugged nonchalantly. "I found Mr. Claeg's return and her agreement coincidental; that is all."

Ham leaned his head back against the chair and massaged the muscles at the back of his neck. Unhappy with this latest development, he privately agreed with his sister. He considered it his family duty to protect Lady A'Court from the artist's machinations.

The figure sitting on the barrel sketching was just the person he was looking for. Crossing the street, he approached the fifteen-year-old from the side. Mallory did not bother calling out, since he would likely be ignored.

Mallory had met Gill in Newcastle Street in front of Astley's Pavilion six months earlier. Dressed in old trousers and a shirt too large, the filthy youth had tried to sell him a sketch of one of the acts: eight horses performing a country-dance. Taking in the shoeless feet and weather-stained cap that probably covered hair crawling with vermin, he had almost walked away. It was not the slender filthy hand on his sleeve that had stopped him but rather the remarkable talent on the paper. Looking into the kid's coffee-colored eyes, Mallory recognized a kindred spirit. There was hunger, not only for food but also for art. Since their first encounter, he had tried to feed both needs.

It had taken the great connoisseur of women four days to figure out the talented lad was a girl.

Peeking over the slender shoulder, he glimpsed a fairly accurate rendering of the British Museum. He deepened his voice and said, "I'll give ye three shillings for it."

"Just three?" the young artist said, sounding annoyed at being disturbed. When she looked up, recognition swept away the annoyance from the coffee-colored eyes. "Claeg! You're back!" Hopping off the barrel, the girl hugged him excitedly.

"Good to see you, too, Gill. I thought I would have to search the museum to find you."

"Nah," she said, closing her book and gathering up her supplies. "Already been there today."

Gill had a peculiar obsession for Egyptian artifacts. She spent many hours perusing the dusty collections. According to her, the museum had been bequeathed in 1756 a valuable collection of Egyptian antiquities owned by the late Colonel Lethulier, which his nephew had later added to. The Harleian curiosities included two mummies, Mallory had been told. And soon, much to Gill's delight, the museum was opening to the public an exhibition of antiquities brought over by the expedition supervised by Sir Ralph Abercrombie. Mallory expected nothing could keep her away when the new building finally opened.

"Been back long?" she asked, falling into step with his casual stride. He had tried to improve upon her appearance once he had learned that she was a girl. Gill had refused. Skirts and frippery were not for her, she had said. Most eyes skimming over her in male togs thought she was a boy and she was left alone. Thinking of his sister, he had wondered more than once what dire circumstances had tossed this poor girl into the streets. Whenever Mallory had tried to get her to talk about her family, she just changed the subject.

"Just a few days." Noticing her crestfallen expression, he added, "Though this is my first day back on Bury Street. My father has been ill." After one night, he knew he could not remain in that house with his father begging him for death and his mother displaying stoic dignity. The distance was not so great that Mallory could not visit them whenever he was called.

"Sorry about your da. Is he better?"

He scrubbed his face with his hand. "Not really. The physician said that his recovery would take months, that is, if he recovers at all."

"Bad luck all around, Claeg. 'Course, who trusts those medical men? A body is worth more to 'em dead than alive."

"Little girl, you are too young to be so cynical."

She grinned at him. The flash of humor reminded him that beneath the grime lay hidden a fascinating face. "Age doesn't necessarily mean sharp, ol' man."

"And did I mention saucy?" he added, jogging up the steps and rapping on the front door of his town house. Gill had lightened the tightness in his chest that had developed after he saw his father. Mallory owed her, but getting her to accept his assistance was akin to pulling the tail of a three-legged donkey.

"Leastways once a day when you are about."

The door opened and his manservant appeared in the doorway.

"Messing, all is well, I trust?"

The servant bowed his head cordially in greeting. "Yes, sir." His gaze flickered over at Gill and hardened in disapproval. Snubbing the ragamuffin, he said, "Lord Ventris has called twice. Your *Seduction of Cressida* has captured his interest. Mrs. Howsen and Miss Nost have sent inquiries about your return. They each are hoping that you are accepting new commissions. Lady Buttrey has issued a standing invitation for you to view her latest addition to her art collection. And ah, Mrs. Le Maye stopped by. She was rather explicit in her, uh—" Recalling Gill's tender age, he falteringly adjusted the message by adding "needs."

Gill wiped her nose and snickered into her hand. There was no fooling the imp. She was too shrewd not to guess most of Mallory's callers were attracted to the artist rather than his art. Of the group, only Lord Ventris was strictly interested in a business transaction.

Mallory had painted a portrait of Miss Nost for her father. He had discerned during one of the sittings that both father and daughter were considering him as a possible husband for the young lady.

He had a very brief and forgettable liaison with Mrs. Howsen a few years earlier. The widow had hinted last month that she was willing to resume their friendship.

Lady Buttrey was another lady who had caught his attention, but he had not pursued her. Never shy, the lady had been aware of his attraction. The private collection she had invited him to view was likely in her bedchamber.

As for Carissa, well, he had cast her aside last year after she had tried to hurt Amara by flaunting her very old friendship with Brock Bedegrayne. Mallory had thoroughly enjoyed punishing the jealous witch, but her spitefulness had prompted him to end their relationship. He could not view her renewed interest in him as anything encouraging.

A year earlier, he had told himself that he had acted for his sister's sake. Now he understood that meeting Brook again had played a part in his decision to part ways with Carissa, although he doubted the countess would be flattered he had discarded his mistress for her.

"We can sort through the business issues later, Messing." Mallory noticed Gill was not following him into the house. "Coming, imp?" he asked, purposely keeping the offer blasé.

It still took some coaxing to get her to enter his house. Sometimes she reminded him of a wary animal mistrustful of its good fortune. Once he got her into his painting room, they could spend hours discussing art. He had discovered she had a keen wit and a hunger for art that rivaled his own. While he fed her mind, he always managed to feed her belly. Considering how scrawny she was, it might very well be the only meal she would eat that day.

"I should leave. You have work." Her movements were decidedly awkward, revealing her sudden discomfort. "I best be off to sell my sketch."

Ah, pride. For some, it was an insurmountable wall. "The

one of the museum is mine," he said decisively, watching her eyes round. "Three shillings was my offer."

Slyness crept into her dark brown eyes. "Four."

"My dear girl, four shillings is outright thievery. Three is highly generous, considering the problems you are having with perspective."

She was so outraged by the insult that she was not aware that she had followed him into the house. Messing wrinkled his nose as she passed but was prudent to keep his mouth shut.

"Problems with perspective? Are you daft? The building all but jumps off the paper." She opened her book, her furious motions demanding that he look at her work and recant his criticism.

He nodded to the woman who appeared behind them. "Why, Mrs. Lane, how pretty you look today," Mallory said to his housekeeper. He removed his hat and handed it to his manservant.

"Mr. Claeg, it is good to have you back with us again." She gave him an apprising look. "You have been starving yourself."

His naturally lean frame caused her no small amount of concern. She fussed over him like an overprotective hen. "If I starve, my raison d'être is motivated by the noblest endeavor."

"Art," Gill said, still stewing about his unflattering observation.

Mrs. Lane grunted. "Likely one of your mistresses is giving you fits. Give me a little time and I will bring something for you and the girl." She glared at Gill in her no-nonsense fashion. "I am leaving it to you to make certain Mr. Claeg eats every bite."

"Y-Yes, ma'am," Gill said, intimidated by the housekeeper. "Every bite."

Satisfied with the promise, the older woman turned to

leave. She winked at him, leaving no doubt that Gill had been expertly manipulated. He was not the only one who worried about the girl.

Sighing dramatically, Mallory said with resignation, "Well, Gill, that settles it. No one disobeys Mrs. Lane's dictates. Put your book on my worktable and we will discuss why your sketch merits less than the four shillings you are demanding."

"But—" The protest was for appearances, since Gill already had tossed her sketching book ungraciously onto the table and was slipping the leather strap of her pack over her head.

"No thanks are necessary, brat," he said, smiling at the similarities between Gill and the countess. Neither female desired his help, and yet their mulishness just made him more determined to meddle in their solitary lives. "The joy of art is derived in sharing it with others."

He laughed when she crossed her eyes in response. Inspiration struck him. Giving in to his spontaneous nature, he said, "I have never contemplated taking on an apprentice before, but your unrefined talent challenges me."

"Unrefined," she sniffed, and wiped her nose with her sleeve. "I've done well enough without you."

"Think of what you might achieve with my assistance, Gill, if you become my apprentice. I rather like the notion of being your master," he added maddeningly.

The young woman grimaced. "Having your man Messing plant his sneering lips on my arse is more likely than me ever calling you master, Claeg."

Chapter Fourteen

With trepidation, Brook watched her servant approach Viscount Tipton's town house. She had told no one about this particular errand. This was private. The last time she had been here, the surgeon had told her that she had lost her baby.

She looked away when the front door opened, regretting her decision to come to Devona first. Perhaps choosing to approach the youngest Bedegrayne first was cowardly, but so much had changed in Brook's absence. Even if she had been brave, she did not know where Wynne lived. Returning to the Tiptons' residence seemed somehow appropriate, that is, if the lady and lord of the house did not refuse her card.

"My lady," the footman said, startling her with his sudden presence. He opened the carriage door. "The family is receiving visitors this afternoon."

The news should have calmed her. Instead she was fighting the urge to order the coachman to take her home. Half-blind by fear, she allowed the servant to assist her out of the carriage. The Tiptons' butler stood stiffly by the open door, giving her no choice but to follow through with her purpose.

"Lady A'Court, the family bids you welcome and await you in the drawing room," the gruff servant said. "Might I say, my lady, that you look noticeably better since our last meeting." He smiled at her, flaunting disturbingly sharp little teeth.

"Ah, thank you, Mr. . . ." she began, floundering for the name of a man she could not recall.

"Just Speck," he said, escorting her to the drawing room. "You were too sickly for introductions." She let the understatement go unchallenged. He opened the door and entered before her. "Lady A'Court, my lord."

She was petrified. The strange-looking butler practically shoved her into the room. A sweeping glance revealed Viscount Tipton was alone. "My lord, I was told the family was receiving visitors."

The oddy-colored bluish eyes from her dreams lightened with amusement. "My servant lied."

How dreadfully awkward! Uncertain on how to respond, she said, "Forgive me, Lord Tipton. I shall not keep you."

"No, stay," the surgeon ordered before she could back out of the room. "I owe you the apology. Much to my dismay, no one seems to appreciate my humor except for my wife. Please, come in and sit."

"Did your servant lie, my lord?"

He guided her toward one of the chairs. "Only at my urging. The family is not receiving visitors this afternoon. Nevertheless, our house is always open to you, Lady A'Court."

His kindness was almost her undoing. Blinking furiously to combat the overwhelming urge to cry, she asked, "Is your wife at home?"

"Regrettably, she is out of the house. I know she will be upset when she learns that she has missed your visit. Will you be remaining in town for the season?"

"Your butler told me that the family was home. I assumed your wife was here."

"A tiny deception perpetuated at my order, I confess." He did not seem repentant for his actions. "I wanted to meet you again and was certain you would not enter the house if you had been alerted to Devona's absence."

Clutching her reticule tightly with both hands, Brook

tried to hide her alarm. There was good reason that polite society treaded cautiously when dealing with this gentleman. "Why?"

"The dire circumstances that brought you to me drove you away from London. It is not a great leap in intellect to assume you would have been content to avoid me."

It seemed rude to agree. "My lord, I may not have been as appreciative as I should have been during those early days; however, I now realize that I owe my life to you."

"To be indebted to *Le Cadavre Raffine* must be terribly burdensome for you."

Brook was taken aback. Not only by his casual use of a nickname she had only heard others whisper but also because he seemed to be teasing her. "Are you mocking me, sir?"

"Only a little," he assured her. He moved closer, disconcerting her further. He was a large man. His size alone was intimidating. She could not quite meet his gaze. "It must have taken a tremendous amount of courage to come here."

"I will admit, I was apprehensive of the family's reaction."

"Really, how so?" He stared down at her as if she were a puzzle he needed to solve.

"Well, it takes a generous soul to forgive the woman responsible for almost getting a beloved member of your family killed."

"You let her leave?"

Tipton winced at the vociferous exasperation directed at him. "My fiery temptress, what did you expect me to do? Have Speck lock her up in the larder?"

"No, of course not," Devona replied, showing no sign of calming down. His wife was a petite woman with bluish-green eyes and curly copper tresses no amount of hairpins seemed able to contain. At four and twenty, she was the youngest of the Bedegrayne siblings. She also had a temper that rivaled her father's. "You knew I was taking Lucian to see Papa. You should have sent someone to summon me home."

"My apologies, but I lack your talent for thinking up grand schemes. Besides, the lady was terrified. Speck had to coax her into the room."

"Good grief! You turned the gargoyle loose on her. Knowing him, he probably dragged her into the room."

Tipton viewed it as more of a nudge, but he wisely kept his mouth shut. Despite her fears, Lady A'Court had stood her ground even if it had taken some prodding on his part to understand why she thought he and the Bedegraynes would denounce her return.

"Pearl would have been a more suitable choice." Devona sagged against him, letting him hold her. "Well, nothing can be done about it. I presume you ordered Speck to follow her once she ran screaming from the house."

Tipton and the young widow had parted genially, both satisfied with their encounter. Out of concern, he had told Speck to follow her at a discreet distance just in case the lady had been less than forthright about her residence. "Give me some credit, Devona. I can exude charm when it is necessary." He nuzzled the top of her head with his chin. "I caught you, did I not?"

"You blackmailed me into marrying you," she said bluntly. She tilted her head back, confronting the full impact of his eerie light blue stare. "It was a devil's bargain I have never regretted."

Moved by her declaration, he gruffly said, "Good thing, since I hold on to what is mine, Wife."

Mallory recognized Brock Bedegrayne's equipage in front of the Keyworths' town house. He had encountered the couple on his numerable visits. While he applauded his sister's dedication to her family, it troubled him that his parents were so unworthy.

"G'morning, Buckle," he greeted the butler. "Are the

Bedegraynes in the library?" If he succeeded at nothing else this day, he intended to ease his sister's pain.

"No, sir. Mrs. Bedegrayne was feeling sickly this morning. I was able to persuade her into eating something for the baby's sake. You will find her and Mr. Bedegrayne in the morning room."

"You are a good man, Buckle," he said, patting him on the back. "Give me some time with my sister before you announce my arrival. There is no reason to upset Amara any more than we have to, do you not agree?"

"Very well, sir."

He found his sister and her husband just where the butler had told him they would be. Like children whispering secrets, they had their heads together. They parted at his entrance into the room.

"Buckle tells me you are unwell, puss," Mallory said, kissing the top of her head.

Amara brushed the crumbs of her toasted bread from her fingers. "A minor stomach complaint, nothing more."

"She was whiter than this table linen," Bedegrayne countered, holding Mallory's questioning stare. "Perhaps we should quit town. The air is not good for her."

His meaning was clear. The man worried that the strain of the Keyworths' refusal to acknowledge Amara was endangering her and the baby she carried in her womb.

"A fine idea, Bedegrayne. If you do not mind having a houseguest in a few weeks, I will join you at Whitmott Park once I have settled my business affairs."

"I am not leaving town," Amara said, glaring at them. "I am not the first lady in England who has found herself in the delicate condition. Do you both think I am so inept that I cannot bear a child, something every female since the dawn of time has done for her mate?"

"Frankly, Sis, *delicate* is not the word that pops into my head when you are screeching like a harpy."

Bedegrayne shot at him an annoyed scowl. "You need rest, dove. Sitting in this house does not count."

"Let it be, Brock," she warned, casting a look in Mallory's direction.

"Hell, Amara, it is no secret around town that your family despises us."

Mallory's sister pushed away her barely touched plate of food and burst into tears. He did not care if Bedegrayne was her husband; he could not stand by and watch him bully her. "That is enough, Bedegrayne."

"Not nearly, sir. While you flit in and out of your sister's life, I have been at her side watching her useless attempts to appease your parents for the astounding transgression of falling in love with the wrong man."

"Brock," she begged through her tears.

"What will you do, dove? Give me up? Give up our child?"

In her outrage, her tears dried up at the suggestion. "Never," she vehemently replied. "I love you." She fiercely hugged Bedegrayne.

Mallory could not quite swallow the lump swelling in his throat. Crouching down beside her chair, he said, "Amara, we Claegs are a selfish clan. I defied the family by running off with my mistress. Doran tried to turn himself into something he was not because he found himself lacking in our father's eyes. And you, you almost sacrificed yourself in marriage to men you could never love because some part of you felt you needed to make up for your brothers' failings."

Amara shook her head in denial. "No."

He smiled slightly. "Perhaps not. I have spent most of my life as the family outcast and it affords me a different view than yours. Bedegrayne also saw the truth. Love is something freely offered. It cannot be stolen or bartered away. Our father will never forgive you because he does not understand this concept."

"Are you telling me to forget about him, to stay away even when he is sick and needs me?" She hiccuped softly.

Mallory kissed her hand. "I am suggesting that you do not settle for less than you deserve. You were brave when you chose a life with Bedegrayne. If our family cannot reconcile themselves to your decision, then you must cast them out of your heart."

"I am not like you, Brother. I do not love carelessly or lightly."

She had inadvertently smitten a ruthless blow by simply speaking the truth. He absently rubbed his heart. "I have not been as fortunate as you, puss. Mayhap one day," he said wistfully.

Her husband touched her on the shoulder. "Your brother is right. If your father needs you at his side, he will have to push aside his pride and summon you. We are leaving now." Bedegrayne, not brooking any disobedience, helped her onto her feet.

"Will you be traveling north to Whitmott Park?" Mallory asked, calculating the distance between his sister and Cornwall.

"No," Bedegrayne said, disgruntled about the decision. "Short of kidnapping, there is no way of luring Amara out of town now that Lyon's prey has returned."

Mallory froze at the mention of A'Court's first name. He had not heard any rumors of Brook's return, although he admitted silently that he was not paying heed to the latest on-dit titillating polite society. It did not bode well for him if the countess had indeed returned to town and yet had failed to tell him of her presence. Recalling his parting words, he privately conceded that it would have been more astounding if she had contacted him.

Unaware of her brother's musings, Amara adopted an intractable expression. "Do not call her that horrid name! After all she has endured, she is undeserving of the *ton*'s mockery."

She appealed to her brother. "Do you recall Lord Lanston's daughter, Brook? She was probably too young and innocent for you to consider trifling with—"

"You have an extraordinarily low opinion of me," he lamented.

"Sadly, Lyon Meylan, Lord A'Court, had no such compunction in marrying a lady ten years younger than himself."

"A difference in age is not a sin, puss. How many years does Bedegrayne have over you? Seven?"

"Six," she admitted, irritated that Mallory had not readily agreed with her. "His age was less troublesome than other aspects. Lord A'Court was courting a lady whose disposition was so contrary to his. Brook's family was naturally ecstatic that she had captured an earl's attention. If anyone had any concerns about the gentleman, they were swept away when the banns were posted."

Mallory lifted his brow. At this stage he was not prepared to reveal his association with the countess. "You speak as if you know the lady intimately."

"I do, or rather I did. Oh, it is complicated. Suffice to say, Brook's unexpected appearance at Tipton's house has caused quite a stir within the family. Once word reaches polite society of her return, I predict she will suffer dearly for her odious husband's misdeeds."

Amara looked miserable. Mallory wondered if she was recalling how she had not been above using the countess's absence to her advantage by telling the family that she was visiting the widow when, in truth, she had been alone with Bedegrayne. His accidental encounter with Brook in Cornwall had revealed his sister's duplicity; otherwise she might have gotten away with it.

"I could never resist a notorious lady," he said, wryly acknowledging it was the key to many of his troubles. "If I offer my assistance in helping the countess, will you stop worrying and allow your husband to take you home?"

Her hopeful appreciation as she rushed up to hug him almost made him regret the casual lies he had spun for his little sister. "You are a good man, Mallory Claeg," she said fiercely.

Returning her hug, he closed his eyes and let her believe one more lie.

Chapter Fifteen

"This is how I imagined it, Cousin," Ham said, caught up in the excitement of the evening as they ascended the grand double staircase of the King's Theatre. Brook was grateful for the earl's arm, because the real performance was about to take place in one of the theater boxes rather than on the stage.

With her mother's assistance, Brook was fashionably attired. The pale green crape train dress she had chosen was worn over white satin. The long crape sleeves were also white and the bodice was in the French style, covering just above the swell of her breasts. Her long hair had been pulled up by a twisting rope of pearls and green tourmaline, with the loose ends a dangling array of curls. White kid gloves and shoes completed the flattering effect.

"I prefer Drury Lane," May complained, looking incomparable in pale blue. Her parents and her mother-in-law completed their small party.

Not even his sister's grumbling could sink the earl's jollity. "For opera ballet, this stage is preferred above all. Besides," he said, patting Brook's hand on his arm. "This evening we embark on the first of many such adventures. We will get to Drury Lane, May, just be patient."

Brook sensed Ham's sister was not satisfied with his response. She could feel the prickle of awareness as the other woman glowered at the back of her head. The suggestion to attend tonight's benefit had been hers and May knew it. Whether the woman resented Brook's influence over Ham or simply was unhappy with the choice of entertainment, she could only speculate. Regardless, she found the animosity between them tiring. One day in the near future, she and May Hamblin were going to have a private chat.

"Do we have a private box, my lord?" Brook's mother interjected, sounding as if she had spent her entire life sitting in private boxes and would settle for no less.

"Naturally," Elthia, Lady A'Court, snapped, outraged that her standing in society had been questioned. "Where else would the A'Courts sit? The pit?"

Mr. Ludlow, too familiar with their baiting discourse, said, "I believe Mrs. Ludlow was asking if the family had leased a box for the season."

Slightly mollified by the explanation, the dowager replied, "Our patronage of the arts has been somewhat limited this generation, sir. Vainglorious actresses were not my son's passion. A practical man, he had invested his resources in Newmarket. Lyon had a keen eye for prime horseflesh. It is a pity this useful skill was not applicable to the human animal."

It did not take any insight to guess who among them reminded the dowager of her son's failings. Usually impassive in her silence, Brook amazed herself saying, "Madam, the travesty is that your son treated everyone like animals." Women, in Lyon's opinion, were willful creatures that needed a man's unyielding dominance.

"How dare you speak thusly about your own husband?" the older woman demanded, shocked that anyone dared to speak ill of her son.

May muffled her indiscreet giggle. Ham quelled her with a patriarchal glare. Leaning down so his mouth almost touched Brook's ear, he whispered, "My dear cousin, whatever Lyon's faults, airing them in public benefits no one."

"I thought that was the entire point of this evening, my lord," she challenged, letting her voice rise in volume. Brook halted on the landing, forcing the people behind them from skirting their little group with undisguised interest. "You and the rest of the family are showing me off to the *ton,* proving once and for all that Lyon Meylan, the former Lord A'Court, was not the gentleman they all thought he was—a sadistic madman who broke his pretty bride!"

The elder countess shook with rage. "You, madam, are the one who is mad if you expect us to believe your lies. Silence her at once!" she demanded of the earl.

Before Brook could defend herself from her mother-in-law's outrageous accusation, Ham gripped her elbow firmly and steered her away from the dowager.

"Lady A'Court," Brook heard her mother say in an apologetic tone that only fueled her ire. "You must forgive my daughter's behavior. Returning to town, where she and your son spent their married life together, has been more upsetting than either one of us could have predicted."

Brook could not bear to hear another word. "Release me at once, my lord," she said through clenched teeth. "You are calling attention to us." She pulled her elbow from his harsh grip and rubbed the abused limb.

"No, my lady," the earl said, clearly aggravated. "I credit you for any attention we have garnered."

Brook's lips trembled. "She says the most awful things to me."

"The lady has been troubled since her son's death."

"I was Lyon's wife. My troubles started long before his death," Brook said flatly, her hostile stance daring him to deny her accusation.

Ham had never seen her so upset. His expression ran the gamut from anger to helpless confusion. It was obvious that he did not know how best to handle her volatile disposition.

"She has suffered a great loss and speaks out of pain. You

have always understood and been patient with her. Why are you acting in this manner?"

She waved away his excuses. "Why is she deserving of patience and understanding and I am not?"

"Good heavens, is that not A'Court's widow?" a woman whispered to her escort as they passed.

The question reminded Brook of her surroundings. Frustration had impelled her out of her silence. Wariness was beginning to slip into her cracking composure as she realized how public their altercation had become. Ham took advantage of her hesitation and seized her by the arm and moved them farther away from the curious crowd.

"This tantrum is beneath you." He nervously nodded to a passing couple who evidently were acquainted with him.

His withdraw of support was just another betrayal. "And your lecture is presumptuous. If being seen with me has somehow tarnished your sterling character, then might I suggest that you take me home." With Mr. Ludlow's assistance, she could be on her way to Loughwydde at dawn.

Comprehension had Ham lifting his brows. "And reward you for your atrocious manners? I think not. Was that your goal all along? Well, madam, your efforts have failed." He leaned, intimidating her with his proximity. He spoke slowly and distinctly, as if she were a child. "Might *I* suggest, Cousin, that you take a few minutes of privacy to compose yourself? When you feel more like yourself again, you may join us in the theater box." He gave her away from him as if he had found touching her offensive. "Do not even think of defying me by leaving this building."

Brook turned on her soft heel and walked away from him while he was delivering his threat. Boorish, sniveling hypocrite! She was too angry to think of crying over his dreadful conduct. Moving blindly down a narrow passage, she hoped to find a quiet place where she could calm down. As much as she regretted agreeing with the pompous earl, in her current mood she was likely to push both May and her mother-in-law out of the theater box.

Brook checked box after box, discovering all of them occupied. She returned to one of the lobbies. Crossing the room, she ignored the fruit woman offering to sell her the libretto and slipped into one of the salons. The chamber was not empty, she discovered. A gentleman and his lady stood near the stove. Disappointed, Brook attempted to back out before they noticed her.

Her movements caught the gentleman's attention. He glanced over at her and froze her with his unwavering stare. Murmuring something to his companion, Brook was about to apologize for her intrusion when the lady whirled and gaped.

"Brook!"

Recognizing her friend Amara Bedegrayne did not ease Brook's discomfort or her desire to leave the room. She backed into something solid while her tongue sought for a lucid comment. Checking behind her, she merely gaped at the cynical twist of Mallory Claeg's mouth.

"Running away, Countess?"

Mallory leaned against the wall with his arms crossed. His position effectively cut off any opportunity for the countess to escape. He did not know what had fouled her temper, but her distraction had allowed him to follow her through the various passages of the theater house undetected. Had the woman no sense? Wandering about dim passages only invited mischief. He had been contemplating instigating a little of his own when she stumbled upon Amara and Bedegrayne.

"I am so happy you have returned," his sister was saying; her high spirits were genuine. "You look wonderful. Do you not agree, Brock?"

"Aye, dove," Bedegrayne readily agreed, meeting Mallory's gaze with a silent question.

He might have fooled his sister, but his subtle possessive stance was recognizable to another possessive male. Mallory shrugged, not disputing the other man's conjecture.

"What about you, Brother?" Amara asked, searching for anything to alleviate the tension in the room.

Mallory leveled his gaze on the countess. "The clouds disperse in the brilliance of her beauty." As she had discarded the dull hues of her widow weeds, the comeliness she had often tried to conceal was wholly displayed. If they had been alone, he would have demonstrated how pleased he was by her transformation.

His sister's censorious scowl informed him that she believed he was insincere in his praise. Women were truly puzzling. Wondering if he had insulted his sister by excluding her, he added, "Puss, you are rather fetching, too."

It was the countess's turn to give him an unreadable glance. He was already regretting bringing them together if all they were going to do was glare at him.

Shaking her head in disgust, she said to Amara, "I heard that you married Mr. Bedegrayne." Brook pointedly did not reveal that Mallory was most likely her source. "And a babe arriving at the end of summer. It appears double congratulations are in order."

"I wish you could have been present for the wedding. I had tried to send word out to you. However, no one seemed to know your whereabouts."

Brook glanced away guiltily. It appeared Mallory's sister could not resist extracting a little revenge for what she perceived as a betrayal of friendship when the countess disappeared.

Since he was responsible for maneuvering her into this prickly situation, he felt determined to assist her whether she welcomed his intervention or not. "When faced with loss, we all deal with grief in our own way. It is not like you to judge so harshly, Amara."

"I am not," his sister denied, her lower lip jutting out at his scolding. "I just have so many questions—"

"And this is not the place to conduct an interrogation," Bedegrayne teased, coming to Mallory's aid. "Why do we not adjourn to our box before we miss the opera ballet you were so adamant to attend?"

"I must go, too," the countess said regretfully, and rose.

Amara jumped up with a grace that belied her growing abdomen. "Join us. I insist." Now that she had found her old friend she had no intention of allowing Brook to escape.

The countess gave Mallory an apprehensive look. "The party I arrived with is expecting me. I have already been gone too long."

"I will warrant your family would be tolerant to old friends laying claim to your attention."

She gave him a rueful smile. "You have not met the elder Lady A'Court. She has little acquaintance with tolerance. Since I have already managed to upset her, the rest of my family will expect me to make reparation before the evening has concluded."

"What have you done?" Mallory asked, not caring if the question seemed rude to Amara and Bedegrayne.

"Spoken too freely." The countess impulsively embraced Amara. "Might I call on you one day?"

His sister nodded. "I will be very vexed if you do not."

"Hmm, I seem to have that effect on everyone I encounter these days. It was a pleasure to see you again." Her neck was a graceful curve as she inclined her head and curtsied. "Gentlemen."

Before Mallory could unwind from his casual stance near the wall, Bedegrayne said, "Lady A'Court, my family would find my actions reprehensible if I permitted you to wander these dark passages unescorted."

"That is absurd, I am—"

"I will return the countess to the protective bosom of her

family," Mallory said crisply, causing Amara to stare at him flabbergasted.

Brook finally deigned to look at him. The temper he had viewed earlier in her expressive eyes was now directed at him. "No."

She offered no flowery apology, nor did she fumble her way through a pathetic lie. Like a mythic queen she judged him and found him lacking. By damn if he was letting her get away with it!

"Reconsider," he said, countering her refusal with a blatant warning. The lady was being unashamedly difficult, a vengeful tactic for his arrogance during their parting. She could sink her sharp claws into him at her leisure now that she was in town. Women's volatile nature was just another aspect he admired about them.

"Brook, please forgive my brother. His wit usually rivals his tact. Lamentably, both are absent this evening," Amara said, not prepared to forgive her brother even if her friend was willing.

The countess did not react to his sister's earnest apology. Still focused on Mallory, she tipped up her chin. "I would rather not."

Her response could have applied to either Claeg sibling. Amara glanced between them, clearly distressed and confused by the charged intimacy. As far as his sister knew, years had passed since he had last seen the countess. Only Bedegrayne was beginning to comprehend the complexity of the exchange.

"A clever lady," Mallory's handsome brother-in-law smoothly interjected. "Claeg is a womanizer. I would not trust my married sisters alone with him."

"Brock!" Amara objected, indignant that her husband was being so provoking to her brother. "You are not helping."

"I agree, Bedegrayne," Mallory retorted. "Do go away."

The countess appeared to be regretting the debacle her

tetchy outbursts had created. "Stay with your wife, Mr. Bedegrayne. I have intruded long enough. I will leave."

"Good. Let us depart," Mallory quipped, pleased she had
circled back to what he had longed for the minute he glimpsed
her in the theater's lobby. When he reached for her arm, she
backed up against Bedegrayne.

"Amara, I do have a helpful suggestion, that is, if you can
resist boxing Claeg's ears," her husband said, finding the escalating predicament vastly amusing.

Three pairs of eyes focused on him with various degrees
of irritation and curiosity.

He puffed up his chest, clearly delighted with his self-
importance. "We will all escort her back to her family."

Mallory's eyes narrowed into dangerous slits of rebellion.
"No."

Chapter Sixteen

"By damn, Bedegrayne, you let her get away!" Mallory spat, his mood a simmering cauldron of frustration and vitriol. "Give me one reason why I should not meet you at the nearest common and put a lead ball in you?"

The Bedegrayne in question was unmoved by the threat on his life.

"I will offer you one," Amara said, her hand resting on her abdomen. "Putting a lead ball into the father of my child would displease me."

"Why, thank you, dove," Bedegrayne said, taking up his wife's hand and kissing it. "Nice to know I would be missed."

"A lead ball can be dangerous," Viscount Tipton interjected, seriously contemplating the machination. He and his wife had missed the antics responsible for Mallory's foul mood, but the man was enjoying the aftermath. "Distance between the duelists, condition of the weapon, location of the impact, not to mention depth of the wound, could make the difference between whether a gentleman lived or died. Unless killing Bedegrayne was your intention all along," the surgeon conceded.

"I was just expressing my thoughts aloud," Mallory said, earning another glower from his sister. "Puss, your daughter will be born cross-eyed if you do not cease frowning at me."

Tipton and his viscountess had been awaiting their return

from escorting Lady A'Court to her companions. It had been an unsettling revelation to see just who was waiting for the widow. Lord A'Court greeted his cousin by marriage as if she were a slow-witted child who had wandered away from her elders. The realization that the countess was equally unhappy with the earl was a soothing balm on the raw edges of Mallory's temper.

"I will hear no more talk in regards to shooting my brother, Mr. Claeg," Lady Tipton cautioned.

"Heed her warning, Claeg. Our Devona is very protective of those she loves," Bedegrayne said, his fondness for his sibling evident.

Mallory had heard rumors connecting the youngest Bedegrayne girl and his brother. His mother had on several occasions accused the lady of seducing Doran. They were easily discounted when one observed how smitten she was with the gentleman most of the *ton* feared. Although slight in stature, she possessed her sire's spirit and her brother's inclination for adventure. Letting his gaze drift from her white dress up to her unusual copper tresses, he could well imagine what those curling flames might look like unbound. Contemplating the possible historical themes in which he might paint her, Mallory wondered if Tipton would grant his wife permission to visit his house.

Noticing his frank admiration, the viscount stirred and leaned forward. "You have enough trouble in your life to think of inviting more." He rested his arm across the back of his wife's chair and idly toyed with the appliqué flower on her sleeve.

Mallory flashed him a grin at the bold display of affection and possession. Flaunting polite society's rules was one thing he and Tipton had in common. "I was considering painting the lady, nothing more."

"If I had thought you were proposing more, Claeg, I

would not have bothered with threats," the man replied with lazy menace.

"I can attest to that," Bedegrayne muttered, his expression reflective of his own dealings with the surgeon.

Tipton's pewter eyes switched to his brother-in-law. "Your presence attests to my bountiful patience."

Bedegrayne replied with a rude gesture. Amara slapped his wrist with her fan, aware that their actions were most likely being observed by the occupants of the nearby boxes.

Mallory listened to the taunting repartee between the two gentlemen while his gaze sought out the countess. He had despised leaving her in A'Court's capable hands, knowing the man was viewing her as his future bride. Distance and the dimness of the theater prevented Mallory from distinctly viewing her expression, but he recognized the pale green dress she wore. She sat between Miss Hamblin and the earl. Brook's prominent position beside the new earl was a public declaration that whatever conflicts had existed between the Ludlows and the A'Courts had now ended. This alliance and the countess's animosity toward Mallory had him questioning the motives that had brought her to town. Any reason not involving him was likely to displease him.

"Claeg," Tipton said, noticing they had lost Mallory's attention. It was no strain on the surgeon's intellect to guess which lady had caught his eye. "Lady A'Court knew her appearance this evening would stir up the old speculation again. She will not thank you for linking her name to yours."

"No," Mallory agreed, sliding the surgeon a wry grin. "Nevertheless, she will just have to learn to accept it."

Brook never understood there were degrees to madness, and she felt like she was experiencing them all as she sat silently beside Ham and watched the opera ballet. A man on the stage gestured broadly to the audience and lamented about his misfortunes in song. Even with the libretto, she was barely following along with the tale.

Seeing Mallory here in London had flustered her more than she could have predicted. She had vowed not to seek him out. Brook had still not forgiven him for his boorish threats. Seeing her again, the arrogant man was probably congratulating himself for bullying her or, worse yet, seducing her to gain her compliance. Had he thought his masterful skills as a lover had enthralled her so that she was lost without his touch? Pish, how mortifying! She stirred uncomfortably in her seat, wishing she could think of a reasonable excuse to leave. Ham would never consent. Learning that she had spent her time apart from them in the company of Mallory Claeg had not improved Ham's disposition. Nor had he forgiven her for losing her temper with the elder countess.

The older woman had been pleased that Lord A'Court had readily come to her defense. Though she quickly learned that his support was finite when she refused to sit next to Brook. The dowager's snide suggestion that Brook sit behind them was promptly rejected. Ham had insisted that she was to sit beside him. It was part of his grand plan to introduce her back into polite society. If he had thought to silence the gossips, he was as misguided as her deceased husband.

She blinked as everyone around her applauded. The voluminous crimson drapery descended with the help of squeaking ropes and pulleys. Intermission. She had been so lost in her own musings that she had missed one of the acts. Staring down into the auditorium, she noticed the patrons below were moving about

"Would you care for a refreshment?" Ham asked the dowager.

Still sulking from her encounter with Brook, she remained seated while the others stood and discreetly stretched. Under the gloomy light given off by the wax candles, her eyes gleamed like glass beads. "You may send someone to fetch me some lemonade. I prefer to watch the activities from here."

"Very well, madam." His stern expression did not soften when he glanced at Brook. "Coming?"

She did not relish mingling with the other patrons in one of the salons. However, her mother-in-law's decision altered her own. "Yes, my lord. My limbs grow weary from sitting."

Excited, her mother approached them. "Did you notice who joined Mr. Claeg and the Bedegraynes in their box?"

"No, Mama." She had not sought out their box. While her parting with Brock and Amara Bedegrayne had been strained, it was nothing in comparison to the undercurrents she had felt when Mallory had said farewell to her. "I was enjoying the opera ballet," she lied.

"How provincial of you," May Hamblin commented; her eyes twinkled in appreciation of her accurate gibe.

"Oh, Daughter, no one but the cits heed what goes on down below. Everything worth talking about occurs in the boxes and salons. Mr. Claeg was sitting near *Le Cadavre Raffiné!*" Brook's mother confessed, breathless at the shocking news.

"Mrs. Ludlow, I highly doubt Viscount Tipton introduces himself by that ridiculous name," her husband interjected, exasperated that his wife was awed by the very subject they had hoped to extinguish for their daughter: gossip. The lines in his face deepened as he shook his head at the irony. "Nor, Wife, do I believe he would appreciate the notion of you discussing him in such a manner."

Mrs. Ludlow's hands fluttered nervously. "Pooh. I am not afraid of him."

Brook wondered if her mother would be impressed or scandalized to learn her daughter had recently gone to the surgeon's house and spent time with him alone in his drawing room. "Papa is correct. The gentleman you speak of is a respected surgeon and connected to the Bedegraynes by marriage. You gain no friends maligning him."

May opened her fan made of peacock feathers and gently

stirred the air around her face. "The man married into a re-spectable family, but his notorious past has been tasty scandal broth for years. How odd of you to fiercely defend a gentle-man I wager you scarcely know."

"May," Ham growled.

"Every word you speak only confirms your ignorance, Miss Hamblin," Brook said with mock sadness. "How fortu-nate most gentlemen prefer a comely face over intelligence. I predict you will secure a husband this season."

The earl stared at her as if truly seeing her for the first time. "Brook!"

"Ladies, please," Mrs. Ludlow said, astonished by her daughter's provoking behavior.

Not finished, May was eager to have her say. "Then again, maybe not so odd. After all, the *ton* calls you Lyon's prey. You and *Le Cadavre Raffine* both share the taint of notoriety."

"You have gone too far, Miss Hamblin!" Mr. Ludlow exclaimed.

Seated several chairs away but possessing excellent hear-ing, Elthia, Lady A'Court, cackled, earning frowns from the Ludlows.

Brook touched his arm to stop him from stepping in front of her. "No. May is entitled to her opinion. A view I assume is shared by many of those same people who impress Mama so much." Her mother glanced away in shame. Brook stepped closer to May, speaking so softly the woman had to lean closer to hear her. "I once lived the paragon existence you highly prize. Beware, Cousin, that lofty perch is precarious."

"There she is," Bedegrayne observed, calling attention to the widow's entrance. The once-empty room was now overflow-ing with people. "She is not alone."

Mallory discreetly watched the countess enter with her entourage. They were a solemn group. Lord A'Court stood at her side as he surveyed the room. His disdain was not feigned.

Brook appeared equally unenthused. Her pallor concerned
Mallory. She kept her lips tightly compressed, and the strain
of what troubled her was evident on her face. Mr. and Mrs.
Ludlow flanked their daughter. The solicitor was stiffly reserved, while his wife valiantly fought the urge to cry. Only
Miss Hamblin, who clutched her brother's other arm, seemed
immune to the friction.

"Who is the young lady?" Tipton asked.

"Miss Hamblin. She is Lord A'Court's sister." The young
woman noticed Mallory's scrutiny and brazenly smiled in
invitation. He did not return her smile. *Ah, foolish little girl,*
he mused when she waved. Did she not realize that reputa-
tions had been ruined for less provocation?

"This one wants you," the viscount said.

Bedegrayne coughed. "I do not comprehend how he does
it, Tipton, but they *all* seem to want him." He was clearly
mystified by their interest.

"A tad obvious, do you not think?" Lady Tipton said to
Amara. Their agreement was conveyed by expressions of
mutual distaste. Miss Hamblin's attempts to gain his notice
were viewed as pitiable, if not vulgar. "Lord A'Court will
be issuing challenges weekly if his sister does not learn
some discretion."

The countess had yet to glance Mallory's way. He was
beginning to suspect her avoidance was deliberate. The notion that she might consider him beneath her to associate
with in public left a sour taste on his tongue.

Tipton, who had been watching him closely, asked, "Why
is it, I wonder, that we always want the unattainable?"

Hearing her husband's question, the viscountess said,
"Oh, it is not complicated to figure out. There is no value in
something so easily won."

Mallory privately agreed. He switched his gaze back to
the countess. Her mother was introducing her to a matron and
her male companion. Brook's curtsey lacked the grace of

ease, and her nerves showed in her eyes as her gaze moved from one face to the other. Although Mallory had touched her body, had given her pleasure, he did not delude himself into believing he had won her.

"I cannot fathom how you convinced the countess into this meeting," he murmured to the surgeon. "Anyone watching her for any length of time can tell that she is terrified."

"In capable hands, fear can be a rather useful tool," Tipton countered.

The countess smiled at something the gentleman was saying. The sadness Mallory glimpsed in its soft curves broke his heart. He doubted there was anyone present in the room who was more acquainted with fear than Lady A'Court.

Chapter Seventeen

Brook surveyed the room, seeing the gauntlet of people as a kind of test. Jousting insults with May Hamblin, nay, even the dowager, was preferable to talking to anyone brave or curious enough to approach her and her family. Nevertheless, she had not come for them. If she did anything correctly this miserable night, it would be this.

"Are you able to go through with this?" her stepfather asked, noting the strain in her expression.

"Of course, Papa," she said lightly. "No one promised this evening would be pleasant."

Unconvinced by her words, Mr. Ludlow said, "Let me summon the coachman. We have accomplished what we planned."

Overhearing their exchange, Ham interjected, "You are a devoted father, Mr. Ludlow. However, your concern is misplaced." He silenced any argument the other man might have had with a stern look. "Since Lady A'Court is enjoying the opera ballet, it would be callous of us to deny her the simple amusement. Do you not agree, Cousin?"

She pretended not to feel the pressure of his fingers on her arm. "Yes, my lord. *Callous* is one of the words that comes to mind," she conceded, breathing a sigh of relief when he released his grip. Their presence was already drawing attention. "Along with one or two other words."

Before he could demand what she had meant by her comment, a woman moved in front of them. Somewhere in her mid-forties and still retaining the figure of her youth, she had a face that contained a beauty the tiny lines near her eyes and mouth could not diminish. "When someone told me that you were here, why, I accused them of lying," she said, her violet eyes softening in affection. "I told them that if Lady A'Court was in town, she would have most assuredly paid me a visit."

"Forgive us, Lady Haslake," her mother said, giving Brook the name she was struggling for. "We have only just arrived and have yet to make our presence known."

"My absence has deprived me of London's fashions," Brook added, and the other woman made a sympathetic sound. "We have been patronizing Madam Courroux since our return. So far I have been pleased with the results." Chatting about the mundane seemed tasking. Her body was so tense she felt her bones grind with each movement.

Ham's visage glowed in approval. She had the astonishing urge to stick her tongue out at him.

"Madam Courroux is an excellent choice for a young lady. Her creations are inventive without being absurd. I do, however, recommend Monsieur Lozier for your bonnets. He does such wonderful things with feathers."

"Speaking of me again, hmm? I thought the feathers were our little secret," Mallory said, intruding on their conversation. Brook had been aware of his presence in the room but had not seen him approach.

The outrageousness of his comment startled a burst of laughter from Lady Haslake. She was extremely devoted to her earl and everyone knew it. She whacked Mallory playfully on his coat sleeve. "Mr. Claeg, that clever tongue of yours will get you in trouble one day, sir!"

Mallory took the older woman's hand and kissed it. Holding Brook's gaze, he said, "I can only hope." It earned him another giggle, as he had intended. Realizing he had been staring too long at Brook, he let his gaze slide away while he issued greetings to her companions. Ham stiffly nodded and mumbled a greeting. The earl then intentionally walked away to speak with a gentleman he knew. It was not a direct cut in the truest sense, but it was rude.

"How are your lovely daughters?"

Brook frowned, wondering if anyone's daughter was safe from the scoundrel. It seemed he was acquainted with every unmarried female in London.

Warming to one of her favorite subjects, Lady Haslake brightened. "How kind of you to remember. My eldest—" She stopped and tilted her head to the side. "Oh, good, here she is now. Laurette, Mr Claeg was asking about you."

That was not precisely true, Brook protested silently, but no one corrected the misassumption. She did not bother concealing her disappointment. No one was paying attention to her. All eyes were focused on Lady Laurette Omant. The twenty-three-year-old woman politely greeted everyone. She was a youthful replica of her mother. With glossy black tresses and violet eyes and claiming a dowry that had most of the fortune hunters salivating, Rett, as her family and friends affectionately called her, had gentlemen dropping at her feet like overripe fruit.

"Mr. Claeg, I am honored you recalled my name," she said, her lashes lowered flirtatiously. "The last time we met, you were surrounded by a legion of young ladies all desiring the chance to be immortalized by your, uh, skillful hands."

Brook had managed not to show any reaction to the image the woman's words conjured. Mallory did not appear embarrassed by or apologetic for the reminder, but his assessing gaze briefly locked onto Brook's before returning to the earl's daughter.

"If I recall correctly, my lady, it was your mischievous announcement during the ball that I was searching for a noble lady to be my Aphrodite that created the farce. I had to talk my way out of two dawn appointments because the furious gentlemen in question thought I was pursuing their wives."

"Good grief, Rett, my dear, you did not," her mother said, unaware of her daughter's role in that old gossip.

"Well, I—" She dismissed her wicked actions by arching her left brow in a charming manner that made Brook feel a tug of envy for the unapologetic ease she possessed.

"Mr. Claeg, I trust my daughter's part did not overly inconvenience you?" Lady Haslake glared at her eldest child, promising with a look that they would be discussing the matter at great length later in private.

The gleam in Mallory's light blue gaze hinted that he was not above stirring his own mischief. "You will be pleased to know that I was not confined to bed because I stared into the barrel of a duelist's pistol."

Taking the imagined outcome to heart, Lady Haslake clasped her hand over her mouth in horror. "Merciful Lord!"

Lusty libertine, Brook sneered. He likely bedded several of those would-be Aphrodites. The mask of indifference she thought firmly in place must have yielded in her ire. The sly humor she had glimpsed in Mallory's eyes erupted into shameless delight. He *knew* she was jealous.

"Never fear, my lady. I am unharmed." Something over Lady Haslake's shoulder distracted him. Frowning, he tried to recall what he had been saying. "I . . ." His concentration was lost again. "With your permission, excuse me." Mallory nodded curtly and disappeared in the crowd.

"That was odd," Lady Haslake mused.

Her daughter was not concerned. "Mr. Claeg is an eccentric, Mama. He once chased down a lady because the blue hue of her dress intrigued him. Do not take offense."

"Oh, I do not. Though do not tell the handsome rascal," she said, including everyone in her collusion. "Our annual ball is approaching and this might be the only leverage I have in gaining his assent to attend our grand function."

"If guilt fails, Mother," her daughter said, her violet eyes, which reminded Brook of a spring meadow, brimming with humor, "perhaps I can dream up another scheme by which to persuade him."

Brook tried to see who had lured Mallory away, but they had both disappeared. It was difficult not to feel resentful, even if she was not talking to the man!

"I daresay the gentleman has endured enough of your mischief!" the older woman dotingly chided her eldest child. "Oh, Lady A'Court, you and your family must attend our ball. I will be upset with all of you if you send regrets."

Relieved that someone of distinction was opening their home to her daughter, Mrs. Ludlow hastily replied, "Let me allay your fears, Lady Haslake, by stating that nothing will keep us from your door on the night of your revered ball. Do you not agree, Brook?" She looked expectantly at her daughter for support.

"Brook?" a soft feminine voice called out to her. She turned, not trusting her hearing. A blond woman stood apart from the others. Seeing her again touched not only memories but also Brook's heart.

"Brook," the woman said, her body tensing as if holding back her affectionate nature. "Dear friend, it is good to see you again."

She closed her eyes in relief. Brook had not been certain she would come even though Viscount Tipton had assured her that her qualms were groundless. "Wynne."

He had to be mistaken. Mallory pushed a path through the crowd blocking the way to his quarry. The women must have thought him incredibly rude abandoning them in that manner. The flash of pain in Brook's eyes as he brushed past her revealed she thought he had grown bored and had found a new muse. He was really going to have to improve on her impression of him. Later. Right now, he needed to prove to himself that he had not glimpsed part of his past.

Mallory stepped out into the passage. Oil lamps provided ample light. He was not alone. People were standing and chatting in small groups. Others were leaving the salon to return to their boxes before the next act of the opera ballet began.

"Claeg, where are you going?"

His departure had not gone unnoticed. Bedegrayne might be related to him now; however, it did not make him privy to all Mallory's secrets. Besides, telling his brother-in-law anything was in effect confessing it to his sister. This part of his life was something Amara did not need to know.

"I saw—I thought I recognized someone I used to know," he said, keeping it as close to the truth as possible. Whoever he had seen was gone. He seized the queue at the base of his neck and tugged it in frustration.

"Now is not the time to be reacquainted with old loves," Bedegrayne said, maddened by what he perceived as lack of control. "You were the one who insisted on joining us. Do not disappoint your sister. Your father's illness and the pregnancy have made her delicate. If you do anything to upset her further, Claeg, I vow you will regret it."

"Alone?" he asked, finally seeing the humorous side of things. "I think not. Now if you added Milroy and Tipton to the threat I might worry." Something in Bedegrayne's expression alerted him. Milroy. So he and his lady had finally arrived. Mallory thought of the countess. *Damn.*

In the distance, perhaps on the stairs beyond their view, they heard a woman's throaty laughter. The sound made the hairs on his arms and neck prickle in reaction. The back view of a tall, familiar woman. A glimpse of red hair. Laughter that haunted his darkest nightmares. They were pieces of a spellbinding riddle he could not let go, even for the countess. "I will not be gone for long."

"Claeg!" Bedegrayne shouted behind him, announcing his presence to everyone.

Damn.

Wynne Milroy risked rejection by embracing Brook. They both closed their eyes, blocking out their audience. Their public meeting was intentional, but not everything was for them. Her friend pulled back. When they had been in Miss Rann's School for the Lady's Arts together many of the girls had mistaken them for sisters. It had not been just their looks that had the girls drawing that false conclusion but also their camaraderie. "When Tipton and Devona told me that you were here . . ." Still clutching Brook's hands, Wynne's eyes filled with tears.

Brook struggled with her own composure. Her friend looked the same. They shared a similar pale hue of blond, which Brook had always blamed for their superficial resemblance. While her eyes were blue, the other woman's eyes were a cool green, much like her brother's and yet similar in shape to her younger sister's. The women were once similar in build, but giving birth to twins had softened Wynne's slender frame by adding more to her bosom, whereas grief and her self-imposed exile had sharpened Brook's face. Two years and so much pain stood between them. Her lips trembled. "I . . ." She tried to smile but failed. "There is so much I have to say."

"I, as well." Wynne's gaze sought out and held her husband's. The connection was instantaneous and strengthened her. "Now that you have returned we have plenty of time."

Those simple, generous words offered so much more than Brook dared to hope. The dread she had been feeling about their encounter melted. She swayed, dizzy from the lightness. "Yes, there is time," she agreed, for the first time believing it.

The race through the passageway and down the stairs had been for naught. Angry at himself for choosing to chase ghosts instead of offering his support to the countess, Mallory had returned to the salon only to discover that most of the occupants had returned to their theater boxes. Hot and sweating from his run, he wished he could have removed his coat and loosened his cravat. Still panting softly, he ducked under the low drapery into Tipton's box. There were only four people in the box.

Amara glanced back, met Mallory's tardiness with a hostile glare, and then returned her attention back to the stage. Lady Tipton was not so polite. Muttering an oath, she started to rise until her husband lazily stopped her. He whispered something into her ear, and whatever he said was enough to quiet her. Bedegrayne, the bastard, had the indecency to grin at Mallory's predicament. He gritted his teeth. He did not care about the others, but he despised disappointing Amara. There had been too much of that in the past. His sister was as temperamental as a hissing kitten when goaded. There was no point in begging her forgiveness. She was a typical woman when it came to vengeance. Unless he was prepared to grovel and endure a little clawing, she would not relent in her silence. A pity he was not in the mood to accommodate her bloodletting.

Then he thought of the countess's hurt expression.

Bloody hell.

He collapsed into the chair positioned behind his sister and leaned forward, forcing her to listen to him. Bedegrayne snickered at his pathetic predicament.

"Are you planning to make me crawl, puss?"

Amara turned to reply and then recalled that she was not speaking to him. Clamping her mouth shut, she mutely stared unseeingly straight ahead.

"Of course you are," he grumbled, desperate to get her to tell him what had happened. The box where the Ludlows and the A'Courts had been seated was empty. "I thought better of you, Amara. Using such an obvious female ploy as silence to punish me for my imaginary infractions."

She attacked him as he had hoped. "Imaginary? You promised—ugh!" she exclaimed, disgusted that she had fallen for his ruse.

"I know I promised," Mallory said, playing with one of the curls near her ear. "I will not bore you with excuses. I tend to brazenly lie when I am coerced into confessions." She swallowed and he watched the fluid movement of her throat. "Suffice to say, I regret disappointing you."

She remained silent.

Heartless wench! By damn, her tactic was working. He felt like the vilest cretin. Furious, he pushed himself onto his feet. "You know, puss, you remind me of someone when you act like this. Oh yes, now I recall. Our mother." He turned on his heel and stalked out of the box.

She waited until he was gone before she winced. "That was low."

"How long will it take for you to forgive your brother?" her husband asked.

"For his last comment alone?" She crossed her hands over her swollen belly. "Never."

Chapter Eighteen

"I feel guilty," Brook confessed. "Like we ran the man out of his own house."

As Tipton had orchestrated it, they had both played out their parts for the public. He had explained that because the families had not spoken of the circumstances surrounding Lyon Meylan, Lord A'Court's death to anyone, most of what the *ton* knew was speculation. Seeing the two women together should quell any rumors that there was discord between them. Several hours later Brook was sitting in the very house in which her husband had died.

"No. I think for Keanan, our visit was just the excuse he needed to prompt him to check on his brother. Besides, he understood we needed to speak privately."

It was something her family had not. Ham had been embarrassingly vocal in his discontentment about her leaving with Mr. and Mrs. Milroy. With the exception of her stepfather, she had not been pleased with any of them. Disregarding Lord A'Court's order had been her pleasure.

They had taken solace in Wynne's private sitting room upstairs. She explained that she preferred to be close to her twin daughters, Aideen and Anna. The girls had been named in memory of the couple's mothers. Pretty miniatures of their mother, they had celebrated their first birthday last February. Brook had peeked into the nursery to view the sleeping girls.

She had not been prepared for the wrenching envy she felt in her heart as she had gazed down at them, and it shamed her. Wynne had already been carrying her children in her womb when Lyon had kidnapped her. If he had known, there was no telling what he might have done.

"Does Mr. Milroy blame me?"

Wynne made a small protesting sound. "Why would he? Brook, no one in my family blames you for what happened."

They had curled up on the sofa and sat facing each other. The intimacy of their positions was not taken for granted by Brook, who had lived too long without the companionship of a genuine friend. "That is highly generous, considering it was my husband who snatched you from a ball and set a trap in this very house to murder your Mr. Milroy," she said, relieved she was talking to someone with whom she did not have to pick her words carefully.

"Did you know he was coming for me?"

The suggestion that she had betrayed Wynne in such a cruel manner stunned her speechless. "No. He talked. Wild talk, but he was married to me. He could not carry out any of his plans unless . . ."

Wynne finished the thought she could not bear to speak aloud. "Unless you died. Oh, Brook, was that his intention when he beat you so severely? I saw the blood," she said; her expression took on a haunted quality. "If it had not been for Tipton's skills, you would have died from the blood loss. Later, we feared the grief and the fever would kill you."

"I should never have come that day," Brook murmured, trying to fit what she had been told with the fragments of her memory.

"Would you have rather perished with your babe?" her friend demanded, surprising her with her vehemence.

"Yes." She took back the words with a small shake of her head. "When I woke up and realized my babe had died inside of me, I prayed that the fever would claim me."

Without saying a word, Wynne reached out and clasped Brook's hand in a gesture of comfort.

"I had failed my son, you see." She glanced down at their joined hands. "I fell in love with a man who saw you when he touched me."

Grief swam in the liquid pool of Wynne's green eyes. "I am so sorry, Brook."

She pulled out the handkerchief she had absently stuffed into the cuff of her sleeve and gently wiped away all traces of her friend's tears. Lyon had once convinced Brook that crying was a sign of weakness. Even after his death, she had not indulged in tears, convinced by his mother that keeping the tears within was proving to them all how strong she had become. Watching Wynne cry reminded her that tears also showed compassion. It was a sign that adversity had not destroyed the gentler passions within. If Mallory had not come along and seduced her out of her complacency, she might have continued to cling to her counterfeit strength and let it eat her from the inside out until nothing remained but a brittle, bitter husk.

"I resented you for a while," Brook admitted, needing to get it all out. "You had so many admirers that you had not even noticed Lyon."

"I was aware of you. I sensed you were developing an attachment for Lord A'Court. In respect to our friendship, I thought I had nipped any affection he had developed in regard to me."

While she had simmered in her jealousy Wynne had never wavered in devotion. "Your indifference fed his fervor. He thought to prove himself worthy of your esteem. When you rejected him, he set out to win you through your father—"

"My father laughed at his offer." Wynne sickened at the notion of her beloved father ridiculing a gentleman who was teetering toward the edge of desperation.

"So he courted me. If he could not have you, he would claim someone who reminded him of you."

"Someone I loved as a sister."

It had been the perfect revenge for a sadistic monster.

Wynne used the toe point of one shoe to toy with the tassel decorating the top of her other. "I understood why you stayed away for so long. We spent much of that first year at Holinshead, our estate in the north. Keanan claimed the estate needed work and the country air was good for me while my waist expanded to amazing proportions. Regardless, I knew the truth. He was shielding me from all of the unpleasant talk."

"It must have been difficult," Brook said, thinking they had both stayed away for the same reason, although she had no one to protect her.

"Harder still when you did not write. Your silence confirmed my darkest fears. I thought you hated me for killing your husband."

"You did not kill Lyon, Wynne." The conviction sounded weak even to Brook's ears.

"Did I deliberately plot his demise as he had Keanan's? No. Honestly, Brook, now that I have brought up the subject I am not so sure I can discuss what happened, even with you."

How could Brook tell her friend that the details of her husband's death had not haunted her, that he had murdered her love months before he had delivered the beating that had killed their child? "I was not seeking an explanation, Wynne. You owe me nothing."

"Your husband knew he was dying, Brook. We had fallen together through a broken section of the railing on the upper story. I landed on some scaffolding, but he had tumbled over. The only thing preventing him from falling was his hold on my dress."

Brook's mouth went dry. "No one said anything."

"No one but family knows what really happened." She rubbed her eyes and sighed. "Your husband knew he was dying. The fall was too great. He had no chance of surviving. So he tried to take me with him."

Brook closed her eyes, but the image of Wynne fighting for her life while dangling several stories in the air did not fade. She was well acquainted with Lyon's ruthlessness and strength.

"I managed to grab something. A brick? A piece of wood? I cannot recall anymore," Wynne said wearily. "All my energies were focused on one goal. To break his lethal hold." Her eyes snapped open and held Brook's. "Now do you understand why I feel responsible? I killed him."

Brook had been so consumed with her own guilt that she had not considered how Lyon's death had affected her friend. "Did you expect me to be angry with you for surviving such a horror? I am not. I am glad he is dead. My only regret is that he had not perished by my hand. Does that make me a monster, Wynne?"

"No. It means you survived the horror, too."

They settled into silence, each thinking of what the other had said. Brook was the first to speak. "There is one matter we have not addressed. We both know Lyon was a dead man the minute he kidnapped you. Either your Mr. Milroy or your family would have seen to it."

Her friend had no rebuttal because it was the truth. Lyon Meylan, Lord A'Court's crimes were too numerous. He would not have escaped with his life.

A mournful wail had Brook jumping up. Wynne grabbed her side and fell against the cushion laughing. "It is one of the girls. I wager it is Aideen."

Feeling foolish, Brook said faintly, "Does she always wake up thusly?" In the life she had dreamed up about her son, she had not imagined him producing a raging cry fierce enough to awaken half of London.

"Often. We blame Papa for her ornery temper." Wynne stood and hooked her arm around Brook. A quavering cry blended with the hysterical wailing. "Ah, that is my Anna. Come along and truly meet my daughters."

The nursery maid was changing the soiled diaper of one of the girls. The other stood in her crib, her tiny face red with misery. Her crying intensified when she saw her mother.

"I tried to get them changed before we disturbed you, madam," the woman said apologetically.

"No need to apologize, Mary." Wynne touched her tender bosom swelling with the breast milk the girls' cries stimulated. "They slept longer than I had expected." She scooped up the toddler reaching for her in the crib. "Poor Aideen. Have you waited long for your mama?" she cooed. Brook was fascinated when the child, all business, grasped the edge of Wynne's bodice and nuzzled her breast, questing for a ripe nipple.

"Shall I mix up some barley gruel for the wee ones?"

Finished with Anna, Wynne pulled down her nightdress and picked the fussing child up. Anna popped a finger into her mouth and rested her cheek on the nursery maid's shoulder.

"A small amount. I will feed them just enough to ease my discomfort." Moving to a nearby chair, Brook's friend glanced up from her daughter's face. "We are in the process of weaning them. None of us seem to want to give up the night feeding. You are welcome to remain if you like. This has become such a big part of my life I sometimes forget that not everyone is thrilled to share every aspect of our routine."

The nursery maid smiled ruefully. "Here now, you have the look of someone who has held a babe a time or two." She reached for the blanket, missing the spasm of pain crossing Brook's face. "I will leave Miss Anna in your care, my lady, and see to the gruel."

Hungry to witness the life she had lost, Brook said, "Is it all right if I hold her, Wynne?"

"Do not be afraid. They are quite sturdy despite their size."

The servant with practiced efficiency placed Anna Milroy into Brook's inexperienced arms and positioned her hands until she was satisfied.

With the help of her daughter, Wynne had worked one breast out of her low-cut dress. Aideen quickly latched her mouth over her mother's nipple and suckled. The fury that had summoned her mother had subsided. Holding on to the edge of the bodice with one hand, the toddler played with her mother's hair with the other.

"She grunts and devours like a little greedy piglet." Cringing at her rudeness, Brook had not intended to speak the observation aloud.

"Yes, she does sound like a greedy little piglet," Wynne concurred, repeating Brook's observation in a singsong manner to her daughter. Reacting to her mother's voice, the child emitted a husky giggle without releasing the nipple and then continued suckling.

Brook pulled away from the poignant intimacy of mother and daughter. She held Anna closer, but the little girl did not seem bothered. Perhaps her demanding sister had already taught her the virtues of patience. Chomping on her finger, she studied Brook with solemn eyes. Uncertain how one addressed a child, she shifted the baby's weight so that it rested on her hip. Brook touched the fine blond hair that curled slightly at Anna's nape. "You have your mama's hair," she said softly, not understanding the tears burning in her eyes. "And your papa's eyes, I think." Lyon had deprived her of more than a loving husband. He had cheated her of the babies she had dreamed of having with him.

"Gah," Anna said, popping her finger wet with slobber into Brook's mouth.

Laughing through her tears, Brook turned her face away in an attempt to dislodge the girl's slimy finger. She supposed the girl had sensed her sadness and decided to share her comforting finger.

"Ack!" The second Brook removed the little finger from her mouth, the mischievous imp popped it back in and gave her a wide grin, revealing her four tiny teeth.

"What?" Wynne glanced up and recognized the game her daughter had discovered with her friend. "Anna Milroy!" The scolding lacked the impact of anger because Wynne was too busy pressing her face into Aideen's shoulder and laughing.

Since Brook was holding the child, it was impossible to avoid her inquisitive finger. "I am so glad you find this amusing, Mrs. Milroy."

"Gah-gah!"

The wiggling child managed to outmaneuver Brook once again. With a mouthful of fingers, she mumbled, "Doeth she tire ovth gum?"

The silliness of the garbled question was too much for Wynne. Laughing uncontrollably, she freed her breast from Aideen and flipped the baby onto her shoulder. She tucked her breast back into her bodice. Gasping for breath, she said, "I am so happy we are friends again."

Brook pulled back. She managed to utter, "As I am," before Anna thwarted her efforts to evade her and continued her game.

The hours Brook had spent with Wynne and her daughters had been healing. Her friend had been correct. They had both survived Lyon's cruelty. The fear Brook had carried around her had lessened, with her knowing that Wynne did not blame her. She was less certain of Mr. Keanan Milroy. There was nothing she could fault in his speech or manners toward her. It was only a feeling. When he had joined them later after visiting his half brother, Drake Fawks, the Duke of Reckester, she had caught his indigo gaze measuring her. Brook had found his size and judging silence intimidating. The lateness of the hour had given her a valid excuse to leave. Wynne had tried to talk her into staying the night; however, all her invitations were refused. Mr. Milroy ordered a coach and bundled Brook into it. She left the Milroys' town house with the promise that she would return. Oddly, in spite of Mr. Milroy's lukewarm enthusiasm toward her renewing her acquaintance with his wife, Brook did want to see her friend again.

Bidding the coachman farewell, Brook watched the coach continue down the street. She had forgotten how London sounded at night. The scent of food and sound of faint music drifted on the evening air; the clopping of hooves on cobblestone and the rumble of coaches as they raced down the narrow streets blended with laughter from a nearby tavern and the cheerful greeting of a drunken gentleman. Unlike rural Loughwydde, the town never seemed to sleep.

The notion of sleep suddenly appealed to her. Turning her back on the street, Brook strolled up the short path that led to the stairs. A noise to the left startled her out of her fanciful musings about London. Peering at the bush where she had heard the scuffling sound, she squeaked in terror and stumbled backward when a scrawny dog darted past her and into the street. The encounter left her heart pounding in her chest. Feeling silly, she straightened and checked the windows of the house for some sense of who was still awake. If she was fortunate, her family had grown weary of waiting for her return and retired.

As she took a step forward, the firm hand clamped over her mouth deprived her of breath and of movement. She clawed at the immovable fingers, but her kid gloves rendered her nails useless. She moaned as her captor dragged her away from the house. Her lungs demanded more air as she struggled. The tight corset she was wearing combined with fear were denying her the precious resource. As her vision grayed, she felt herself being lifted. The sensation reminded her of flying. Too light-headed to resist, Brook floated into the mist.

Chapter Nineteen

Brook felt something wet on her face. She turned her head away wondering how she was going to convince one-year-old Anna Milroy that her soggy fingers were no longer amusing. The stinging slap on her cheek had her eyes opening.

"Bastard!"

"The last time I woke you up, you were more pleasant," Mallory said in lieu of a greeting.

"The last time I was not recovering from being smothered." Coatless, he still wore the evening clothes he had donned for the theater. Sitting up, she realized her head had been resting on the crumpled remains of his dress coat.

"Quit exaggerating." He sat next to her, his hands resting on his knees. "You just became faint with all of the excitement."

For a kidnapper, he was not very resourceful. Now that her eyes had adjusted to the gloom, she recognized her whereabouts. When she had fainted on him, he had carried her to the back of the house and into the gardens. At the back of the property the owner had built a small greenhouse. In the center of it a fountain had been installed to provide water to the tender plants and create a tranquil environment. The greenhouse was a pleasant retreat from the frenzied activity of the household.

"What were you doing grabbing me like . . . like you were planning to murder me?" she demanded, her spirit reviving now that she knew she was safe.

"If I had known having a private discussion with you in London would be so difficult, I would never have asked you to join me."

"Asked?" Her voice had raised an octave. "There was no asking. There was only demanding and insults, you lout." She punched him in the heart.

"Ow, what was that for?" He rubbed his injury.

"Do you want me to make a list? Oh, why do you care? On second thought—" She punched him again. "—that is for *not* caring."

He eyed her warily. "You are insane. Next time I am hitting back, do you understand?"

"No, I do not understand. What is this all about? Why am I here, sir? Does it amuse you to seduce one woman and then have her watch you move on to the next?"

"No."

Her eyes narrowed at the laugh blended with his denial. Maybe she had not worked out all her problems, but she was not allowing another man to manipulate her.

"No? No, there is no pleasure in it, or no, there is no woman?"

"You are jealous."

It was absolutely the wrong thing to say. Screeching, Brook launched herself at him. Not bothering to hide his laughter, he wrapped his arms around her as she tried to pummel him. Landing on his back, he winced. "Calm down, Countess. You have had your revenge. Damn, I think I hit my head on a rock. Does not anyone clean up this place?"

"I hope you have split your skull open on it. You deserve nothing less for scaring me half to death!" She despised feeling helpless, and his surprise attack, albeit harmless, had stirred up some old fears.

Mallory was quickly losing his good humor. "I wanted to see you," he said through clenched teeth.

"If you recall, Mr. Claeg, you encountered me twice at the theater. Then you flirted with Lady Haslake's daughter and, oh yes, ran off after some mysterious woman. Who was she? A new mistress or one of your careless discards?"

"Allow me to clarify: I wanted to see you alone."

She let some of the anger drain out of her. "Now you have." She tried to stand but discovered her skirts were tangled with his legs.

"Not so fast, Countess." He tumbled them so that he was on top. "Let us address some of your other accusations."

"I would rather not," she primly replied.

"Stop being childish," he ordered. Grabbing his wrinkled coat, he belied his angry command by stuffing it under her head. "To begin with, I was not flirting with Lady Laurette Omant. The young lady has never been overly impressed by my charms. Second, I am not searching for a new mistress. Why would I, when I have you? Although, I confess, as a lover you are a maddening one."

She might have been appeased if he had not tacked on the last part. "You do not have me, Mr. Claeg."

"Hmm, don't I?" he purred, his husky voice doing crazy things to her insides. His hair had come undone and was a dark curtain around his face. "You constantly provoke me into proving myself. Fortunately for you, I happen to feel the predilection to accommodate you."

"Enough. Let me up before someone hears us and decides to search the greenhouse."

Mallory bent closer so his long hair covered her face. He nipped her earlobe. "Then we best be quiet. You have proven to be a screamer when aroused, so I will have to think of something. I swear not to smother you. If you faint, it will be from the pleasure of our lovemaking."

Fainting from pleasure. The idea had merit. *No,* she

thought, letting common sense intrude upon the fantasy. She was not going to let him seduce her on the floor of a greenhouse. "I cannot see this benefiting either one of us." She turned her head, giving him access to the curve of her neck.

"Then I need to work on my persuasive skills." He licked her neck and she shivered. "It is only fair that I be allowed to practice on you."

Mallory had vowed himself that if he caught the countess alone he would woo her gently. The oath had been declared hours earlier when he was still feeling guilty over breaking his promise to Amara. Once he had his hands on Brook, all his good intentions evaporated. He did not understand how this noble woman had the power to turn him into a howling beast craving the delicious heat of mating. Although she had yet to admit it to him or even to herself, he sensed the wildness in her. It was his absolute pleasure to incite her hidden nature.

"There is no reasoning with you."

"None," he heartily agreed, and kissed the skin exposed above her breast. His hand expertly slipped beneath her skirt and skimmed over her stocking-clad calf. The flesh under his hand quivered as he trailed his teasing fingers upward.

"You are the worst sort of libertine," she accused, fighting to maintain her composure even though her body was softening at his touch.

"Definitely wicked. You might as well surrender."

"You—" She bit her lower lip when he lightly tickled the soft nest between her legs. "You cannot be trusted."

"You can trust me, Countess," he whispered in the darkness. He glided his thumb seductively along the soft, yielding flesh. "Your body already does." He demonstrated by using her wetness to draw a teasing spiral on her inner thigh. She lifted her leg up, silently inviting him to indulge his hunger. "Cracking through that stubborn brain of yours will take some work."

Mallory quieted her parting lips with a kiss. For some unfathomable reason she was determined to talk him out of
making love to her. He refused to let her deny both of them.
There was no doubt she inflamed him. She simply had to
brush against him and his unruly cock hardened. He nibbled
her lower lip and tasted the coppery flavor of blood from
when she had bitten it earlier.

She gasped and turned her face away. "This is insane."

"Denying ourselves is insane." He tugged on her bodice,
exposing as much flesh as he could without ruining the dress.
She surprised him by pulling his head to her breast. Pleased
that she was getting into the spirit of being deliciously rav-
ished, he suckled her nipples in turn. She groaned, holding
his head to her bosom as he plumped her responsive flesh
with his tongue and teeth.

Brook shook her head, overcome by what he was building within her. "I can—I cannot."

He laved the cleft between her breasts. His fingers felt
clumsy as he unfastened the buttons on his breeches. "With
us, everything is possible."

Since lighting a candle might summon an audience at an
inopportune moment, Mallory relied on his other senses. He
anointed his fingers in her wetness and she moaned softly.
The scent of her arousal triggered all manner of primitiveness
in him. Rolling on his side, he frantically worked his breeches
down his hips and legs. He kicked them into a dark corner.

In his heightened awareness, his head lifted at the sound
of rustling fabric. Mallory did not know if he could trust
himself if she was about to refuse him. His hand shot out to
catch her before she moved away. Instead of grasping fabric,
his fingers curved around her thigh.

The countess wanted him.

The knowledge was an intoxicating chemical in his brain.
Cupping his scrotum, he moved and positioned himself above
her. His hand stroked and then encircled his rigid length,

anticipating the claiming. She fit against him perfectly. He groaned as her wetness coated the head of his cock, coaxing him deeper into her core.

Mallory held himself back. "Say the words, Countess."

She hesitated. He sensed she was puzzled by his command. Even in the gloom her eyes were a beacon for him. He stared down at her, willing her to speak. She lifted herself up on her elbows and the motion had him sinking deeper into her. He could feel himself expanding within her. In a few minutes, he was no longer going to care about words. The countess tilted her face up to his. He accommodated her by lowering his so she could kiss him. She was not interested in a kiss. Instead she moved her mouth and shyly whispered into his ear.

"Fuck me."

His body jolted at the unexpected vulgarity. The beast she often accused him of being awakened. Fully aroused, he speared his cock into the heart of her. They both cried out in ecstasy. Mallory's mind blanked as he surrendered to the pleasures of a willing woman beneath him. Wildly he battered himself into her. There was no resistance. Her slick, hot feminine core took him deeply, encouraging speed and less finesse. The countess's hands roved over his back as if searching for purchase. Finally clasping his hips, she disrupted his frenzied rhythm by forcing him to slow down and linger, as her impending release grew nearer. Crying out, she lifted her hips, demanding more. Mallory blindly obeyed. Cupping her buttocks, he shortened his thrusts, letting her orgasm pulse against him. As he took her, he allowed himself to be taken. As he was grinding against her, the violence of her release milked his cock. Claiming her in the most primitive manner was impossible to resist. He did not even try. As he muffled his shout of completion into her shoulder, the streaming of his seed seemed never-ending.

Only when his head cleared did he recall their parting words to each other at Loughwydde.

The choice is yours.

Choice, you black-hearted villain . . . what choice?

The choice of whether you are my woman or some pitiful lonely widow I fucked for sport.

Still deep within her and panting into her hair, Mallory realized now that the countess had never believed he had been offering her a choice. She had never trusted him of being capable of offering her more.

Fuck me.

Black-hearted villain. He had been so bloody obliging.

She was getting rather apt at slipping into houses unnoticed, Brook decided as she prepared for bed. There was no doubt it was Mallory Claeg's wicked influence. Dressed in a night rail, she climbed into bed. She groaned in pleasure. Her back felt bruised from Mallory's frenzied lovemaking. His impulsive nature created some interesting predicaments, she mused, but next time she preferred that they make love on a soft bed instead of the stone flooring of an old greenhouse.

Perhaps that explained his odd mood afterward. As she was used to his teasing chatter, he seemed too quiet. He did not speak until they had straightened their clothing.

"We have been reckless, Countess," he said, coming over to her. He smoothed the hair from her face.

"We were quiet," she said, lowering her voice just in case she was wrong.

Mallory smiled at the horror in her tone. "I was not speaking about the sounds we made but rather the fact that I have been treating you more like a wife than a mistress."

Blinking at him, he thought she was being deliberately obtuse.

"I have spent my seed in you on numerous occasions, Countess. You could be breeding."

A child. She had long given up the hope that she might be blessed with another. Holding Wynne's little girl had resurrected those old needs. Bitterly she met his gaze. "I knew something was troubling you."

"A woman who knows her lover usually commits her heart as well."

She sensed he spoke more to himself than to her. "Are you worried about it? There is no need. My husband had his revenge on me. Losing his son has left me barren."

Mallory's silence as he contemplated her confession unnerved her. "Do you know this as fact?"

Brook shrugged and stepped away from him. She was careful to remain close because she had no desire to crack her head on the fountain. "There was a great amount of blood, I was told. Tipton warned me that I might never completely recover from the damage done to my womb. So you see, you have worried needlessly." It was so painful for her to speak of it to anyone. Saying it aloud made it real.

"Hmm, that remains to be seen." He came closer and embraced her. They stood there for a while. She closed her eyes and pretended he was attempting to draw some of the pain out of her.

His next words confirmed her wry suspicions that he was relieved by her news and not above enjoying it. "However, I am never one to turn away or reject good fortune. Besides, I rather like being reckless with you."

"A strange declaration, Mr. Claeg. Still, I like being reckless with you, too."

Mallory backed them up to the concrete edge of the fountain. Sitting down, he pulled her onto his lap. He touched her ankle and she knew what he wanted.

"Your stamina is remarkable," she said, her nipples puckering at the thought of him inside her again.

"Thank you, m'dear." He planted a wet kiss on her mouth. "Oh, let us be clear on one matter. If we discover you have more in common with the lush Gaea than we had erroneously assumed, you will marry me." He pushed against the hidden nubbin, softening his threat with pleasure. "Do you agree?"

She was so slick, there was nothing he could not do. The fiend was trying to seduce her into agreeing with him! She tried to shift away from him to think clearly, but he was relentless. "This is something we need to seriously contemplate." He kissed her throat and wiggled his fingers deeper. "I . . . oh . . ." She sucked in her breath. He was not playing fairly. "Marriage . . . I do not desire it."

He murmured against her throat, "Let me persuade you." He licked her ear. "You will not regret it. In fact, you will insist that I persuade you again—and often."

A man of considerable talent, he had worked his manhood free from his breeches while he kept her too busy to think of the hundred reasons that she did not want to marry him. He lifted her and shifted her balance so that she straddled him. This new position thrust him so wholly, she thought she might weep from the pleasure.

Lying on her bed, Brook tightened her legs together, recalling the cries he had wrung out of her. The man had shown her several times before he sent her off to bed how persuasive he could be. She furrowed her brow trying to recall all that she had promised in the throes of passion.

Yes, I desire you, Mallory.

Yes, only your masterful touch will satisfy me.

Yes, if we make a child, I will marry you!

Yes, please!

The scoundrel had used her own body against her. He had seductively extracted each promise he had demanded and she had joyfully succumbed to the rewards of her compliance.

Let me persuade you.

Oh yes. Even despising the method by which he had gained her oath did not prevent her from wanting him to persuade her again.

Chapter Twenty

"His Lordship is having a good day," the servant announced to Mallory when he entered the room. His mother had retained the man, personally trained by the physician seeing to Lord Keyworth's care, to take care of her husband's personal needs while he carried out the physician's day-to-day instructions.

As the weeks passed there had been some improvement in the viscount's condition. He was able to sit now unassisted. Mallory had immediately purchased him a wheelchair. Although he needed help moving from the bed to the chair, the chair freed him from the chamber that had become his prison.

"Good day, my lord. Forgive me for interrupting your meal." Mallory was usually more thoughtful of the time of day at which he visited Lord Keyworth. His father was easily frustrated. It was not Mallory's intention to add to his humiliation.

"Veal broth," the cheerful man explained. "Very fortifying to the weakened constitution."

The permanent frown contorting one side of the viscount's face and his slow tongue were still making speech difficult for him. "Cow pish," he grumbled.

It had become an old argument. Until the physician was satisfied Lord Keyworth could swallow bits of food without choking on them, he was confined to the plain diet of the infirm.

"Well, Father, if we could all recover as quickly as you

have, the entire *ton* would be swilling a pint of cow piss daily."

Mallory was pleased to glimpse the familiar gleam of humor. His sire's chuckle was slow and sounded like he was out of practice.

"Really, Mr. Claeg," the servant complained when the viscount refused another spoonful of the broth. "His Lordship becomes uncooperative in his excitability. I do not think it is a behavior we should encourage."

Mallory did not view stubbornness as a flaw. It was a trait he admired in the countess even when he wanted to strangle her for it. The Claegs were also known for their various degrees of stubbornness. When the trait flared to life, it gave him hope that his father had not given up.

"Perhaps he tires of cow piss," Mallory said, earning another hoarse chuckle from his father. "Now that I am here, why don't I take Lord Keyworth for a stroll through the gardens? If he becomes difficult I will dump him in the cistern."

"Co' try," the older man said; his breathing had become more pronounced with his efforts. He turned his head into the pillow and coughed.

Not liking his routine tampered with, the servant offered the older man another spoonful of broth. "Perhaps, after he has finished his meal." Lord Keyworth evaded the spoon at the last second and the broth dribbled down his neck.

"He does not want it," Mallory said through his teeth, not caring if he was interfering with the physician's or his mother's rules. The servant ignored him.

The viscount struck out at the next feeding attempt. He had lost the dexterity of his hand, but that did not keep him from swinging his arm at the servant's head. He missed. Instead, he knocked the bowl of broth out of the man's hand. Perhaps that had been the viscount's goal all along. The china shattered against the leg of a nearby chair.

Wearing a fair amount of the broth down the front of his shirt, the servant sputtered in outrage.

"He warned you, and so did I," Mallory smugly said. "Perhaps if you quit treating him like a child, you might discover he will be less temperamental." He grinned at his father. "What do you think, my lord? Shall we check out the cistern?" Mallory leaned over his father, planning to carry him to the wheelchair in the corner of the room.

"No-no-no-no-no," Lord Keyworth complained when Mallory touched his shoulder.

He stepped back, uncertain what to do. "I was jesting about the cistern," he said, appalled that his father might believe he was serious.

"G'way. . . . Go 'way," the man sobbed.

Mallory felt an obstruction in his throat at his father's rejection. Whirling away, he was brought up short by the servant standing in his way. The sympathy in the man's expression was unexpected.

"Mr. Claeg, permit me to walk you to the door."

Not trusting his voice not to break when he spoke, Mallory did not bid his father farewell. The servant maintained his silence until they reached the door.

"Mr. Claeg, do not be offended by Lord Keyworth's reaction."

He swallowed the growing lump in his throat. "Is his mind so scrambled that he thought I was actually planning to hurt him?"

"Of course not, sir," the man denied. "I know you do not think highly of our attempts to keep your father quiet and adhere to routine, but we proceed cautiously because he does not benefit from the excitability. He has shown remarkable improvement and will continue to do so if we give him the opportunity to heal and work around his limitations."

The reasonable explanation made Mallory ashamed that

he had ridiculed the man earlier. "Are you asking me to stay away?"

His job required patience and his solemn expression exuded it. "No. Despite his reaction, he is comforted by your presence. It eases his injured brain knowing that you are looking after your mother and his business interests."

Mallory thought of the letters on his father's desk and the meeting his solicitor had arranged for later in the afternoon. The viscount had employed good men to look after his interests. Acting in his stead had not been as burdensome as Mallory had once imagined it would be.

"What did I do to cause his upset?" Seeing his strong father cry disturbed Mallory more than the rejection.

"Nothing dire," the man said assuredly. "His Lordship was enjoying your banter and it was clear he wanted to join you outdoors."

"Then why was he so upset?"

"You can blame the injury he has suffered. Sometimes he cannot control his reactions. He feels, sometimes too much. When he is overwhelmed he reacts like any of us would. Only Lord Keyworth's tolerance is decidedly lower than it used to be. He understands this, but it does not negate his feelings."

Mallory remained silent. He had half a dozen questions, but the servant who was used to working with slower, damaged minds worked at a different pace.

"When he realized that you intended to pick him up, your father lost the delicate balance he had with his emotions. His pride would never permit him to accept such assistance from you."

He glanced away and nodded abruptly.

"Why do you not go down to His Lordship's study and assist your mother with his correspondence? I will clean up your father and give him a chance to calm down. Later, if his disposition improves, I will help him get into the wheelchair and the two of you can enjoy the gardens as you suggested."

"Why did you not warn me that the encounter betwixt you and Mrs. Milroy was planned?" Ham demanded.

He had arrived an hour earlier at their house with the purpose of inviting her along for a carriage drive through Hyde Park. Brook assumed the invitation had been an excuse for him to deliver the lecture she was enduring.

"My lord, you are not privy to all of my activities, nor do you have the right to exert a claim," she said pointedly. "Berating me for a past deed is a waste of time."

"She and Mr. Milroy were in the house when your husband had his accident," he argued. "Renewing the acquaintance will only remind the *ton* of the connection."

If Lyon had gotten his way, Mr. Milroy, Wynne, and anyone else who had interfered with him would have been discovered dead in that house. "The connection was made when Lyon kidnapped my friend from her carriage."

"Was that what she told you?" He sneered derisively. "Have you forgotten that you were missing from your household? Lyon was questioning everyone who might have encountered you that day."

If Ham believed the lies, there was nothing she could say to dissuade him from casting the Milroys as villains. "I refuse to continue this discussion, my lord."

"Elthia, Lady A'Court, was inconsolable when she learned you had left with those people. It took hours and a liberal dosing of sherry to calm her down."

Ah, the crux of his ire. "Be reasonable, Ham. There is nothing I do in my life that does not upset Mother A'Court. Since I did not have the decency to collapse dead at the foot of her son's coffin—"

"She does not—"

Brook overrode his protest. "The very least I can do in her esteemed opinion is spend the rest of my life not upsetting her!"

"The dowager recognizes that you are still a young woman, with the desires of youth. Children. . . ." He let the word linger tantalizingly on the air. "Marrying me would ensure the A'Court line, Brook. I could give you back the son you lost."

Brook curtly held up a silencing hand. No one could ever bring back the son she had lost. "Please, my lord. Say nothing more on the subject." If by some miracle she was able to have a child, she was not breeding to continue the A'Court line.

Ham refused to give up. "She would support the match, Brook. If you were kinder to her."

"Kinder?" She laughed bitterly. "Being kinder implies I have been cruel, which I have not."

"More patient, then," he entreated, coming around the table so nothing separated them. "You are not the only member of this family who remembers the past. Facing the old rumors has been difficult for all of us."

She quietly conceded that he was correct.

"That is why meeting Wynne Milroy in the middle of the salon of the King's Theatre was inappropriate."

So he had circled around to make his point. "Argh, I will not listen to this!" Brook slapped her hands over her ears and walked away from him, disgusted. She was too gullible, she thought, berating herself. She actually had believed Ham could be reasonable.

"Brook, we are not finished!" he yelled, charging after her. "Let us sit down. I will summon a servant for some tea."

"My lady, I beg your pardon," the housekeeper said, but her cynical expression hinted that it was the earl who should be doing the begging. "You have a gentleman caller."

The implication that Ham was not was amazingly clear to everyone but the earl.

"Send him away. Tell him Her Ladyship is indisposed," he said dismissively.

"I take my orders from the Ludlows and Lady A'Court, my lord," the woman sniffed, her hands fisted on her broad hips. She was the mother of fifteen, and eight of them were males. A snotty lord did not impress her. The housekeeper looked to her mistress. "The gentleman told me that he did not want to bother the family. He asked if you would meet him out in the gardens."

Brook could think of only one man who was so bold.

"Tell him I will be there momentarily."

"Aye, madam." The housekeeper dipped into a quick curtsey and left to deliver the message.

Ham stilled Brook's exit by holding her arm. "A stranger comes to the door asking to see you and you just rush off without finding out who he is?"

"That is the point, Cousin," she said, slipping from his hold. "No stranger would ask me to meet him in the gardens. I regret I will have to decline your considerate invitation for a drive through Hyde Park this afternoon. Mayhap another day when you do not feel the need to lecture me about my friends."

She was not surprised to find Mallory pacing near the greenhouse. Rushing toward him, she could see something was terribly wrong. She was not fashionably attired to receive callers; however, something in his expression told her that the troubles weighing on his mind were not superficial.

"My lord, you asked for me?"

He took the last two steps to close the distance. Cupping her face in his hands, he said, "I feared I would be turned away." The kiss he pressed on her mouth was light, almost reverent. Brook tasted the flavor of tears on his lips.

"What has happened? Is it your father?"

Mallory was usually so lighthearted. Only when he had

spoken of his wife and the Hennings had she glimpsed this troubled side of his nature.

Mallory slid down onto his knees. He was beginning to frighten her. Wrapping his arms around her waist, he laid his cheek against her stomach. "I need you, Countess. You have so much strength. Do you mind sharing it with me?"

She had never thought of herself as a strong person. Odd, how someone telling you that you were somehow made it true. Brook removed his hat and let it down to the ground. He had not tied back his unruly hair, so she stroked his head, giving him the comfort he sought.

"Can you tell me what happened?"

Holding her tightly, he said with his eyes closed, "Later. Right now, I need this." Mallory burrowed his face into her stomach. "To touch, to smell you . . . I need *you*. Is it enough, Countess?"

Like him, she did not believe in forever. However, Mallory had come to her craving comfort. She could not turn him away, even if letting him closer meant that one day he would shatter the remains of her heart. "For as long as you need me," she murmured, brushing her fingers over the rough stubble on his cheek.

They held each other in the garden, unaware that their tenderness was being observed. Ham watched them from an upper-story window. With clenched fists he fought the urge to march into the garden and tear Brook out of Claeg's embrace. He was a generous man. Had he not offered his own sister up to Claeg for his amusement as long as it meant that he kept away from Lady A'Court? Claeg was not interested in May. The loving scene below revealed how close he and the countess had become. Something had to be done, Ham thought as he sipped Ludlow's brandy to stop the tremors in his hands. Something violent.

Chapter Twenty-One

"I had despaired that Mr. Claeg would ever summon me," May Hamblin said. She gingerly touched her new bonnet in several strategic spots, fretting that it was spoiling the curls she had spent over an hour creating.

Brook had not known of Mallory's interest in completing May's picture until her brother had sent a messenger politely requesting that she act as chaperone for May. Feeling guilty about their argument days ago when she had abandoned him for Mallory, Brook had agreed. Besides, she did not trust May Hamblin. The ambitious young woman had her eye on Mallory Claeg. With his father so ill, the notion of becoming the new Lady Keyworth probably was an added enticement.

"He returned to London for his family. Everything else became secondary."

"Not everything," May countered slyly. "Mr. Claeg was at the Vining sisters' card party two evenings past. You should have joined us. Miss Nost made such an embarrassing fuss when he entered the room."

"Oh really." Ham had not mentioned the Vining sisters' card party. "What did Miss Nost do?"

Enjoying that her connections in the *ton* exceeded Brook's, May was happy to share all the details. She shifted in the carriage seat so they were face-to-face. "Well, the poor girl has been pining, absolutely *pining*, for Mr. Claeg since her father commissioned a portrait in honor of her twentieth birthday. According to Miss Grearson, who heard the tale from Miss Swern, who swears upon her mother's grave that what I am about to tell you is entirely true, Mr. Claeg had expressed a desire to paint Miss Nost disrobed."

Since he had expressed the same desire about her, Brook was beginning to wonder how many other women had received his generous invitation. *Duplicitous scoundrel.* "I assume Mr. Nost called him out."

"Miss Nost never told him."

She just told a few gossiping women so that everyone within a twenty-mile radius knew about it. Recalling some of the vile gossip Brook had heard about Lyon and herself, she sighed. She silently apologized for the unkind name she had called him.

"Miss Grearson went on to say that Miss Nost, although shocked by his outrageous suggestion, later relented when she recognized the course her errant heart had taken. Wanting to prove her love, she was prepared to deliver herself completely and succumb to the passions he inspired."

Brook, catching herself pouting, bit her lip in punishment. "Pray continue. I cannot wait to hear the rest."

Engrossed in the retelling of the scandalous tale, May leaned closer. "I was told Miss Nost had arrived in the painting room at Mr. Claeg's town house before him. Stripped bare all the way to her toes, she presented herself like a nobleman's succulent feast on Boxing Day."

"Good grief," Brook said, suddenly feeling pity for the young woman. "I am guessing this tale does not end well."

"Indeed, it does not!" May exclaimed with malicious relish. "Mr. Claeg entered the painting room as Miss Nost had imagined he would, but he was not alone. The girl's father had just arrived and a friend from the Royal Academy had joined them. The housekeeper was behind the trio with tea and cakes!"

"What happened next?"

"Miss Nost was so overcome with humiliation, she just stood there and screamed. It was Mr. Claeg who hastily produced some drapery so the housekeeper could respectfully cover up the poor girl. Miss Swern says the friend from the Royal Academy was so impressed with Miss Nost's lungs that he offered Mr. Nost twice the value of the painting. Out of respect for his daughter, the man naturally refused all offers."

Brook laughed at the ridiculousness of the tale. "So what happened at the Vinings' card party?"

"This part of the tale I witnessed firsthand. When Mr. Claeg entered the room, Miss Nost was visibly upset by his presence. Unaware that he was the source of her agitation, Mr. Claeg innocently approached Mr. Nost and his daughter to pay his respects. Before he could speak, her face went white and she fainted. Her skull would have been bashed in by one of the tables if Mr. Claeg had not caught her up into his arms when she slumped over. The circumstances that led up to her ignoble fall were what everyone was talking about for the rest of the evening. Disgraced, Miss Nost left soon after she was revived."

Brook could not wait until she cornered Mallory for his version of the tale. "With the exception of Lady Lumley's dog choking to death on Mrs. Sheers's ruby and diamond ring one evening, nothing interesting ever happened at the card parties I attended."

As they climbed up the stairs of Mallory's town house behind the housekeeper, Brook noticed the strong odor of linseed oil and turpentine was pervasive throughout. She glanced at May and watched her nose wrinkle in reaction.

"I suppose one grows accustomed to it," Brook said, unconvinced. The house smelled worse than the cottage in Cornwall.

"I barely notice it myself anymore," the housekeeper replied. "He'll be in the painting room with Gill."

Mallory had not mentioned Gill. It was a reminder of how little Brook knew about his life in town. She and May paused at the threshold, allowing the servant to announce them.

"Mr. Claeg, you have guests, sir. A Miss Hamblin and Lady A'Court."

Peering around the large canvas he was working on, Mallory smiled and devoured Brook with his hungry gaze. "Ladies. Welcome." Coatless, he had donned an apron to protect his clothing. When he lifted his arms in greeting, she noted his rolled-up sleeves were splattered with green and black paint. "Gill, come out from your hiding place and meet my friends."

"I'm moving as fast as I'm able." A small youthful face popped out from the doorway to the left of them. "Which one is which, Claeg?" The adolescent stepped completely into view. "Wait, I recognize this one." Pointing at Brook, Gill said, "This is your bluebell countess."

"That's right. This is Lady A'Court," Mallory said, pleased his companion was able to recognize the lady who had inspired his work. "Come closer. Mrs. Lane is promising us sweets now that my model has arrived. Gill, the other lovely lady is Miss May Hamblin."

"A pleasure, ladies," Gill said, tugging the worn edge of his cap.

Something about the dress May wore lured Gill closer. She shied away when the adolescent tried to stroke the fabric. "You will get it dirty," May said, moving closer to Brook.

Not offended, Gill snickered, looking at Mallory to share in his amusement. "Not worth a farthing if it can't be petted a little."

May gasped. "Mr. Gill, I find your coarse manners revolting."

Gill held his sides and collapsed onto the floor laughing.

May's puzzled frown became more pronounced when her insult was met with laughter.

Mallory's grin widened. Brook could tell he was thinking about how much he liked petting her. He chuckled at her blush. "I cannot fault your logic, Gill. However, you have to treat some ladies like the Egyptian artifacts you prize at the museum."

Understanding the odd explanation, the adolescent nodded. Brook wondered how the fifteen-year-old was connected to Mallory. Something about the upturned gaunt face was familiar.

"I prefer touching." Gill let Mallory haul him up.

Winking at Brook, he said, "As do I, Gill. As do I."

Brook's curiosity was soon satisfied about Gill's presence. Once Mallory had settled May into her old pose and begun to paint, Gill retrieved a sketching book from a leather satchel on the floor. As the adolescent flipped through the thick pages, even Brook's inexperienced eye recognized talent.

"You are an artist."

Gill's gaze locked onto hers and narrowed. Accepting Brook's words as a compliment, the youth shrugged. "Aye. That's what I keep telling Claeg, here."

"Gill is my new apprentice," Mallory said from behind the canvas.

"His temporary apprentice," Gill corrected. "We are still haggling the finer points of our arrangement."

Selecting a black lead pencil, Brook watched as May Hamblin's face was defined with a few hastily scrawled lines. Mallory's new assistant was very good.

"Gill is demanding cakes every day. This provision has forced me into renegotiating Mrs. Lane's wages."

"An apprentice is akin to a servant," May argued, unable

to move her head, so she missed Gill's scowl and furious slash with his pencil. "An unpaid servant, I believe. What is there to bargain?"

Brook gazed down at Gill's sketch and choked on her laughter. The youth had given May three eyes and horns. Hearing Brook's laughter, Gill stiffened his shoulders. As the child looked back, something in his expression triggered why the face seemed so familiar. When Lyon was still alive and tormenting Brook, she had glimpsed the same frightened expression in her own mirror.

"Gill is a girl," Brook flatly stated.

Grinning up at her, Gill said, "That's five shillings you owe me, Claeg."

"There was some kind of wager?" May asked. As she waited a beat, Brook's observation sank in. "That's a girl?"

Disgusted, Mallory slapped down his brush. "Damn! It took me days to figure out the lad was a she. What gave her away?"

Everyone stared at Brook. "I am not sure." She did not want to talk about the past in front of Gill and May. "A feeling more than anything, I suppose."

Mallory gestured at the cheeky fifteen-year-old. "Ladies, meet Gillian, or Gill, as everyone calls her."

Holding out a paint-smudged hand, the girl said primly, "Miss Gillian Revil." Brook shook her hand.

"Gillian Revil." Mallory shook his head. "Changing your last name again, are you?"

"I like it," Gill shot back. "It suits me. A lot like the extra five shillings I will have in my pocket."

Mallory had been pleased with how he had maneuvered Brook into visiting his home until it was obvious that getting her alone was bloody unlikely with shrewd Miss Hamblin watching over them.

"You can move about, Miss Hamblin. I need to mix up

more paint before we continue." Mallory made a soft clicking sound with his tongue as he thought up excuses to pull the countess into the smaller workroom. So far, *Lady A'Court, would you like to help me stir?* was his best effort. Pathetic.

"Thank goodness," Miss Hamblin said, wincing as she stretched her arms and wiggled her fingers. "If I had held that pose a minute longer, it would have been permanent."

"And a lovely addition to the other useless garden statues the birds make use of you would have been, too," Gill mumbled under her breath.

"Did you say something, Miss Revil?"

"I says, Miss," Gill said, overenunciating, much to Mallory's merriment. "What you need is a tour."

"Half the time, I have no idea what you are saying," Miss Hamblin said, giving her a pitying look.

"To move about . . . put the blood back into your scrawny limbs." Gill walked in a circle, waving her arms. "This is only a workroom. You haven't seen the other rooms. The ones Claeg keeps up nice and clean for high-and-mighty patrons."

"Gill."

"Let me show her," Gill pleaded to Mallory. "I won't touch anything. I swear. Miss Hamblin will keep me honest. Come on, what have you to say?" she cajoled.

Gill, bless her, had innocently handed him the perfect excuse to separate the countess from her charge.

"If you run into Messing, tell him that you were under orders to show Miss Hamblin the drawing room."

"Aye, Claeg. It'd be my pleasure." Gill reached for Miss Hamblin's hand and then thought better of it. "Come along, Miss. Something tells me that you and that fancy dress will fit nicely in this room."

Not knowing how to refuse the enthusiastic girl without offending her host, Miss Hamblin beseeched her chaperone, "Brook, are you joining us on our tour?"

Mallory stepped between them. Smoothly he lied, "The

countess has seen the room. She can lend a hand stirring the paints." He shrugged at Brook, who looked at him in genuine disbelief. It had sounded better in his head.

"Off we go, Miss." Gill spurred Miss Hamblin along by reaching out for her dress. She shrieked and hurried out the door. The girl paused. "Showing her everything will take some time. You'll be owing me double the amount of cakes for this favor, Claeg." Whistling, Mallory heard Gill order Miss Hamblin to slow down.

The imp knew what he was about all along. Solving his dilemma of distracting Miss Hamblin had earned Gill extra cakes for an entire month.

Chapter Twenty-Two

"Mallory," Brook said the instant they were alone. "Where did you meet Gill?"

"I really do not want to talk right now." He grabbed her hand and dragged her over to the sofa guests sometimes used to observe him at work. There were nights it had also served as his bed when he was too tired to climb the stairs to his bedchamber. Plopping down, he dragged her onto his lap.

Struggling to get free of him, she could not help but think of the last time he had pulled her onto his lap. "Release me, you fiend!" Ignoring her, he began kissing the side of her neck. She laughed because it tickled. "This is hardly appropriate. Anyone could walk into this room."

"I prefer doing the inappropriate with you," he murmured against her throat. "Besides, Gill will keep Miss Hamblin distracted. She is rather good at it." He bit the curve of her neck.

Brook sighed against him and then shook herself when she realized what he was doing. Gill Revil was not the only one who had a talent for distraction. "Oh no. I refuse to let you get away with this." She gave him a shove and stumbled out of his tempting embrace. Brook tugged on the sleeve he had pulled down. "I was asking you about Gill. Who are her people?"

Glowering at her through the strands of brown hair that had come loose, Mallory was not happy that he was being denied. "Are you asking if she is related to me? Mayhap my

natural daughter from a youthful indiscretion?" The prominent muscle in his jaw ticced his displeasure.

Appalled, she exclaimed, "No! The thought had not occurred to me." It truly had not. From the look of the girl's
odd tattered attire and her rough dialect it was clear that she
came from humble circumstances. Brook could not imagine
Mallory denying a child of his anything. "I was simply curious about how you had met. The young girl obviously adores
you, though why that surprises me I do not know. You seem
to enthrall every female you meet."

Taking advantage of her being distracted, Mallory rose
up from the sofa and captured her. He spun them around,
and they collapsed onto the sofa. This time he pinned her in
place with his body. "Are you enthralled, Countess?"

Oh yes. There was something about Mallory Claeg that
coaxed even the most sensible woman into doing the unthink-
able. Loath to admit it, she said, "You will have to figure that
one out for yourself. Now about Gill . . ."

Mallory groaned and lightly pressed his head to hers.
"Egad, you are persistent." Understanding that she was not
likely to melt in his arms until she had gained the answers
she sought, he said, "Gill was selling her sketches on the
street when I met her six months ago. Her natural ability impressed me and since then I have been trying to help her.
Naturally, this chafes against her independence, so she re-
jects most of my attempts to assist her. Her life and family
are a mystery. Often she reminds me of you."

She was positive the observation was not a compliment.
"Is she living with you?"

"No. She is too wary of me. The pair of you share that in
common. Nevertheless, I have spent enough time with her to
understand how her mind works. It is one thing to accept a
meal here and there from me. Sleeping under my roof gives
me power over her, and that she will not accept. Piecing
together what she has told me over the months, I suspect

someone, probably a man, has given her trouble. As to whom, I cannot say."

Trouble with a man was something she understood. It was not a far leap to identify with Gill. Nibbling her lip, she wondered if she could approach the girl.

"Your face is so expressive, I can see what you are thinking," Mallory said, tracing the line of each brow with soft kisses.

"Do you?"

"I doubt she will accept your help. Neither one of us understands what it is like to live on the streets, enduring poverty and running off the predators that want to enslave you. Gill does not trust anything offered without a price. The key to helping her is to go about it slowly."

His hand playfully skimmed her breast. "And you are a man of immeasurable patience, hmm?"

"Tremendous," he assured her. He kissed the soft swell of her breast. "Leave Gill to me. I have a plan."

"Uh-huh."

"Unconvinced?" He unexpectedly lifted his head and she felt the impact of his sorcerer's eyes. "I have coaxed her into accepting the position as my apprentice, have I not? Six months ago she would have spat on the offer." His grinning confidence was so engaging that she found herself smiling, too. "See, patience."

"Astonishing," she marveled. "You waited six months to make the generous offer of making her your personal slave. How kind of you."

"No," he countered, sensing he was being teased but showing all the signs of an aggravated man reaching his limits. "I will be her teacher. If she can learn to accept instruction from me regarding the arts, I will persuade her into accepting other gifts." He suddenly leered at her. "It is you who I hope to charm into the position of my personal slave." He caged her head with his arms, and she was trapped. His long lashes lowered seductively as he focused on her mouth. "I can envision the benefits of keeping you by my side day and night."

She could as well, so she said nothing. Unless she wanted to give his servants something to gossip about, one of them would have to be sensible. It appeared she was elected. Placing her hands on his shoulders, she pushed. "A lovely fancy for you, I am certain. However, there is nothing endearing about slavery to a man. So off. May will not remain in Gill's company forever, and we have paint to stir."

He hesitated. When he realized she was quite serious, he climbed off her. "You are not dressed properly to play with paints."

"It was your excuse, not mine," she blithely replied, and sat up. "Though why you thought I would be interested in such a task is beyond me."

"As you said, it was an excuse. You were supposed to be interested in *me*," he grumbled. "Come on, you can watch me while I do all of the work."

Following him into a smaller room that reminded him of a tiny kitchen with its wooden sinks, she said, "It sounds like the perfect job. I like watching you."

He gave her a measured stare. "Well, is it not fortunate that I like having you watch me?"

Moving away from her, he went to the wall lined with sturdy shelves and chose a glass jar. Removing the top, he sniffed the contents.

"You are not going to drink that?"

"No. This is linseed oil. If the scent is sweet, then I know the oil is not rancid." He set the jar down on the worktable and returned to the shelves and studied his inventory.

"What do you do if it is rancid? Toss it out?"

"Not necessarily. I could add some pulverized quicklime to a pint of oil and heat the mixture until it neutralized the acid." Selecting a small bottle, he said, "Interested in becoming my apprentice, too?"

"No, just curious," she said, watching him add a small amount of pigment to a palette. Next he added the oil. Picking up a wide-bladed painting knife, he began to vigorously mix the two into a semi-dry paste. "Does this ever get tedious?"

"At times," he conceded. "I could purchase my colors. However, the quality is never the same as mixing your own pigments. Of course, grinding colors for me will be one of Gill's tasks as my apprentice."

For a few minutes she listened to the faint sounds of the blade striking the palette as it scraped and rubbed the paste. "Are you expecting me to assist you in this endeavor?" She had produced a number of watercolors until her mother had proclaimed her accomplished at the task. Art was never the passion it seemed to be within Mallory.

"Your lack of enthusiasm, Countess, tempts me into agreeing. Luckily for you, this is proof of our chasteness. Be grateful."

"For what?"

"That I cannot think of a good reason to lock our companions out," he said, giving her a heated glance. "If I had, we would be lying on the sofa enjoying a lazy afternoon of love-making instead of standing here grinding color."

"Is that how you imagined our little visit when you invited May to your town house so you could finish her painting?"

Since his hands were occupied, he used the side of his arm to scratch an itch on his nose. "Not exactly. When I saw Miss Hamblin and her brother at the Vinings' card party, I acted on impulse. An impulse, might I remind you, which brought you to me without offending all of your sensibilities about causing a scandal."

"Unfair," she accused, feeling like he was ridiculing her concerns. "Just because I ask you to be discreet while we are in public does not imply I am—"

"Ashamed of what we share? Afraid to defy the family?

Or simply hypocritical?" Mallory helpfully queried. The paste he was grinding was looser and had a glossy elastic quality to it.

"Blast you!" She put her hands onto the rough worktable and leaned toward him. "Mayhap I should admit all apply and leave you to your work. Alone." Sometimes she felt so transparent around him. She did not like that he stripped her fears so neatly and then made her feel foolish.

"Calm down. Everything is fine." Tipping the palette, he scraped the paint into a small empty jar. He sealed the jar and plucked a rag out of the sink. "You have a right to be vexed. What I said was low and undeserved. Stay." Mallory wiped the painting knife clean with the rag and then scrubbed the palette clean. Wiping off the smudges on his hand, he carelessly tossed the soiled rag back into the sink.

"Why should I?"

He came around to her side of the table and gently eased her into his embrace. "Because seeing you and not being able to touch you properly will torment me. You should especially like that part." He kissed her on the tip of the nose.

"Do not start," she begged.

He exhaled noisily. "I hate that you are right. Still, I am pleased you came." Mallory could not resist kissing her. "Talk to me. Ask me something."

Thinking of May's earlier tale, Brook said, "I heard you attended the Vining sisters' card party recently. So tell me, what happened betwixt you and Miss Nost to cause the poor woman to collapse at your feet?"

Mallory's eyes rolled upward at the mention of the young woman's name. Groaning, he laid his forehead on Brook's rigid shoulder. "The swiftness with which gossip circulates through the *ton* boggles my brain."

Bracing his back against the framing of one of the windows overlooking the street, Mallory was perched with one leg dangling out the window as he watched the activity below. The scene below rarely changed. Carriages and wagons rumbled down the street on their way to their destinations. Street hawkers mingled with pedestrians, singing out their goods. Children ran a zigzag course between all of them. Some played games. Others were not so innocent, plying their sly craft of pickpocketing on the unwary. Mallory recognized all the scents and sounds of his street. It was home. Since his return, it was rare for him to have time alone. If he was not tending to his father's business interests, then he was catching up with his own business that he had neglected. He grinned slightly, thinking of his recent meeting with Lord Ventris. It had been a very profitable day indeed.

Hearing a scratching summons at the door, he ducked his head and shouted his permission to enter.

"Mr. Claeg."

"It is you, Messing. Good. Did you deliver my *Seduction of Cressida* to Lord Ventris?" he asked, not bothering to leave his post at the window.

"Yes, sir," the servant replied. "The proportions of the picture were not appropriate for the wall His Lordship had chosen."

"Ah well, the man had been warned," Mallory said unsympathetically. There had been an occasion years past when he had had the opportunity to view the interior of the gentleman's house. The former owner had been a notable opera singer who had enjoyed entertaining after her performances. The lady had been a generous hostess, he recalled fondly.

"Yes, m'lord. We remained with His Lordship as you had ordered. I took the liberty of offering a few suggestions when the gentleman seemed overly vexed with his quandary."

"I knew you would not disappoint me, Messing."

His face impassive, the manservant straightened his shoulders. This was the only indication he was pleased by his master's praise. "The gentleman eventually decided due to the subject of his new acquisition that-the library was an appropriate location. It appeared to be the perfect setting where he might admire your work and yet not offend the gentle spirits of his lady visitors. Lord Ventris desired me to pass along his compliments."

Rubbing his palm on his breeches, he said, "This went well for us, Messing. I do not believe we have seen the last of Lord Ventris."

"I agree, sir."

At the man's hesitation, Mallory asked, "Was there something else?"

"Yes, my lord. There is a lady downstairs who wishes to see you."

The countess. Could a man be so fortunate twice in one day? The day had started with a profitable business transaction and now Brook had come to him. Three days had elapsed since the ladies had departed his town house, and he was already missing Brook. Perhaps she had found a respectable excuse to escape Miss Hamblin. Slipping his leg through the window, he jumped down. "Who is it? Lady A'Court?"

"No, *mon cher*," Mrs. Carissa Le Maye announced from the doorway. As she had heard his question, her brandy-colored eyes narrowed dangerously. "If you desire a widow, then I should do, *oui*?"

"It is not like you to be so difficult about a dress fitting."

"If given a choice, I would prefer that the chore be accomplished at the house," Brook said to her mother as she waited for the groom to assist the other woman descending from their carriage. Patronizing the shop of the well-known dressmaker in the afternoon was akin to parading about Hyde Park in half dress. She had been highly selective regarding her amusements and the timing of her errands. According to her mother, Brook had been too discriminating.

"Madam Courroux's skills are in high demand this month,

and we cannot have her tarry on your dress. The Haslakes' ball is one of the highlights of the season. It is not to be missed. Not receiving an invitation can be likened to being refused a ticket to Almack's."

"Mama, I was not given admittance to Almack's," Brook said dryly, pretending not to feel dejected. It had hurt more than she had expected when tickets had arrived for her mother-in-law, Lord A'Court, and his sister. The earl had been outraged by the patronesses' intentional slight toward Brook and had offered to ignore the coveted invitations. His sister had threatened never to eat again if he tried. Elthia, Lady A'Court, added weight to May's view by reminding the earl of his position in polite society. In the end the trio had attended without Brook.

Mr. and Mrs. Ludlow had also been refused tickets because of their connection to Brook. Her mother had been humiliated by the omission. "Gaining a ticket to Almack's would have been a sterling stamp of approval on your character, my dear. The *ton* respects the opinions of the patronesses. Their support would have assisted us immensely."

"I do not care about Almack's, Mama. Nor will I truckle to a gaggle of females who think they are better than the rest of us."

Mrs. Ludlow fluttered her hands, checking all directions to make certain her daughter's contumely had not been overheard.

"Do you know what I do miss?" She sighed wistfully. "Being worthy of belonging. I am not one of them anymore."

"You will be again, my dear. The Haslakes' ball is just the beginning for you," her mother said soothingly.

"Is it?" Or had her beginning started with Mallory on the cliffs in Cornwall? "This is pointless, Mama. I should have remained at Loughwydde."

"Drivel. Once you see what a lovely ball gown Madam

Courroux has created for you, your melancholy will lift. Just
wait and see if it does not."

"What are you doing here, Carissa?" Mallory asked, deliberately keeping his gaze fixed on her face as she unbuttoned
her striped spencer and revealed the low-cut bodice of the
dress beneath. She handed the garment to his manservant.

"Is this how you greet an old friend, I ask?" She pouted
her painted lips. She untied her bonnet and placed it on top of
her spencer. "Messing, be a good man and take care of my
property."

"Sir?" the servant queried Mallory for confirmation of
his guest's dismissal.

Sensing an audience would add to the dramatics, he said,
"I will summon you when we need you."

"Very well, my lord." He closed the door behind him.

Before Mallory realized her intent, Carissa jumped into
his arms. His arms closed around her to prevent her from
falling. "Bastard! You have been in town for days and still
you make me come to you. I should not be rewarding you for
your arrogance." She let her head tip back so she could be-
stow a kiss on his waiting mouth.

His body stirred at her womanly scent. Mallory pulled
her upright abruptly and stepped aside. "More than half a
year has elapsed, Carissa, since either one of us has been
concerned about the other."

"Poof! A man who counts the days is one who has been
missing me. I have missed you, too, lover." She teasingly
counted the buttons on his waistcoat.

He grabbed her hands and squeezed them to gain her attention. "I am no longer interested in playing games."

She burst into laughter at the obvious lie. He was a man
who adored games, and she had known him long enough to
understand some aspects of a man never changed.

"Games with you," he clarified.

"Ah, you have found someone else to play your bed games with, no?" she asked. There was brittleness to her merriment that she could not conceal in her eyes.

"Kissing and telling was one of your favorite games, not mine," he coolly informed her.

"Lady A'Court, how kind of you to grace my shop with your presence." Madam Courroux approached them. Her genuflection was greatly exaggerated. She clapped her hands together and two assistants appeared at her side. "Bring me the Countess of A'Court's ball gown."

Brook glanced around, anxious at all the attention the other patrons were giving them. "Perhaps we should retire to a private room for the viewing."

The suggestion wounded the dressmaker. "My lady, I am not ashamed of my work. A dress by Madam Courroux is of the highest quality."

The woman was working herself up into a state of agitation. Brook exchanged helpless looks with her mother. "I am positive the dress is lovely. I just wanted some priv—"

The dressmaker fended off her protests with a hand gesture. "Even on an unfinished dress, the skills of my seamstresses are unmatched. No one is ever cheated in my shop."

"Your reputation precedes you, madam," Brook said, pulling her aside. "It was one of the reasons why I insisted to Lady Haslake that only a dress from your shop would satisfy me. Your establishment provides excellent workmanship and respects the confidentiality of your more distinguished clientele."

Madam Courroux's eyes rounded. "Of course, my lady." She lowered her voice to a whisper. "You desire to make an entrance at the Haslake ball. This I understand. You want everyone who sees you to wonder where such a splendid ball gown was created."

Brook would consider herself fortunate if that was the

utmost question on the tip of everyone's waggling tongues.
"Naturally, I will be proud to tell everyone who created my
wardrobe for the season."

One of the assistants approached them carrying a gown.
Madam Courroux gasped. "Idiot! What are you doing?" She
made a tsking sound. "Lady A'Court is accorded all the cour-
tesies of a respected patroness. Where did you intend for the
countess to change into her new ball gown? The street?" She
smacked her forehead, aggrieved with her staff. She gave her
assistant a shove in the direction she required. "Go . . . go!"

"Now, now, *amoureux*," Carrisa chastised, gliding away from
him. She eased onto the sofa. Her movements were a seductive invitation. "How you have changed if this is how you treat
your very good friends."

Mallory stared down at her. The woman was trouble. He
did not know why he was hesitating when the logical action
would have been to have Messing toss the exotic witch into
the street.

"Were we friends, Carissa? So many months have passed,
I cannot recall."

"Typical man," she said, sighing, letting her fingers dance
across the back of the sofa. "I, on the other hand, do not suffer the lethe a discarded lover often induces."

"Strange, considering the legions of men who have fallen
for your impressive charms only to find themselves abandoned for someone new."

"Mallory, you speak as if I was the one who ended our
affair." She teasingly traced the edge of her bodice. Like all
fools, he fell for her flirtation. Encouraged, she said playfully, "Then again, you and I both know which one of us
was the callous villain."

Picking up a chair, he turned it backward and straddled it.
He rested his chin on his hands and admired the little performance she was giving. Shaking his head, he said, "You are a

passable actress, Carissa, but you will never convince me that you shed a tear over me."

Her passionate nature ignited into a spectacular storm of outrage. Rising off the sofa, she paced in front of him. "Bloodless swine!" she exclaimed, losing the French accent she preferred to affect. "You touched me. Your mouth tasted my flesh as your rod pierced the very heart of me. I closed my eyes afterward with your musky scent stirring my senses. I awoke with your hungered panting teasing my ear. Our coupling was unparalleled. How could you know my body and not know me?"

"Can any man who has lain in your bed answer your question truthfully?" he countered, trying to keep hold of his temper.

"Damn you for your cruelty, Mallory Claeg," she said, her eyes brilliant with tears.

Hating himself for being the cause of her tears but not fully trusting them, he warily approached her trembling figure. "Carissa, neither one of us was seeking a permanent arrangement when we tumbled into bed." Needing to soothe, he gently clasped her shoulders and massaged. "It is unlike you to look back. You were fine when we parted. The last I heard, you were dallying with a Prussian nobleman, or was he a spy?"

She laughed at his puzzled expression, as he had hoped she would. "And what if I told you he was both?"

"If there is such a man, leave it to Carissa Le Maye to discover him in London. Did he break your heart, minx?"

"*Non*," she said, sliding her hand up to his nape. Her damp lashes fluttered up and she held his concerned gaze. "It was already fractured when you left me."

"What we had between us was not about hearts."

"You are quite right. It was about *le feu*. This." Before he grasped her purpose, she pulled his face down to hers. Latching on to his mouth, she poured all her anger and desperation into the kiss. Their lovemaking had always been tempestuous. His body reacted from recollection rather than actually being aroused by her kiss.

Despite her catching him unawares, Mallory did not want to hurt her. As he struggled against her, she had the agility of a snake. Her tongue pushed into his mouth, demanding that he respond. Whipping his head back, he took an unsteady step backward. The indulgence he had felt because of their past had been purged with his humor.

"My lord, are you there?" a cheerful feminine voice said from the other side of the door. "Good news." His new visitor managed to open the door. It swung open, carrying the flowery scent of her on the breeze. "Lady A'Court is occupied this afternoon, so we must carry on without her . . ." Miss Hamblin paused when she noticed he had a visitor. ". . . alone."

An innocent, perhaps, but the lady was shrewd enough to notice Mallory's wrinkled shirt and Carrisa's swollen, wet lips. His gut chilled at May's false smile.

"Forgive my intrusion. Your man told me you were working. When he kept me waiting in the drawing room, I did not think you would mind me sneaking a peek."

Carissa's smile revealed plenty of teeth. "You are welcome to watch, *petit agneau*. Neither Mallory nor myself has been troubled by modesty. Who knows? You might even learn something that your prudish governess never taught you."

Miss Hamblin was a weak opponent for the experienced courtesan. She blushed; the confidence she had shown when she entered the room began to waver. "I-I thought . . . you said something about meeting again to finish my portrait."

The situation was damnably awkward. Furious at being caught at doing nothing but looking guilty all the same, Mallory said with an edge to his voice, "There was no need to trouble yourself on my account. I was able to finish the picture in your absence."

He had never needed her. The invitation had been a ruse to see the countess. Mallory closed his eyes in agony. The sensation he was experiencing took a second to recognize. It was fear.

Messing rushed into the room. Blast his bloody hide for being less diligent about Miss Hamblin.

"Good. There you are, Messing. Why do you not escort Miss Hamblin to the drawing room?" Not caring if he was rude, Mallory took the meddlesome miss by the elbow and literally pushed her at his manservant. "Miss Hamblin, you deserve to view your portrait in the proper setting."

She opened her mouth to argue.

"I will join you shortly. It is there you may thank me for immortalizing your beauty. Though the pleasure was all mine." He shut the door on her and leaned against the wood.

Carissa clutched her heart and laughed. Spinning once, she could not seem to contain her amusement.

"Thank you," Mallory snarled. "I am thrilled my thorny predicament amuses you so. Do you know what kind of tale that young miss will spin? Or how many people she will tell?"

Laughing heartily, she said, "Oh, I can fathom a wicked guess or two."

His mind was already moving on to the countess's reaction to Miss Hamblin's version of what she had witnessed. "I am blameless, madam. You threw yourself at me!"

"Quite true. I will tell everyone that I instigated the kiss."

"No!" he said, even more horrified by what his former mistress might concoct. "Swear on all of your dead husbands' souls that you will not entertain anyone with the tale. The less said the better."

"I do not understand. You have never cared about gossip or anyone's opinion. It was one of the things I have always admired about you, *mon coeur.*"

"It is complicated," he said tersely.

"Ah," she replied; sadness chased away her initial amusement. "It is not anyone who concerns you, but someone. A particular someone."

Mallory remained silent.

"Some of the rumors I have heard are true then, no? You and the A'Court widow. I am surprised the little mouse had the courage to take on a big nasty wolf after being mauled by a lion."

"Your beauty fades when it takes on that greenish cast, Carissa."

"What do you see in such a woman? Her looks are passable, but what of her spirit? It was crippled by her husband's heavy fists. Is it her weakness that lures you? Do you find her vulnerability a challenge to your jaded nature?"

"Enough, Carissa. I have no need to explain myself to you or anyone." Mallory was unsure of his own feelings. He refused to allow his former mistress to twist his feelings for the countess into some kind of sick game.

"Love, forget A'Court's widow." Sensing she had his interest, she moved closer. "Forget the virgin. The seduction is sweet. However, the bedding is *pénible*." She tentatively stroked his chest. "Invite me back into your bed. I can become any kind of woman you desire. You do not have to hold back for me."

It was a tempting offer. His former mistress was known for her creativity and her fortitude. He believed her offer to be genuine.

It also left him indifferent.

"Carissa, my dear, a man is never so foolish as to offer up everything to a mistress. They tend to be greedy, irksome creatures."

She was the one who stepped away from him.

"There is no need to act like the woman betrayed," he said, annoyed that she was forcing him to be cruel. "No promises were spoken between us. You moved on to a new protector days after we broke. Do not blame me for his failings or yours."

"No, Mallory, I only blame you for *yours*."

He had the decency to wince at the accuracy of that stinging remark. "Was there a point to your visit?"

"Curiosity, I suppose," she said after a momentary pause. "You have changed, I think. I do not know if I like this new man."

"Once you are finished hating me and think on it, you will realize you never really liked the old one, either."

"Maybe you are right. For now, I will relish the hating, since you have left me nothing else." She opened the door. Messing stood nearby, holding her spencer and bonnet. Grimacing at the lack of privacy a competent servant afforded, she said, "I also came to offer you a warning."

"Carissa."

"Not me, *mon ami*," she said bitingly. "We are finished. I speak of another who despises you. Lord De Lanoy. He is in town this season and is asking questions about you. I thought you might be interested."

"Carissa!" Mallory called out to her. "Thank you."

The courtesan arched her brow. "Do not thank me. I hope he castrates you." She glided out of the room with Messing chasing her.

De Lanoy. Mallory had not seen the man in years. The gentleman could not be holding a grudge after all of these years for his stealing Mirabella away from him.

Dismissing the marquis from his thoughts, Mallory preferred to focus on more pertinent matters. How the hell was he going to keep Miss Hamblin from revealing what she had seen to Brook?

Chapter Twenty-Three

Madam Courroux's creation was spectacular. Tucked away in a private room, Brook stared at her reflection in the full-length looking glass. She had paid little attention to the cerulean fabric her mother had waved under her nose several weeks past. The dressmaker had transformed the bundle of fabric into an enchanting ball gown. Reverently Brook touched a floral swirl of seed pearls and sequins on the skirt. The seamstress must have been blind by the time she had finished. The bodice was daring and cut lower than Brook would have chosen for herself. The sleeves were short and puffy, with matching bows on each cuff. A bright yellow ribbon was tied under her bosom, the only relief from a sea of blue. It was the sort of gown that made every woman feel like a goddess.

"When I saw her at the theater, I could not believe my eyes."

"Did she truly believe everyone would forget what happened? What audacity! If she was sensible, she would slink out of town and burrow into whatever hole she has been hiding in."

The ongoing conversation between the two unidentified women froze Brook in place. The joy she had felt when viewing her gown had withered into numbness. It was rude to eavesdrop. The ladies could have been talking about another woman. Alas, Brook did not believe it.

"They say the new earl is offering for her once he has secured the dowager's blessing," one of the women confided.

"It will never happen. The old biddy disliked her then, and I doubt her precious son's demise has improved on her first opinion. She never approved of their marriage but indulged him for the prospect of having grandchildren."

"Some say she was too indulgent. The stories you hear."

"I disagree. You have to have affection for indulgence and there was always something cold about that family. The earl had many appetites and most of them were unsavory. Of course, did the little wife ever thank me for slaking his dark needs before he could stomach crawling into her virginal bed? No, the lady was too preoccupied playing his countess to realize her husband had secretly brought his mistress along on their wedding trip to Italy."

Brook doubled over at the woman's confession and gagged. Old wounds she had thought were healed reopened and bled freely. Suddenly the need to escape the shop rose within her until she thought she might scream for her release. Reaching behind, she tugged on the loosely tied laces and shook her shoulders free. She let the gown drop to the floor. Stepping out of it, she began working herself into her carriage dress.

"She ruined everything by getting pregnant. Do you think the foolish chit thought a child would soften his unpleasant disposition? I, too, had caught several of His Lordship's babes in my womb and I had the good sense to rid myself of the tiny complications before he learned of it."

"Do you like this color?" her companion asked, changing the subject.

Dressed, Brook leaned heavily against the door. She shoved her knuckles into her mouth. The action did not prevent the tears from flowing down her cheeks and into her mouth.

"Not for you, my dear. It makes your face sallow."

Brook's breathing was ragged as she fought not to break down into hysterics. Lyon's duplicity seared her heart. While he had offered Wynne Bedegrayne his ardent devotion for her being the perfect woman, he had kept a mistress to pleasure his body. What had Brook been to him? An indulgence, the other woman had said. A fragile butterfly he could plunge a pin into the heart of and tear her wings off one by one?

The door smacked her in the face, snapping her out of her stupor, as someone tried to open it. Wiping her eyes, Brook moved to the side. The two ladies poised at the threshold were startled to discover her in the room. She did not know the short dark-haired woman. However, Brook did recognize the tall, slender blonde. It appeared when Lyon chose a woman, certain characteristics appealed to him.

"A thousand pardons, my lady," the shorter woman said after a brief recovery. "We did not realize this room was occupied." She sent her friend a meaningful glance. "Come, Letty. We will seek out another room."

They closed the door. As they walked away, Brook heard the woman say, "Do you think she overheard us?"

"Do not fret about it, dear friend. The lady has all of London agog by her return. She could have spared herself this notoriety if she had stayed away. Do you know which certain gentleman has his name linked with hers?"

"Tell me!" the woman pleaded, with eagerness to hear the latest calumny.

They were too far from the door for Brook to hear the man's name.

"No!" The exclamation was followed by distant laughter.

The door swung open again.

"Daughter! Why, you are not dressed!" her mother said, moving past Brook. Mrs. Ludlow cried out when she saw the discarded ball gown on the floor. "I have raised you better than this." She scooped up the blue gown, handling it as if it were a foundling. "If the gown displeases you, just say so. There is not much time. Nevertheless, Madam Courroux will strive to accommodate your dictates." Draping the gown over her front, she critically studied it for flaws. "I do not understand your rashness, Brook. From all accounts, this gown suits your tastes and your coloring."

Brook was barely listening to her mother's prattle. It was taking all of her concentration to hold her composure. "The gown is fine, Mama," she assured her mother.

Mrs. Ludlow frowned at her image. "You do not think it requires lace at the bodice and hem?"

"No lace. I yield to Madam Courroux's refined opinion." Brook touched her head. The women's laughter still resounded in her head.

"I suppose you are correct," her mother said, pouting at her daughter's terseness.

The control she was exerting was causing her body to tremble. "Mama, I trust you to conclude our transaction with the dressmaker. I must leave you."

"What is this? Where are you going? You cannot just go wandering where you please, young lady!"

"The stale air in this room has made me ill. Whether I sit in the carriage or walk the street, I do not care, as long as I am not in this shop a second more." She could not abide having those women staring at her and whispering their secrets.

Finally, when Mrs. Ludlow had recognized that what she had perceived as temper was in fact illness, her brow furrowed with concern. "Of course I can handle Madam Courroux by myself. If you prefer, the coachman can take you directly home and return for me later."

She hugged her mother. "I do not deserve you, Mama."

Flattered by the display of affection, Mrs. Ludlow patted Brook's cheek and said, "What a nonsensical observation.

You deserve a great many things, Daughter, least of all a mother's love."

The lump in Brook's throat swelled, doubling in proportion. With a quick nod, she walked away from her mother. Grateful that she was blinded by the gleam of her tears, Brook briskly walked out of the shop. She did not have the heart to confess to her sweet mother that perhaps her daughter had gotten everything she had deserved, after all.

Mallory had gotten rid of one uninvited female. He hoped his luck held and the other would depart with less dramatics.

"Ah, the fair Miss Hamblin," he said, entering the drawing room. She set down her teacup and saucer and rose to greet him. He had taken the time to comb his hair and put on a clean coat. When he worked, he cared little about his appearance. After what Miss Hamblin had witnessed, Mallory was determined to win her approval. Bowing over her hand, he said, "Are you pleased with the portrait?"

"Your technique is flattering, Mr. Claeg," she said, returning to her position on the plump sofa.

"My model was inspiring."

Miss Hamblin visibly fought not to be charmed. Forcing a frown, she cleared her throat. "I do have some minor quibbles about your work."

The artist in him flared in indignation. "Do you?"

She seemed oblivious to the edge in his voice. "Almost too minor to mention, really. However, as I am so intimate with this particular work, it is difficult to set aside my criticism."

"Pray continue." If she had known him better, she would have recognized the danger and changed the subject.

Miss Hamblin rose and approached the picture. "For example, my eyes. The color is slightly off in hue. And the space between them too close."

He silently fumed. There was nothing wrong with the color or the distance. Mallory was seriously wondering if the vain Miss Hamblin was in need of a decent pair of spectacles. "Your face is perfection, my lady. Mayhap beyond my humble talents as an artist." He nearly choked on the false flattery.

"Oh," she said, covering her mouth with her gloved fingers. Some of his annoyance must have shown. "I meant no offense, sir. Honestly. I blame our too few meetings for these minor flaws. The strength of your work lies in your ability to paint from life. Recollections can be faulty."

So was her eyesight, but Mallory held his tongue. He wanted to endear himself, not make an enemy. "I hate displeasing a lady. After you leave I will prime the canvas with white lead and wipe out all trace of the imperfections."

Destroying her portrait had not been her goal. She had been searching for a way for them to spend time alone. "Oh no, that would hardly be fair. You put so much of yourself into your work. It would be criminal to deny the world your talent."

"It is flawed," he said flatly. He was willing to play her game.

"Minor. Very minor. So minor I doubt anyone will notice," she said, gazing at him earnestly. "Unless you think we should begin again?"

Mallory crossed his arms. "I regret I cannot take advantage of your generous offer, Miss Hamblin. My father's illness and other commitments prevent me from taking on new commissions."

"Is Mrs. Le Maye one of those commitments?" she slyly guessed.

"No. I have already painted Mrs. Le Maye's portrait. I seldom repeat a subject." Since the vindictive Carissa was hoping De Lanoy was planning to castrate him, he was keeping his distance from her.

"Is she your mistress?"

He gaped at her impertinence. "You are too young and sheltered to be asking such shameless questions. I think it

is time for you to leave." It would not hurt suggesting to
A'Court that he take a leather strap to his sister's backside.

"According to my sources, you and Mrs. Le Maye flaunted
your connection."

"Even if we did, I am not prepared to discuss the details
with you." Where were the chaperones, he wondered, when
young misses were free to discuss the gentlemen of the *ton*
and their mistresses? He did feel compelled for the sake of
clarity to add, "Though it is none of your concern, Mrs. Le
Maye and I no longer share an intimate friendship. If I hear
any tale to the contrary, then I will know who is to blame."

He supposed he looked downright intimidating to her, but
he was beyond caring. The infuriating chit had worn out his
patience.

"I am good at keeping secrets, Mr. Claeg," she said; the
manner in which she said it was a pealing bell in his head.

"There is no secret, Miss Hamblin," he insisted, feeling
the claws of desperation. "Whatever you think you glimpsed
when you walked into my painting room is riddled with mis-
assumptions."

"She wants you back."

So she had a better understanding than he had initially assumed. Tugging on a sleeve, he said, "She left disappointed."

With an expression too experienced for her tender years,
Miss Hamblin said, "I assumed as much. Mrs. Le Maye was
muttering French expletives when she left you."

He gained a new appreciation for the young woman's de-
viousness. "Eavesdropping is vulgar."

"Just viewing the departure of the vanquished," she said
blithely. "I truly do not know what you saw in a woman like
her. She was too obvious, in my opinion."

Mallory neither agreed nor disagreed. Sometimes that
was the only sensible option a man had when dealing with a
woman. He eyed her warily, like he would a snake that was
about to strike in his direction.

"I wanted to speak with you without Lady A'Court hovering around. Her presence prevented us from speaking freely."

He made a noncommittal noise in his throat. Mallory raised his brows quizzically when she daringly touched his wrist.

"I immediately saw through your machinations at Lough-wydde."

"How clever of you," he mused.

"The way you stared at me, your touch, and the cunning way you deceived my brother into giving his blessing for us to respectfully meet each other."

"How clever of me."

"I just wanted you to understand that I do not need to be seduced." She demurely lowered her head. "I may not have the experience of your former mistress. Still, I am yours for the taking."

Christ! He would genuinely be the bounder everyone purported him to be if he accepted Miss Hamblin's offer. "You do not know what you are offering," he said, feeling the weight of his years.

"Everyone knows of your preference for widows."

He covered his face with his hand. Each word she uttered made him feel vile. "If true, then you do not meet my expectations." Where was Messing when he needed him?

"I have reasoned this out," she said, pursuing him. "Widows appeal to gentlemen because they cannot accuse them of stealing their virtue. They have also sampled the marriage bed and are often eager to resume the lost pleasure."

He could not fault her logic. Hearing an innocent speak aloud his jaded thoughts was immensely disturbing. "Sound reasoning, do you not think? It also disqualifies you, Miss Hamblin." He opened the door and bellowed for his manservant.

"You are being shortsighted, Mr. Claeg. Ravishing an innocent should hold a novel appeal to someone of your expertise. I am unlike Miss Nost and her father. I am not trading my virtue for marriage. I am content to be your mistress."

For now.

It was one of the reasons that he preferred carrying on with widows. Many of the women he had bedded in the past were satisfied with the physical arrangement. Innocents like Miss Hamblin convinced themselves they were worldly creatures but like all children required the protection of tradition. That translated to marriage.

As he leaned against the door frame, Miss Hamblin took a bold step closer to him. He wanted to flinch when she caressed his cheek but that would have unmanned him. Rigidly he withstood her gentling caress.

"Compared to me, you are a child."

"I am two years younger than Lady A'Court. Her age does not seem to trouble you."

It was not the countess's age that troubled him; it was the lady herself. He doubted the young lady trying to lure him into an affair would appreciate the distinction. "You are an admirable, desirable siren, Miss Hamblin. Sacrificing your virtue on a notorious scoundrel is so much less than you warrant. Instead of aspiring to become an artist's mistress you should be applying that intellect toward capturing a worthy husband."

Her silence confirmed his worst fears. Despite her denials, Miss Hamblin had hoped the temptation of her body would seduce him into the notion of marriage. His relief was visible at his housekeeper's appearance.

"Mrs. Lane, your timing is impeccable. Miss Hamblin has finished viewing her portrait and pronounced it satisfactory. Could you alert her coachman that his lady is eager to depart?"

"But I am not," she protested.

The housekeeper switched her disapproving gaze from her employer to the young woman clutching his coat sleeve.

"Hmm," was all Mrs. Lane articulated before leaving them to see to her task.

Ignoring Miss Hamblin's arguments, Mallory hastened her down the stairs and out of the house. He had her seated in her carriage in what must have been record time.

Resigned that he was getting rid of her, Miss Hamblin said, "Just think about my offer." She wrapped her arms around him and kissed him on the mouth before he could escape. Pleased that she had managed to surprise him, she ordered her coachman to drive on.

A carriage passing in the opposite direction caught his eye. Brook proudly met his hunted gaze. She had witnessed Miss Hamblin's parting kiss. Looking beautifully fragile, she did not order her coachman to stop as he had expected. She just stared at him with her face tight with the pain of betrayal.

Brook!

He started to run after her. Mallory gave up after a half-dozen steps. Watching the back of her carriage fade in the distance, he wanted to howl at the injustice.

Wiping his mouth, he muttered an oath and stepped away from the dust the carriages had stirred. "Bloody perfect!" he sputtered, glaring at his somber housekeeper. "I did not encourage the brazen chit."

"You rarely have to, given your enthralling charm," she said so impassively, he suspected she was being sarcastic. "I thank God I am immune."

Chapter Twenty-Four

Brook was upset. Though her troubled mind was not mulling over the erroneous conclusions Mallory had most likely surmised. May's bald-faced pursuit of the gentleman might have unsettled Brook initially, but she had foreseen the embarrassing predicament. How he chose to handle the impetuous lady was his decision.

She ruthlessly squelched her parting image of the artist. Through the swirling dust he had tried to chase her passing carriage when she made no attempt to stop. He had mouthed her name. His wild brown hair was slipping its confining queue. There had been anguish in his light blue eyes that called to her, demanding that she wait for him. She had ignored the summons.

Instead of heading for the house, she had the coachman stop at a nearby hotel. If Mallory Claeg chose to seek her out, the Ludlows' town house was a logical starting point. She was irritated enough not to make the quest easy for him. Besides, she wanted some time alone to compose her thoughts. Strange how a large room filled with people could be the loneliest place.

The waiter, noticing she was alone, had respected her expressed wishes to be seated at a less-coveted table. She was not seeking recognition, nor did she feel the need to sit at a table befitting her title. Sipping the lemonade the waiter had brought her, Brook tried to banish Lyon's mistress's words from her thoughts.

Do you think the foolish chit thought a child would soften his unpleasant disposition? I, too, had caught several of His Lordship's babes in my womb and I had the good sense to rid myself of the tiny complications before he learned of it.

The lemonade surged over the side as she set the glass down. She had not been the first to conceive Lyon's child. It was a foolish endeavor to feel envious of the mysterious Letty. Neither she nor Lyon had wanted the children who had been created from their passion. Brook had desired those unrealized children, she thought with a pang. If her child had survived, she would have cherished him even while despising his sire.

"Lady A'Court. Am I intruding?"

Brook's visage was enigmatic while she tried to recall the gentleman's name. She easily recognized his square jaw and high forehead. His eyes were a pleasing dark blue with gold flecks. The muscles in his face were firm; only his eyes and the deep lines running from his nostrils to the corners of his mouth revealed his age. She guessed him to be somewhere in his early forties. One of her mother's acquaintances had introduced him the night they had attended the theater. Brook had been so anxious about seeing Wynne Milroy again that she had almost forgotten the encounter.

"Not particularly, my lord. I have spent the afternoon shopping and required a refreshment before I continued," she said; her excuse was as false as her smile.

He was well dressed and his speech bespoke an elevated education. If she was not still tottering from the revelation of Lyon's betrayal, she might have found him appealing. It was a flaw in her character, she dourly mused. Older gentlemen had brought her nothing but grief.

"You are attending the Haslake ball, I assume," he politely inquired.

"Yes. With everyone attending, the shopkeepers are over-whelmed." She lightly clasped her glass of lemonade, using it to anchor her.

"The coins weighing down their pockets are ample compensation for their troubles."

"I suppose so. Still, I am not used to crowds," she admitted.

His grin was sheepish. "You cannot recall my name, can you?"

She responded to his smile. Giving up the pretense, she said, "No, my lord. My recollection of names is embarrassingly transitory."

"Avery Hitchons, Marquis De Lanoy, my lady." He accepted her hand and bowed. "We were introduced—"

"I recall the meeting, my lord. I have just returned to town and the list of names I am required to memorize is longer than my arm." The gentleman's friendly demeanor prompted her to say, "Would you care to join me or are you with friends?"

"If you have no objections, I would enjoy your company. My companions are late in their arrival and I detest sitting alone. It makes me feel like a one-eyed dwarf with red hair." She burst into giggles at the idea. As he recalled that she was also alone, he grimaced at his rambling candor. He tugged on his cravat as if it were strangling him. "That is not to say that sitting alone does not have its own advantages."

"Please, my lord. There is no need to dissemble on my behalf. I detest being on display." She encompassed with a gesture her tiny table stuffed between the wall and some overwatered shrubbery. "Hence my enviable view of the kitchens."

Lord De Lanoy chuckled and sat down in the chair across from her. "It appears we are kindred spirits, madam." Pausing while the waiter poured him a glass of lemonade and refilled hers, he used the silence to admire her. "How fortuitous," he said after they were alone again. "That your thirst and my companions' tardiness brought us together." He held up his glass and she clinked hers against his in a toast. "To fate."

"Fate," she murmured back. The marquis' presence had calmed her faster than any private lecture she could have given herself.

She noticed he had kept his walking stick. Odd, since most gentlemen surrendered them with their hats. He positioned it upright, tapping it occasionally on the floor to punctuate his words.

"I have been traveling, Lady A'Court, and have been absent from London for several seasons."

"Where did your travels take you?"

"Jamaica for a year to oversee a new investment. Virginia and New York because I had never been to America," he explained. "You have also been absent from London, I am told."

She brought her glass to her lips and sipped. The tart refreshment did not ease the tightness in her throat. "Yes. It seemed best to retire after my husband died."

Compassion shimmered in the marquis' eyes. "Forgive me. This—the earl's death—was mentioned to me. It seemed uncouth to bring up such a grievous subject."

"No, I have had two years to reconcile myself to my loss. My family agreed, which is why they encouraged me to join them." There was no point in explaining that she had been bullied and blackmailed into the decision.

"However, you are unhappy."

She circled the rim of the glass with her finger. "Partly. If you know of my husband's death, then you are aware that he perished in an unfortunate accident."

"Yes," he kindly replied. "Violent deaths often involve the participants in scandal. Returning to where it began must be very disconcerting for you."

She found comfort in his presence. He seemed genuinely

interested in her and nonjudgmental regarding her choices. "I
thought I had given myself time to heal, had prepared myself
to face the rumors about my husband. I have learned since
my return that I truly did not know the man I was married to,
nor is anyone willing to let me forget the mistake in marrying
him." She could not fathom why she had confessed her inner
thoughts aloud.

The marquis reached over and encircled his hands over
her hands, which were clutching her lemonade. "Loss affects
all of us differently. No one should be allowed to judge which
path is the correct one to walk. You are a remarkable woman,
Lady A'Court."

"Ho, De Lanoy!" a gentleman called out.

They both turned to acknowledge the greeting. A gentleman slightly older than the marquis and a red-haired woman
stood waiting at a respectable distance. Fashionably attired,
the woman was taller than her companion, and there was a
marked difference in their ages. They did not seem inclined
to join their friend, nor did Marquis De Lanoy invite them
closer.

He released Brook's hands and sat back. "Would you care
to join our table, my lady? My companions will not care.
They always enjoy making new friends."

If the offer was made out of politeness, he gave it warmth
by sincere expression. She was flattered by his attempt to extend their acquaintance.

"You are kind, my lord. Regrettably, I must decline. I must
finish my errands if I want to attend the Haslake ball." He
stood and walked around to her side so he could pull out her
chair. Rising, she gifted him with a slight smile. "Thank you
for listening."

"My pleasure," he said, tapping his walking stick twice
on the flooring. "I look forward to our next meeting."

"As do I, my lord," she said, allowing him to bow over her
hand. He looked up and caught her staring at their clasped

hands. The blue in his eyes was so clear she could count the gold flecks in the depths.

"I am a great believer in fate, Lady A'Court. I predict you and I are destined to be very good friends."

Entering Sir Thomas Bedegrayne's town house was akin to treason in his mother's estimable opinion. Mallory had no quarrel with the Bedegrayne patriarch. Once, their families had been bound together in friendship. Rivalry and petty disputes had divided his father and the old Bedegrayne. Mallory had thought his sister marrying into the family would have mended the breach between the two families. Sir Thomas had seemed willing to put aside their differences. However, Mallory's parents were less forgiving. He pitied Amara, for she was the one who was hurt most by the discord.

The butler did not react to Mallory's name when he offered it. He simply escorted Mallory through a maze of halls to the conservatory. Bedegrayne was not alone. The scene looked more like an intimate family gathering than a business meeting. Brock and his father were seated at a wrought-iron table playing cards. Amara was also present. A three-year-old boy clutched both of her hands. Tipping his head back, the child was giggling as she stepped side to side while he stood on her shoes. Another young woman moved into sight as she carried a potted plant to a makeshift worktable. The raven-haired beauty was muttering to herself. Mallory did not know her intimately. The Bedegrayne men, not to mention her steely-eyed older brother, Viscount Tipton, would have had something to say about him befriending Miss Madeleina Wyman.

Amara noticed him first. He responded to her joyful smile with an identical one. "Mallory. No one told me you were coming for a visit." She lumbered toward him, her young charge in front of her.

He shot the Bedegrayne men a questioning glance. "It

came as a surprise to me, too, puss." He kissed her on the cheek. "Who is this scamp?" It was a game they played together.

"I'm Lucien Gorgon Thomas Wyman," the boy said, grinning up at him.

He was a beautiful boy. Angelic, really, with his blond locks and gray eyes. It was difficult to believe Tipton was his sire. "Someone actually named this poor child Gorgon? You have my sympathies."

Swinging in Amara's arms, he giggled. "Gorgon."

"He is saying Gordon. Luc has troubles with his *d*s," Brock dryly said, setting the cards in his hand aside. Sensing his wife was tiring from their play, he got out of his chair and picked up his nephew. Brock tossed the boy over his shoulder and let him hang upside down.

"Bedegrayne, you are a natural with children," Mallory quipped. The position must have been part of their usual play. The boy let his arms dangle, perfectly content to have all of the blood in his body rush to his head. "I predict the overprotective mother here might allow you to hold your daughter when she is old enough to run away."

"Not fair," Amara protested. "Who says I will be overprotective?"

"Instinct. With Bedegrayne as her father, she will need it."

Heeding Lucien's pleas, Brock flipped him around and let him do a headstand. "What brings you here to Bedlam? Has something happened to Lord Keyworth?"

"No. Father is improving each day," Mallory promised his sister, since her husband's question alarmed her. "Good evening, Sir Thomas. My apologies for arriving late. I was out of the house when the messenger delivered your note." He had spent hours searching London for the countess. She had not returned home as he had hoped she would. Frustrated and maddened by what she had perceived as his sins, he had done what most gentlemen did when their lady was angry. He went to the nearest jeweler to find a bauble to placate her.

"Claeg, it is good to see you, sir," Sir Thomas said in a low, gruff voice. "We were sorry to hear about your father's illness. Please pass on my best regards to your dear mother."

"I will, sir. Thank you."

Built like a grizzly bear, the intimidating man with the booming voice had lost his beloved wife twenty years earlier. He had raised his children in the best manner a grieving father could and chosen not to remarry. Rumor had it that occasionally one of the older ladies of the *ton* tried to entice the baronet, but he had remained devoted to his Anna.

"Maddy! Quit dawdling in the dirt and come pay your respects to Mr. Claeg," the older man ordered. Mallory watched Brock and Amara exchange private looks. Only Sir Thomas was able to get away with bullying Miss Wyman in such a manner.

She had been fourteen when her mother's death had placed her in her older brother's household. The young woman who was wielding a sharp-looking trowel was almost nineteen. If she shared any traits with Tipton it was her stubbornness and temper.

"I never dawdle in the dirt, Papa," she said sweetly testing the edge of her tool. Amara had once told Mallory that Sir Thomas had been a soothing influence on the frightened, defiant girl, compared to Tipton's threatening tactics. In those early months after her arrival, Bedegrayne and the young girl had formed a lasting bond. He had become an adopted father for her, easing the bittersweet pain of watching his daughters leave his protection. "I was repotting the Spanish broom I gave you. You should sack your gardener."

Since the plants in the conservatory had become a hobby of sorts to Sir Thomas, the gardener she was referring to was the old man himself.

"Blast you, gel. I was getting it done in my own way. Do you not have half of London under your fingernails? Must you poke them into my pots?" he bellowed.

"Up," Lucien demanded of his uncle. If the scamp did not have a headache, Mallory would have been surprised. He was getting a mild one just observing the boy.

"Quick, Luc, have your Aunt Maddy show you her pots before she breaks one of them over your grandfather's head," Brock said, sparing them the angry rebuttal.

"Aunt Mag!" the boy exclaimed to no one in particular.

"Come with me, my sweet boy," Miss Wyman said, crouching down and opening her arms so her nephew could run into them. She wrapped them around his tiny frame and carried him off. "I will teach you the proper way to pot Spanish broom. Then you can show your *granga* how to do it," she said, using Luc's word for *granddad*. As they strode away, their voices faded into indistinguishable murmurs.

"I cannot imagine your dawdling in the dirt, Sir Thomas," Mallory said, earning the flinty stare that had made lesser men twitch.

"It's a quiet way of spending time," he said, deliberately raising his voice so Miss Wyman could overhear him. " 'Course, it's only soothing when I don't have the gel fussing over me."

"I am surprised the police have not carried you off." She said nothing more. The young woman knew how to use silence to rile the patriarch.

Mallory wondered privately if Miss Wyman might be interested in meeting Gill. His mysterious apprentice could use a lady's influence. The garden nymph had benefited from the Bedegrayne polish without it ruining her uniqueness.

"And why is that?" Sir Thomas eventually replied, swallowing her bait whole.

"You have murdered your yellow azalea," she retorted.

Satisfied with having the last word, she returned her attention to Lucien.

"Sir Thomas, why send a messenger to my brother?" Amara asked, subtly distracting him.

"When I was at my club, I saw something in the betting book that might interest you," the baronet said shrewdly.

Mallory could not conceive how anything in a betting book would concern him. "Really. What?"

"It concerns a certain widow." The baronet nodded to Brock. "The lad here says you have an eye out for Lady A'Court."

All secrets, it appeared, were fair game to family.

Mallory gave Brock a surly look. "I do not recall making any grand confessions, Bedegrayne."

"No, you just acted like you wanted to heave A'Court over the balcony for sitting with his cousin."

The earl was aspiring to marry Mallory's new mistress. It would make any gentleman disagreeable. Naturally, he had the sense not to offer up that grumbling excuse in front of his sister, so he said defensively, "The man was bullying the lady. I was just doing my part in helping Amara's friend."

He was not convincing anyone.

"Brother," Amara said, taking her husband's place at the table. "Your exchanges with Brook hint at a familiarity I cannot fathom. She told me that she had been residing at Loughwydde. Did you encounter her during your excursions to Cornwall?"

Three pairs of eyes were watching him so closely, he doubted he could concoct a passable lie. "The area is not so vast. The countess and I have met a time or two."

"You never said a word about it. Even knowing I was worrying about her."

He bravely faced his sister's ire. "She extracted my oath,

Amara. Are you planning to censure me for honoring a friend's request?"

She bit her lower lip and held her tongue. His silence had been laudable; she just did not like that she had been excluded.

Mallory returned his attention to Sir Thomas. "You read something in your betting books about Brook? It is no secret that the new A'Court covets her hand in marriage." Not while he was still breathing, he thought with uncharacteristic violence on his mind.

"No, this was not about A'Court," the baronet denied, freeing the air in Mallory's lungs. "Some jackass wrote down in the book that Marquis De Lanoy would claim A'Court's widow as his mistress within the month. There are several entries after it from members accepting the wager. If we can figure out who made the initial entry we can send Reckless Milroy after him to pound some respect into him for a lady's virtue. The fighter has some experience in such matters."

While Sir Thomas proposed schemes to reveal the guilty member, Mallory's thoughts focused on De Lanoy. Was it just a swaggering boast or had De Lanoy met the countess? If the marquis had discovered his interest in the lady, he might have decided to avenge himself for Mirabella by seducing the lady Mallory considered his. He would kill De Lanoy if he chose such a dangerous path for vengeance.

"Forget about digging up your old dueling pistols," Brock told his father. "You might accidentally shoot one of the servants."

"Or your foot," Miss Wyman added, clearly listening to their exchange.

"Bah, I was a fine marksman in my day."

"Your eyes were younger," Brock replied. "Besides, Claeg has more sense than to challenge an old rival because some sot scribbled a childish dare."

Seething about De Lanoy's plot to steal the countess from him, Mallory could think of nothing to assure the Bedegraynes.

Brock sighed. "Or I could be wrong."

Chapter Twenty-Five

"Stay away from De Lanoy."

Brook had managed to avoid Mallory for two days before he had cornered her at Lady Malion's garden party and issued his inane threat. The lady had spent an exorbitant amount of money to restore the old gardens and she had invited several hundred of her dearest friends to admire the efforts.

"Who told you about the hotel?"

"Hotel?" He seemed to grow larger in his fury. "You met him at the hotel when you dream of every excuse to avoid me in public?"

"It was merely chance. We sipped lemonade in front of a room filled with witnesses. It was all very sordid. I am astounded no one printed an announcement in the papers." Brook did not care what he thought. She was the one who should be angry. When she needed him to comfort her, he was standing on the street kissing May Hamblin.

"There is no need for sarcasm," he said, striving to keep his voice calm so that no one paid attention to them admiring the laurel hedges. "Just follow my dictates."

"Or what? You are not my father or my husband. There are no consequences, Mr. Claeg," she sneered, using his surname to provoke him.

"Defy me, Countess, and I will give you a wagonload of

consequences. Starting with my hand paddling your luscious backside."

He looked like he wanted to throttle her rather than paddle her backside. Neither threat worried her. "I am not afraid of you."

His light blue eyes blazed with unholy light. "Come closer so I may convince you."

She was courting danger challenging him in such a public manner, but he was being ridiculous about a lonely gentleman who had treated her with kindness and respect. Brook stepped closer.

Mallory closed his eyes. Shaking off some of the anger, he said, "Why do I admire you when you are doing your best to provoke me?"

"A few minutes ago, I reasoned out that you were insane." She grinned up into his face, completely disarming him.

"I must be for letting you get away with it." His expression told her he wanted to be alone with her. A second later, he was dragging her away from the other guests. He chose a flowering bush to conceal them.

"Why were you meeting strange gentlemen at hotels, Countess?"

He had inadvertently given her the opening she needed without sounding like a jealous harpy. "Well, you were my first choice. Unfortunately, you were too busy kissing Miss Hamblin, so I rejected the notion."

Mallory covered his eyes as if in pain. It was cruel, but she liked the flash of fear she glimpsed before he recovered. "A'Court should have a chat with his sister about offering her virtue to known scoundrels. It is fortunate I have my hands full of you." He grabbed her to him and pressed a possessive kiss on her mouth.

"May offered to become your mistress?" Brook was about to issue a few threats herself with this latest revelation.

"Do not fret. I have developed a preference for demure blondes."

"Oh, that was your twin brother who was kissing the brazen chit?"

Her words caused him to grin wickedly. "She ambushed me. It was you I wanted to chase after, not Miss Hamblin." He nuzzled her hair with his chin. "I swear."

"I believe you."

His relief was palpable. "I was prepared to be more convincing, mayhap grovel if it were required."

"A lovely suggestion. Let us save it for later when I can savor it."

He kissed her again. This time softly. "I have not changed my opinion about De Lanoy. Avoid the man."

"Mallory, I have encountered the gentleman on several occasions and he has been civil. He is certainly not the sort of man who grabs a lady and drags her into the bushes so he can steal a kiss."

"No, he is the other sort who might use a trusting widow to gain his revenge on the gentleman who married his favorite mistress!"

Finally, he had managed to rattle her. The light, mocking derision that had her looking down her nose at him vanished from her face.

"Marquis De Lanoy was Mirabella's protector?" An endearing dimple appeared as she furrowed her brow in concentration. "I do not recall you ever mentioning his name."

"I may have not. I am not particularly proud of my dealings with the gentleman." He had been an arrogant, boastful bastard, drunk on the reckless passion of his and Mirabella's stolen love.

"Many years have passed since you and Mirabella created a small scandal by running off to Gretna Green. The gentleman

I met did not seem to harbor any ill will toward anyone. Nor did he mention you."

Mallory had no inclination to argue over the man's integrity. "And you are an excellent judge of a man's character? Lest you forget, madam, your flesh bears the scars resulting from your high opinion of another monster."

She sputtered at his callous remark. Before he could apologize, she said, "How true. The fact I am standing here with you is another hallmark of my stupidity." She glared at his offending hand when he halted her flight. "Let me pass."

"Damned inflexible woman! I am trying to protect you from being hurt by my past." He thought about revealing what Sir Thomas had told him about the betting book in his club and then discarded the notion. Her disposition was too unpredictable at the moment. Further provocation might have her packing her belongings and returning to Loughwydde.

"If I heed you on this, sir, where does it end? From your telling, I would have to avoid half of England's inhabitants in order for you to shield me from your past wickedness."

Mallory took her sword thrust of righteousness without uttering a sound. It was a bloodless wound, but the poison of her words coursed through him.

"Brook, there you are," Wynne Milroy said, pretending that she had not overheard her friend's outrageous comment about his past. "Lady Malion told me you were out here. She did not mention your escort. It is good to see you again, Mr. Claeg."

"Good afternoon, Mrs. Milroy," he said in an abrupt manner. Although the lady possessed all the traits that made the Bedegraynes a handsome clan, it was not the first time that Mallory had marveled over the former Lord A'Court's folly for coveting the wrong woman. The countess was definitely more appealing than the ethereal blonde.

As she sensed her timely appearance had effectively stalled out their argument, Wynne Milroy's pale green eyes reflected her cheerfulness. "Mr. Claeg, perhaps I can impose upon you."

"You may try."

Undeterred by his surly tone, she continued, "Most of your historical paintings have strong themes involving women."

"Mr. Claeg cannot resist women," Brook said, her face sorrowful with regret. "It is in his blood. Like a fatal disease."

Mrs. Milroy pursed her lips to hide the irresistible impulse to smile. "Your work is remarkable, my lord. I had hoped you might persuade my husband to model for a future endeavor. Mayhap your representation of Hercules? His physique is most impressive."

"What is your husband's position toward your latest scheme, madam?" Mallory relished the notion of working with the retired fighter. He could see Reckless Milroy as Hercules or even a weary Titan Atlas.

"If he objects, give me time. I will convince him. I feel it is my duty to preserve his magnificent shoulders for the forthcoming generations."

Reconciled that he no longer had the privacy to extract the countess's oath to avoid De Lanoy, Mallory bowed. "It seems we share a mutual aspiration, Mrs. Milroy. I will go speak to your husband."

"Excellent."

He bowed over Brook's hand. "Do not disappoint me, Countess." With a parting scowl, he turned on his heel.

"I have a surprise for you, Brook," he heard Mrs. Milroy confide to her friend. "Keanan was able to convince his half-brother to join us. It was a formidable task, I can assure you. The man prefers his business ledgers to polite society these days, since he inherited the Reckester title. And he is still unmatched. Was he not one of your admirers the season you were brought out?"

Mallory stopped, wanting to hear her response. He gritted his teeth at the notion of Reckester courting his countess. The handsome rake had a reputation for seducing women that almost equaled his!

"I believe so," was Brook's hesitant reply.

"Well, you are twice as beautiful now as you were then. I think you should remind the Duke of your admirable qualities. Just think. If the man has any sense we might become sisters!"

Not if he stopped the meddling Mrs. Milroy. He started back toward the two women.

"Mr. Claeg. What providence has brought us together this day?"

Mallory stilled at the feminine voice. The throaty, almost lyrical tone stirred flashes of old memories and past nightmares. Milroy was forgotten. The lecture Mallory had been intending to deliver to the countess would have to be postponed. Flashing a charming grin, he greeted the lady he had pursued through the dim passageways of the King's Theatre before she had vanished.

"Mrs. Henning. Well, well . . . you were never one to lack nerve. I suppose that is why you were always managing to surprise me."

Brook discreetly observed Mallory as he chatted with an unidentified woman. Something about her was vaguely familiar. One thing was apparent. He knew her, Brook thought, disgusted at his never-ending popularity. Sleek like a thoroughbred, the woman exuded an erotic thrall that made Brook feel plain ordinary. Her quivering lower lip betrayed her hurt feelings when he placed his hand on the woman's arm and strolled out of sight. She was never allowing the horrid man to touch her ever again!

"What are you doing here?"

Mrs. Edda Henning gave him a coy glance. "Like many of the guests here, I have come to see Lady Malion's gardens."

They strolled down the stone path, which led to a man-made pond. Mallory stepped off the path. Picking up a small stone, he sent it skipping across the water's surface. His companion remained on the stone path. Mindful that the hem of her skirts was likely to become soiled, she kept lifting them slightly to adjust their position.

"Do not act dense, Mrs. Henning. I long ago credited you with intelligence. A pity I cannot claim the same for myself."

Unperturbed by his hostility, she allowed her gaze to slide over him admiringly. "You have benefited from the passing years, sir. Mr. Henning has not been so fortunate. Last winter a lung fever weakened him."

"And here I thought it would be some angry gentleman granting my fondest wish by discharging a dueling pistol at him. A shame. Henning always did have Satan's own luck for escaping the aftermath of his mischief."

Her dark eyes were liquid with compassion. "You are still bitter after all of these years."

Mallory made a rude noise. "Thinking of Mirabella moldering in her cold grave tends to sour my disposition."

She risked ruining her hem by moving to the edge of the pond. He whipped the stone in his hand with such ferocity that it sank immediately. "Mr. Claeg, no one, not even you, could have predicted that your wife would meet a tragic end," she said, seemingly earnest to convince him.

Most of her red hair was tucked under her stylish bonnet. The few tendrils that were free teased her rosy cheek. She had barely changed. He could understand why Henning had picked her to be his wife.

She sadly lowered her gaze. "Do you blame me? Is it because we were . . ." Edda Henning struggled to find a polite word to describe the blind rutting frenzy of their joining. He held up a warning hand to silence her. She ignored the curt command. ". . . because we were intimate the day your lady died?"

"It was a mistake," he said flatly. The vague recollections of the encounter had always troubled him. They aroused him in his dreams and made him angry when he was fully awake. "I have never been clear on how I ended up in your bed at all."

"Now you are being deliberately insulting," she said with a brief laugh. "How I have missed your wit, my lord."

The lady was up to something. "Spare me the nostalgia, madam. I am assuming that your husband orchestrated our tender reunion. What has changed? You and Henning have been calculatingly elusive since I glimpsed you both at the theater."

"Forgive me for being so mysterious. Seeing you at the theater so unexpectedly that evening startled me. I, too, have memories of the night Mirabella died in your arms. I was uncertain of your reaction, so I chose the coward's path and ran."

"Why seek me out now, Mrs. Henning? I no longer participate in those vulgar games you play with your guests. Being covered in Mirabella's blood cured me of such destructive vices."

"My lord, can you not believe we were changed, too, by your wife's death? Mr. Henning gave up his exclusive gatherings."

"So you have been living the fat squire's life since we parted," he said, unconvinced that someone like Henning could shed his perversions like a snake sheds its skin.

Her playful expression begged him to share her amusement. "Not exactly. My husband decided that we should spend some time abroad."

The soulless bastard must have been worried about Mallory exacting retribution for Mirabella's death to bundle himself and his wife abroad for a few years. If Mallory had not been consumed with self-recriminations about his own part, he might have given life to Henning's fears.

The land around them brightened as the drifting clouds

parted, revealing the sun. Edda Henning opened up her parasol in defense. "Contrary to what you might think, my husband is no villain. You are a fair man, Mr. Claeg. Why do you not join us for a late supper? You will see for yourself that your false impression was formed from the extraordinary circumstances."

He did not trust what he might do if he were forced to sit across a table from Henning. "I must decline your generous invitation."

Her lovely visage showed her disappointment. "Very well. I will not attempt to persuade you."

In his mind, he saw a hazy vision of them together. Her hair was unbound and she was sitting on his lap. She was holding a goblet to his lips, encouraging him to drink. When he turned away, she poured the wine over her bare breast and invited him to imbibe. Yes, the lady could be persuasive. "It is a pointless endeavor, madam." Mallory had spent the last few years thwarting his reckless tendencies. He had not always succeeded. The countess was living proof of that. However, it cost him nothing to refuse Edda Henning.

"Oh, I disagree," she countered. Something in her expression reminded him of the woman of the past, not the proper-lady pretense she had donned with her dress. "Convincing you might have proven diverting for both of us."

Chapter Twenty-Six

Brook stared at the cerulean ball gown the maid had pressed and laid out on her bed. It was so beautiful. She despised everything it represented. The notion of feigning an illness to avoid the Haslakes' ball was immensely appealing.

"Brook!"

Hearing the excitement in her mother's voice, Brook groaned and covered her face with her hands. She listened as Mrs. Ludlow's rushed footfalls approached her door. There was no hope of evading this ball. Her mother had placed her high ambitions on the event reestablishing Brook's place in polite society.

"Mama, you have not finished dressing," she observed upon her mother's entrance.

"Do not worry about that." She held out a jeweler's leather case. "This is for you."

Brook accepted the wide, flat case, moved by her mother's generosity. "Mama, this was unnecessary. Although I relinquished my claim on the A'Court family jewels immediately after Lyon's death, I do have what you and Papa have given me through the years. There are also several fine pieces that I have inherited from my sire."

She did not add that Elthia, Lady A'Court, had sent her solicitor to Brook a day after Lyon's death and demanded that her daughter-in-law hand over all of the A'Court family jewelry. Still suffering from the heartache of losing her baby and being betrayed by her husband, Brook had surrendered even the jewelry Lyon had purchased for her. She had wanted nothing to remind her of the lie she had endured.

"Oh no, dear, this is not from Mr. Ludlow and me. This was just delivered by messenger for you."

Since a mysterious jeweler's case was just too tempting for her mother's inherent curiosity, Brook said wryly, "And I suppose you could not resist a tiny peek." She placed the leather case on her dressing table and fumbled with the clasp.

"Only the briefest glimpses, I swear. Hurry and open it!"

She opened the lid and uttered a soft sound of approval.

Mrs. Ludlow peered over Brook's shoulder and beamed. "Who would believe he of all people would send you a matched set? And an elegantly appropriate *en suite* at that."

Nestled on a luxuriant bed of velvet rested a double-strand pearl choker. Picking up the necklace, Brook admired the luster of the pearls, which had been carefully matched for their size and color.

"Take a look at the earrings," her mother urged.

The size and unique shape of the pearls made them a prize any woman would treasure. A pearl, about the size of a fox's eye, was designed to lie on the earlobe. Attached by tiny gold rings from behind, a two-inch pear-shaped pearl dangled.

"Here, allow me to assist you."

She stood patiently while her mother secured the clasp of the choker. Her fingers stroked the bracelet, a delicate miniature of the necklace. "This is too costly. Ham should not have bothered." She had to remind herself that he was still waiting for her consent to his marriage proposal. Perhaps the pearls were a bribe to hasten her decision.

Mrs. Ludlow gasped and covered her mouth with her hand. "Did I not give you the card? The jewelry is not from Lord A'Court." She searched the pocket of her dressing gown. "Where did I put it?" she muttered, distracted by her search.

"Who sent it?"

"Ah, here it is."

Brook accepted the note and quickly read the lazy scrawl of cursive writing:

Trust can be likened to a pearl, Countess. To wholly realize its value, it must be nurtured slowly. Is it not fortuitous that I am a patient man?

Yrs,
M.C.

Mallory had sent her the pearl jewelry. She had not seen him since he had warned her to stay away from Lord De Lanoy and then walked off with another woman. The man completely bewildered her. "Well, this only reaffirms my opinion. Mr. Claeg should not be sending me costly gifts."

"It appears the gentleman is courting you. How wonderful!"

"Mama! Mr. Claeg is not courting me," Brook protested. He had never proposed a respectable arrangement, just a convenient one. Unless, she amended privately to herself, she was miraculously carrying his child. "I cannot keep this jewelry. Accepting his gifts will only encourage him."

This argument did not dissuade Mrs. Ludlow. Reaching for an earring, she beckoned for her daughter to present her ear. "Though I believe Ham would make a better husband for you, since you share similar temperaments, one must not dismiss Mr. Claeg. He is the Keyworth heir. With his father's health failing he may be viscount sooner than expected."

There was no malice in Mrs. Ludlow's heart when she spoke so casually of Lord Keyworth's demise. She simply viewed herself as practical. Admiring the earring she had attached to Brook's earlobe, she said, "Pearls suit you, my dear."

Brook attached the second earring herself. Straightening,

she studied her reflection in the mirror. She concurred with her mother's opinion. The pearls seem to glow against her complexion. Mallory had discerning taste for choosing the appropriate gewgaws. *He must have had a great amount of experience,* an insidious voice in her head whispered tauntingly. She thought of the endless number of past mistresses who had preceded her and the women who were likely to follow her. Some of the admiration in her face faded at the thought.

"It would not be honorable to accept his gift. I have no intention of marrying."

Ever.

"Naturally you will marry again. Your income is too modest for you to be content with the rural seclusion it will force you to maintain. Marriage would provide you with a gentleman's protection and children. Brook, dearest, you cannot tell me that you do not desire to have children?"

She picked up the bracelet and rubbed the pearls against her lips. "You are wrong, Mama. Marrying Lyon denied me both."

Mallory paced at the bottom of Keyworth's staircase awaiting his mother. She had sent him a note three hours earlier stating her desire for him to escort her to the Haslake ball. An ill husband would never prevent the viscountess from attending one of the season's larger balls.

He looked up at the murmur of voices coming from the above landing. With her maid following behind her, Lady Keyworth made her entrance, which was worthy of a queen.

"Mother, I will be the envy of all the gentlemen." He dutifully took her hand and kissed it.

Used to his debonair spirit and not believing there was a dram of sincerity in her wicked son, Lady Keyworth accepted his compliment with a nod. "I am pleased you have chosen appropriate attire."

He quirked a brow. "Did you expect to find smudges of paint on my shirtsleeve?"

"Or on your hands."

"Sweet Mother, why do you think I wear gloves?" he teased, earning a reproachful stare.

"You are letting your hair grow too long," she fretted minutes later when he removed his hat in the family coach.

He shifted in the seat so he could stretch his long legs out. "I manage to keep from dipping the ends in my paint pots."

"The fashionable styles lean toward the classical." At his wordless reply she tried appealing to his vanity. "A shorter length would strengthen your jaw."

His long hair was an old argument. Mallory yawned. "Not a wise choice. I might poke someone in the eye with it."

She huffed. "You have no intention of heeding my advice."

"None," he replied pleasantly.

"Can you think only of yourself? The other day Lady Buttrey made the observation that your hair reminded her of a savage. I was exceedingly embarrassed. Your eccentricities invite comment."

Mallory tugged on the neat queue that was so irritating to the viscountess. He did not like the notion of Lady Buttrey with her fantasies of showing him her private art collection having intimate conversations with his mother. "It was rude of the lady to comment on me at all. Since you are the duchess of propriety, I pray you put the chit in her place."

"How could I?" she wailed, unhappy that he was finding fault in her actions. "It is you who continue to place me in these awkward predicaments. The next time I receive her card I may very well send Buckle out to tell her the family is not at home."

It was a decision that had Mallory's enthusiastic approval. He settled back into his comfortable slouch. "Do not place high value on Lady Buttrey's opinion. Her predilections are too Philistine for a Claeg."

She slipped into a bewildered silence while she debated whether his remark was praise or an insult to the family. Mallory had made similar accusations toward his mother and father.

"Besides," he drawled lazily, "some discriminating ladies of the *ton* find your wayward son appealing." He was thinking fond thoughts of the countess. She liked how his long hair tickled her face.

Lady Keyworth's eyes narrowed into mere slits. It was clear he had not inherited his appreciation of absurdity from his mother. "Mrs. Le Maye is not someone I would consider discriminating. In fact, some have said that in regards to gentlemen she has little preference at all."

He tried not to flinch under her icy stare. "She is very particular about money." And she highly prized the skills of her lover. It seemed prudent not to mention the latter.

Her face reddened. "I do not care about the woman's preferences. I care about your connection to the courtesan."

"I suppose with Father's illness and all, it has been almost impossible to keep up with all of the current gossip."

"Do not mock me, Mallory."

"I dare not. You might lock me in my bedchamber and deny me supper." It was his mother's favorite punishment for wayward children. No doubt, Amara had endured an empty stomach on countless occasions. He stilled her scathing retort with a gesture. "Mother, your concern about Mrs. Le Maye is belated. Seasons have passed since our parting."

The revelation mollified her slightly. Still she could not resist pushing her observations on him. "I know I have no say in who you choose for companionship."

"On this we agree."

"Your father tells me to close my eyes to your scandalous mistresses. Nevertheless, I must speak my piece."

"The drive to the Haslakes' town house might seem quicker if you do not."

"The women you choose to consort with are beneath you."

"Not always," he denied. "The same position becomes tedious when overdone."

"Mallory Claeg!" she thundered. "I do not want to hear the details of your lewd wantonness. By God, must you turn everything into a jest?"

"I must."

He laughed at her shriek.

Telling her how holding on to his laughter had saved his sanity after Mirabella's death would be pointless. His marriage had been the ultimate effrontery. Her death had probably been a relief to his mortified parents.

The coach slowed to a halt. Now began the endless caravan of coaches inching their wheels toward the Haslakes' town house. Mallory felt obliged to hand her an olive branch. No man withstood the stony silence of his mother for any great length.

"I promised Lord Keyworth that I would look after you. It will be an impossible feat if you rebuff me all evening."

She stared out the window. "Do not exert yourself. I can look after myself."

The coach lurched forward and then abruptly stopped. Mallory's teeth snapped together in frustration. He was bound by his word. Otherwise, he would have just opened the door and horrified his mother further by walking to the Haslakes' front door.

He slumped back into his seat and pretended to sleep.

Chapter Twenty-Seven

"Brook Meylan, Countess of A'Court."

She held her breath as the servant announced her. There were a few curious glances, but the activity in the ballroom continued indifferent to her arrival. The orchestra had not ceased playing. The guests who were engaged in conversation or dancing had not frozen into statues. Nor had the walls of the ballroom crumbled into dust. Everything seemed ordinary. The relief she felt was almost intoxicating.

Waiting for her parents to be announced, she noticed Ham had arrived before them. He lifted a hand in greeting. He said something to his companions and then worked his way to her side.

"Cousin," he said, marveling at her appearance, since he was still unused to seeing her in anything but her dull widow colors. "You are enchanting. Pray tell me that no one has claimed your first dance."

Thrilled by his reaction, she curtseyed. "No one has asked, my lord. You are the first."

His gray eyes glinted in delight. "I would be granted my fondest wish if I could claim all of your first dances, my lady."

Not giving her a chance to respond to his bold hint at wanting her for his bride, he pulled her closer and began guiding her away from the entrance.

"Ham, my mother and father—" She looked back to see if

they had appeared. Lord Haslake had delayed Mr. Ludlow by asking him questions about a mutual acquaintance.

"Your parents are not expecting you to remain at their side all evening. Besides, we have had little time these last few weeks."

"My lord, I am aware that you have obligations that extend beyond me. No one, least of all I, planned for you to personally see to my daily amusements."

"If I had been free to do so, I would have gladly taken the pleasurable task."

The earnestness in his expression stirred her guilt. "Where is your sister?"

She had her answer seconds later. He brought her to his family. Mother A'Court sat beside her younger sister, Lady Kerbey. May hovered dutifully behind them, but she was obviously feeling burdened by the chore. She forlornly watched the couples dancing while she longed for a partner. The sisters' elderly mother, Mrs. Byres, was nearby immersed in a conversation with Mrs. Molly Bedegrayne. Brook smiled fondly at the older woman, remembering the afternoon visits she and the Bedegrayne sisters had spent together at Aunt Moll's house. She had heard that the lady had recently married. Hopefully, there would be a moment sometime during the evening when they could become reacquainted. Brook greeted the ladies. May praised her ball gown and she returned the compliment.

"My lady, what is your opinion of our cousin? Is she not the jewel in the A'Court crown?" Ham said, anxious for the dowager's reply.

Elthia, Lady A'Court, raised her lorgnette and critically scrutinized Brook's appearance. On tenterhooks she awaited her mother-in-law's pronouncement. "Mrs. Ludlow did well to choose bold colors," she said after deliberating. "The bodice is lower than I anticipated. An excessive display of flesh is vulgar. Unmarried ladies and widows in particular must guard against drawing unwarranted attention. Luckily, you are not burdened with much aloft. You have my compliments, madam."

"Thank you," she replied, trying not to stare at her bosom.

The older woman leaned forward to get a closer inspection of the pearl bracelet adorning Brook's wrist. "This bracelet is exquisite. I do not recall this piece as belonging to the family collection."

"If you recollect, Mother A'Court, I relinquished all of the A'Court jewelry to your solicitor." She had not kept a single bauble, not even the betrothal ring Lyon had put on her finger. "The pearls belong to me."

Ham stood proudly beside her. He squeezed her arm, showing his pleasure. "Your praise is most welcome, madam. One day soon I hope you will be offering us your blessing."

"My lord," Brook begged, not wanting to set false expectations. Her gaze impotently sought out May's assistance. If Ham were given further encouragement he would be announcing their betrothal sometime this evening.

"You are distressing our cousin, Brother," May said, holding Brook's panicked gaze. "Let her enjoy the amusements of the season before speaking of marrying her and bundling her off to the country again to birth your heirs."

The accuracy of her statement caused the earl's ears to redden. "May, you are being indelicate."

Elthia, Lady A'Court, surprised them all by saying, "I have been giving this match you have proposed some consideration, my lord. My son would be honored by your diligent care of his widow. Though I had initially disapproved of Lyon's choice in bride, the years have matured her frivolous nature. When the moment comes that you are prepared to claim her publicly as your countess, you will have my support."

Stunned, Brook blinked rapidly as Ham rushed past her

and kissed the dowager's hand. He said, "Madam, your generosity overwhelms me."

"Before you post the banns," May interjected, noting that her future sister-in-law was not as enthused by the older woman's declaration, "you might want to court the lady who holds your affections."

Lady Kerbey chuckled and gave Brook a commiserating look. "A gentleman's arrogance. A'Court, continue this high road and see if our Brook does not reject you."

They were simply teasing Ham. Nevertheless, Brook welcomed their hindrance. She would listen to no further talk about marriage. "All that I have promised is a dance," Brook warned. "The hand I offer is impermanent."

"Ho! That is the spirit," Lady Kerbey crowed. "Give our cousin a merry chase so he might appreciate the prize."

Mallory did not linger as the servant announced their names. His light blue gaze searched the crowded ballroom for a blonde in cerulean blue. Days ago, he had made inquiries about the color of her gown because he wanted to purchase a jewelry suite that complemented it. He had considered bribing Brook's maid. However, Mrs. Ludlow had proven most cooperative. He had sworn the older woman to secrecy and she was too much of a romantic to deny him.

"You are not planning on abandoning me for the card room?" Lady Keyworth inquired.

"Not at all." A flash of blue caught his eye. Cocking his head, he said, "You will be pleased, Mother. My father's illness has reminded me how neglectful I have been about my duties."

Startled by the admission, she dropped her fan. Mallory gallantly retrieved it. Accepting it, she asked, "What are you planning to do?"

Ah, there she was. His pleasure diminished slightly when

he realized A'Court had partnered her for a dance. "Hmm . . . what? Oh, you will approve. I plan to marry a countess."

"You are angry."

No. She was furious. She rapped his hand with her fan when he tried to soothe her like she was a horse. "You promised that if I came to London you would cease pressuring me into accepting your proposal."

The master of ceremonies called for the dancers to form their sets. Too upset by Ham's imperious manner, she did not have the heart to feign enthusiasm for a country-dance. "I require some air," she muttered, leaving him standing with his mouth open.

"Lady A'Court!"

She heard his frantic whisper to stop, but she ignored him. As she stepped outside, the fresh air revived her. The earl caught up with her. Grabbing her arm, he steered her away from the windows.

"Did you not hear me?"

"Yes, Ham, I did. And like you and Mother A'Court, I chose to ignore your wishes." She opened her fan and used it to keep away the tiny insects hovering near her face.

"Dearest," he entreated. "I know I promised I would not press you. Still the outcome will never change. Why fight it? There are so many benefits in marrying."

"Name them."

He stepped back, slightly perplexed. "Name them?"

Brook closed the gap between them and poked him on the shoulder. He jumped as she hit a tender spot. "These wonderful benefits you claim. I want to hear all about them."

"You will remain Lady A'Court."

She wrinkled her nose. "I have never experienced any pleasure being the Countess of A'Court. Another."

"Wealth and status," he said, suspecting that she was ridiculing him.

"Through my Lanston lineage, I claim both. More."

Her haughty demeanor was stirring his ire. He was unused to anyone questioning him, least of all a woman. "Loughwydde."

"It is mine!"

His gray eyes hardened. He reminded her briefly of Lyon. "Loughwydde is yours because I desire for you to have it."

"Cornwall has meant nothing to the A'Courts. The acreage is too small to deem profitable and the distance too far from London. Ham, Loughwydde has been in my family for generations."

He handed her his handkerchief. Until then, she had not noticed her tears. "Then you do not want to give me a reason to strip you of your quaint rural estate."

Locking his wrists behind his back, he strolled back into the ballroom. Her fearful expression heartened him. He suspected she would come to heel when he chose to announce their betrothal.

Mallory watched A'Court as he disappeared into the crowded ballroom.

Pompous prig.

Moving out of the shadows, Mallory approached Brook. He studied her profile. While many of the ladies within had spent hours pinning and curling their locks into complicated confections, the countess had striven for simplicity. Single braids draped like gold ropes from her temples. She had combed her tresses high and tethered them at her crown. The luxuriant cascade fell down her back in soft, natural curls. He longed to bury his face into the softness. The blue silk shimmered in the moonlight as she walked to one of the stone benches and sat. She hiccupped softly and dabbed a handkerchief at her cheeks.

"Your tears glitter like diamonds in the moonlight."

She started at his voice and then relaxed. "It sounds poetic. In truth, crying makes me soggy."

He fingered the pear-shaped pearl dangling from her earlobe. "Mayhap pearls. Though they tend to glow rather than glitter."

She choked on her laughter. "It hardly matters. It still means I am too hideous to show my face in the ballroom."

Hideous? Did the woman not look in the mirror? Finding her lack of vanity mildly irritating, he snatched the handkerchief from her hand. "Let me see if I can improve upon you."

Mallory thought she was perfect. He just wanted an excuse to touch her. Folding the handkerchief around his finger, he began at the corner of her eye and lightly followed its contour. He repeated the action on the other side until there was no trace of her sorrow.

"Thank you for the pearls." She touched the necklace. "You were thoughtful to purchase them."

"You astound me, Countess. I was prepared for arguments about how you could not accept such an expensive gift."

Chagrined, she gave him a hesitant smile. "I drafted in my head a similar argument."

"What changed your mind? Pray do not tell me that you have developed mercenary tendencies," he said in feigned horror.

"Your kindness," she blurted out, quieting his teasing. Surprised at herself, she tried to make light of her confession. "Trust me, this is an aberration. On the morrow, I will likely come to my senses and blister your ears with all my sound reasoning for not accepting gifts from notable scoundrels."

Unable to resist, he murmured, "Do you know what ladies say about charming rogues and moonlit gardens?"

"No."

His cheeks dimpled as he roguishly grinned. "Why, nothing at all, Countess." Bending his head, he fitted his mouth over hers. She touched his arm. Intense in her concentration, she clumsily moved her lips over his. Her soft butterfly caresses were a potent arcanum. He wanted nothing more than to lead her deeper into the shadows and teach her the decadence of making love under the stars.

"Very sweet."

Brook's eyes widened at Carissa Le Maye's mocking opinion. Wanting to reassure the countess, Mallory kissed her on the nose, and then turned to deal with his scorned lover.

"How can you tell, Carissa, when the bitterness of vitriol coats your tongue?"

The widow did not respond to his question. Sweeping past them in a gown of wine and gold, she rested her hand on a stone balustrade, which overlooked the formal gardens. With her back to them, she said wistfully, "I love nights like this. Do you recall the eve we crept like thieves into the Holbecks' garden? We had attended a party earlier that day and I admired their charming belvedere."

Mallory knew where she was going with this tale. Christ, he had heard her recount it to unsuspecting listeners on numerous occasions just to see their eyes pop at their audacity. "Lady A'Court is not interested in old history."

Carissa glanced back at them. "On the contrary, I think Lyon's little *souris* would twitch her tiny ears in rapt regard." She continued her tale. "The columns of the circular structure were comprised of pink marble. Have you ever pressed your warm breasts against cool marble, Lady A'Court?"

Carisa would tell the entire sordid tale if he did not surrender. "Enough! You want something from me, Mrs. Le Maye. What?"

Triumphant in her easy victory, she caressed the balustrade. "Nothing naughty, *amoureux*. I am merely the messenger. An old friend desires your company in the library."

"Who?"

She touched her tongue to her upper lip. "I think I shall not tell you. You always did love my surprises."

"Countess," he said, his hard gaze fixed on his ex-mistress, "my sister must have arrived by now. See if you cannot find her before my mother does." He pinched Carissa hard on the chin. Instead of wincing, she purred. "Lady A'Court is off-limits for your games. Defy me and I will introduce you to another tale that you will make you weep in remembrance of it."

"Avoid Carissa Le Maye," Mallory warned as they entered the ballroom again. His demeanor had changed. Grimness had replaced the lighthearted tenderness he had shown her after Ham's casual threat of taking Loughwydde from her.

Brook was getting weary of everyone bullying her. "That might be difficult. Mrs. Le Maye does not seem like the kind of woman who allows anyone to ignore her."

His jaw tightened at her observation. "That is the truth," he muttered. "Hell, Countess, the fault is mine. Carissa has not forgiven me for breaking with her first."

"She wants you back," she starkly said.

Mallory's uninviting expression softened. He took her hand before she could stop him and reverently kissed it. "Well, she will survive the disappointment." He released her hand as they came up to his sister. "I should have known Bedegrayne could not keep you home where you belong."

The silver sequins on Amara's fan winked under the candlelight as she fanned herself in agitation. "Thank you for your concern, Brother. However, Brock has already lectured me about tiring myself." She appealed to Brook. "I believe I can endure the strain of standing."

"Have a little tolerance, puss." Without thought to appearances, he pulled her into his arms and kissed her cheek. "This is Bedegrayne's firstborn, and my first niece. We are bound to get excitable about your welfare."

"Brook, I had hoped you would attend. Your gown is magnificent!" Amara also looked incredible in her cream and amber ball gown.

"I need a favor, Sis. Could you look after the countess for

me?" He sent Brook a meaningful glance reminding her that he wanted Amara protected from any hurtful confrontations with her mother. "Carissa Le Maye has sharpened her claws and is of the mind to use them on Brook."

"Oh, that horrid creature!" Amara said with uncharacteristic vehemence. "I do not understand how you could have ever involved yourself with that woman."

Mallory contrived to look repentant. "A regretful lapse, I must admit. Just watch over your friend until I return for her." He rudely pointed at Brook. "Stay." He left before either one of them could argue.

Her friend cocked her brow in a mischievous fashion that reminded Brook of Mallory. "My brother appears overly concerned about you these days. Tell me, what is going on between you?"

Brook noticed Mrs. Le Maye had entered the ballroom. She was chatting flirtatiously with a gentleman. The woman never seemed to lack for companions. Still, it did not prevent her from bestowing Brook with a malevolent glare.

Recalling that Amara was awaiting a reply, she said distantly, "I believe your brother has reasoned out that I might make him a less vexing mistress than some of my recent predecessors."

"My brother goes too far," her friend said, outraged on Brook's behalf. "Someone needs to teach him that not every lady he encounters is merely another potential mistress!"

The library was empty. Mallory stood in the middle of the room and wondered at Carissa's game. Had this merely been a ruse to separate him from Brook?

"So you did get my message, Mr. Claeg. I despaired that I had not made the right impression on your mistress."

"My former mistress," Mallory corrected. He pursued the disembodied voice up three steps and through the open doors to a private balcony. "There seems to be much confusion about this. I am almost persuaded to post the news in all the papers."

The gentleman stood with his back to him as he watched the activities below. There was nothing about the man from his walking stick to his somber attire that hinted to the stranger's identity. "Arrogant and reckless. It was my first and lasting opinion of you. That, and the certainty you stole my betrothed from me."

"Lord De Lanoy." Mallory inclined his head. The marquis' encounter with Brook at the hotel had troubled him since he had learned of it. "Oh, I have relished meeting up with you again."

"Will you lower your voice, Amara?" Brook pleaded, regretting her confession. "It is my family's fondest wish that we put to rest any lingering scandal about my husband's death. Sending your husband after Mallory on my behalf will only link further speculation to my name."

"While having Brock pound some manners into Mallory has merit, I was thinking about murdering my brother myself!"

Amara was showing no signs of calming. Her brother and husband were likely to throttle her for it, albeit for slightly different reasons.

"What wicked tales have you both been whispering behind your fans?" Wynne Milroy asked. Her sudden presence had them parting guiltily. "Come now, Brook, we have been friends too long for me not to know when you are keeping secrets. Should I fathom a guess on what you were discussing before my arrival?" The emerald gown she wore enhanced the pale green hue of her eyes.

"Do not bother. You would be wrong," Amara said dismally. "It was not as we had assumed. It is *worse*."

Good grief, her own friends had been speculating about her. "You have been talking about me?"

"Nothing grievous. We simply noticed a certain gentleman's interest and it aroused our curiosity," Wynne said reassuringly. "Is that not right, Amara?"

Amara was no longer listening to either one of them. She was staring past Brook's shoulder at the woman determined to ignore her.

"Good evening, Mama."

"I wondered if you would remember me." The light from the open doors of the library revealed De Lanoy's austere hawklike features. "I had assumed my name and face had been lost amongst the multitude of victims resulting from your selfish pursuits."

"You speak as if I have spilt more English blood than Napoleon," Mallory marveled, pitying the man for obsessing about a lady who was lost to both of them. "My only sin was loving Mirabella Tantony enough to marry her."

"You seduced her."

"Come now, sir. Let us be blunt. Mirabella was fourteen when she sold herself to her first protector for food and a warm bed. How many gentlemen had known and discarded her before you took notice? If I had not bruised your pride by running off with her, how long would it have been until you tired of her and cast her aside for a less demanding creature, or a wife?"

The silver handle grip gleamed between the man's fingers as De Lanoy thumped the walking stick down against the ground in agitation. "She was content with our arrangement."

"Actually, she was bored with rural life. Mistresses rarely are content with home and hearth, De Lanoy. Mirabella had traveled very little and lusted for adventure. Even if I had not met her, you would have eventually lost her."

The man scoffed, "Is that how you condone your actions, Claeg?"

"I apologize for nothing. Mirabella was mine," Mallory said in a clipped tone. "If you cared for her, be content that she was happy."

"I only have your word, do I not?"

"It is all rather moot since the lady is dead. You surprise me, De Lanoy. I had hoped the years had extinguished your bitterness about the affair. Let her go, sir. I can promise you, Mirabella had set her feelings for you aside when she agreed to run off with me."

"You lie!"

The marquis swung his walking stick at him wildly. Mallory leapt backward into the library, and felt the breeze of the violent arc. The stick struck the wooden frame of the door. Several of the glass panes cracked from the impact.

"She never uttered your name in my presence. Your vengeance is misplaced." Stumbling down the three steps, Mallory avoided another blow. "My regret is that she is not here to tell you herself."

The man howled and charged him. Mallory grabbed the walking stick with both hands as they collided. In tandem, they tumbled over one of the chairs. Having the slight advantage of youth, he recovered first and straddled the furious marquis. Breathing heavily, he pressed the length of the man's own walking stick to his throat.

"Now that we have revisited our old business, let us address the new. For the sake of your health, keep a respectful distance from Lady A'Court."

The marquis glared defiantly at him. "Why would I want to keep away from such a charming creature? We enjoyed a pleasant hour together at one of the hotels, but then, you know all about it. What do you fear, Claeg? Are you afraid I might seduce the lady?"

Mallory increased the pressure against the man's throat. De Lanoy choked. As he turned an unflattering red, he clawed frantically at the unyielding stick. "I have nothing to fear

from you. You cannot say the same. Do not annoy me again."
Mallory stood and watched impassively as the man desperately filled his lungs with precious air. "Otherwise, I may do more than wrinkle your cravat."

Brook held her breath, praying the viscountess was not so callous as to cut her own daughter directly. The older woman paused. She was clearly torn by her loyalties. Ignoring her daughter also meant ignoring the ladies who flanked her.

As she positioned herself subtly in front of Amara, Brook said, "Good evening, madam. I trust your presence this evening is a sign Lord Keyworth is improving."

Grateful to address someone other than the daughter she and her husband had sworn to disown, Lady Keyworth said, "You are kind to inquire, Lady A'Court. Yes, my husband has exceeded the physician's expectations. We anticipate that one day he will make a complete recovery."

Amara swayed slightly at the news. Wynne slipped a supportive arm around her friend. The discord in the family and her father's illness were unrelenting burdens. "Mama, if the crisis has passed, might I visit Papa?" Amara cleared her throat and swallowed her grief when the viscountess looked away.

"Madam, how long do you intend on punishing your daughter for marrying my brother?" Wynne demanded. It took a great amount of provocation for her ire to flare, but this silent impasse with the Keyworths had exhausted her patience.

"Wynne, thank you, but leave it alone," Amara said, her shoulders slumping in sadness. "Mallory thinks your grandchild is a girl. Will you ignore her existence, too, Mama?"

Lady Keyworth flinched at the question. She parted her lips as if to respond, and then thought better of it. The armor of her pride seemed impenetrable. She addressed Brook, who seemed the least threatening of the trio. "Your absence from friends has been long, Lady A'Court. Please extend my regards to your family." The viscountess stiffly nodded. "Mrs. Milroy." She did not spare her daughter a glance as she left them, and joined the next small group of guests.

Amara sniffed and dug into her reticule for a handkerchief.

Able to sympathize with her friend too easily, Brook whispered, "Do not give her the satisfaction of seeing your pain." She met Wynne's cool green gaze. "Go find a quiet spot for Amara to compose herself while I send for her husband." And Mallory. Brook was positive he would not let his mother go unchallenged for her vindictiveness.

Brook found Brock Bedegrayne leaning negligently against one of the walls in the front hall as he conversed with Wynne's husband, Keanan Milroy. She was so intimidated by the pair that she almost backed away. It was concern for Amara which gave her the courage to approach and recount the brief encounter with Lady Keyworth. The gentlemen thanked her and hastened to find their wives.

Mallory Claeg, on the other hand, proved frustratingly elusive. The library was empty. Mrs. Le Maye had told Mallory his mysterious acquaintance was waiting for him in the library. Had it been a ruse? The only thing odd about the room was a chair lying on its side. Respectful of its value, Brook carefully righted the piece. In the past hour, late arrivals had filled the ballroom to crushing capacity. There was no hope of locating Mallory in that huge room unless she accidentally bumped into him. Resigned she had done her best, Brook started for the door.

The indistinct murmurs of approaching guests had her backing away from the door. She crossed the room to the other door and pulled on the latch. It was locked. Glancing around for a place to hide, she reminded herself that she had as much right to be in the library as anyone else. Still, she was feeling too vulnerable to be caught alone.

Brook escaped through the open doors of the balcony and she heard the door on the inside opening. The distinct crunch of glass under her slipper had her wincing as she stepped deeper into the shadows. It appeared she was not the only one who was avoiding the ballroom.

"Who wants a drink?" a drunken male queried to his companions.

There were numerous voices of concurrence. The panes of glass from the other door reflected the blurred movements of the library's occupants. Brook guessed there were four or five people. One or two sat while the others seemed content to explore the room. She allowed her head to rest against the rough exterior stone and prayed no one would come out onto the balcony.

"Pour me a drink, *mon ami*. And do not be stingy with the earl's sherry," Carissa Le Maye said, boldly stepping out onto the balcony.

Brook watched from her hiding place in wide-eyed horror as Mallory's former mistress braced her arms against the railing and sighed. The humiliation of discovery might have been bearable if it had been anyone but this woman.

"Your drink, madam," a male voice called out. "Unless you want company out there."

Tell him no, Brook silently begged the widow, and inched deeper into shadows. The balcony was embarrassingly over-crowded as it was.

"*Non,*" Mrs. Le Maye replied, giving up her view with a mutter of regret. "The night is too young for exclusive games." She turned away and returned to the library's interior.

It took everything within Brook not to whimper in relief.

There were some indistinct murmurs, and then, a woman giggled. One lady with a high grating voice asked, "Did he beg you for an introduction?"

"Who? Lord A'Court? Yes. I refused, naturally," the woman to the right of Brook replied. "The poor man must be besotted with the little widow to humiliate himself in front of the *ton* as he has lately on her behalf."

"I met the lady once. I recall she had a comely face," a gentleman interjected.

In an amused tone, Mrs. Le Maye retorted, "When did you look, my lord? Your inclinations are decidedly below a lady's neck."

Everyone chuckled. Brook peered over the side, realizing she was too high off the ground to slip off the balcony unnoticed. She was a prisoner until the merry little gathering abandoned the library.

"Someone told me her face was the only part of her body that is not scarred," the high grating voice confessed, sounding horrified and pleased by the notion.

"I heard Lyon used the cat on his countess."

"Naw, a whip is too brutal," the drunken gentleman disagreed. "She is a bitty thing. Likely to cut her in two."

Two of the ladies gasped.

"I heard it was birch."

"Or maybe the earl burned her flesh with an iron."

Brook buried her face in her hands, trying to block out their speculation about how her husband had marked her. Amidst their laughter and murmurs she could summon in her mind an image of Lyon chasing her. His gray eyes glinted like the winter sun on ice as he pushed her to the floor and used his body and fists to keep her there. She could have told them that her husband had not used a whip or an iron on her. Lyon had used his teeth to tear, his sharp nails to gouge, and the ring on his finger to slice her flesh.

She bit her finger to prevent her teeth from chattering.

"Why would Lord A'Court want to marry someone so—damaged?" the woman on the right wondered aloud.

"Perhaps this sickness infects all of the A'Court heirs," Carissa Le Maye suggested. Brook could envision her tiny shrug of indifference. "I suspect the A'Court family prefers to keep the widow away from polite society. What better way than to marry the new heir?"

"A'Court seems interested in making a place for the countess and himself in town," a male companion said, unconvinced by Mrs. Le Maye's reasoning.

"It is simply a ruse to gain her trust, you fool!" the widow snapped. "Just wait. A'Court will be making excuses to send her away once his betrothal ring is on her finger."

"You just do not like the thought of Mallory Claeg courting Lady A'Court," the lady with the high voice said slyly.

"Mr. Claeg does not court widows. He beds them. I should know. I have heard him say those words often enough. He should adopt them as the family motto."

"What a wicked thing to say, Carissa!"

"When has she been anything else?" the drunk quipped.

The ensuing silence troubled her. Leaning to the side, she tried to see what they were doing. Realizing the widow was standing close with her back to the open doors, Brook quietly retreated.

"I tire of this waiting. Let us leave," Mrs. Le Maye said, her voice warming to the idea. "He can catch up to us later."

"Does the countess know she shares him with you?"

"Not for long," the widow assured her companions. "Men may be initially charmed by innocence, but they lose interest once it has been corrupted."

Brook listened to the fading laughter and ribald jesting as the door closed behind them. With her arms crossed against her chest in a protective gesture, she leaned against the wall and made her own plans.

Mallory was not in the best humor when he climbed into the coach's compartment and glared at Brook. "I have been searching the Haslakes' town house from top to bottom for you." Since he calculated the chances of her jumping from a moving coach as remote, Mallory signaled the coachman to commence. "The evening is not half over. When I came across Lady Haslake, she told me of your leaving. What is all of this about, Countess?"

"The concept should not be difficult, sir. I am going home."

The interior was just too dark for him to see her face clearly, but he did not like the flat quality in her voice. "Did someone say something to upset you?"

Brook choked on a bitter laugh and shook her head. "Spoken or unspoken, it no longer matters to me. I was a fool to hope enough time had passed for . . . "

"For what?"

"For everyone to forget!" Brook stifled a sob. "Oh, just go back to your mistress. She and your friends are waiting for you."

"Have you been drinking the Haslakes' punch? You are making less sense than you usually do," Mallory muttered, not understanding what had caused her upset.

The countess lunged forward. Instead of attacking, her goal was the small trap door that allowed the occupants within the compartment to issue instructions to the coachman. While Mallory held her trembling figure, Brook pounded on the door. "Stop the coach!" The coachman called out and the horses slowed at his barking command.

"Countess, let me get you back to your parents' house. Then you can tell me what happened at the ball that has you acting crazy."

"I am not crazy. I am ending this bout of madness," she hissed. "Get out!"

Suspicion had him narrowing his eyes. "Is this about Carissa?"

Emitting a low growl, Brook opened the coach door. Fearing she was planning to climb out, Mallory blocked her escape. He had fallen neatly into her plans. As she braced herself with her arms, Brook kicked him in the chest. He fell backward through the open door. Mallory landed on his back. The impact of the dirt street knocked the wind out of him.

While he gasped for air, the countess poked her head through the opening. "Farewell, Mr. Claeg." She slammed the coach door and ordered her man to proceed.

Brook had left his pride as bruised as his arse.

Mallory decided in view of her hostility and his raging need for retribution to allow the night to pass before he forced a confrontation the lady well deserved. The following morning, he discovered the countess had been one step ahead of him all along.

Brook had returned to Loughwydde.

Chapter Twenty-Eight

"Gill, I expect you to visit Mrs. Lane in my absence." Mallory placed his hand on her shoulder and gazed down sternly at her. "Since I am depriving her of an empty stomach to cook for, it would not hurt if you ate whatever she put in front of you. For appearances." He winked.

"Aye, Claeg. I could probably choke down a few of her sweets for your sake." The young girl shrugged. "Messing surely doesn't need 'm. Too many of his parts are drifting south, if you catch my meaning."

Hooting with laughter, Mallory impulsively kissed her on the top of the head. "Do not tell Messing. I prefer that you keep your fingers intact. I will need my apprentice when I return." He mounted the gelding.

"How long will you be gone?" She squinted at him, pretending that his answer did not mean anything to her one way or the other.

"For as long as it takes." He looked down and realized she was unhappy with his reply. "Do not worry, Gill. I am not abandoning you. If you need anything, tell my housekeeper or go to my sister. She is residing at Sir Thomas Bedegrayne's town house. Do you remember the street where he lives?"

She scrunched up her face. "I can see to myself, Claeg."

"I haven't the time to debate you, imp. It would please me if you stopped by the Benevolent Sisterhood, too."

"A house of charity." She sneered. "Not even for you."

"Fine." Mallory let the matter rest. For now. He could introduce Gill to Miss Maddy Wyman when he returned with the countess. "I will miss you, Gill. Keep out of trouble, if you please." He touched the brim of his hat and nodded. He clicked his tongue and signaled the horse with his heels.

"Trouble? Heed the warning yourself!" she called out to him. "I'm not heading off to Cornwall after a lady who likely wants your head on a pike!"

Mallory headed east, hoping to see Amara before he left town. The obligations to his father had delayed his departure by a day. He was not overly concerned, since he was not traveling by post chaise. *Unlike the countess,* he thought with grim satisfaction.

The congestion of horses, equipage, and pedestrians forced him to slow the bay's gait. Maneuvering the animal around one carriage and then another, he jerked on the horse's reins abruptly when he recognized the lady.

Edda Henning.

The bay whinnied and shook its head at the abuse. Mallory had a few things he wanted to say to this woman. It was apparent his sudden appearance distressed her. She bent down and murmured to the child sitting beside her.

Until then, Mallory had not noticed the little girl. Mrs. Henning had birthed a child. Viewing her as a mother was almost beyond his imagination. The girl saw him and smiled. She looked like a beautiful doll. Her long blond hair already had a hint of her mother's red coloring and was curled. The pair wore matching carriage dresses and bonnets. He estimated the child's age to be around five years.

His blood congealed at the revelation.

"Order your man to halt!"

Something in Mallory's forbidding expression must have frightened her. Mrs. Henning called out to her coachman. He followed closely, wondering if she was so foolish to think she could escape him. Impossible. Mallory intended to get some answers from the lady.

Tethering his horse, he approached them, deliberately putting the child at ease with a friendly smile. "Mrs. Henning. A pleasure to see you again." He shifted his gaze on her daughter. Mallory softened his voice. "And who is this?"

Wary of him, and rightly so, Mrs. Henning placed a protective hand on her child. "Mr. Claeg, this is my daughter. Effie, Mr. Claeg is a friend of your Mama and Papa's."

Beaming at him, she suddenly was overcome with shyness and buried her face into her mother's bosom.

"What a fine little lady you are, Miss Henning," Mallory said admiringly, fighting the thickness forming in his throat. "And how old are you, pretty?"

She held up five tiny fingers.

His gut churned with acid, threatening to betray him. "Well, that is deserving of a celebration, do you not think?" At the girl's eager nod, he said, "Gunter's is in sight. Why do we not let the coachman watch over our horses while we sample some sweets?"

"Mama?" the girl pleaded.

"Two against one," Mrs. Henning said faintly. "How can I refuse?"

"You never mentioned that you had a child."

Mallory had treated the ladies to pineapple cake at Gunter's. Afterward, he had suggested that they walk the square. Mrs. Henning reluctantly agreed. They set a leisurely pace behind Effie as she raced ahead attempting to capture a butterfly.

"That is not unusual. Gentlemen rarely have the tolerance to listen to an indulgent mother."

He ignored the weight in his heart. "Is she mine?"

Edda Henning pursed her lips in contemplation. "No, Mr. Claeg, she is mine."

Forgetting about not wanting to frighten the child, he grabbed the woman's arm harshly. "Try again."

"You want to know who is the father of my child?" The corners of her mouth slyly curled. "Honestly, I do not know."

She was toying with him. Contemptuously he released her arm. "I do not believe you. I can add, madam. I wager if I ask Effie what month she was born, I could place her conception around the time of your husband's infamous country house gathering."

Edda Henning did not deny his accusation. "Oh, those were the days, were they not? My husband always preferred gatherings that were rather wild and dissolute. I warrant most of the participants awoke with few memories of the previous night's activities."

And some never awoke, he mused, thinking of Mirabella. "I recall enough, madam, to know there is a *possibility.*"

She glanced away from him and shouted to her daughter, "Effie, dear, do not wander so far from us!"

"Yes, Mama."

While he debated on how to get Mrs. Henning to answer his questions, she solved his dilemma by saying, "You may not believe this, but my husband loves me. He could take to his bed a thousand lovers and still he would return to me."

Mallory knew he would murder anyone who laid a hand on the woman he loved. "I am pleased it is a love match for you," he said sarcastically.

"Oh, it is," she assured him. "Two years passed in our marriage before we had to face that my husband could not get me with child."

"How do you know—" He halted at her eloquent expression. Her carnal appetites had been relentless and she had been given her husband's blessing to sample other men's beds. At some point, it was obvious, she had miscarried a child who was not Henning's.

"By the time we had met you and Mirabella, I had grown weary of our life. I desired children but had a husband who was incapable of providing them. The solution seemed simple." She had the audacity to laugh at his appalled expression. "Oh, Mr. Claeg, if you could see your face."

"You stole that child," he said, feeling used.

"On the contrary, she was given to me unreservedly and quite gratifyingly. It was all carefully planned. The gentlemen invited were handpicked. Wine and narcotics flowed freely to vanquish any inhibitions."

"Why me?"

She offered him an odd glance, since the answer seemed apparent to her. "You were unexpected. I did not know my husband had invited you and your wife. It added spice to our game. He knew I was attracted to you, so perhaps you were there to present an enticing challenge."

"And what of my wife? Her feelings?"

"I am not a cruel woman. She would have never known." She frowned, thinking about that night. "My husband never cared about the others. We have never spoken of it, but I can only assume that jealousy prodded him into summoning your wife when he found us in bed."

"What?" he starkly demanded.

"You do not remember? I am not surprised. It is one of the side effects of the potion. I confess, you imbibed more than the others, but they were not as resistant to my charms as you." She emitted a soft sigh of remembrance. "Once you forgot about your wife, you were magnificent."

"And Mirabella?"

The pleasure left her face. "My husband had told her that you were searching for her. He helped her check each room, saving our bedchamber for the last."

Mallory's jaw grew rigid in anger. "She saw us together."

Edda Henning nodded guiltily. "I noticed her when I peered over your shoulder. She did not remain long."

The pain of the past surged forth renewed. Although he had been a victim to the Hennings' machinations, too, Mirabella had died believing he had betrayed her. He staggered a few steps, sickened.

"Effie is my daughter."

"I cannot say, Mr. Claeg."

"Damn you! Cannot or will not?"

"All games of sport have rules," she said calmly. "Mine were simple. My husband insisted that I bed all five of the handpicked gentlemen within a specified amount of time. It was his way of ensuring that the identity of Effie's true sire could never be ascertained."

"Are you telling me the truth? You do not know who fathered her?"

"Mr. Claeg, I have no reason to lie. I risk nothing even if I stood here and confessed that you are indeed Effie's sire. No court would favor you with rights and the *ton* would ridicule you if you tried to get them. The purported mother in question is a reputed whore. My daughter could have been sired by anyone. Let it be."

There was no way for him to learn the truth. Mallory had spent so many years tormenting himself over his wife's death. Was he planning to squander the remainder torturing himself over a mere possibility? "I should escort you back to your carriage. I am leaving town for a while."

"Mr. Henning and I are also arranging another trip. I doubt we will meet again."

Mallory nodded. He stood quietly as Mrs. Henning summoned Effie to her side. He knelt down and said farewell to the child. Her resemblance to her mother was striking. He saw nothing of himself in her. The fact that the child had blue eyes and her mother had brown meant nothing. He was not the only man she had bedded who had blue eyes. The relief he desired never surfaced.

"Know one thing, my lord. Mr. Henning loves his daughter. She will be denied nothing.

"Except . . ." she let the word hang between them, ". . . a brother or sister. Would you consider . . ." She licked her lips and grinned wickedly.

Mallory stalked off without replying. He did not think he could stop himself from striking down the manipulative witch, because her version of the truth left him wondering if this was just another game to her. Only this time, she was the one who made up the rules.

Chapter Twenty-Nine

Loughwydde had changed little during her absence. The air was warmer and the smell of the sea called to her. Brook had missed walking her cliffs and listening to waves rushing over the rocky beach. This was home. The A'Courts might try to take it away from her, but she would fight them. She was a Lanston. The land had been in her family for generations. No one valued it more than her.

Mrs. Gordy had fussed over Brook the night of her arrival, cooking all of her favorite dishes. After the confusion of London, the silence in the house was disquieting. She had taken her meal in the kitchen with the staff because she was not quite ready to be alone. She had plenty of remaining years to live out for that.

When she had climbed into her bed, she did not question why she chose to sleep in the pearls Mallory had given her. Although she thought parting from him was best, wearing his jewelry comforted her.

Upon awakening, the wetness on her cheeks revealed that she had been weeping in her sleep. She simply wiped the evidence of her grief away. Mallory's pearls were returned to their leather case.

"Up already, madam," Mrs. Gordy said, noting the dark shadows under her mistress's eyes. "I'll tell Cook that you are ready for your breakfast."

Instead of heading for the morning room, Brook moved toward the front door. "I will eat later. It has been ages since I have visited the tidal bathing pools. The tide and weather seem right for it."

One of her ancestors had had a wife who suffered from a deteriorating spine. The physicians had claimed that cold sea bathing would cure her, so her husband had cut three bathing pools at different levels in the rock to capture the tide. The shallow water warmed quickly under the sun and the pools had been a delight for Brook as a child. Regrettably, the pools had not cured the lady for whom they had been hewn.

"Afore you hurry off, you'll be needing some towels. I will not be having you catch your death just 'cause you have an itch to dip your toes in salt water."

Brook smiled at the no-nonsense tone of her housekeeper. "Yes, mum." She hugged the older woman. "It is good to be home again."

Brook slid into the pool and clenched her teeth to keep them from chattering. She might have been hasty when she had declared the weather warm enough for sea bathing. Cold seawater had not deterred her as a child and she did not let it stop her from enjoying the water. Besides, the water was supposed to be restorative.

Tilting her head back, Brook closed her eyes feeling the tingle of salt and sunshine on her face. Mrs. Gordy would be upset with her if she put freckles on her nose, so she planned on limiting her time in the water. Otherwise, the fretful servant would be slathering freckle cream all over her face and arms.

"You present an inspiring picture, Countess."

Her eyes snapped open. Shielding them with her hand, she glanced at him. With his hands arrogantly resting on his hips he leered at her.

"Is this the Temple of the Sun?" Mallory walked around

the edge so that Brook was not blinded by the sunlight. Crouching down, he looked at her submersed body. The shallow depths and her wet chemise left nothing to the imagination. "I thought four white horses were sacrificed to Helios, not delectable innocents."

What was he talking about? She could not fathom that he was here. "I—I do not know."

Mallory dipped his hand into the water and cupped her breast. "Or maybe you are Circe," he mused aloud. "Should I gag you before you utter one of your incantations and turn me into a beast?"

"When have you been anything other?" she quipped, and he tossed his head back and laughed. "Mallory, why have you come?"

Brook covered her breasts. Now that her eyes had adjusted to the glaring sunlight, she glimpsed the anger Mallory had kept from his voice.

"Is it not obvious? I have come for my farewell kiss."

Mallory could not have anticipated a better spot for his ambush. Brook sat in the water and glared at him. He could see that the cold seawater had hardened her nipples. She might as well have been naked, for her chemise was sheer under the sun and the water. It did not matter to him if she chose to remain in the water or climb out. Either choice would prove entertaining.

"I have been waiting two days for you." He had almost killed himself and the horse to arrive before the post chaise.

Brook sputtered in indignation. "I left before you!"

"I had an incentive," he said, bemused that she had never considered that he might pursue her once she left. "My kiss."

Mallory discarded his coat and sat down on the warm rock to pull off his boots. These were his favorite pair and he did not want to get them wet. He had given her the night to recover from her journey. Now she was going to have to face the consequences of running away from him.

"No one travels this far for a mere kiss."

He gave her a roguish grin. "Fine. You can give me more." Without warning he crawled into the pool and positioned himself so that he straddled her legs. Christ, the water was cold!

"Miss me?"

"No—umph!"

Mallory muffled her false denial with a swift kiss. What it lacked in passion it made up for in frustration. Between the countess leaving him and Edda Henning's devastating confession, he had a bellyful. Blindly he pulled the pins out of Brook's hair. He ended the kiss and surveyed the results. Her long blond hair was an improvement over her chemise for concealing her body. He had bruised her mouth with his hard kiss. Her lips were red and slightly swollen. Arousal had softened the anger his arrival had incited in her blue cat eyes.

"I had planned on behaving and paying you a proper visit at Loughwydde. I like your idea much better." Mallory stood and unbuttoned the falls on his breeches.

Brook found her voice when he shoved them down and plopped them next to his coat. "Put those back on!" His burgeoning arousal poking out beneath his shirt left no doubt to his outrageous intentions.

"I cannot love you properly with them on, Countess." She lunged away from him, but he was quicker. Wrapping her in his arms, he rolled so that she was on top. He preferred taking the brunt of the rock that risked bruising her tender flesh. "Say that you missed me." Touching her between her legs, he was not amazed by her readiness. The passion was always there for them, just under the surface. He pulled her closer, nudging the head of his cock against her cleft. There was a brief resistance and then he slid deep into her warmth. He groaned at the rightness of their joining.

"Tell me."

Mallory rocked her against him and she shuddered. "I

missed you," Brook whispered into his shoulder. "I slept in the pearls you gave me because it was the closest thing to having you."

His chest rumbled with laughter at her admission. She had slept in the jewelry he had given her while he had spent the night drinking brandy and mooning over the picture he had painted of her lying in bluebells. Their stubbornness bordered on stupidity.

"You have me now." He quickened his movements, forcing her to hold on to him. "And I have you. Let me show you."

"I need . . . I need—" she chanted in his ear, too befuddled to finish her thought.

This was not a leisurely mating. Mallory been separated from her too long and the fear he had felt when she had departed London without a word had been his constant companion until he saw reclining nearly naked in her bathing pool. As he slammed her down on him, the sun blinded him, and he threw back his head and roared while his release gushed into her. The countess responded and her high-pitched cries of bliss blended with his. She rested her forehead on his shoulder. They were both panting.

Mallory lifted his head and kissed her on the temple. "I had heard of the restorative powers of cold seawater but have never tried them until now."

He had not allowed her to return to Loughwydde.

Gently Mallory had pulled her dress over her head and slipped her shoes on. Using the towels that her housekeeper had supplied, he had bundled Brook up. Once he was satisfied that she was warm, he had dressed. The ascent was too hazardous for romantic demonstrations, so he had waited until they reached the summit before he lifted her into his arms. No amount of begging had gained her freedom.

The crazy man had carried her into his cottage, passed a very astonished Mrs. Whitby, who had been polishing the hall floor, and went up the stairs. Calling down to the woman to alert Loughwydde of Brook's whereabouts, Mallory had kicked the door shut. Shedding their wet clothing, they had climbed into bed and promptly fallen asleep.

It was almost dark when Brook awakened. She had not slept well for days. How odd that she found the solace she craved in this man's arms. With his breath in her ear, he held her tightly against his chest as if he feared that she would escape him even in sleep. His arm was slung over her breasts and his right knee rested high between her legs. She impulsively kissed his forearm and felt his manhood stir against her buttocks. Brook smiled at his response.

"Did you sleep?" Mallory murmured sleepily, his embrace tightening instead of easing.

"Yes. I just awoke," she confessed. "Sleep has been elusive."

He burrowed his face into her neck and bit her shoulder lightly. "You just needed someone to tire you out properly."

"I just need you," she said, not censoring her words. His nibbling on her shoulder stopped.

"Do you mean it?"

She could hear his uncertainty and she was puzzled by it. The Mallory Claeg she knew was nauseatingly confident around women; he was usually telling *her* how she felt.

"There had been times I wished it were a lie," she slowly admitted.

He rolled her onto her back so he could see her face. His light blue eyes gleamed with intensity in the fading light. "This is about my past. There have been too many women. You doubt my sincerity."

"No. It is not that. I have never encountered a man like you. You feel passionate about everything! Each woman was not an idle conquest. I believe you loved each one of them, however fleetingly."

"You think you are like them. That I am devoted until my heart sends me into another woman's arms."

Brook remained silent.

"Little fool!" Mallory leaned over her earnestly. "Have you not considered that with each woman, I was striving to recapture what I had with Mirabella? Lust, it fades with the dawn. No one has meant anything to me, until you."

Brook's heart knocked against her ribs. "What about Carissa Le Maye?"

She flinched when he pounded his fist into the pillow. "This is about what Miss Hamblin saw in my painting room, is it not?" He sighed wearily.

"Your mistress confirmed it."

"She lied. What Miss Hamblin witnessed was a pathetic attempt of a former lover to rekindle an affair that ended weeks after the first time I met you on the cliffs."

His anger gave her hope. "That was more than—"

"A year—yes, I know," he said, finishing her sentence. Mallory caressed the side of her face and then suddenly gripped her hair and gave her a little shake. "You touched something in me that day. I could not stop thinking about you, but I did not know how to approach you without frightening you away, so I started slowly. A few trips for my art, I told my friends and family. In truth, I was coming to see you. Courting you."

"I rejected Ham's offer for marriage."

"Good. It saves me from having to challenge him. For all our differences, I happen to like A'Court. But I would have shot him without reservation if he had pressured you into accepting his proposal."

The fierce adamancy in his tone had Brook soothingly stroking his back. "Mother A'Court is encouraging Ham to take Loughwydde away for my defiance."

"He is a decent gentleman. I believe he will not bow to the dowager's wishes. If he does, then we will fight them.

You will not lose your home, Countess," Mallory vowed, echoing her earlier sentiment.

He lowered his head and she lifted hers to meet his kiss. Brook boldly slipped her tongue into his, tasting and claiming him. Keeping his lips molded to hers, he moved and settled between her legs. Anticipating all the delightful sensations he wrung from her body with each coupling, she widened her legs, giving him access. Mallory teasingly rubbed his firm, turgid manhood against her moist cleft. "I am no longer satisfied with you being my mistress."

"Oh really," Brook said, raising her hips so there was a subtle shift in their position. He slipped smoothly into her. She grinned impishly up at him. "I disagree."

Embedded to the hilt, Mallory held himself still, refusing to be distracted. "Being my mistress is too limited, too temporary. I want you in my bed every night. I want you sitting at my table each morning. There are other pictures I envision you posing for, so many they will take the rest of my life to complete. I want you to marry me."

Brook swallowed the panic she always felt when she thought of marrying again. "Mallory."

His handsome face contorted in pain, but he recovered swiftly. The determination that replaced it made her wary. "You require convincing."

"Not really."

"You are a demanding wench, Countess. How lucky you are that I have the stamina to ravish you into a quivering, boneless slave of my will." He withdrew and drove himself into her tight passage. The power of his thrust forced the air out of her lungs. "When I am finished, you will scream my name. Saying *no* to me will be pushed from your stubborn head."

Brook screamed his name six times before he was satisfied. Exhausted, she fell into a dreamless sleep with Mallory wrapped around her.

Chapter Thirty

Mallory lifted his head and gazed down at his sleeping lover. Tenderly he kissed her hand and gently disengaged himself from her embrace. It heartened him that sometime during the night she had reached out for him.

Rising, he slowly stood and stretched. Mallory was not particularly concerned with her waking. Brook was exhausted, he thought, feeling a significant amount of masculine arrogance. He scratched his backside and reached for a shirt. His lovemaking had taken the countess beyond her self-imposed boundaries to heights she had not conceived. He was not proud of himself, but his relentlessness had been calculated. With each cry he had wrung from her lips, he had hoped he would weaken her resolve to avoid marrying again. Her first husband had shown her pain. Mallory had given her pleasure. Was she so blinded by her fears that she could not see he offered her more?

Love.

Mallory had felt its sharp tug when he saw her on the cliffs, but he had existed without it for so long, he had not recognized it. Once dressed, he left her sleeping in his bed. If he had his way, she would never leave it. He was working on a plan.

The sun was high when he walked out the door. He was astonished that Mrs. Whitby was not around. Considering how he and the countess had burst through the door of the cottage, perhaps the woman had decided they needed some privacy. He assumed she had told the staff at Loughwydde that their mistress was safe. Needing the walk, Mallory decided it would not hurt to walk over to the main house and tell the housekeeper not to worry. While he was there, he could pick up a clean dress so Brook would not have to wear the one drenched with seawater.

Imagining how she might reward him for his thoughtfulness, he heard the noise too late. The walking stick connected with his forehead, bringing him down. His vision dimmed for a few seconds as he fought not to lose consciousness.

"Good. I was hoping you would not make it simple for me by passing out," Lord De Lanoy said, leaning on his weapon.

"I barely felt your tap," Mallory lied. Gingerly he touched the lump swelling in the middle of his forehead. It hurt like the very devil. The bastard had dented his skull.

"Get up! We do not want to draw any attention." He kicked Mallory's foot to enforce the command.

"I would rather not. Maybe you should have thought about that before you started swinging your stick," Mallory said sullenly. He was wounded and weaponless. It also bruised his pride acknowledging that he had permitted a pretentious coward like De Lanoy to gain the upper hand.

"I will not ask again."

Hearing the warning, he squinted up at his attacker. Laughter bubbled out of Mallory when he saw the pistol aimed slightly lower than his heart. "The countess will be sorely vexed if you geld me." He glared malevolently at him. "And so will I."

Brook blearily opened one eye. She rolled over, her hand seeking Mallory. Whether or not he admitted it, the man liked to cuddle. He always kept close to her. She opened both eyes when all that she felt was a cool sheet. Sitting up, she searched the room. Mallory was gone.

"You know, De Lanoy, I usually have my sketching book when I prowl the cliffs," Mallory said conversationally, ignoring the tiny fact that the man who once was his rival for Mirabella's affections had a pistol aimed at his spine and was very angry.

"I fear you will not have the opportunity to sketch today. You are otherwise engaged."

Mallory glimpsed the churning sea and sandy cove below. "Is it your plan to force me into jumping?" If he was going over the edge, he was taking the madman with him.

"Who says I intend to kill you?"

The pistol and the cliff were big indicators, but Mallory doubted the marquis would be appreciative of his wry sense of humor. "What is next? We are running out of land."

Brook returned to Loughwydde. Her irritation had turned to concern when she realized she was alone in the cottage. After what had transpired the night before, she could not believe Mallory had left her.

She closed the front door, not caring who heard her arrival. Mrs. Gordy poked her head through a doorway. "You are looking better. Will you be wanting to eat *this* morning?"

Better? Was the housekeeper daft? She looked worse than a dockside whore with her crumpled, stained gown and messy hair. "Did Mrs. Whitby stop by and give you a message?"

"Aye, madam. She stayed for tea and gave me an earful about you and Mr. Claeg." The older woman gave her a cheery grin. "Considering the time of day it is, I'd say all that talk about his skills as a lover were not flummery."

Brook found that even after everything Mallory had done

to her body, she could still blush. "Have you seen Mr. Claeg this morning?"

"No, my lady. Did you send him over to collect a clean dress? If you do not mind me saying so, there is no hope for the one you are wearing."

Where was he?

"Send Morna up to my bedchamber. You can tear this dress up later for rags." She rushed up the flight of stairs.

Had a messenger come with news that his father had died? He came to the main house the last time to let her know he was leaving. Brook could not forget his promise:

When I am finished, you will scream my name. Saying no *to me will be pushed from your stubborn head.*

She had not uttered the word he wanted banished from her thoughts. Nor had she agreed to marry him. He had given her so much, and still, lying beneath him writhing from the pleasure he had coaxed from her body, she had resisted. Perhaps he had finally decided to stop bloodying his head against the stone walls of her heart.

Mallory's head felt like he had been battering a wall with it. Grimacing as he assessed the swelling with his finger, he realized it was bleeding. When he untied his bound hands, he was going to beat the marquis to death with his walking stick.

Unused to the area, De Lanoy nervously eyed the uneven stone steps that led down to the beach. "Down there. You first."

Still shaken from the hit he had taken on his head, Mallory carefully made his descent. "Why are we here? In London, you tried your hand at seducing Lady A'Court and were rebuffed. Do not tell me this is about revenge?"

"You were always astute, Mr. Claeg. Yes, this is about revenge. However, you guessed wrong about the lady."

Mirabella. So many of his regrets in his life went back to

his first love. "She is dead, De Lanoy. Killing me will not bring her back."

"She was not supposed to die!" the man roared.

Mallory had raged at the heavens for the same reason. "I understand that you blame me, but the rumors you heard about her accident were not exaggerated. I arrived too late to prevent her from picking up that pistol."

"I do blame you, sir!"

Mallory took a staggering step onto the sand. De Lanoy was too close for him to attack. "For what? Mirabella choosing a mere artist instead of playing mistress for you?"

"I wanted to marry her, Claeg." The pistol wavered menacingly. "She would have accepted my proposal if you had not lured her away with the promise of adventure. I seemed too staid and homely when compared to the bravura of Mallory Claeg."

Anger was the best weapon he had at the moment. Mallory prayed he would not go too far and goad the man into shooting him. "We were young and reckless. We dazzled each other. I was too arrogant to apologize for what you perceived as stealing her away from you. I can offer it now. I regret that you were hurt by our selfishness."

De Lanoy howled in fury. "Keep your regret and apology. I do not want either!"

They had moved down the beach. Several more feet and Mallory would be standing in the surf. The water was likely to slow him when he attacked.

"She promised she would return to me. I had shown her how unworthy you were."

His ramblings made no sense to Mallory. It was a clear sign he was witnessing the crumpling of the marquis' sanity. He figured it was time to give the man a little prod. "I did not coerce Mirabella into running off with me to Gretna Green. She was the one who suggested it."

"Seeing you rutting with that whore Edda Henning had her regretting her decision."

Mallory's eyes turned glacial at the mention of Edda Henning's name. Very few people knew what had occurred in that bedchamber. He still only recalled pieces. He doubted the Hennings were so foolhardy as to brazenly admit what they had done in order to have a child.

De Lanoy curled his upper lip into a sneer. "I have not waited years for my revenge, Claeg. I have already had it. Who do you think held your head up and pried your mouth open after you had collapsed in a drunken stupor so Edda could pour her foul aphrodisiac down your throat?" His expression became gleefully evil. "You never knew how close I was, did you? Watching you and Mirabella. . . . Did you think I would allow you to walk away unpunished? Who do you think quietly pointed you out to Henning and his ilk? Their exclusive little group of freaks did not stumble across you by chance."

They had stopped and faced each other while the surf lapped at their boots. "You must have hated Mirabella to have pushed her toward people you knew would exploit her weaknesses."

"I was trying to save her!" he said, waving the pistol. "To show her that you were a beast under all that charm. She did not believe me at first." De Lanoy nodded briskly. "But I convinced her. Or should I say, your zealous claiming of your host's wife convinced her."

Forgetting about the pistol, Mallory took a threatening step forward. "It was an illusion. A defilement of my mind, my body, and you let my wife believe I wanted it, you pompous bastard!"

"Stay back!" he bellowed; his eyes darted back and forth in agitation. "You should have seen her face when I removed the blindfold. I held her arms and forced her to watch you lose yourself in that whore. Mirabella cried, you know. She finally saw the devil in you and cursed you back to the hell where you belonged." De Lanoy slumped and lowered the pistol to his side. "I just did not predict the duel."

Mallory had his opening to attack, but he did not take it. The marquis had answers to the questions that had plagued him since Mirabella had bled to death in his arms.

"I was told the duel was her idea."

Troubled by his own memories of that night, De Lanoy blindly nodded. "She hated you for betraying her, but she despised Edda Henning. It was she who Mirabella challenged."

Mallory rubbed his head. His head was pounding and he felt nauseous. "It was Edda Henning who shot her." It was only now that he realized that he had not seen Mirabella's opponent. When he saw her raise her pistol, he had been blind to everything else around him. "I was told it was just another game for the guests."

"That was what everyone believed. Only the Hennings, Mirabella, and I were aware that the pistols would discharge something deadlier than gunpowder. Later, the Hennings encouraged the tale to protect themselves."

"You should have stopped her."

De Lanoy's mouth moved soundlessly. "Everything occurred so fast. Henning was loading the pistols for them when I learned of it."

Mallory thought of the vivacious, beautiful girl he had been so entranced by that he had defied his family and married her. He then thought of Henning and his love for his wife. He had given her the child she had craved by the foulest means. Could the same man calmly load a pistol for his wife's opponent and hand it to her, knowing it might the instrument that killed his wife?

Mr. Henning and I are also arranging another trip. I doubt we will meet again.

The truth blazed like righteous fire in Mallory's eyes. "Henning would never have risked his wife's life, De Lanoy.

You watched him load Mirabella's pistol with only gunpowder. Only Edda's had been loaded lethally correct."

The Hennings had shot his wife, but De Lanoy was her executioner. Mallory lunged for the pistol.

Brook had returned to the cottage, but there was no indication that Mallory had returned in her absence. Worried, she ran through the woods. It was there on one of the paths that she tripped over the ornate walking stick. Picking it up, she recognized it as the one Lord De Lanoy had held when they had shared lemonade at the hotel. Why was it here? Keeping the stick, she headed for the cliffs. She did not know what possessed her, but the urgency to find Mallory was mounting. As she peered over the edge, the wind snagged her unbound hair and the strands danced on the air.

She saw two men on the beach. The coatless one with his hands bound was Mallory. At this distance and angle, she did not recognize the man holding the pistol. The walking stick in her hand revealed his identity as Marquis De Lanoy. Suddenly Mallory charged. Brook screamed. The wind carried her horror up to the clouds. Heedless of her own safety, she ran for the stairs. She did not understand what had provoked this confrontation, but she was not going to let De Lanoy shoot Mallory. As she descended the steps, she felt helpless. The marquis, too shaken by Mallory's attack, had dropped his weapon on the sand. Instead of picking it up, her reckless lover swung his bound fists and struck the man in the jaw. They both staggered backward from the force.

"Mallory!" she cried, frustrated he could not hear her.

Lord De Lanoy lowered his head and tackled him. They went down hard. Twisting to unbalance his attacker, Mallory brought his bound hands down on the man's head. The lord clutched his head. Scooting backward, Mallory kicked out. His foot caught the marquis in the chest and he fell facedown

in the sand. A murderous fury possessed her lover. He straddled the fallen man and curled his bound hands around Lord
De Lanoy's neck.

"You are going to kill him!" she shrieked. Brook did not
bother with the remaining steps. She leaped. Her knees collapsed under her when she landed on the sand. Climbing to
her feet, with the walking stick still firmly clenched in her
hand, she ran toward the fighting men.

She noticed the pistol as the marquis reached for it. He
aimed it at Mallory's chest and fired. Screaming his name,
she watched her love cover his wound and collapse.

De Lanoy shuffled to his feet. "I did not kill Mirabella!"
He gestured with the empty pistol. "You were the one." Raising the butt of the pistol, he intended to strike Mallory in the
temple. If the wound in his chest did not kill him, the blow to
the head might finish him off.

Brook was not going to lose Mallory Claeg to a madman!

She swung the walking stick at Marquis De Lanoy's head.
The impact was sickening. Retching, she realized the small
jutting handle was imbedded in the side of his head. The
man fell sideways toward the surf. Blood quickly darkened
the sand under him.

"Countess!" Mallory called out to her, pulling her away
from the violence she had committed. "Your aim is remarkable." As he clutched his chest, his chuckle turned into a
cough. To her horror, the circumference of blood was expanding beyond his hand. "Remind me to throw out all of my walking sticks."

Dropping the offending weapon, she literally fell on her
hands and knees beside him. Terror gave her the strength to
rend her skirt. She wadded the piece of fabric into a pad.
"Move your hand. I need to press this to your wound. You are
losing too much blood."

He leaned heavily against her. "Mirabella . . ."

"We can talk about it later," she snapped, and clamped her hand over his to stop the bleeding. The knot on his head was ugly and sticky with blood. "How am I going to get you up those steps?"

"I was wrong—wrong about many things. De Lanoy was responsible for us meeting the Hennings. He . . . he thought she would return to him if I—"

"Hush. You will make the bleeding worse if you move."

"Edda Henning shot my wife. I was right about the drugging. Mirabella saw . . . misunderstood." He grimaced at the pain. "I hope you killed him!"

Brook did not know if the marquis was dead or alive. At the moment, she did not particularly care, since the horrid man was responsible for so much of the pain in Mallory's past. A whistle aloft had her looking up at the cliffs. She waved, recognizing the men.

"Hold on, Mallory Claeg. Help is coming," she promised.

"No," he rasped, stopping her heart.

She felt her lids sting with unshed tears. "You must. I cannot bear to lose you."

A faint imitation of the smile appeared. "That sounds like a declaration, Countess." He struggled to sit up. "Help me up so you can propose to me properly."

"You must be delirious from the pain. What are you trying to do? You will bleed to death if you keep flailing."

"Gentlemen never flail. It stresses the seams of one's coat and looks rather ridiculous. Besides, I am not dying." Mallory sneered derisively at De Lanoy's body. "The man had the barrel pressed against my chest and still managed to bungle it. If I perish it will be from disgust at his incompetence."

Brook covered her mouth with her hand and quietly sobbed. No one dying of a mortal wound would have the vigor to mock his attacker. If Mallory said he would not die, she believed him.

"Are you hurt, Lady A'Court?" her headman asked, rushing to her side.

"I am fine."

"Check him," Mallory ordered, through gritted teeth, the groom leaning over De Lanoy. Despite his assurances, Mallory's wound was not as paltry as he wanted to believe.

They turned the unconscious man over. One of the men pressed his ear to the marquis' chest and listened. "He lives."

"A pity. I suppose I will have to be content his new residence will either be Newgate or a prison hulk." Mallory motioned the men. "Get him out of my sight. And have someone ride for a surgeon. This lead ball will have to be dug out."

"Aye, my lord." Picking the marquis up by his arms and legs, they hauled him toward the stone steps.

"Why do we care what happens to Marquis De Lanoy?" Brook challenged, outraged that Mallory had ordered her men to attend to his attacker first. "I want you off this beach. You need to be in bed."

"It might be best for the surgeon to bandage the wound before I am moved." At her alarmed expression, he said, "Merely a precaution, Countess. I have too much to live for now that we are getting married."

"I never agreed to marry you."

"You cannot bear to live without me," he reminded her, settling his head against her breast. Mallory closed his eyes.

"Moreover, at the moment, it looks like marriage to you would make me a widow again." Brook pressed harder on his wound and prayed her men would hurry.

"I love you."

Her heart swelled at the simple words. "I love you, too."

"We are getting married," he said drowsily. "I devised a plan."

"This was before you were hit in the head, bound, battled an old rival, and were shot with a dueling pistol?"

"I will admit De Lanoy distracted me for a few minutes."

She merely lifted her brow at his arrogant statement. "Give me a few days to heal and we can act on it."

"Hmm," he sighed, cuddling her closer. "Kidnapping."

Uncertain she had heard him correctly, she asked, "I beg your pardon?"

"I was planning to kidnap you from Loughwydde. Dashing off to Gretna Green sounded romantic until I estimated the miles. Too bloody far."

She kissed his head. "So you have given up on your plan?"

"A Claeg give up? Never." Brook smiled at his indignation. "We will go to London. Special license. Give our friends and family a chance to fuss."

She gazed down lovingly at him. He had saved her from despair the day he found her standing at the edge of the cliff. Brook had fought him every step as he dragged her back from the precipice and forced himself into her life. With him she had discovered passion and pieces of herself that she thought Lyon had destroyed.

In turn, she had returned something Mallory thought he had lost when Mirabella had died. His heart. And hope. He desired a family and if it was possible, she wanted to give him that precious gift.

Mallory opened one eye. "Do you think my plan will work?" She had thought he had fallen asleep. Instead he was patiently waiting for her to mull over his proposal.

"When you feel up to it, I will let you convince me."

Satisfied with her answer, he let his eye close. "Two days. Three at the most."

Brook was already anticipating how he would go about persuading her. After all, it only seemed fair to let the wicked scoundrel have his way.

Epilogue

Three weeks later . . .

"This has been too much for you," Brook fretted when she caught him leaning heavily against one of the balcony doors. Mallory had slipped away from the festivities for a few minutes because he had not wanted anyone to know how easily he still tired.

He responded to the worry he heard in her voice by wrapping his arms around her. Being able to claim her as his bride had been worth the weariness and discomfort that had plagued him for weeks. Amara, with the assistance of the Bedegraynes, had taken care of the wedding preparations in London while he had patiently endured the countess's fussing at Loughwydde. Though they had not made a romantic dash to Gretna Green, Mallory was rather pleased with the results. Brook's back bumped against his bandaged chest and he grimaced in pain. "Tired of me already, Countess?"

"No," Brook said, offering him her profile. She wore the cerulean gown she had purchased for the Haslakes' ball and the pearls he had given her. He leaned into the light caress of her fingers along his jaw. "I should not have allowed you to talk me into returning to London so soon. Although I appreciate what everyone has done for us, the wedding could have been postponed until you were stronger."

Swaying them gently to the music coming from the

drawing room, he said, "I would have spoken my vows from my bed if you had consented."

She smiled, recalling his arrogant assurances on the beach the day De Lanoy had shot him. "Two days, you had said. Three at the most."

Mallory playfully nuzzled her cheek with his chin. "So I was somewhat optimistic in my recovery."

"You view everything too optimistically. It was nothing short of a miracle the bullet glanced off your ribs, breaking them instead of—"

"Knocking my heart out of my chest? Too late. I lost it that day on the cliffs when you were glaring down at me, demanding to know if I was mad or simply drunk."

"Well, I have my answer, now. You are mad." Brook fidgeted in his arms. "Will you please sit down? You have been on your feet too long. If you do not trust my opinion I am certain Tipton would concur."

Accepting her nagging with affable resignation, he led her to the sofa and pulled her into his lap. At her soft protest, he said, "Yes. You have been entirely too gentle with me, Countess. I miss having you in my bed."

After the misfortune on the beach, she'd had him taken to Loughwydde. There she had remained by his side throughout his convalescence. The fear of losing him had crumpled her remaining defensive walls more effectively than sweet flattery or calculated seduction. Her unwavering devotion had been humbling to a man who had not thought to find love again.

"You jest, sir. I have rarely left your side, and well you know this."

Overlooking her protest, Mallory said, "I have not shared my bed with my wife. There is a difference."

She rested her cheek against his. "Yes, there is a difference."

While he had been bedridden, he had told her the sorrowful tale he had pieced together from what he had learned from Edda Henning and De Lanoy. He did not spare himself by glossing over his role in the affair because Mallory had not wanted to build their life together on a foundation of lies. She had listened without interrupting him. Then she had pressed her face into his shoulder and cried. She understood too well how it felt to be used as someone's pawn. Brook had cried for Mirabella and she had cried for him.

Through Tipton's discreet contacts, Mallory had learned the Hennings had left London again. Their selfish machinations would leave him wondering always if that shy, beautiful little girl was connected to him by blood. Even if she were, the Hennings had denied him any means of proving it.

"What are you brooding about?"

"My past," he replied honestly. "It haunts me at odd moments. My life before you came along, Countess, was not devoted to honor or duty. Nor have I loved wisely. I would not have you hurt by mistakes."

Brook sighed against him. "Whereas I devoted myself to the virtues you shirked and still managed to marry a man who hurt me and twisted passion into something ugly. The scandal of his life and death will be talked about for years, Mallory. It pains me to know that you are suffering for my ill choices."

He assumed she was referring to his parents' notable absence from the wedding festivities. An invitation had been extended to them, but his mother had sent a note that morning regretfully declining. She had used Lord Keyworth's poor health as the reason for their refusal. Mallory was disappointed in his mother's decision. It was not his father's health that kept his mother away, but rather, whom he had invited to share their special day. He foresaw a future sea of notes from his mother extending her regrets since he had no intention of cutting his sister out of his life to punish her for marrying into the Bedegrayne family.

"The Keyworths' absence had nothing to do with you, love. My mother was truly ecstatic to learn I had aspirations of marrying an A'Court."

"She will be less enthused when she hears the A'Court family is not very pleased with me for refusing Ham's offer of marriage," Brook said glumly.

"Well, not to worry, my family thrives on discord. It is the family motto."

She pulled her cheek away from his and stared. "You are making that part up."

"No," Mallory leered wickedly at her. "It's some fancy Latin phrase . . . goes something like, *est thriva discardo.* When they put it in Latin, you know it is old."

Brook pleased him by laughing. The sound of her joy warmed his heart, his very soul. He could be content spending the rest of his life devising mischief to humor her.

"I am acquainted with the language, Mallory Claeg, and that phrase you uttered was not Latin."

"No? Well, how about—" Cuddling her closer, he whispered an indelicate Latin phrase he did know. Noticing that her ears were turning a charming pink, he bit her tender earlobe.

"Gad," Gill muttered, scowling at them with disappointment. "I should've known I'd find you two kissing. Claeg, you are missing everything!"

It pleased him that his young apprentice was enjoying herself. With the exception of art and Egyptian artifacts, he could not think of anything that induced such enthusiasm. "You underestimate me, Gill. If you will be a good girl and close the door behind you I will make certain I get my everything." He and Brook had talked Gill into coming to the Bedegrayne house for the wedding, but no amount of coaxing had put her into the pretty dress Mallory had purchased for her.

"There is always time for *that*," the girl sneered, unimpressed with his hint for her hasty departure. "Have you seen the cakes? One even has a mix of candied fruit and nuts on it!" The wide-eyed excitement in her young countenance made his heart ache.

Mallory and his new bride exchanged amused glances. Without being asked, Brook slid off his lap. The lingering touch on his shoulder was a silent signal that she was willing to make, as Gill so delicately put it, time for *that* later when they were alone. For now, they had family and friends waiting for them.

He linked his hand in Brook's. "Well, Countess, there are few things that surpass cake."

"Especially, with fruits and nuts on top," Brook said, winking at Gill. Satisfied they were on their way to rejoin their party, Gill dashed off to tell the others they could start cutting into the desserts.

Mallory nuzzled her ear. "Of course, when we are alone, I would be delighted to demonstrate what does outdo my hunger for sweets."

His teasing torment of her ear had her shivering. Turning her face up to his, Brook said, "No, love, the delight will be all mine."

With a wistful smile on her lips, Maddy Wyman watched along with the rest of the guests as Mallory and Brook Claeg kissed in front of their guests. The clapping and bawdy cheering made the bride blush. It was a small intimate gathering. Almost everyone was connected to the Bedegraynes by blood or marriage. Sir Thomas Bedegrayne had commented on Lord and Lady Keyworth's absence since they had not deigned to attend either one of their children's weddings. His elder son had efficiently squelched his querulous diatribe by reminding him that this was a day of celebration.

Maddy was about to join the hungry group eyeing the table

of desserts when she noticed her three-year-old nephew, Lucien, entering with her poor little dog clamped fiercely to his chest. Flora was an exuberant white Maltese who was used to entering a room on all four paws. Maddy had locked her in the conservatory to avoid any embarrassing incidents.

Her brother noticed his toddling son with his cumbersome companion. They simultaneously approached the boy from opposite directions.

Lucien brightened as he saw her. "Aunt Maggy, Flaw-ra!" he exclaimed, butchering her and Flora's names. He tried to hold out the struggling dog. Flora took advantage of his divided attention and wriggled out of his grasp. She hit the floor with an ungraceful splat when her short legs buckled under her when she fell.

"I thought you locked her up?" Tipton asked accusingly as he watched the dog run away from the gleeful boy and under one of the tables.

This was not her fault. "I did," Maddy said, through clenched teeth. Paying no heed to her elegant dress, she crouched down to grab the frolicsome dog. "Flora!" she called out in frustration as a flash of white hair charged past her just out of reach.

"I'll help, I'll help. Here, Flaw-ra," Lucien yelled, chasing after her.

Amara snickered into her husband's shoulder as Maddy pursued the boy and dog. Great! She had become the evening's entertainment. At least, they were not browbeating her into playing the pianoforte. She should be grateful for small blessings.

Tipton caught his son with one arm and hauled him into his arms. He gave his sister an impatient look.

"I know, I know. I will capture Flora and lock her up." She playfully pinched her nephew's nose as she walked past father and son. "Little imp. Maybe we should lock you up, too."

Maddy headed out of the room and into an outer hall. Hearing the telltale sounds of tiny nails clicking across the marble flooring below, she rushed down the stairs. "Stubborn dog," she said, her tone promising a retribution she never intended delivering to her beloved Maltese. The sight of a stranger hunkered down petting her dog had her skidding to an abrupt halt. She slipped on the last step and landed smartly on her backside.

The gentleman looked in her direction and grinned at the very salty utterance she had borrowed from one of the garden jobbers she occasionally worked with. Maddy felt the impact of his smile even from a distance. He appeared to be somewhere in his late twenties. His face was lean and tanned by the sun. If not for the subtle charm of his smile, she might not have considered him handsome. She could tell from where she was sitting that his nose had been broken once or twice. There was an aura of severity emanating from him that had nothing to do with his dark brown hair or coloring. He seemed to be as curious about her as she was of him. Unwilling to give him more of an advantage than he already had, Maddy climbed to her feet when he stood.

"Who gave you leave to enter this house?"

"Not exactly the greeting I was expecting." He picked up Flora and tucked her under his arm. The smitten dog was arching her little body up to lick him on the jaw. He bore the animal's affectionate nature better than most. "Though somehow befitting the prodigal son."

Clutching the newel, she braced herself as he approached. "Who are you?"

"Exactly the question I was about to pose to you," he replied, his gaze too bold to be considered admiring. "Who do you belong to, fair nymph? Sir Thomas Bedegrayne or his heir?"

Maddy's brow furrowed in bewilderment. There was a familiarity about him that she could not place as he circled around the interior of the hall and halted in front of her. "Neither, sir. Now give me my dog." She held out her arms, but a sound from above caused them both to look upward.

Brock Bedegrayne stared down at the gentleman. He made no attempt to conceal his astonishment. "Christ."

Stroking Flora, the man's brow crookedly cocked in amusement. "Not quite. Father always likened me to the fallen one. It is good to see you as well, Brother."

"Nyle," Maddy whispered, almost as stunned as his sibling.

The Bedegraynes' dark seraphim had returned home.